Ride the Wave

Ride the Wave

KATHERINE REILLY

HEAD
of
ZEUS

An Aria Book

Bloomsbury Publishing Plc
50 Bedford Square, London, WC1B 3DP, UK
Bloomsbury Publishing Ireland Limited,
29 Earlsfort Terrace, Dublin 2, D02 AY28, Ireland

HEAD OF ZEUS LTD
5–8 Hardwick Street
London EC1R 4RG

To find out more about our authors and books visit
www.headofzeus.com
For product safety related questions contact productsafety@bloomsbury.com

For my Wolders girls,
who make the whole place shimmer.

Prologue

It's late and the beach is empty, shrouded in darkness. The wind is battering dramatically against the coastline, the crash of the waves echoing around the natural amphitheatre of the cliffs. As he makes his way unsteadily down the wooden steps to the sand, his board tucked under his arm, he pauses to lean on the rail and peer out. His eyes are adjusting now and he can make out the mass of white foam tumbling towards shore from what must be towering waves. He can hear the roar of them in his ears.

If this was yesterday, he would make the decision not to go out.

The conditions are bad and getting worse. It's too risky. His instinct is to turn back.

But things are different now and tonight he will ignore that instinct. He will ignore it because for as long as he can remember he has had an aching need to surf, a need that burns through every cell of his body and has the capability to override any rational sober thoughts he may have. He will continue down the steps and he will stumble across the sand towards the waves with his board, because this is all he is. This is the only way he knows how to be.

And he is too heartbroken to pay attention to instinct.

Later, when he is struggling underwater against the current that is crushing his lungs, when he helplessly tumbles and rolls through the pitch black, when he thinks *this is it, I've fucked it*, his instinct will kick in again.

It will tell him to fight.

One

'Iris, we'd like you to go to Portugal to interview...' Toni leaves a dramatic pause hanging in the air as she clicks on her mouse and then swivels her desktop to face the screen towards me '...him.'

As I peer at the image, the editor-in-chief of *Studio* magazine leans back in her cushioned, black office chair on the other side of the desk and removes her designer, black, square-frame glasses, a smug smile stretching across her lips as she awaits my reaction.

I raise my eyebrows a little, intrigued, but doing my best to keep a neutral expression. A professional expression. It's no use, though. Toni knows *exactly* what I'm thinking; that's why she's smirking. But it's impossible not to think what I'm thinking. This guy is hot. No, more than hot.

He's beautiful.

It's a striking picture too. The photographer has captured him mid-stride across the sandy beach, carrying a surfboard under one arm, fresh out of the sea with his wetsuit peeled down to his waist, the low light of the sun bathing his muscled arms and ripped abs in a warm orange glow. His dark-brown hair is wet and tousled, beads of water trailing down his cheeks towards his strong, chiselled jawline, his full lips parted slightly, and his dark eyes locked on the camera lens as though he's just noticed he's being photographed.

I try to fight the fact I suddenly need to swallow, but I can't help it.

Toni notices my throat bob.

'Good. I hoped you'd say yes,' she says, placing her glasses down by the keyboard, her hazel eyes flashing at me.

'I haven't yet.'

'You will.'

I uncross my legs to cross them again the other way, which isn't as easy as it sounds in the fitted, black skirt I chose to wear with my black, cashmere, roll-neck top and over-the-knee heeled boots today.

Whenever I come to the *Studio* office, I tend to wear all black. It's safely stylish and the staff here are not messing around. You step through the elevator doors out onto this floor and you know instantly that you're surrounded by people who work for *the* leading fashion and lifestyle magazine in the UK. Toni is also in mostly black today, a sharp trouser suit with a white blouse and Louboutin heels, and flawless, barely-there make-up, her light-brown hair in a stylish short cut that complements her oval-shaped face.

I don't mind making the effort to ensure I don't look out of place when I have meetings at *Studio*; I happily took my time getting ready this morning. I've always taken a lot of pride in my clothes and make-up. I'm of the mind that if

I try to *look* in control then I *feel* in control, even if my life is all over the place.

Which, to be frank, a lot of the time, it is.

But if you looked at me now, hopefully, you wouldn't realise that, not with my long, dark hair swept up into a neat ponytail, bold, black, winged eyeliner framing my green eyes and carefully applied statement red lipstick.

'Who is this guy?' I ask, fiddling absent-mindedly with the butterfly of one of my small, gold, hoop earrings. 'Some kind of model, right?' I drop my hand, giving her a pointed look. 'You know that's not my area of expertise.'

Ever since I started writing on a freelance basis for *Studio*, its editor Toni Walker has been trying to get me to broaden my scope of work; sports journalism, my specialism, is 'a bit niche', she likes to remind me. I know that. I also know how lucky I am to be on *Studio*'s radar at all. It's a glossy brand that everyone has heard of and it has numerous international editions. But the British *Studio* is the original.

It's a stroke of luck that I got into Toni's good books and found myself in the comfortable position of receiving regular commissions from the country's top magazine. I used to be a sports writer for *The Daily Journal* newspaper, but with the way things were going there – like with all print media – I knew I wouldn't have a job for long so I took voluntary redundancy at the first opportunity and made the leap into freelance journalism.

Suddenly, I didn't have a stable income and I had to pitch ideas constantly to various publications in the hope of keeping up regular work. Then, former professional tennis player Kieran O'Sullivan offered me an exclusive interview. At first, I didn't believe him. I know him well now – he's the fiancé of my best friend Flora – and Kieran is notoriously private and hates any kind of press intrusion in his personal life. For years, he shunned interviews, even after he retired the summer before last, and despite my teasing when they were first dating, I've never broached the subject of speaking to him in a professional capacity.

That's not my style.

But Kieran isn't an idiot and he knew that a bit of press would do wonders for the charity he founded, so he approached me last year with the idea of an interview about, well, everything: his career, his history, his relationships. Once we'd talked through how it would work, I didn't hesitate to write to Toni Walker at *Studio* to offer her the exclusive. I got a reply within two minutes and it was a big, resounding *yes*. No surprises there.

Toni's exactly the no-bullshit-type editor I like working for and, luckily for me, I'm the type of journalist she likes to work with: I'm passionate about what I'm writing and I've never missed a deadline. She's commissioned me to write several high-profile pieces about sport celebrities, but recently has tried to convince me to consider expanding my portfolio.

I guess that must be what is going on here with this handsome beach model she's presenting me with. It's going to be hard to say no to interviewing this dark-haired, half-naked Adonis, but I'm determined to stay focused on what I do best: sports journalism.

'He isn't a model,' she says to my surprise. 'He's a pro surfer. A former pro surfer, I should say. He retired a while ago. His name is Leo Silva. You heard of him?'

I shake my head.

She quirks a brow. 'And here I was thinking you were a sports expert.'

'Surfing isn't exactly my thing.'

'Well, you might want to make it your thing,' she suggests, clasping her hands in front of her on the table. 'I take it you know the name Michelle Martin.'

Of course I know Michelle Martin. She's the Australian media proprietor who owns Bind Inc., the international umbrella company of many media titles and brands, of which *Studio* is one. But most people know her because of a TV show she did years ago, *Pitch*, a documentary that followed her and her core team for a couple of months in her London offices as her largely-print media company battled to stay relevant in a digital world. Her ruthless opinions and tendency to interrupt people with a curt, 'Boring! Next!' became iconic.

She's always had a fiercely unapologetic, powerful and demanding reputation, but her popularity has dipped recently thanks to interviews that went viral for all the wrong reasons – mostly clips of her giving sneering responses to reasonable questions. She also likes to share her sharp opinions on social media and snap back at anyone who thinks differently, hurling personal insults without any thought.

'Yes, I know Michelle Martin,' I confirm. 'We're sitting in her building.'

Toni taps at her screen with her long, red, manicured fingernail. 'Leo Silva is her son.'

'This surfer is Michelle Martin's *son*?' I glance back at his picture. 'Whoa.'

Toni fights a smile. 'I know.'

'I'm not sure I knew she had a son. Maybe it rings a bell...'

'He hasn't appeared in any of her TV work, she never talked about him in front of a camera, and he's not affiliated with her company,' Toni explains frankly to clear up my confusion. 'They haven't been on the best terms.'

'Oh. Did you say he's in Portugal?'

'That's where he's been hiding since he left Australia twelve years ago on his retirement from pro surfing at the age of twenty-four. Michelle's assistant tells me it's where his father resides. He stuck around to help with Leo while he was growing up, but moved back home to Portugal when Leo bought his own place at eighteen.'

'Okay, so Leo did well for himself early on, then.'

'There was a time that Leo Silva was the World Champion, a huge surf star.' She leans forward conspiratorially, resting her forearms on her desk. 'But he was also a notorious party boy: booze, drugs, famous flings. He was a tabloid favourite on the other side of the world. None of Michelle's rags, of course. His wild behaviour wasn't a great look for his mother, who was busy building her empire there and overseas. Fucking Christmas for her rivals. They plastered his antics all over their platforms.'

'I bet.'

'He lost his sponsors and damaged Michelle Martin's reputation by association at the time. You know how the business sharks think, especially of a woman back then: she couldn't handle her out-of-control son; what else couldn't she handle?'

'Okay, you've painted the picture. Fame, fortune and wasted potential. What's the hook? Why do you want this feature on him now?'

Her lips curl into a gratified smile at my impatience and curiosity. We both know she would be asking the exact same questions.

'Leo was meant to be the next Kelly Slater,' she says. 'But his partying streak destroyed his career. Then he... disappeared. Retired early and fled overnight. No more parties, no more press, and no more surfing. Strange, right?'

'So, what happened?' I ask, unable to fight the urge to gaze at his image. 'He woke up one morning and decided to just... give up? Did something happen to him? Why leave the country altogether?'

Toni lifts her finger, pointing it at me. 'These are the questions I want you to answer and more, Iris. What is his story? Why has he been hiding away all these years? And why has he chosen to come back now?'

'He's surfing again?'

'Here we come to the hook of our piece. Yes, and he is, in the words of his mother's publicist, a "changed man". In case it wasn't obvious, this feature was pitched by Michelle's team. Difficult one to say no to, if I'm honest.'

I grimace. 'We're doing an article at the behest of the magazine's owner.'

'*You're* doing this feature at her behest, yes. So no pressure,' she confirms unashamedly. 'I don't know whether you're aware, but Michelle is the subject of a new documentary. Cameras following her day-to-day life, that sort of thing.'

'Hasn't she already done that?'

'A long time ago. This is a new one. Her team are currently guiding her through a bit of a...' she pauses to search for the word '...publicity crisis. Or, as one of her team put it, "a PR shitshow." There are rumours that the Bind Inc. board isn't thrilled by her reputation – and neither am I, to be honest. I assume you've seen the backlash she's had on social media?'

'I heard that there had been calls to boycott the Bind Inc. publications after some of her more… brutal remarks,' I say, trying to tread carefully.

'Exactly. Not helpful at all in today's climate. We're struggling to retain readers as it is. But a glittering documentary is hoping to change all that. Give the people the *real* Michelle Martin behind the fiery façade and win them over.' She rolls her eyes.

'Fine. But what does a feature on her surfer son have to do with her documentary?'

'Ah.' She straightens. 'Apparently, our boss wants the world to know that her wayward son is a new man. The reformed son of a supportive and loving mother, a surf star who hasn't given up on himself, an inspiration to budding athletes everywhere.' She gives a wave of her hand. 'You get the gist. They want to go big on his comeback.'

'Which is?' I prompt.

'Leo has accepted an invitation to take part in Australia's famous Rip Curl Pro Bells Beach contest this April. Michelle and her camera crew will be travelling there to cheer him on. Good optics, that: the devoted mother as well as a savvy businessperson. And to add a dash more entertainment to the already-moving narrative, one Ethan Anderson – Leo's old rival, apparently – has also decided to emerge from retirement to face him once again.'

I take a moment to let this all sink in.

'It's a good story, Iris,' Toni presses. 'The troubled son of a famous media proprietor, a surf prodigy who went off the rails, disappeared from public life and hid away in a tiny town in Portugal. Now he's back in his mid-thirties to face his former rival once again and is ready to heal old wounds with his mother. I sense it will be quite the tear-jerker and, if he wins...' she exhales, tilting her head at me '...it's a Hollywood movie in the making.'

I roll my eyes. 'It also sounds like it's been constructed and contrived by an overzealous production team and camera crew.'

'Tell me you're not tempted,' she says, jerking her head at the screen.

'Honestly, I don't know anything about surfing and I'm not sure how I feel about writing a feature for the head of this corporation,' I say bluntly.

'Her team has assured me we have full control, no funny business.'

'What, she's not going to ask to see it pre-publication? Let's be real.'

'It will go to press how I see fit,' she assures me impatiently. 'I'm sure she trusts me to do what's best for the magazine.'

'If she trusts you, then why don't *you* write it?'

'With my boundless free time? Iris, I barely see my daughter as it is. I don't have time to write articles. Editors rarely have time to actually write,' she says with a hint of regret. 'Besides, according to her team, Michelle Martin asked for you specifically.'

I stare at her, waiting for her to laugh her statement off as a joke, but she doesn't.

'Really? But why?' I stammer, bewildered she's even heard of me.

'Apparently, she was distinctly impressed by your last piece for *Studio*, the one on the playboy skier who no one took seriously until your piece on him went stratospheric. She also mentioned your article on the gymnast who got injured, became addicted to painkillers, went to rehab and came back to win gold. And Kieran O'Sullivan's interview of course: the lost tennis champion saved by love.'

'So... Michelle Martin likes the way I write sport stars.'

'She likes the way you write *redemption*,' Toni emphasises. 'You remind readers that athletes are human. You make them relatable. *Likeable*. That's not easy. This is Michelle's son. She needs to know that it's in safe hands.'

I sigh. 'It's a lot of pressure, and I'm really not a beach person...'

She snorts. 'You're not a gymnast or a cyclist either, are you? But you managed to capture those worlds beautifully. I'm talking about sending you to *Portugal* here, Iris. You'll have two weeks there to shadow him. Don't be a moron; take the bloody job.'

I hesitate. 'Isn't the big competition in Australia?'

She quirks a brow. 'Don't push it. Our budget won't stretch to cover those long-haul flights. But you needn't worry; Michelle will be out there to cover that part of the story with her documentary crew. You can get back to England and she can tell us how it ends.'

'Let's say we'll play it by ear.'

Toni allows a small smile. 'You know, Iris, I had a meeting this morning with Elena Cerenzo, our European editorial director. We discussed the idea of creating a role of a sports feature director, an editor who would work across our European publications. Your name was mentioned in that discussion.'

I stare at her, my stomach twisting.

'I appreciate you are a freelance journalist,' she continues, 'but out of curiosity, might you ever be tempted to consider a fixed role again?'

Oh my God. This is... this is *huge*. A dream job.

I nod thoughtfully, trying to play it cool. 'It might be something I'd think about, yes.'

She looks satisfied. 'Good. Well, should you produce yet another one of your winning features on our lead surfer here, I'd say you'd be in a very good position to prove to the executive leadership team that you'd be a good fit.' She pauses. 'But I'm getting ahead of myself. You haven't formally accepted this commission yet.' She straightens, reaching for her glasses and putting them on as she returns her attention to an email on her screen.

I sit in silence, well aware that she's making a point. She needs an answer on this now. It's rare for a freelancer to turn down work and even rarer to say no to work that offers the opportunity to go abroad. But there's a reason surfing isn't my thing – a reason I can't admit to her – and if this big job wasn't being dangled in front of me, I'd probably say no.

Toni coolly taps away at her keyboard, knowing I can't turn this down.

'All right,' I say to absolutely no one's surprise. 'When am I flying to Portugal?'

Two

'Monday,' Mum repeats to make sure she's heard me right. 'But it's Saturday! You only had the meeting yesterday. She's given you two days to get everything sorted.'

I was meant to be going to Mum's today for lunch but changed the plan for her to come to my flat instead so I could make a start on preparing for the trip. She arrived this afternoon, has been here two minutes and has already plumped every throw cushion on my sofa. Standing in the doorway to my bedroom, she's now eyeing up the ones resting on my pillows. I can see her fighting the urge not to sort them.

Selecting a black, halterneck dress from my wardrobe, I free it from its hanger and begin to fold it carefully, turning to my suitcase that's lying open on my bed.

'That's right,' I confirm. 'The surf competition is in April, so Leo Silva will be in full training now. The sooner I can get to him, the better. You know athletes start clamming up the closer they get to the competition. The editorial assistant at

Studio sent over my itinerary late last night and the flight is booked for Monday.'

'Toni might have given you a little more warning,' Mum says, leaning on the doorframe as I go back to my wardrobe to pick out the next outfit. 'How are you going to fit in time to research the piece before you get thrown into things? It all seems very rushed. You have to drop everything and cancel all your plans so suddenly.'

I snort, folding a pair of cream linen trousers. 'It's not like I had that much to cancel, Mum. This is a great opportunity and I get to go to Portugal for two weeks.'

'Out of season,' she notes.

'It's still *Portugal*,' I emphasise, but grabbing a couple of jackets all the same and folding them into my case. 'The village where he lives is meant to be lovely; I looked it up last night. It's a former fishing town, really small and beautiful. My first meeting with Leo is scheduled for Tuesday morning, so I have this weekend and Monday to research him.' I straighten, putting my hands on my hips. 'Not that there's much to research. He's got no socials, and after a quick google, pretty much all that comes up is old celebrity gossip on him back in Australia during his party days. Nothing new. No *actual* interviews.'

'Strange,' Mum agrees, 'when his mother owns so many publications.'

'That could be the reason he avoids them,' I remark, giving her a knowing smile. 'Maybe having an insider's knowledge of the media industry put him off.'

'It *is* very impressive that Michelle Martin has asked for you specially,' Mum says proudly. 'She doesn't seem the warmest of personalities, but at least she has good taste.'

I chuckle, opening a drawer to pick out some tops. 'Thanks, Mum.'

'I only wish I could come with you. It would be nice to escape for a bit.'

I stop rummaging through my drawer to look up at her as she sighs, pretending to pick a piece of fluff off the collar of her crisp, pale-blue shirt. There's no fluff there, of course; Mum never looks anything less than polished. She was the one who instilled a sense of pride in the way I dress. I suppose I've always aspired to appear as put-together as she is.

'Mum, will you be okay?' I ask quietly.

She looks startled and then appalled at the question. 'Of course! I only meant that I'd love a holiday. You know I've always been keen to do more travelling – of course, it's hard to find the time. Life is busy, but that's a good thing!'

Her poise is instantly back into play, any hint of vulnerability gone.

'I won't be away for very long,' I assure her.

'No, it will fly by! And, as you say, it's a wonderful opportunity.'

I nod. She must know what I'm thinking though because she says, 'Iris, I'll be *fine*. You mustn't worry about me in the slightest.'

She does her best to convince me of her words through a fixed smile. I've been watching her do this for weeks. Months, even. Ever since she and Dad invited me over for dinner to tell me they were getting a divorce.

I wasn't surprised when they told me. When I'd been in between flats a couple of years ago, I had to move back in with them for a while and I had front-row seats to their bickering. I'd overhear their muttered, snide remarks and witness first-hand their diminishing respect for one another. It's like they'd completely forgotten what it was about the other that they fell in love with. Eventually, they gave up on fighting for whatever it was they'd lost.

I see Mum as much as I can around work, and I've tried to make an effort with Dad. It's a bit awkward when I see him; we don't talk about Mum or anything serious or real. We talk like we've always talked: about sports.

Mum has hardly been chatty about the divorce either. She continues to put on a brave front and won't discuss details of it, which is still ongoing. To anyone else, she might seem perfectly fine. But I see the underlying sadness behind her demure smiles and immaculate appearance, the hurt and pain she wouldn't dare admit to having.

It breaks my heart.

'Mum, I already know what you're going to say, but I would like to point out that I don't *have* to go to Portugal,' I tell her now in a soft and serious voice. 'If you need me around then I can let Toni know and she can find someone else to write this one.'

'Oh, Iris,' Mum says, shaking her head and striding over to me, the comforting scent of her Chanel perfume wafting over me as she reaches for my hands and clasps them in hers. 'I don't need anything of you! I *want* you to go. You are so brilliant at writing these stories and I love reading them. I'm not surprised that *Studio* have picked you for something like this.' She hesitates. 'I'll miss you, that's all.'

'I'll miss you too, Mum.'

She pats my hand. 'Right, that's enough of that. I bought

some bits and bobs for lunch. Shall I go get that ready? Do you need my help with packing?'

I shake my head. 'I'm good.'

'Of course you are. A pro.' She gives me a knowing look. 'Learnt from the master.'

Giving my hand a squeeze, she turns around and marches out of the room.

The conversation has blunted my motivation, so I take a brief pause in packing.

Sitting down on the edge of my bed, I grab my laptop from the bedside table and open it, checking the details of my trip. Everything looks good but when I google the Airbnb I've been booked into, I gasp. The studio apartment is *tiny* and doesn't even look clean in the photos. The bed is one of those ones that pull out from the wall and the bathroom looks to be the size of a phone box, separated from the main room with just a curtain.

Now, I understand that magazines are working on a tight budget and they can't put their journalists up at swanky, five-star hotels, especially for a project that requires a long stint like this one, but *come on*. If Michelle Martin wants me to be in a good mood to write nicely about her son, she might want to make me a little more comfortable.

I groan, running a hand through my hair, already dreading the phone call to Sam, the lovely editorial assistant at *Studio* to argue my case. Then, I have a brainwave: Naomi. My best friend from university who has a fabulous job in luxury travel PR. I don't waste any time, grabbing my phone and giving her a call.

'Hey Naomi,' I trill when she answers, 'my wonderful, brilliant friend.'

'Okay,' she sighs. 'What have you done and/or what do you need?'

'What makes you assume I've done something?' I say defensively.

'You just called me your "wonderful, brilliant friend",' she points out, chuckling. 'Out with it, Iris; I have to get back to this press release. I'm on a deadline here.'

'It's a Saturday.'

'Have you met my boss? And you're one to talk. I can't remember the last time you weren't working. Anyway, What can I do for you?'

'Okay, I might need your help with something,' I admit, biting my lip.

'Uh-huh.'

'I'm writing a piece on a pro surfer and they want me to shadow him for a couple of weeks in Portugal from Monday.'

'Ooh! Nice.'

'Yeah, it is. Except the apartment they've put me up in isn't at all. And you know what their budget is like; it's unlikely they'll agree to book me somewhere nicer.'

'Ah.' I can hear her smile down the phone. 'I have a feeling where this is going. Where in Portugal are you staying?'

'It's a small village called Burgau,' I inform her hopefully. 'I really hate asking you for favours, but when you see the place they want me to stay—'

'Let me see what I can do.'

'You're my icon.'

'Stop it, you.'

'There's more where that came from if you find me a nice room in Burgau,' I promise her, smiling as she laughs.

'And, look, I'm not expecting anything fancy or big. Just somewhere clean would be nice.'

'Leave it with me,' she says before I thank her profusely and we hang up.

Jumping to my feet, I select an upbeat playlist on Spotify and get back to folding.

'I want you to try this wine,' Mum announces, appearing again in my doorway but this time with two glasses of white wine, one of which she passes over to me. 'A friend brought it over last night for dinner and it really is delicious. A Gavi di Gavi. It's currently on a deal at Sainsbury's. What do you think?'

I swirl it around the glass, have a good sniff and take a sip.

'Very nice,' I say, impressed.

'I thought the same. He always gets it right. I wish I knew more about wine, but you know that was your father's expertise. I should have listened to him when he talked about it. I'm glad you got an interest in it, at least.'

'Hang on.' I hold up my free hand to her. 'Did you say "he" gets it right? Who is this friend who came round for dinner?'

She gives me a pointed look. 'Don't, Iris. He really is only a friend. Purely platonic.'

I nod, clasping my glass with both hands. 'I wouldn't mind if…'

My sentence trails off; I can't quite bring myself to say it.

'Thank you, darling, but I'm not there yet,' she says simply but firmly. 'It will be a long time before I'm ready for romance again.' She pauses. 'What about you?'

'What *about* me?'

'Any love interests I should know about? You don't tell me things like you used to.'

'That's because I have nothing to tell. Nothing serious anyway. All good fun.'

'As long as you're happy,' she says with a sigh. 'It's been a while since anyone really took your fancy; you've been keeping them all at arm's length. Might be a good thing to let someone in for once.'

'I'm too busy for a relationship.'

This is mostly true.

But it's also that I prefer to keep my romantic entanglements short and uncomplicated. If I were to analyse that, I might put it down to Dylan, my last long-term boyfriend who broke up with me the day after my twenty-fifth birthday. I was so hungover, I listened to his prepared break-up speech and then promptly vomited into a bin on the street outside *Les Misérables*, the matinée show of which he'd booked as my gift. We'd been together for three years and I really did think he was it. But he'd been offered a job in Amsterdam. He didn't want to do long distance, he said; it would be too hard.

You're not worth the effort is what he meant.

It was one of the worst days of my life and I didn't even get to see the show. Dylan took a long time for me to get over and from then on, I've protected myself from that pain. Putting yourself in that position – it's terrifying – and no one I've met since has seemed worth the risk.

Mum glances at my open suitcase. 'I am proud of you, darling, and impressed at how you take these trips all over the world to meet such impressive people,' she says.

'You could travel too, if you wanted, Mum. Nothing

is holding you back. Now's the time to… grab life by the balls.'

She rolls her eyes, muttering, 'Really, Iris, no need to be so crass.'

I can't help grinning. She's so prim and proper, she makes it easy to tease her.

'Sorry, Mum. I'm not wrong, though.'

She sighs. 'Hm. Anyway, I'll let you get back to your packing.' She stops in the doorway, turning back to me. 'Iris, are you sure this is the right feature for you to take on? A surfer? Only, I know how you are around the sea—'

'I'll be fine,' I assure her, not wanting to think about it.

She watches me carefully, nodding. 'If you say so.'

'I do say so.'

'All right. Both of us are fine, then.'

'Exactly. We're *more* than fine,' I insist.

'Yes, we are. We both need to make sure we – what was it?' She looks pensive, pretending to search for the right expression. 'Grab life by the balls.'

My jaw drops open.

'What? You think I can't be crass too sometimes?' She shrugs, leaving the room before calling over her shoulder as she heads down the stairs, 'One thing you can count on, Iris, is that people will always surprise you.'

Three

I owe Naomi BIG time.

She called me Saturday night to say that she'd found me an ocean-view apartment in a building owned by one of her company's big clients in Portugal that was free for me to use – if I might consider reviewing it for the travel section of *Studio*.

When I arrive there on Monday and open the front door, my jaw drops. I have to double- check I'm in the right place and then phone her immediately.

'Naomi,' I gasp when she picks up, 'this place is beautiful! Thank you, *thank you*!'

'No problem. It wasn't that hard to find you somewhere considering it's March.'

'Oh my God,' I continue, gliding across the cold stone floor of the spacious lounge and opening the doors out onto the balcony. I gaze out at the stretch of golden sand and, beyond it, the turquoise-blue sea. It's a beautiful evening, and I breathe in the cool breeze, strands of my hair whipping round my face. I may not like being *in* the water, but I sure do love looking out over it. 'Naomi, this view. It's... I can't describe it.'

'You're meant to be a writer.'

'That's how good it is.'

She sounds relieved. 'I hear Burgau is stunning. I've never been.'

'I've only just arrived, but yeah, you could say it's picturesque.' I smile, leaning an arm on the balcony. 'When you go down the hill nearer the beach, the roads become all cobbled and quaint.' I turn my head to admire the high, sloping cliffs that frame the end of the beach. 'Wow. Burgau is seriously spectacular. A nice place to hide out.'

'Who's hiding?'

'Leo Silva.' I force myself in from the balcony to explore the rest of the apartment. 'He's the subject of my article.'

'The pro surfer you mentioned,' she recalls.

'*Former* pro surfer,' I correct, opening the door to the bedroom and grinning at how spacious it is with a modern ensuite bathroom. 'He retired and disappeared.'

'And he's been living in Burgau ever since? Makes sense, it's a pretty good surfing spot. That's what it says in my notes, anyway. So you're going to write one of your big features on him for *Studio*? Like you did with that skier?'

'Uh-huh,' I say, flopping down onto the bed and lying back to stare up at the white ceiling. 'Not a bad gig.'

'Sure.' She hesitates. 'Iris, have you thought this through?'

'Honestly, no, not really.' I laugh, kicking off my shoes. 'The whole thing came about very quickly, but hey, it will be fine. You know I can research fast.'

'Yeah, but... didn't you *immerse* yourself in the skier's

life?' She reminds me cautiously. 'That's how you write these pieces so well – you don't do these interviews by half; you throw yourself into their lives. Like with the skier, you were out on the slopes with him at the crack of dawn, watching him train. You wrote about the feeling of skiing, all that cool stuff about the exhilaration and sense of freedom you experienced as you followed him down the mountain. As a reader, I felt like I was there with you.'

'Is this your weird way of asking if you can come join me out here?'

'I wish.' She pauses. 'Actually, I'm worried about you.'

'What? *Why?*' I blurt out, bewildered.

'Because of Mallorca.'

A lump forms in my throat. I realise what she's getting at.

'I don't want that to happen to you again,' she continues. 'Are you really the right person to write this article?'

I swallow. 'Of course,' I manage to croak, shutting my eyes, determined to push those memories from my brain. 'I appreciate what you're trying to say, but I'm fine. I'll be fine.'

'Are you sure?'

'Yes,' I say firmly in an attempt to persuade myself more than her. 'It will work out. It always does. I'll find a way. And anyway, it's too late to back out.'

'Okay, but I'm here if you need to talk about it.'

'Nope, I'm good!' I say chirpily, forcing myself to open my eyes and sit up. 'I do, however, have to go. I need to… unpack.'

'Let me know how everything goes!'

'Thanks so much again, Naomi. I'm so grateful to stay somewhere like this.'

'Well, in return, if you meet any single surfers who make a mean piña colada...'

I smile into the phone. 'I'll book you on the first flight out.'

We say our goodbyes and I get up, ready for action. As soon as I arrive anywhere, I have to unpack before I can even think about relaxing, so I drag my case into the bedroom, haul it up onto the bed and get to work. By the time my clothes are all hanging up in the wardrobe or folded neatly into drawers, and the bathroom is decked out in my numerous skincare and beauty products, I feel much more at home and ready to begin this new project. It's like I can't get my brain into order until my space is organised.

It may have been a short flight, but I feel gross from the plane, so I shower and throw on a pink dress that has spaghetti straps and a thigh slit, applying make-up and getting excited to explore. It's the first night after all; I should eat out and there's something exciting about dressing up for dinner when you're abroad. Just being somewhere new feels exhilarating; you don't know what will happen or who you'll meet. And for me, it's all part of the writing process. I have to bring the readers here to Portugal and I can't do that staying cooped up in a flat. Experiencing the delights of Burgau, such as dining out, is technically research.

At least, that's how I justify my expenses.

As I sit on the sofa to do up the ankle straps of my heels, I glance over at the balcony, which seems to be calling to me. I eye up the chairs and small round table out there, picturing myself enjoying a coffee out there every morning, writing up my notes in peace, casually procrastinating by watching the sailboats floating by on the horizon.

I think I'll like it here.

Smiling to myself, I spritz some perfume on my wrists, gather the contents of my handbag together, grab the keys from the counter and finally head out the door, locking it behind me. I'm practically dancing down the steps of the building, my hand trailing round the curve of the bannister, when I almost collide with someone on their way up. The shock sends me off balance and I would go tumbling down the steps if he didn't act so quickly, reaching out to take my arm, holding me steady.

'Oh my God!' I exclaim, regaining my balance as my fingers grip into the solid arm of my companion. 'I—'

Whoa.

The lips of the man I almost took out tilt upwards into a smile that sends my heartbeat into overdrive. Dressed in a smart, tailored suit, the sleeve of which my fingernails are currently digging into, he is in his late thirties, I'd guess, tall with swept-back, dark hair, glasses and designer stubble. And he smells delicious: an aromatic, expensive cologne.

'I'm sorry,' I say, relaxing my shoulders and smiling back at him, as I release his arm from my grip. 'Thank you for catching me.'

It suddenly occurs to me that I'm not in London, I'm in Portugal and I've made the most classic Brit-abroad mistake in the book by assuming everyone everywhere speaks English. I blame his handsomeness. It's thrown me off my game.

'Oh God, that's so rude,' I blurt out, aware that I'm still doing it, the heat flushing across my cheeks. 'Uh... *desculpa.*' I grimace at my terrible pronunciation and hope he'll forgive me.

By the way his smile is widening, I think he might.

'That's okay,' he responds in English with a Portuguese accent that makes my whole body almost melt right there on the stairs. He is *muito* sexy. 'It was my fault. I shouldn't run up the stairs.' He takes a step up so we're on the same level. 'Have you just arrived here?'

'Yes, I've flown in from London.'

'Ah. Welcome,' he says warmly. 'So, you like the apartment?'

'Yes, very much. Do you live here in this building?'

'Uh, no,' he says. 'Actually, my family owns it.'

'You're kidding.'

He smiles modestly, sliding his hands into his pockets. 'You're the journalist.'

I'm grateful to Naomi for organising my accommodation and everything, but *hello*, she could have given me a heads-up that her client was smoking hot.

'Yes, that's me. Thank you so much for letting me stay.'

'It's not a problem. If you need anything or have any questions,' he brings his eyes up to meet mine, his voice sincere and serious, 'don't hesitate to contact me.'

'Will do. And thanks again for saving me from falling.'

'Any time.'

Blushing, I tuck my hair behind my ear and, with a polite parting smile, carry on down the steps.

When he calls out, 'Wait', I turn back to see he hasn't moved. He's been watching me go.

'I… I didn't ask your name,' he notes apologetically.

'Iris.'

'Iris,' he repeats. 'Beautiful.'

'Thank you.'

'I'm José.'

'Nice to meet you, José,' I say before calmly carrying on down the stairs. I open the door and step out into the cool, evening air, unable to stop a smile.

I think I really will like it here.

I would like to know why the people who built Burgau decided that cobblestones were a good idea. Yes, they're charming, but wearing heels on these streets is a *nightmare*. Especially as the village is basically one giant slope.

I probably should have gone with a different pair of shoes, but these heels really do work well with this dress. I remind myself of that as I make my way back to the flat after dinner, trying to convince myself it was worth it for the look. I move at a snail's pace in fear of going over on my ankle.

'Fuck's sake,' I mutter under my breath as I stumble, stopping to regain my balance.

Luckily, the streets are pretty much empty so few people can witness my helpless tottering. I like that it's quieter at the moment here; I can enjoy Burgau without any crowds.

It's been a great first evening. I've done enough travelling to meet interviewees to have no qualms in eating out on my own; in fact, I enjoy it. I read or research on my phone while taking in the sounds and sights of a new place. It was difficult to find any restaurants that were open – obviously, a lot of Burgau closes up during the off-season – but the tapas place I (quite literally) stumbled upon was just what I was after: family-run, nothing fancy, with a small table in the corner by the window. The staff were so lovely and welcoming, and I spent the evening reading about Leo Silva's past achievements and antics while feasting on *presunto ibérico* (ibérico ham) *queijo fresco com doce de abóbora* (cheese with pumpkin jam) and *camarão cozido* (cooked shrimp), washed down with a glass of Alvarinho.

I read through old articles on Leo from Aussie celebrity gossip sites that showed photos of him in his late teens or early twenties with a beer bottle in one hand and a cigarette in the other, exiting a club or bar clumsily, his hair slicked back with sweat, his eyes bleary.

I've also discovered that Leo was a surf prodigy. According to the articles I found, he was the 'surf star of the future', the 'one to watch', a 'grom with fearless style, making waves in the surf world' – I have since learnt that 'grom' is a term for a young surfer. One journalist stated that he was honoured to have witnessed Leo surf at eighteen, an athlete who he felt 'would surely make history with his command of the oceans'.

Talk about pressure.

But Leo's partying started to take its toll on his professional achievements. His supporters began to wane, his critics got louder, his achievements deteriorated. Ethan Anderson suddenly popped up out of nowhere as the surfer on the up, while Leo couldn't seem to get it together. 'This star's light has ebbed and dimmed' declared a national paper's headline after Leo lost out on the world championship to Ethan. The second time Ethan won the title, Leo barely gets a look-in. Press interest in him has distinctly lessened by that point.

Then it disappears altogether.

I may not know anything about surfing but I'm already

excited to hear Leo's side to his story. Hopefully, my readers will be too. I finished my solo dinner feeling positive about meeting him tomorrow.

As I get nearer to the apartment, I follow the road round the corner and realise that I've been concentrating so hard on not face-planting the cobbles that I haven't been focusing on where I'm going. The beach is straight ahead of me. The road widens and leads right down onto the sand, with space for cars to park on the cobbles either side of the main path. There's one dark truck parked up in the spot nearest the beach: someone who perhaps had one too many in one of the local bars and has left their car overnight.

It's quiet and tranquil. I should turn back, but something stops me. I hear the sound of the rolling waves and breathe in the salty air. Perhaps this is a good time to remind myself how it feels to be near the sea. I can do a practice round now, when no one is around, before coming back here in a professional capacity over the next couple of weeks.

Making my way down onto the beach, I stand still at the edge of the sand and will myself to take my shoes off so I can make my way towards the water. It takes me a good minute or so, but eventually, I crouch down to undo the buckle of the strap round one ankle and slip off the shoe before following suit with the other. I straighten, my heels dangling from my fingers. I step forwards.

It may have been a long time since I've walked on sand, but I've been on a beach since the incident and I can do it again. Yes, this is *fine*. I knew it would be. I'm going to have no problem conducting this interview standing here.

Then again, it's not the sand I'm afraid of.

Taking a deep breath, I force myself to take a few more

steps, hope growing with every shuffle forwards. I come to a stop near the water, hitting the limit of my bravery. I curl my toes into the soft sand beneath my feet, my heart beating faster as the sound of the waves is much nearer now. Back on the road or the balcony, the sound of the water rolling and crashing is calming, therapeutic even. I know I'm safe there.

But here.

The sound and the overpowering smell of the sea begin to crack through the walls I've carefully constructed in my mind to block traumatic memories. My breathing quickens, coming short and shallow, as I remember the swirling darkness, the salt water hitting the back of my throat, the paralysing feeling of being completely powerless.

I know that I'll spiral if I don't get a hold on this quickly. I try to steady and deepen my breathing, shutting my eyes to try to focus solely on remaining calm, but without my sight, the sound of the waves only feels louder. My hand pressing against my chest, I open my eyes wide with panic.

And that's when I see someone.

A silhouette far out in the ocean. I gasp, fear gripping my heart as I realise they're alone out there. I fumble for my phone in my bag to call for help. As I clutch it in my hands, trying to remember the emergency number here, I glance up to see them still out there, their torso bobbing in roughly the same place above the water.

I slowly lower my phone.

They're not in danger at all. They're surfing.

I watch in bewilderment as they lean forwards on their board and begin to paddle. This person must know this area well to surf it in the evening alone, but whoever they are, they're clearly an idiot. That water must be *freezing*.

This man – and I can tell it's a man now from his body shape as he pops up on his board – is, however, a welcome distraction, dredging my mind out from unwanted memories and a place of panic. He's mesmerising.

I can't tear my eyes away from him as he glides effortlessly through the water, the wave carrying him along as though it's working with him to bring him into land. When he disappears into the water, I wait for him to emerge, that bubble of panic coming up in my throat again as it does any time I see someone go underwater. But there he is, trudging his way out of the water a way along the beach from me, shaking his hair and pushing it back out of his eyes, bringing his surfboard in with him. He makes his way up the sand and then stops, looking up to find me staring right at him. I start. He stands still, peering back at me, a strange figure watching him alone on the beach.

Turning on my heel as quickly as soft sand allows, I rush back to the safety of the road and scamper up it as fast as possible barefoot, back round the corner and onto the straight towards the apartment building, my cheeks flushed with embarrassment.

When I get back, I hurry up the stairs and into the flat, placing my keys on the counter and lining up my heels on the stand by the door. I move across the room to the balcony, quietly opening the doors and peering down to the waves below.

The beach is deserted. He's gone.

Four

I check my phone again. Yes, I'm definitely in the right place at the right time. It says it right here in the email from the editorial assistant at *Studio*: I will find Leo Silva by Marina's Bar on Praia do Burgau beach at 7.45 a.m. today. I've got the date correct and I'm standing next to Marina's Bar, where I've been waiting on my own for ten minutes.

No one is here.

I'll give him five more minutes and then I'll call his mobile number that was included in the same email. Normally, I'd have phoned my interview subject in advance or at least made contact with them over email, but he didn't offer an email address and since I haven't had long to prepare myself for the trip, I figured there wouldn't be much point in introducing myself before I met him in person today.

I smooth out non-existent creases from my black jumpsuit, adjusting the high-waisted belt. The quaint and charming cobbles threatened to fuck up my outfit choice again, but I decided to meet them in battle head on, donning a pair of black, open-toe, ankle-strap heels. These shoes have never let me down and they are surprisingly comfortable. They make me feel powerful and ready for any challenge that comes my way, and on the first day of an interview, I like to have that kind of confidence.

Of course, these shoes are not exactly ideal for the beach, but there's a path of uneven, wooden slats leading from the road to the front of the beach bar, so I'm able to avoid sinking into the sand. My phone vibrates and I check the screen hopefully, but it's not him. It's a message from my mum wishing me luck today.

Before calling Leo, I decide to quickly scope out Marina's Bar, just to make sure I'm not being stupid. He might have been waiting inside for me all this time. It looks closed, which isn't surprising this early in the morning, but the sign does say it serves coffee, so maybe it opens its doors earlier for locals like Leo. Careful not to topple over on the rickety, wooden pathway around the front of the bar, I knock on the door before stepping aside to gingerly peer through the windows.

As the door swings open, I jump back from the window, embarrassed to have been caught trying to see in. A woman stands in the doorway watching me with a bemused expression. At a guess I'd say she's in her thirties with thick, curly, brown hair messily tied back, bright-brown eyes and flawless skin. She's wearing a white strap top and shorts over a bikini with small, gold, hoop earrings. Her eyes travel briefly down to my heels and back up again, and I feel distinctly overdressed.

'Hi,' I begin, offering a warm smile. '*Olá*. Do you—'

'We're closed,' she says in perfect English, but not in a

rude way, more just stating the obvious. 'We don't open for another hour.'

'Oh no, that's not— Thank you, I was actually looking for someone,' I explain. 'I'm meant to be meeting him here and I wanted to check he wasn't inside.'

'Who are you meeting?'

'Leo Silva,' I say, already typing his name into Google so I can show her a picture. 'I don't know if you know him, but he said he'd be here at this time. Unless I've made a mistake.'

'Ah. No mistake.'

'He's here?' I ask hopefully, glancing back through the window at the empty chairs and tables inside.

'Not exactly.' Looking past me, she smiles gently over my shoulder. 'He's out there.'

Following her eyeline, I turn around to look out to sea and spot a man in the distance, straddling a surfboard, bobbing on the water.

'Oh. He's surfing,' I say stupidly, lowering my phone.

'His natural state. He's usually the first out there.'

'I didn't see him,' I admit, as I notice a smattering of other surfers striding across the beach to join him in the waves. 'You'd think I would check the sea for surfers since I came here to interview one, but I didn't even think to look.'

She raises her eyebrows in surprise. 'You're interviewing Leo?'

'Yes, I'm a journalist working for *Studio* magazine,' I say, putting my hands on my hips as I look back out at the sea. 'I'm writing a piece on him.'

'He didn't mention it.'

'You know him well?' I ask curiously, turning my attention back to her.

'We're friends.' She nods, her brow furrowing as she keeps her eyes fixed on me, as though she's trying to solve a puzzle. 'I'm surprised he agreed to an interview. No offence, but I didn't think he was fond of the press.'

'Yeah, well, having read what people have written about him in the past, I'm not surprised that he might be... cautious. But this article isn't showbiz gossip. It's a profile piece; I'm writing about his big comeback.'

'Bells Beach.'

'Exactly.' Glancing back over my shoulder at him paddling further out, I heave a sigh and shrug. 'I guess I'll... wait for him to come back in.'

'It's a good day for surfing. He might be out there a while.' She grimaces. 'He should have mentioned it to me if he was planning on talking to you here. I would have opened up early for you if so.'

'Maybe he forgot.'

As I stare out at him, he looks in this direction. Then, he calmly turns to look the other way. Considering the empty beach and my non-beach-friendly outfit, I can't imagine I'm difficult to spot. He saw me, I know it.

'Or he didn't forget at all, he just decided not to talk to me without letting me know,' I mutter, feeling like an idiot. 'Great.'

'Leo never does give a great first impression,' she says, giving me a sympathetic smile. 'He grows on you.'

'I hope so.' I reach for my sunglasses in my bag. 'Thank you for all your help.'

'You want me to give him a message?' she offers.

'No, that's okay. I'll give it to him myself. I'll wait until he's done.'

'Like I said, could be a while.'

'I flew here from London solely to interview him and follow his training for the next couple of weeks, so I genuinely have nothing better to do. It's fine; I'll go get a coffee somewhere nearby and come back to check in a bit.'

She sighs, waggling her finger at me. 'No, no, I'm not letting you risk missing him after all this. Come in, I'll get you a coffee.'

'But you're not open yet; I'd hate for you to go to any trouble.'

'It's no trouble, come in. I'm Marina.'

I point up at the sign above the door. 'You own this place?'

'No, that's another Marina.'

'Really?'

'No. I was being sarcastic.' She grins, holding the door open for me.

'Oh.' I laugh, following her in. 'I'm Iris.'

'Nice to meet you. Take a seat out the front on the decking. You've got a great view there; you can keep an eye on him,' she suggests, heading behind the bar to fire up the coffee machine.

'Okay, will do,' I say, hovering by the bar a little longer. 'So, you seem like you know Leo pretty well. Have you been friends a long time?'

She glances suspiciously over her shoulder at me. 'Is that a question for the article?'

'I would tell you if I was asking you an official question,' I assure her. 'But it's helpful to get some background and a feel of his life here: who he hangs out with, where he goes, that sort of thing.'

'Aha. You want a particular type of coffee?' she asks, distracted.

'*Meia de leite, por favor*,' I attempt. 'Coffee with milk, right? Did I say it right?'

'Very good,' she smiles, selecting a mug and placing it at the machine.

'It's important to know how to order coffee in every language,' I declare, while she nods in agreement. 'So, you and Leo are close friends? Have you known him a long time?'

'Since he moved here, yes,' she tells me to the background hum of the coffee machine. 'He's very much a part of this community now.' She smiles at me. 'I'll bring your coffee out to you.'

It's polite and friendly, but it's a direction rather than a suggestion. I get it. It's rare that anyone is forthcoming to a journalist and even rarer for someone to willingly give up information on a friend. Appreciating that Marina has already done a lot for me to open up early in the first place, I take the hint without any push back. Thanking her, I stroll outside to sit at a table right in the centre of the decking that overlooks the beach.

Sliding my sunglasses on, I notice an older gentleman on the beach with a shirt on and his hands in his short pockets, also watching Leo. At first, I think he's observing all the surfers out there, but it soon becomes clear that he's only interested in what Leo is doing.

Sipping on the delicious coffee Marina brings over, I watch the surfers doing their thing. They're making it look very easy. They casually straddle their boards, hanging out in the water, chatting to each other as they float, their legs dangling in the water. Then one of them will decide that this wave is the one to surf, paddling with the swell of the water before popping up on their board and riding it towards the shore, gliding swiftly up into powerful turns, pumping their board if the wave slows. I can't take my eyes off them.

The waves aren't that big here today, definitely not as big as the ones I've seen Leo surf in old videos online, but no one seems to be out here determined to catch the biggest wave coming. It's more of a relaxed vibe, I think.

Eventually, Leo looks to be finishing up and as he strides out of the water in his wetsuit carrying his board, I take the last gulp of my coffee and ask Marina if I can pay up.

'It's on the house,' she insists, refusing to take my card.

'I will be sure to mention Marina's Bar in the feature as the coffee in Burgau with the best view,' I promise her, standing up.

'*If* there is a feature,' she says, joining me in watching Leo as he stops to talk to the older man waiting on the sand. 'I hope you haven't come all this way for nothing.'

'This is a minor hiccup,' I say, trying to convince myself as much as her. 'He approached us about writing the feature in the first place.'

She looks at me, baffled. 'Really? He did?'

'Sort of. His mum did.' I grab my bag from under the table. 'I'll see you soon. Thanks so much for the coffee.'

Without risking any more delay, I rush out of the bar and totter back down the pathway that meets the road, waiting at the car park and making sure that he cannot miss me. I watch him like a hawk, observing the older man pat him on the shoulder and leave him, going towards Marina's. Leo, on the other hand, heads straight for the car park, his head bowed, his eyes on the sand ahead of each of his steps. When he finally looks up long enough to see me waiting for him, his frown deepens but he doesn't stop to acknowledge me.

In person, he's even more gorgeous than the photos. Tall, tanned, sharp jaw, tousled, dark hair that's still wet from the salty water, he walks across the beach as though he should be in slow motion and have his own theme tune. But his expression is not inviting.

If anything, I would call it hostile.

Still, I'm unperturbed. It's not like I haven't cracked through hostility before.

'Hi, Leo,' I say with a winning smile, waiting until he's close enough to hear me. 'I'm Iris Gray, the journalist from *Studio* magazine. It's a pleasure to meet you, I hope you…' I hesitate as I consider the correct expression '…had a good surf?'

He doesn't respond, instead marching right by me. I'm stunned at being blanked, but not put off. He's on concrete now and, although the threat of cobbles looms, it's better than sand. Here, I can chase him down, hurrying to fall into step with him as he approaches his pickup truck.

'As I said, I'm here from *Studio* magazine; we were due to meet this morning for our first interview? It would be great to talk to you about how this is all going to work,' I say brightly as he puts his board in the back. 'I'm really looking forward to the next couple of weeks and learning as much as possible about your world.'

'I have to say,' he says in an Australian accent, turning round to look down at me, tall enough to tower over me despite the extra height of my heels, 'I'm surprised you hung about as long as you did, Iris Gray. I thought you'd leave as soon as you saw me out there surfing. Takes dedication to hang around this long.'

'I—'

My words disappear as he starts peeling off his wetsuit right there in front of me, revealing his perfectly sculpted torso, the water beads on his skin glistening. I swallow and determine to keep my eyes *up*, firmly focused on his face, refusing to let them linger on the way his arms are flexing and his abs are tightening as he reaches down to pull the wetsuit off completely. He straightens, standing in front of me in only his blue board shorts.

Fuck me. His shoulders are so muscled and broad.

I want to reach out and dig my fingernails into them.

I won't, obviously.

'I… um…' *Stop thinking about his shoulders, Iris; focus on the job.* 'I am excited to start work on this feature; of course I waited.' I clear my throat, ignoring the way the corner of his lips twitch as though he knows why I'm stumbling over my words. 'Look, if you forgot about our meeting this morning or if you're a bit nervous, that's fine. We can take this at a pace that's comfortable for you. How about we go for a coffee now you're done surfing?'

He throws his wetsuit in the back of his truck. 'I'm afraid that doesn't work for me. I'm busy. I have to go home and take a shower before work.'

He opens the driver's door and jumps in, slamming it shut behind him. The window is wound down so I make a bid to continue our conversation as he starts the engine.

'If you're worried about the feature, that's normal,' I assure him quickly. 'It's daunting to let someone in, but you can trust me. All I want to do is tell your story.'

He puts on his sunglasses, resting one hand on the wheel. 'No offence, Iris, but you're a journalist. I know you.'

'Excuse me?'

'You don't want to tell stories; you want to sell copies by whatever means possible.'

'That's not—'

'Plus, I don't want anyone to tell my story. All I want to do is surf.' He puts the truck into gear before turning to look at me through the window. 'And how come you didn't learn your lesson from last night?'

I frown, confused. 'What?'

'Next time, don't wear heels to the beach.'

With that, he reverses out and drives off up the road, leaving me staring after him.

Five

'Yes, Mr Silva may have been… uh… a little reluctant to come on board with the piece at first,' admits *Studio*'s editorial assistant Samantha over the phone as I tap my nails impatiently on the railing of my balcony.

I close my eyes in despair. 'How reluctant?'

'Uh.' She pauses. 'I think the general feeling was that he'd rather not do it.'

'Sam, please can you ask Toni why I am here in Portugal to interview someone who *refuses to be interviewed*?' I ask through gritted teeth.

'As I said, she's in a meeting right now,' Sam insists, although it's difficult to believe. 'But she did mention that this issue might crop up and she said to assure you that Mr Silva did eventually agree to the interview at the request of his mother. She said to tell you that he may need a bit of persuading to spend so much time on it. You know, maybe he thought it would only take, like, a day.'

'He didn't seem open to giving me a one-sentence quote

just now, let alone an interview, *let alone* a full-blown profile set up,' I huff, running my fingers through my hair. 'I'm meant to be shadowing this guy for two weeks!'

'If it helps,' Sam says, her voice going higher and squeakier as my exasperation grows, 'Toni did say that if anyone could get him to open up, it would be you.'

'Flattery, huh. Nice try, Sam, but that shit won't work on me.'

'She really did say that! Promise.'

'This is a disaster.'

'But you've turned disasters round before, right? Look at Kieran O'Sullivan! He never spoke to the press before you came along.'

I sigh, leaning forward on the balcony and looking out at the water, trying to be calmed by the therapeutic view. I think about the sports feature director job. No wonder Toni implied that if I landed this story, I'd be in the running for that role. I have to get an athlete who hates journalists to trust me, a journalist.

'Fine,' I say finally, straightening. 'I won't give up that easily. You sent me his phone number on that email but he's not picking up my calls or replying to messages. Do you have an address for him?'

'I'll see what I can do.'

'Thanks Sam. Oh, and he mentioned going to work, but I can't find any information about him having a job anywhere. If Toni could fill me in on what he does and where he works, that might help too. And I remember Toni saying his dad lives here somewhere? See what you can find out about that. Anything and everything that might help.'

'Got it.'

'I'd rather not hang around the beach all day every day hoping he shows up to surf.'

'I don't know, that sounds nice to me,' Sam says wistfully. 'Don't worry, Iris; as soon as Toni is out of her meeting, I'll speak to her and when I have more information, I'll ping it across to you.'

'Thanks. Have a good day.'

'You too! Enjoy lazing around the beach!'

Rolling my eyes, I say goodbye and hang up. This definitely isn't the best start to this project, but maybe I can use this to my advantage for the feature somehow. A prickly athlete who starts to lower his guard and reveal the cuddly character beneath the hard outer shell. It's a nice angle with an intriguing hook. Why has he put up this wall around him in the first place? What are his true feelings about his mum and her media empire? Is he ready to step back into the spotlight? And what will it take for someone to break through this barrier?

I smile. Yes, this might actually be a good thing.

Bringing my laptop outside, I google Leo for what must be at least the hundredth time in the last couple of days and continue trawling through the old videos on YouTube of him surfing. I thought I'd watched all of the few interviews that he did – even when he was winning and at the top of his game, he didn't seem too keen to speak to the press – but I discover one more, a much older one I'd missed before.

It's captioned *Australia's Groms: the Next Big Things in Surfing*. It features footage of a young teenage Leo, along with another boy and a girl heading out to surf together on Bells Beach. They're all fearless and brilliant, despite being barely thirteen years old, and clearly good friends, laughing and joking together as they jog down the beach with their boards and make their way into the water. It's only when they speak to camera afterwards briefly that I realise the other boy is Ethan Anderson.

'I thought you two were enemies,' I say to my laptop screen, pausing the video to confirm it is definitely him. 'Huh.'

Opening a new tab, I search for more information on their relationship. There isn't much – most of the press surrounding the two later on only seems to care about their professional rivalry. It seems to be a well-known fact that the two of them hated each other. But here they are on camera, laughing and teasing one another, talking about how they plan to spend the rest of their lives surfing and travelling the world to compete. I do find one piece that mentions the two came up the circuit together and were friends once upon a time, but it doesn't elaborate on what happened between them. I click back onto the previous tab, looking at the two boys grinning together.

My phone vibrates making me jump. It's Sam.

'I've got two addresses for you,' she tells me proudly. 'One is his home address and the other is for the surf shop and school he owns. You should have them in your inbox now.'

'Thank you, Sam,' I say, jumping to my feet and looking round for my keys. 'I don't remember reading anywhere that he owns a surf shop. Did we only just find that out?'

'Toni said Michelle's assistant mentioned it in passing; she had to chase it up.'

'Okay, great. Thanks so much for everything, Sam. Speak soon.'

'Good luck!'

Before setting off, I search for the surf shop online and discover that it's near the beach front, moments from here, but it's not open yet. I could wait until then, but I've done enough waiting this morning and I'm impatient. I decide to pay him a visit at home first.

There are some beautiful, big villas in Burgau, right up on the hillside, that boast spectacular views of the coastline and village, and when I type in his address, I assume it's going to be one of those. Considering his surf achievements and sponsorships once upon a time, not to mention his outrageously wealthy mother, I've assumed he's always been very comfortable financially speaking. I've also seen the house he used to live in when he was based in Victoria, Australia and it did not disappoint; it was the ultimate beach house with state-of-the-art architecture, all huge open spaces, glass doors and an infinity pool.

But apparently, his taste has changed. He doesn't reside in one of those gorgeous villas I was eyeing up on the drive into the village. He lives in an apartment building that's on the other side of the village, a bit of a walk from here.

When I think about it, it makes sense that he'd favour somewhere more understated. Clearly, he made the decision that he didn't want to stand out anymore. Like Marina said, he's part of this community now. He may not want to tell his story, but I'm determined to hear it.

I grab my bag and head out the door.

It takes me a while to get to his place in these shoes – why is everything here *uphill*, for Christ's sake?! – and I have to take a couple of breaks to catch my breath but eventually, I arrive at his building in one piece. I double-check the number to his flat – four – and press the buzzer. No one answers. There's no camera, so I don't think he's screening me, unless he saw me coming down the road. Luckily, a young guy who looks like a surfer himself in his swim shorts and backwards cap comes out of the building just at that moment and I slip in through the door before it closes. Maybe Leo has already left for work, but I might as well check he's not here. The building only has four flats; his is right at the top. There is a lift, but it's out of order.

'Course it is. Thanks for nothing,' I mutter bitterly, shooting evils at the broken elevator before reluctantly heading to the stairs.

I take a moment when I reach his floor to collect myself before knocking confidently on his door. Nothing. I knock again, louder this time.

'One moment,' he calls out.

I steel myself. The door swings open and he stands in front of me wearing nothing but a towel round his waist, a startled expression on his face.

Oh God. Why is he always half-naked and *wet* when I speak to him?

It's incredibly distracting.

He looks so… solid.

'Hi,' I say brightly, keeping my eyes firmly on his face and refusing to let them drift down to his perfectly sculpted torso. 'It's me again.'

'I can see that,' he says, alarmed.

'We didn't get the chance to rearrange our meeting back at the beach, so I thought I'd pop over and we could book something in.'

He stares at me. 'You thought you'd… pop over.'

'I know you have to be at work soon and I wasn't sure if you'd want me to visit you there, so I thought—'

'You thought you'd come to my home,' he finishes for me, his brow furrowed.

'I'm sorry for disturbing you when you're... uh—'

I gesture in the general vicinity of his abs, accidentally glancing down to the deep-cut V muscles leading into the top of his towel.

Jesus. Did someone carve this man out of marble?

'Showering?' he prompts to finish the end of my sentence, my eyes flying back up.

'Right. I thought you'd be done by now. You've been in there... a while.'

He narrows his eyes at me. 'I made some breakfast before I showered.'

'That makes sense. None of my business.' I hold up my hands to show I come in peace. 'But it's really important that we get this first chat booked in so we can work out the best way of me shadowing you.'

His jaw tightens. When he doesn't respond, I continue confidently.

'As I was trying to say at the beach earlier, I understand that this process can be really daunting, and it might seem a bit invasive, having someone follow you around, but I promise I'm very discreet.'

'You? Discreet.' His eyes travel down to my heels and back up again. 'Really.'

'Yes,' I bristle.

He looks sceptical.

Despite the fact he's pissing me off, I try to level with him. 'You're not the first athlete who has been unnerved by the idea of a profile piece, but you'll soon realise that it's absolutely fine. Most of the time, the athletes I shadow end up loving it. You get to speak about your passion all the time to someone who's really listening, you can show me how important certain things are to you, you can talk through your hardest challenges and feel pride at overcoming them. It can actually be therapeutic.'

He rolls his eyes. 'Oh please. This kind of bullshit isn't going to work with me, okay? You can save your manipulative speeches for someone else.'

'I'm not trying to *manipulate* you,' I say, stunned. 'All I want to do is talk to you and learn about your life. That's what I do.'

'I can't do this now.'

Shaking his head, he goes to shut the door in my face. But I step forwards, jamming my foot in the way to stop him. My patience is starting to wear thin.

'Hey,' I say abruptly, frowning at him. 'You agreed to this interview and, whether or not you want to do it now, I've flown out here from London and the least you could do is be civil. Don't you think?'

He looks taken aback by my candour and has the decency to look a little ashamed, his eyes falling to the floor. He doesn't say anything, his lips pressed into a hard line, but at least he's not forcing the door shut anymore. I sigh, putting my hands on my hips.

'Leo, I don't get it. This is your big comeback. Why wouldn't you want to do this interview? This isn't any old publication; this is *Studio*. Most athletes would kill for this kind of publicity.'

'I don't speak to the press,' he states plainly. 'My mum

wanted me to do this and I said I would do an interview because her team kept going on at me about it and I...' he pauses, a muscle twitching in his jaw '...owed her one.'

Interesting. Clearly, there's some guilt there about everything that happened more than a decade ago, or perhaps she did him some kind of favour. I make a mental note to tease that out of him at some point during our interviews. Which I *will* get.

'But her assistant said it would be a quick chat,' he continues, frowning at me. 'Then I discover that a journalist has been flown from London to shadow me for *two weeks*. This isn't what I signed up for. I'm meant to be focusing on Bells Beach, not my mum's image.'

'What about *your* image? Don't you care about that?'

'I care about surfing,' he snaps.

'Great, then surf,' I say, shrugging. 'I'll take care of your image. If you choose to work with me, it will make things easier, but if you decide not to, then I'll get what I can from other sources. I can easily learn about your surfing from what I witness from the beach. This morning, you seemed okay out there. A *lot* of falls – wait, what do you call them? Oh yeah, "wipeouts" – but you have time to work on that before the contest. I'm sure you'll improve.'

'There were no wipeouts,' he counters.

'Sure there were! You fell off all the time. Don't be disheartened. You'll get there.'

'They weren't...' He looks at me, aghast. 'Those falls were me *dismounting* the board safely after catching a wave.'

'Oh. I see. Sure. *Dismounts.*' I tilt my head, giving him a sympathetic smile, lowering my voice to a hush. 'Fake it' til you make it, right? Love that. You tell yourself what you need to; our readers will totally relate.'

I wink at him. He glowers at me.

'I should make a note of this, actually; it's all good insight to your character,' I say, rifling through my bag for my notepad and pen. 'I think it's nice that you're starting out with those gentle waves today. Build up your confidence.'

'I'm not… Look, you try to surf every day, no matter what, even if the waves are small. It all matters to the training, the feel of the board and the water, even if it's not the level you'll be facing in a contest and—'

He stops talking abruptly. He stares at me, wide-eyed.

I smile up at him sweetly, pen poised.

'Oh,' he says, nodding slowly, 'you're good.'

'Good at what?' I say innocently.

He folds his arms across his chest. 'Okay, Iris Gray, not bad.'

'I don't know what you're talking about.'

He sighs, rubbing the back of his neck with his hand. 'Shit. You're really not going to let this article go, are you.'

'No,' I confirm. 'I'm writing this piece with or without you.'

'Is that because of who my mother is? *Studio* is one of hers.' He tries to appeal to me with an exasperated expression. 'Do we really need to go through all the motions of this? Can't she just tell you what to write? Then everyone wins.'

'Firstly, no one wins if a journalist is being told what to write,' I say pointedly. 'Secondly, wouldn't you rather have some say in what's going to be written about you? If you don't talk to me, I have to go on what I've experienced, which is currently kind of… stand-offish.' I hesitate. 'But Marina tells me you grow on people.'

He allows a small laugh, his face relaxing a little.

'But honestly, Leo, out of everyone involved in making this happen, I thought you'd be the one who wanted this article the most.'

He tips his head back, lets out a loud 'HA!' and then looks back at me, amazed. 'Why would you think that?'

'I thought you might want to let the world know that not only are you back, but you're back to win,' I say calmly, looking him dead in the eye.

His jaw tenses. My words have struck a chord.

'I want to be the one to tell your story, Leo,' I say in a low and serious tone, desperate not to lose one inch of the ground I've made here. 'Help me to tell it properly.'

He doesn't say anything. *Come on.*

'You might inspire someone, you know,' I add hopefully. 'A young kid out there dreaming of mastering the waves. Or someone who feels they've lost their way. You can be the guy who gets to show them it's okay to not have all the answers straight away, and that it's possible to find your way back to something you love. You could inspire them to get back on that board and ride the wave to see where it takes them.'

'Christ.' He quirks a brow. 'You must be desperate with cheesy soundbites like that.'

'I'm being honest. I think you're selling yourself short – your comeback could mean a lot to someone out there. If it's told in the right way.'

He groans. '*Fine.* How would this whole thing work?'

'We can sit down for a casual chat to talk that through and then schedule in our first interview,' I say, my heart lifting at his decision. 'When would work for you to do that?'

The corners of his lips tug up into an amused smile. 'You need to *schedule* in a casual chat so that you can *schedule* a first interview?'

'I… yeah. We could do the chat now, though. Maybe I could come in.'

'I'd rather be dressed if that's okay,' he says drily, his hands gripping his towel. 'I'm also going to be late for work.'

'Of course, your surf school. I only just found out you owned one.'

Leo scowls. 'Who told you that? Wait.' He holds up a hand. 'Let me guess. My mum?'

'Well, it was actually *Studio*'s editorial assistant who told me, so I'm not sure where she got the information but maybe there was some kind of mix up—'

'No, Mum and her team would love for you to write that I own a successful surf school and shop so it doesn't look as though I've been doing nothing all these years,' he mutters bitterly. 'I'm afraid if you want the truth, I just work at one, okay? I'm an employee. I teach surfing and help out in the shop. I don't run anything.'

'You see? This is why it's great to talk to me and make sure I don't get anything wrong,' I point out, clinging to any positivity I can muster.

He looks unconvinced.

'So when works for you to meet?' I ask hastily, getting my phone out to schedule it into my calendar. 'I could come during your lunch break? Or after work might be better?'

He sighs, still obviously pissed off. 'After work is fine.'

'Okay, great. Do you know a good coffee place? We can go wherever you like.'

He glares at me. 'I'll need something stronger than coffee if I'm talking to a journalist.'

'How about Marina's Bar?' I suggest. 'She's your friend, right? It's a good idea to go somewhere you know and feel comfortable in. Does that setting work for you?'

'Yeah, fine, whatever.'

'And what time do you finish? Do you want me to come meet you at the shop or would you rather I see you at the bar?'

He rubs his forehead.

'God, are you always this...' he waves his hand about, searching for the right word '...busy? It's like your brain is set to a hundred miles per hour.'

'I will take that as a compliment. If you mean, am I efficient? Then, yes. It helps to have all the facts of when and where you're meeting someone.'

'You're on city mode,' he mumbles.

'What's "city mode"?'

'You know.' He gestures at me. 'You're very... London.'

I don't really know what to say to that. 'Oh. Well, I *am* from London.'

He sighs heavily as though I'm not getting it, which is fair because I'm not.

'I finish at four,' he says gruffly. 'Don't come to the shop; I'll meet you at Marina's.'

'Great, I'll be at Marina's for four o'clock,' I repeat, typing it into my calendar and shuffling back from his doorway. 'Have a good day!'

'It already feels like a long one,' he mutters before closing his door in my face.

Six

'Ten minutes early,' Leo announces on my arrival, sitting back in his chair. He glances at the clock hanging on the wall above the bar amongst all the framed photos of surfers. 'I had a bet with Marina that it would be at least fifteen.'

Marina rolls her eyes and mouths, 'He's lying,' from behind the bar while I make my way across the decking to our table, pulling out the chair opposite him.

'I had a feeling you might be one of those being-on-time-is-late kind of people,' he adds, squinting at me across the table.

I offer a polite smile but refuse to give him the satisfaction of confirming that he's correct. Besides, this isn't about him getting to know me; it's the other way round.

'You were here even earlier,' I point out, placing my handbag on the chair next to mine. 'I'm impressed. I was worried you might not show up at all.'

'I'm a man of my word.'

'You weren't at 7.45 a.m. this morning,' I say curtly.

Whoops. What am I doing? This is a meeting. I'm not meant to be scolding him; I'm meant to be wooing him. In a professional sense.

Luckily, he doesn't seem insulted. He reaches forward for his bottle of chilled beer that's sitting on the table. 'If it makes you feel any better, I already got told off by Marina for that.'

'It's manners, Leo,' Marina comments, having strolled over to our table to give him a stern look. She turns to me. 'I told him it wasn't fair to leave you waiting on your own like that, especially so early in the morning.'

'Even though, technically, you left *me* waiting,' he remarks to her, taking a sip of his beer. 'You were supposed to be joining me out there this morning, remember?'

'I was busy,' she shoots back.

'Hang on a minute,' I interject, looking from one to the other. 'Marina, were you supposed to be surfing this morning when you were making me coffee?'

'It's not a problem; I can surf any time I want,' she says with a shrug. 'And unlike some people,' she glares at Leo, who pretends to ignore her, keeping his eyes fixed on the wave, 'I like to make guests feel welcome here.'

'Well, thank you so much,' I say, smiling gratefully up at her. 'I really appreciate it.'

'Like I say, it's no problem. What can I get you to drink?' she asks, distracted by some other customers wandering in and giving them a wave.

'A sparkling water, please.'

'Ice and lemon? Coming right up,' she says, leaving us to it.

Leo watches me carefully as I get my notepad and pen out my bag. Knowing his eyes are on me makes me strangely nervous. There's something about the way he's looking at me, as though he's scrutinising every move I make, waiting for me to mess up. I'm suddenly aware of everything I do, the way I do it and how it might look. That's why I checked my appearance several times before leaving the apartment to make my way over here, why I refreshed my red lipstick, brushed my hair and spritzed perfume on.

It has nothing to do with his shoulders.

Or arms.

Or eyes.

And God, his lips are so full and striking. They look so soft.

Damn it, Iris, concentrate.

'Hey,' he says, jolting me from my thoughts. 'You with us?'

'Sorry?' I say, shifting in my seat. I bring my focus back to the task at hand and sit upright, scribbling the time and date in my notepad. 'We can begin if you're ready.'

He arches a brow. 'I thought this was a casual chat.'

'It is.'

'Do you always announce the start of casual chats and take minutes of them?'

'I'm not recording this interview,' I assure him, tapping the screen of my phone. 'When I do that, I will let you know and, if it's all right with you, I'll record them so I don't misquote you. This is a chat to talk through how the next two weeks are going to pan out.'

'Right. So what's with the notepad?'

'It's so I can note down anything useful you tell me today,

like your general routine, where and how you like to train and exercise, who it might be a good idea to speak to – stuff like that,' I explain, before lowering my pen as he shifts in his seat. 'You know what, you're right. I'm going to put this away.'

I shove my pad and pen back in my bag, annoyed that I've already made an error. I need to make him feel relaxed. Instead, I've automatically gone into full on journo mode, pen at the ready to note down anything he says. He made it clear that he needs to be eased into this process. I'm going to have to work to make up for my mistake in creating an unnecessarily formal atmosphere.

'Sparkling water,' Marina says as she approaches our table again, placing it down in front of me. 'Anything else?'

'Glass of white wine, please.' I smile. 'One from the Algarve if possible.'

'No problem,' she says. 'Another round, Leo?'

I turn to see him watching me again, a small smile playing across his lips.

'Sure. I'm having a cheat day.'

As Marina leaves, I sit back in my chair and gaze out across the beach.

'Not a bad view. I can see why you'd want to live here.'

'Mmm,' he says non-committedly.

'I really appreciate you talking to me, Leo,' I emphasise, watching a seagull swoop down along the top of the water before rising again. 'I understand your hesitation, but I'm on your side. This isn't about tearing anyone down. If you want, I can send you a selection of my previous features that have been a similar format so you can read—'

'I've read them.'

I turn to him in surprise. 'You have?'

He knocks the last bit of his beer back and Marina arrives with my wine and another bottle for him. I try not to drink when I'm working, but I'm making an exception to the rule. If he's more comfortable in an informal atmosphere, that's what I'll create.

'What did you think?' I ask tentatively, taking a sip of wine.

Leo considers my question before answering: 'I can see why my mum chose you.'

I wait for him to expand on that but he doesn't. I don't probe him any further. From his neutral expression, I'm guessing that my writing didn't overwhelm him with joy, and I'd rather not have a confidence knock. Better to leave it there. I don't need his good opinion. What matters is that Michelle Martin and the *Studio* team think I'm the person for the job.

He's stuck with me and there's nothing he can do about it.

We fall into silence, watching the waves rolling in and out. I decide that he needs to be the one to make the first move and I can be very stubborn when I want to be.

Finally he sits up, leaning on the table.

'So, how will this work then?' he asks, tapping his fingers on the coaster. 'A couple of interviews and we're good to go?'

'I don't like to give an exact number of interviews at first, because we'll sometimes naturally fall into conversation, but yes, roughly two or three formal sit-down talks would be about right, depending on how long they are,' I say breezily as though I haven't been waiting to talk about this since

I landed in this country. 'If you can also give me a rough schedule of your training, that would be helpful.'

'My training is surfing,' he mutters. 'You won't learn much from it.'

'I'll learn plenty,' I counter, unfazed. 'Just like I learnt about freestyle skiing from watching a professional skier ski. You don't need to worry about that side of things; you focus on doing what you do and let me worry about capturing it all for the audience.'

'Fine. A couple of interviews and you watch me surf a bit,' he grumbles. 'I'd say that can be wrapped up in the next two days or so.'

'I'd rather not squeeze it all in in a short amount of time. I'm here for a couple of weeks so there's no rush. It's not just about the training and what you tell me; to really get inside your head, I have to experience your lifestyle a little. Training for your comeback in a surf competition isn't only about surfing, right?'

'That's exactly what it is,' he says defiantly, swigging his beer.

'Really?'

'Really.'

I smile innocently at him. He can try to play me all he wants, but he won't win.

'How else do you keep up your fitness? Are you telling me you don't go to the gym or do any other form of exercise? And what about diet? That must come into play. You just mentioned a "cheat day" so I take it you don't normally drink.'

He tilts his head at me. 'I allow myself the occasional beer or glass of wine.'

'Sure, but I doubt you will as we get closer to the contest. How about looking after your mental health? A lot of athletes meditate or put a lot of focus into wellness. It's not just about physical preparation. It can't only be about watching you surf a couple of times – I'm looking at the big picture here, Leo.'

He leans back in his chair, shoving his hands in his pockets. 'Who would agree to this kind of intrusion into their life? I don't get it.'

'It's not an intrusion, it's an... exploration,' I say, ignoring his snort of disapproval. 'And *you* agreed to it, remember? A fact you keep forgetting.'

'I was *tricked* into it. One quick chat, they said. What a load of bull.'

I watch him grumpily swipe his bottle up from the table and drink from it.

'But you're here now. You didn't have to be; you could have stood me up again, but you still showed. And you came early. Why? If you really don't want to be here talking to me, then why did you come?'

He takes a deep breath, watching me in an unnerving way. It makes my stomach flutter. I have to drop my eyes for a moment to gather myself.

Eventually, he exhales, his brow furrowing. 'Maybe a part of me wanted to prove to everyone that I haven't given up yet. Prove to them I still have what it takes to win those points and ring the bell trophy at Bells Beach.'

I smile softly at him. 'And maybe prove it to yourself, too, along the way.'

Something flits across his expression, a vulnerability or flicker of hope, but it's gone as quickly as it came. Soon enough, he's back to narrowing his eyes suspiciously at me.

'I can tell you're fishing for soppy quotes for your article,' he says haughtily. 'This isn't one of our assigned interviews.'

'I'm not fishing for anything; we're talking.'

'This is how you get your subjects to open up to you: luring them in with a drink in a nice, chilled setting and then – bam,' he claps his hands together, 'you get them to say something without thinking, something they regret. But you've got your snappy headline.'

'I've never had anyone experience regret over something I've written about them. More often, I get sent wonderful presents from my interviewees thanking me for a feature that shows them in a candid but honourable light.'

He lifts his brow. 'Isn't that bribery?'

'*After* the piece is published,' I say, fighting the urge to roll my eyes. 'They have no say on what I write. You read my pieces – did you read anything in there that led you to believe the subject might regret talking to me? Or did you finish it willing them to win?'

'I don't care if people will me to win,' he insists. 'You don't win something because others want that for you. You win because you're better than everyone else in the competition.'

'And how do you become better than everyone else?'

'You work hard, you focus,' he shrugs, 'and you hope that the conditions and swell on the day work in your favour. Sometimes, you get that perfect set; sometimes, you don't. It's got nothing to do with the number of people cheering for you.'

'People cheering for you can help your mentality, which can lead you to win, though, right?' I point out. 'I'm no athlete but everyone needs someone in their corner. Someone to keep you calm when things get rocky, someone to be there when the doubts creep in and help to remind you that you have what it takes.'

'Not surfers. We're lone wolves.'

'I've read that the surf community is a strong one. A lot of surfers are friends, competing all over the world together, and they have plenty of supporters watching the contests and cheering from the shore. I've seen the videos.'

'You can't hear the cheers above the roar of the waves.'

He's trying to shock me, I surmise. Maybe he wants me to gasp or think badly of him. But I've heard this line of nonsense from athletes before and I know that it's all a façade. Doing this job has taught me that strength lies in numbers. The ones who really want to win are well aware they can't do it on their own.

'No,' I say calmly, 'maybe you can't.'

'You see? I'm not going to make a very interesting subject for your article.'

I take a sip of my drink. 'Can't say I agree with that.'

He glares at me. 'There will be some questions I won't answer, Iris. I may have agreed to do this thing for my mum's sake or whatever, but I'm not going to bare my soul. There has to be some boundaries.'

'It's rare that there aren't.'

'Your other interviewees may be happy to go back to their childhood or discuss their past or go into detail about the profound meaningful motivations that encouraged them to pick up a ball again or whatever,' he waves his hand, 'but that stuff is off limits with me. It's not relevant. I'm just a surfer, doing my thing, and I'm going to win Rip Curl Pro Bells Beach this year. That's it.'

'Works for me.'

'Okay, then. Good.'

'Great.'

He shoots me a sceptical look but my sincere expression doesn't falter. If he can put up boundaries, so can I. But, honestly, it's really quite amusing that he thinks I won't be leaving here with the story that I came for.

I take another drink of my wine. He takes a swig of his beer.

We both look out at the beach. I fight a smile.

Out of the corner of my eye, I catch him glance at me.

'What?' he demands to know. 'Why are you smiling like that?'

'No reason,' I say, before my grin widens. 'Okay, I was thinking about you saying, "profound meaningful motivations" that made them "pick up a ball again". It was funny.'

His scowl softens. 'It's true. Their motivations were profound.'

'I know.' I lean back in my seat and stretch out my legs, still chuckling. 'It's the way you put it. So casual about some of the best athletes in the world. But, hey, whatever, they're just… picking up a ball.'

He edges towards a smile. 'You know what I mean.'

'Uh-huh.'

'I'm just picking up a surfboard.'

'Right.'

We fall back into silence, but this time, it feels different. He seems a bit more at ease. It's too soon to tell, but I think there's a teeny, tiny crack in his armour.

His phone vibrates and he checks the screen, before

downing the last few swigs of his beer and jumping to his feet. 'I should go,' he announces.

'Okay,' I say, sitting up. 'This was great, thank you. When would it suit you for our first interview? Does tomorrow work? We could do same time, same place if you like.'

'Sure. Fine.' He gives me a pointed look. 'You'll soon see that there's not much to write, Iris. I'll have my game face on.'

As he turns away and leaves, I sip my wine smugly, enjoying the tranquil view.

Go ahead, Leo Silva, put on your game face.

I've had mine on all along.

Seven

When he messages to say he's not going to make the interview while I'm sitting waiting for him at Marina's Bar on Wednesday afternoon, I'm not surprised.

Am I pissed off? Yes.

Do I think he's a selfish jerk who wants to make this as difficult as possible? Yes.

But am I surprised? No.

At least this time he'd had the decency to let me know he wasn't going to come; he had my number because I messaged him this morning confirming our appointment. He didn't reply to that, but hey, he's messaged. A marked improvement from yesterday. Maybe next time, he'll make even more progress and cancel *before* we're supposed to be meeting.

God. What an arsehole.

I've dealt with athletes reluctant or nervous to talk to me, but it's the first time I've been stood up. It's not very nice.

I stare at his message, trying to work out my next move.

'Marina,' I call out while she's wiping the table of someone who's just left, 'could I switch my order from an iced tea to a white wine again please?'

'Next time you come, I'm going to get you a white wine no matter what you order.'

'You already know me *very* well.'

She bursts out laughing and I return my attention to my phone.

Steeling myself, I start typing.

No problem. We could do tomorrow instead?

Blue ticks. He's typing back straight away. That's got to be a good sign.

Maybe. I'll let you know.

I roll my eyes. Fucking hell, he's so annoying. I know what he's doing. He knows when my flight is booked back to London and that I have a limited amount of time here. He's going to keep putting things off until the last minute so everything will be a big rush.

But I won't let him win. For now, I have to keep my cool.

Great, thank you. If you're busy surfing, it would be great if I join? Just to observe your training. I wouldn't get in the way

Grey ticks. And now he's offline.

Fuck.

'Boy trouble?' Marina asks, setting the glass down in front of me and putting her hands on her hips.

'Leo can't make our interview.'

'That's why I said "boy" and not "man",' she tells me with a wry smile. 'He can act like a spoilt child sometimes.'

'He wants me to give up and leave, but I won't.'

'I know that. I could tell when we met that you were a woman who gets shit done.'

I break into a smile. 'You're very observant, Marina.'

'How are you liking Burgau?' she asks, gesturing out to the beach. 'I know the weather is not as good at this time of year, but I personally prefer it in the down season. Not for my business obviously,' she nods to the empty tables, 'but the town itself is quieter. More relaxed.'

'So far, I love it,' I reply earnestly. 'I've been exploring today and there's such a nice atmosphere here. The village is so beautiful, there's great coffee, great food—'

'Great people,' she tags on.

'And yes, that.' I grin at her. 'I'd like to come back in the summer when all the bars and restaurants are open, but you're right, it's nice when it's quiet. It suits the setting. I'm not a beach person, so I wouldn't be lounging around in the sun or swimming in the sea anyway.'

She raises her eyebrows. 'Not a beach person. No wonder Leo is upset with you.'

'He doesn't like me because of my job,' I sigh, throwing my hand up in exasperation. 'In his head, I represent the entire British press.'

She watches me curiously as I drink my wine. 'I said he was upset with you; I didn't say he doesn't *like* you.'

'It's okay, Marina, my feelings aren't hurt,' I assure her. 'I'm used to it. It comes hand in hand with this kind of work. Certain journalists give the rest a bad name; my best friend is with a tennis pro and he has told me *exactly* what he thinks about reporters. Obviously, I'm an exception.'

'Obviously.'

'If Leo would give me a chance then maybe he'd agree. I'm on his side. This article is about his big comeback and how exciting that is. I'm not here to make him look bad.

I'm here to... I don't know...' I throw my hands up in the air '...be inspired?'

She nods pensively.

'Sorry,' I mutter, taking another sip of my drink. 'I don't mean to rant.'

'It's okay,' she assures me. 'I know what he's like. He's stubborn.'

Glancing over her shoulder to check she's not needed, she quickly pulls out the chair next to mine and perches on the edge of it.

'He is also scared,' she says simply, her seriousness prompting me to lower my glass to show I'm listening properly. 'People like Leo don't like to let others in. He's mistrusting at first, guarded – but once you get to know him, he's sweet and easy-going. He knows his mum wants this and I think he does want to help. But now you're here and maybe... maybe you surprised him.'

'You think I came in too strong?'

'No. What I mean is, it's obvious you can't be fooled.'

I sit back in my chair. 'What was he expecting? A journalist who would accept a couple of soundbites and hop on a plane back to London?'

She shrugs. 'Maybe. He hadn't even told me about the interview. I think he was trying to convince himself it wasn't a big deal.'

'Then I show up and freak him out completely. Okay, so what do I do?' I ask, frowning at her. 'How do I get him to trust me?'

'That I can't help with, mainly because I have no idea whether he *can* trust you myself. We only just met.' She smiles mischievously at me, jumping to her feet and tucking her chair in. 'But I can help in giving us the opportunity to get to know you. My girlfriend's birthday is this weekend and I'm throwing a party here Saturday. You want to come? It would be nice to have some new blood.'

'Really? Yeah! I'd love to,' I say warmly. 'Thanks.'

'Leo will be there,' she assures me. 'He's said he'll show up at some point.'

'From my experience, I'm not sure that means much,' I warn, gesturing to the empty chair on the other side of the table.

She waggles her finger at me. 'See? You're wrong there. If Leo says he'll show up, he'll show up.'

'Not today.'

'When it matters.'

'Marina,' I sigh, leaning forward on the table and looking up at her, 'that's the Leo I'm desperate to meet. *That's* the one I want to write about. I'm writing this feature whether he talks to me or not, and right now, the Leo Silva that's going to appear in it isn't that great.'

'I'm not going to persuade him to talk to you, Iris,' she says sternly. 'All I want to do is make your stay a little more comfortable.'

'Well, you're definitely succeeding there,' I tell her gratefully, tipping my glass at her. 'And I get that you can't help me with him. It's frustrating, that's all. I want to do him justice. I don't believe that he's a lone wolf, or whatever he was going on about yesterday.'

She looks confused. 'Lone wolf?'

'Apparently, surfers don't need anyone but themselves,' I mutter. 'He's out there alone and that's it. But I've followed sport all my life, and I know that that's not how it goes. Nobody gets that far alone, not really.'

Marina watches as I knock back the last of my drink and then she takes a deep breath.

'Have you been to the surf shop yet?' she asks.

'No, not yet.'

'I think you should go. You should go to the surf shop.'

'Leo finished at four; he won't be there.'

'I know, but still, you should go.'

I look at her strangely. She stares me down.

'The surf shop,' I repeat, pushing my chair back and getting to my feet.

'You might find what you're looking for there.'

'Thanks Marina,' I say, grabbing my bag and phone.

'Nothing to thank me for. I always recommend Adriano's surf shop to tourists,' she says with a shrug, sauntering away. 'It's not far from here. You should get there in time before it shuts.'

The bell above the door rings as I push it open and step into the surf shop and school.

It's a small, white, unassuming building down a narrow street close to the beach front, and according to the sign at the front, it closes in half an hour. The shop is silent and empty.

'Hello?' I call out.

No one responds.

Wandering towards the back, I run my eyes along the four framed charcoal sketches on the wall: drawings of surfers riding waves. I realise that a similar one hangs in Marina's Bar too. Must be a local artist.

'Hello, can I help you?' A man's voice says behind me, making me jump.

'Hi!' I smile, turning round to see an older gentleman emerging from the back room and coming to stand by the counter. He looks familiar but I can't place him. 'I... Marina recommended I come here. I'm Iris.'

'Yes, the journalist from London.'

My heart sinks. 'Ah. I take it Leo has told you about me.'

'He mentioned you.'

'Oh dear.' I grimace, before holding out my hand for him to shake. 'You are...?'

'Adriano.' He smiles, taking my hand. 'Leo's father.'

I inhale sharply, my fingers still grasping his.

He chuckles, patting the top of my hand before releasing it and turning away to go back to the counter. 'He hasn't told *you* about *me*, then. Welcome to my shop, Iris.'

'I... sorry, I knew you lived in the area but he didn't say you owned the shop where he worked,' I explain hurriedly.

Now I know why he seems familiar. He was on the beach watching Leo surf yesterday morning. *Why* didn't I think that's who he could be?!

'I'm so sorry, Mr Silva,' I repeat, moving over to the counter where he's now putting on some glasses to read the till screen. 'I should have known this was your shop and that Leo worked for you.'

'I'm working for him, too,' he tells me without looking up.

'Leo was insistent that he is an employee here at the shop and surf school you run.'

'Yes, he works for me in here, but out there,' he gestures in the direction of the beach, 'I work for him. I'm Leo's surfing coach.'

I blink at him. 'You're his coach.'

'Yes.' He lifts his eyes up to meet mine. 'It's a recently appointed position.'

'I see. I was under the impression that he didn't have a coach. That he was... alone.'

'Surfers are never alone,' he says coolly. 'And certainly not my Leo.'

'Nice to know I'm right about something,' I murmur, glancing around the shop. When I return my attention to him, I notice he's still watching me. I plaster on a smile. 'I know that this is a longshot, but is Leo here, Mr Silva?'

'Adriano, please. No, he's surfing.'

'I didn't see him out there.'

'He doesn't just surf here; he goes to several places along the coast,' he explains. 'He goes where he wants, wherever has the best waves.'

'Do you think he'll be back soon?'

He shakes his head. 'He didn't leave too long ago and he seemed... agitated. Was he meant to be meeting you?'

'We can rearrange.'

'Probably a good thing. He wasn't so easy to talk to today,' he says with a shrug. 'He was angry at himself after our session this morning. He thinks he surfed badly.'

'*Can* you surf badly? You mean he fell a lot?' I ask earnestly.

'You can read the water wrong. Sometimes, you ignore your gut; sometimes, your instincts lead you awry. Leo puts a lot of pressure on himself to always be the best and that's when he makes mistakes. He should be out there for the love of it. It's my job to remind him of that when he gets inside his head.'

'And what's it like? Coaching Leo?'

A knowing smile spreads across his face. 'I can tell from the way that you ask that you haven't seen the best side of him yet.'

Damn it. I'm usually good at masking my feelings about someone.

'The most complex subjects tend to be the most interesting ones,' I say coolly.

He laughs. 'I like that. Complex, eh? A nice way of saying he's been a shit to you.'

I grin at his bluntness. 'He's… nervous. How do you feel about him doing this feature?'

He leans an arm on the counter. 'Are you asking me that as his coach or as his father?'

'Depends on how you answer.'

He looks satisfied with my response. 'I have read your other articles, Iris. You must be good at getting people to talk about themselves.'

'It's not that difficult. People like to talk about themselves.'

'That is true.'

'What about you? Would you be happy to talk about yourself and your son for the piece?' I ask cheekily, going straight for my chance to secure him.

He takes a moment to consider my request.

'Despite what Leo may have told you, I promise I haven't come here to write an article that in any way upsets your family,' I insist. 'I just want to hear his story. Maybe you can help with that.'

Stroking his chin, he finally nods. 'Yes, I am happy to talk to you. I'm very proud of Leo; he deserves a bit of good press.'

'Great! When would it work for you to meet? Shall I come here tomorrow?'

He brushes the idea off with a wave of his hand. 'No, no. If we're going to do this, let's do it properly. I shall take you to lunch at my favourite restaurant.'

'No, Adriano,' I say, beaming at him. '*Studio* will take us to lunch.'

'I won't say no to that.'

'Thank you.' I pause, a question on the tip of my tongue but hesitant to push my luck.

'Yes, Iris?' he says, tilting his head at me and looking at me expectantly.

This guy really *is* good at reading people.

'As his coach, would you be happy for me to observe some of his training sessions?' I ask hopefully. 'I don't think Leo is going to be very forthcoming about when and where he's surfing. I don't want to do anything to distract him of course, but this feature is centred on his big comeback. I need to build in the work in the lead up to it.'

'I understand. Of course. I can let you know where we're going to be and you are welcome to come watch him surf.' He shrugs. 'It's not like you're out there in the water with him, getting in the way.'

I shudder at the thought. 'Exactly. Thank you, Adriano.'

After exchanging numbers and saying goodbye, I leave the shop in a completely different mood to when I walked in. I'm uplifted by his warmth and willingness to cooperate.

It finally feels like I'm getting somewhere.

Tonight, I'm taking myself out for dinner.

Eight

I feel like celebrating so I take myself to this amazing restaurant I passed earlier today when I was exploring and thought it looked nice. One of the few occasions when I was right to judge a book by its cover: the food is delicious, the staff are lovely and it's a relaxed but sophisticated setting. I bought a book in the airport on the way here, a thriller set in a beach house, and I've been able to eat my dinner completely engrossed in the pages.

'I think my perfect date might be a book,' I announced to Flora a couple of weeks ago when I was round her house for dinner. 'Aside from you, of course.'

'You can say that sort of thing all you like, but I don't believe you,' she told me curtly, twisting a cap back on its bottle. 'You love dating. Remember when I first broke up with my ex-boyfriend Jonah? You told me how wonderful dating was. Fun, romantic, exciting, dramatic – those were the words I believe you used.'

'Those are also the words I use to describe some of my

favourite books,' I countered haughtily. 'And you don't get to have an opinion on the matter. You were on the dating scene for about one whole minute before you fell head over heels with your accidental roommate.'

'Iris, I love books as much as the next person, but you can't date one,' Flora said, before taking a sip of her drink.

'I suppose. You can't have sex with one either.'

She spat Appletiser out all over the table. I smiled, delighted with myself.

'You can *read* about sex though,' I considered, 'which can be just as satisfying.'

'Iris,' she giggled, dabbing at her mouth with a napkin. 'Come on. Be serious. I know dating can be tiring and I also know that you're happy on your own – but it would also be okay for you to admit you might want to meet someone.'

'I know that,' I assured her, before heaving a sigh. 'But I don't have space for that sort of thing in my schedule right now.'

'Sometimes, it comes along when you least expect it and before you know it—'

'You're living in a mansion in Wimbledon carrying the offspring of a professional tennis player,' I finished for her, gesturing around her spacious, open-plan kitchen.

'Exactly. Oof.' She shifted in her seat, placing her palm over her belly. 'Don't I know that this is the kid of an athlete. The strength of the kicks!'

I'd jumped to my feet and run around the table to feel the movement and our conversation had naturally shifted onto something else. I know she's looking out for me, but I meant what I said: I don't have time for real-life romance right now.

I really would rather go on a date with a book.

'Iris?'

I snap my head up from my page-turner to look right up into the stunningly beautiful eyes of—

'José.' I smile, flooded with relief at remembering the name of my current landlord.

If it's possible, he looks even better tonight than he did when we bumped into each other on the stairs of my building on Monday. His dark hair styled perfectly, he's wearing a dark-navy suit with no tie, the top of the shirt unbuttoned, and a pale, silk pocket square. I can smell a hint of his cologne, nothing too overpowering. Just right.

He glances around the restaurant before his eyes return to me, his forehead furrowing in confusion. 'You are... dining alone?'

'Yes, that's right,' I say, marking my page.

'No, I can't allow it,' he says, his eyes flashing dangerously at me. 'You must join my table. I'm eating with some friends; they wouldn't mind you joining us I'm sure.'

He nods to a table behind me where two other well-dressed men are already sitting, perusing the menu. I didn't even notice them walk in. My book had distracted me from absolutely everyone else in the room. They glance up at José's comment and smile at me.

I smile politely back.

'That's kind, but I've finished,' I tell him, gesturing for the waiter to come over with the card machine so I can pay the bill. 'Thank you, though.'

'How are you enjoying your stay here?' he asks, stepping aside as the waiter awkwardly holds the machine out for me, his eyes darting to José nervously as though he's some kind of local celebrity. 'I hope it hasn't disappointed you.'

'Not at all. It's beautiful and it has a wonderful sense of community. Everyone has been so welcoming.'

'Good.'

As I move to stand up, he steps swiftly behind me to hold out my chair.

'Allow me,' he insists.

I pretend not to notice his eyes trail down the neckline of my dress as I turn to face him.

'Thank you, José. It was nice to see you again. Enjoy your dinner,' I say, before thanking the waiter and making my way towards the door.

'Iris,' José says, stopping me in my tracks as I hoped he might. I turn to face him. 'I really don't like the idea of you dining alone for your stay here. Perhaps I could take you out some time.'

'Perhaps. You know where I'm staying if you ever want to ask,' I say coolly, before turning away from him and strolling out of the restaurant.

I suppose one date without a book wouldn't hurt.

If Leo was half as charming as his father, I'd be in danger. Lunch with Adriano the next day is so easy and entertaining, I keep forgetting that I'm working – which is always when I do my best interviews. I'm so naturally interested in what he's saying that I'm not really thinking about the questions I'm asking him. The conversation moves all by itself without any kind of plan, and I have no idea where it's going to go, but by the end of it, I know I'll have way too many brilliant quotes than I can possibly fit into my word count.

'Hang on,' I say, holding up my hand to interrupt him mid-story as he chuckles away, 'did you say Leo was *six* years old at this point?'

'Yes. Six years old.'

'And he was late for a school trip because he was surfing? At *six years old*.'

'That's right,' he confirms, enjoying my stunned expression.

'I had no idea that you could start surfing that young!'

'Not on his own, I was there with him,' Adriano emphasises. 'We both got in plenty of trouble with the school that day. He missed the coach, so I had to drive him to the museum instead. You should have seen us in the car,' he chuckles at the memory, 'both of us sulking because we knew we were missing some great waves.'

'That's amazing that he was out on a board so young.' I return my attention to the delicious salted cod dish I've ordered – Adriano has taken me to what he claims is the best fish restaurant in town and so far, I'm inclined to agree with him. 'So I take it he gets his love of surfing from you then?'

'I grew up here in Burgau, so I've always felt connected to the ocean,' he tells me, linking his fingers together and resting his chin on his knuckles. 'That connection is something I saw in Leo from a very young age. You are born with it. He was lucky to grow up in Victoria where he could learn to surf. I'd been travelling, you see, and when I met Michelle, I decided to stay in Australia. I loved living out there – it's such a beautiful place – and it was a joy to teach him as a young boy and see him grow to love the sport like I did. More so, I think. He's wonderful to watch, like he was meant to do it – you can always spot him out there on the water, no matter the crowd.'

I smile, glancing at the screen of my phone to make sure it's still recording and got that gorgeous quote. I always have the fear that at the end of an interview, I'll check my phone and it won't have recorded anything, which is why I also have an old-fashioned Dictaphone in my bag recording the whole conversation, too, as back-up. No harm in being safe rather than sorry.

'When you were teaching him as a kid, did you always plan for him to surf professionally?' I ask, placing my glass back down.

He shakes his head. 'Not at all. You can't plan your child's destiny, that I strongly believe. But anyone could tell from watching him that he was special. He has a gift. I made sure that when Leo was learning to surf, he was having fun. That was absolutely key to my teaching and a technique I hope we bring to the surf school here.' He leans back in his chair pensively. 'The best surfers in the world, Iris, are not those who are in it for the competitions, but those who get on the board for the *feeling* of it.'

'The feeling of surfing.'

'Yes. There is nothing like it. The freedom and exhilaration of surfing a wave. But even if you don't surf, simply being out there in the ocean is enough. That is when you understand what matters in life.'

I keep my eyes fixed on his. 'And what does matter in life, do you think?'

'The small things,' he says simply. 'The simple, everyday

moments of joy and love and respect.' A sadness flits across his expression. 'That is what Leo needed to come here to remember. He forgot that for a while. It's easy for that to happen. I only wish... I wish I'd persuaded him to come with me when I first moved home from Australia. We wanted different things at that time and... Anyway, he got here in the end.'

'Do you think he has rediscovered those small moments of joy here in Burgau?'

'When you watch him in the water, Iris, you will see for yourself. I am so proud of how far he's come. He's found himself again. It's not easy to rediscover hope and confidence when you've been swallowed up by such sadness and misery. But like I told him when he first came here, it's like coming off your board in a wave. You can feel uneasy and lost, your confidence shattered, but you will come up for air and everything will make sense. And then you bring what you've learnt from that to master the next wave, because that's the most important thing to remember – there will always be another wave coming.' He shoots me a grin. 'I had to word it in a way he would understand.'

'I think it's a lovely way of putting it. Even if you're not a surfer.' I hesitate. 'Adriano, you seem passionate about Leo finding his love of surfing after everything – do you worry about him entering the Rip Curl Pro Bells Beach contest again, being in a competitive headspace, and what it might do to his mentality?'

He ponders the question. 'I trust Leo,' he answers eventually. 'If this is what Leo needs to do, then he has my support. Bells Beach... means something to him.'

I notice something flash across his expression – fear,

maybe – but it's gone too fast for me to read. As if he can tell I'm studying him, he collects himself, fixing a smile.

'Why is Bells Beach so important? Because he grew up around there?'

'I'll leave that for him to answer,' he says softly.

'I suppose everyone wants to ring that iconic bell trophy,' I say, steering away from the personal angle now that he's shut it down but still hoping to get something else from him.

'Oh yes,' he chuckles, his expression lighting up. 'Bells Beach is the longest-running event in the surf calendar. So much history in that wave. The champions of Bells have been some of the true greats of the sport. The bell trophy is iconic – Leo has rung it before and I believe he has what it takes to ring it again.'

'And what about Michelle?' I ask gingerly. 'She seems fully supportive of his comeback. What are her thoughts on his return to the surf scene?'

'Mmm.' He sighs, giving me a pointed look. 'I won't talk about Michelle.'

Oh well. It was worth a try. 'I understand.'

He smiles gratefully before gesturing to our empty plates. 'Ah, now we have finished our lunch, I think we should finish the interview. You press stop on that thing,' he gestures to my phone, 'and we can have a proper drink.'

I burst out laughing, reaching over to press stop on the recording, dropping my phone into my bag and turning off my Dictaphone too.

'Thank you so much, Adriano,' I gush as he waves over his friend who owns the restaurant, asking for a bottle of wine that the owner recommends. 'That was wonderful.'

'Probably a lot of nonsense, but hopefully you have something there.'

'There's plenty, trust me.' I grin, leaning back so the waiter can clear the table. 'I have to say that it's very unusual I speak to a family member before the subject themselves, but never mind. I've made a start.'

'Leo will come round,' he assures me, beaming at the owner who comes over with the bottle, clapping Adriano on the back before he fills our glasses.

'He really does not want to do this.'

'No, but he gave his mother his word. And you, also.' He holds up his glass to toast. 'To your article. I hope that the world gets to see the real Leo.'

I clink my glass against his. 'Me too. Cheers.'

'*Saúde.*'

We sip our drinks and I smile my approval of his wine choice.

'So, do you surf, Iris?' he asks.

'No,' I say, tensing.

'You should. I think you would like it. I read your articles and I like that you give the sport a go yourself. The greats make it look so easy, but you show your readers what that takes to achieve,' he says, watching me as I fiddle with the edge of the tablecloth. 'The article about the skier was very moving.'

'Thank you. I've skied before, so it was fun to try it again. I wasn't exactly his level, but...' I force a laugh, trailing off.

'Leo will take you out on the water if you wish. I can speak to him.'

'I don't think that will be necessary,' I say quickly. 'I've read a lot about surfing and I can watch Leo while he's out there.'

'Reading about surfing is not the same. To really understand it, you need to be on a board moving with the water, focusing only on the steadiness of your body, the shifting of balance, the feel of the tide.'

I take a large gulp of wine, placing down my glass. 'You know, I think I've drunk wine every day that I've been here? I keep forgetting that I'm here for work. It's easy to do that in a place like this. It must be hard for you to avoid going to Marina's every day: a bar on the beach with that view so close to your shop! She wouldn't be able to get rid of me!'

I'm speaking too quickly, rambling. If he notices my nerves, he pretends not to.

He offers a warm smile. 'Yes, it is tempting.'

'Your shop is in such a great location.'

He inhales deeply through his nose. 'You're not the only person to notice that. A property developer has offered to buy it. They want to build a block of flats there.'

'Oh! Well, that's... How do you feel about that?'

Adriano knits his eyebrows together in a frown. 'It breaks my heart. The locals are all against such development, but that is what is happening here now. Tourism is growing and that can be a good thing... and a bad thing. Costs are high. I may not have a choice.'

'You might have to sell?'

He nods slowly. 'This is not for your article, Iris—'

'Off the record,' I interject firmly. 'You have my word.'

'That is one of the reasons Leo has agreed to the competition and the article,' he says softly. 'He knows that if he wins, the spotlight will be on him again and our shop and school will likely be saved; after a comeback like this, if he's successful, business would boom with his name attached to it.' He sighs, concern etched in the creases on his forehead. 'I wish he didn't put that pressure on himself, but he cares deeply about my business.'

'I'm so sorry. That's a lot to shoulder. For both of you.'

'Yes, it's one of those things. The modern apartments here, they are beautiful for visitors, but too many and suddenly, what makes the village what it is, that is lost. The new replaces the old. Change is good but not when you lose the spirit of a place, you see?'

I feel a stab of guilt at staying in one of those new modern apartments. 'Yes.'

'There are lots of people here who support me and the surf school, people like Marina and others who live and work here all year round. I have not lost hope yet.'

'You have my article too,' I remind him eagerly. 'People will want to book some lessons and come visit your shop once they read about it, I'm sure of it.'

'I hope. Another reason why Leo agreed to the article. But it's easy to say you'll do something, and then when it comes to it…'

'I've met reluctant interviewees before. I'm sure I can win him over.'

'I know that, Iris,' Adriano says, his eyes glinting at me. 'I knew as soon as I met you that Leo didn't have a chance.'

'Maybe I'll try to speak to him this evening,' I suggest, straightening. 'He knew we were having lunch, right? So he might be quite keen to talk, wanting to know what you and I have spoken about. Where do you think I'll find him tonight?'

'Yoga.'

I blink at him. 'Yoga? Leo does yoga.'

'I was the one who encouraged him to try it,' Adriano tells me proudly. 'He was too focused on his gym workouts in between surfing, and I said he should try yoga so he could learn the importance of breath. That is as important to surfing as building muscle. He loves it now and practises often.'

'Huh.' I pick up my glass again, swirling the liquid round.

Leo leans back in his chair to observe me. 'You're quite like him, you know.'

'Who, Leo? Is that because we're both stubborn?'

'Determined, smart, self-sufficient,' he corrects gently. 'And something about you that draws everyone in – yet you hold them at bay.'

'Here I was thinking I was difficult to read.' I take a sip of wine, blushing. 'Am I that easy to crack? We've only had one lunch.'

'You'll have to let me know how it goes with Leo,' he says, brushing over my embarrassment with a secretive smile. 'I think you two might just get on.'

Nine

In the end, it's Flora who reminds me what I'm here to do.

We're on a video call as I sit on the balcony of the flat, looking out at the ocean, the breeze tickling my shoulders, and when I've told her that I still haven't spoken to Leo, she's understandably confused.

'But you've interviewed his dad,' she checks, pottering about her kitchen.

'Yeah, he's great.' I inhale deeply. 'Flora, you really need to come here, especially as an artist. You need to paint this view. The beach is so beautiful, framed by these amazing cliffs – can you see them in the distance? Hang on, if I move the phone—'

'Iris, why are you talking to me about the *view*? You need to speak to Leo!'

'I've tried.' I shrug. 'He'll come round.'

'Yeah, once you've persuaded him to,' she says, her brow furrowed. 'When he was playing Wimbledon, there's no way Kieran would have chosen to speak to a journalist. If this guy is the same calibre, you need to make an effort.'

'What do you think I'm doing?'

'I think you're enjoying a lovely holiday in a place that is clearly starting to distract you from your job. All you've told me about so far is how amazing Burgau is and your subject's charming father.'

'He is charming. And nothing could distract me from my job! This is delicate. I can't force him to talk to me. I'll make him see the light. Eventually.'

'Uh-huh.' She gives a sceptical look down the camera. 'Can I give you my opinion?'

'It sounds like I don't have a choice in the matter.'

'You're not fighting for this story.'

'Hey!'

'You're not!' she maintains. 'If he was a tennis player, you'd be out on those courts every day. Look at that ski dude that everyone fell in love with – you basically followed him on a pair of skis every day.'

'Did you use the word "dude"?' I ask, appalled.

'I'm saying that I think your... worries might be affecting how much you want this story. The Iris I know would immerse herself in the world of her subject whether they're ready for her or not.'

'What do you want me to do, Flora?' I sigh huffily. 'I can't follow him into the sea. You... you know I can't do that.'

'Maybe this is the opportunity you need to finally face your fear, Iris.'

I groan. 'Flora, I *can't*.'

'Okay, fine. Well, is he in the sea right now?'

'No, he's... he's at yoga.'

A satisfied smile appears on her lips. '*You* like yoga.'

I take a moment, letting her point sink in.

'Out of interest, when did you decide that Leo Silva got to make the rules?' Flora continues breezily, propping up her phone on something so she can light a three-wick candle on her coffee table before she plonks herself down on the sofa. 'I get that you need him for the story, but doesn't he need you, too? He needs this publicity.'

Damn it. She's right.

What am I doing?

'Flora, I have to go,' I say, jumping to my feet. 'There's somewhere I need to be.'

'That's my girl,' she grins. 'Oh, and Iris, wear the teal yoga leggings and matching bra. You packed that set, right?'

'Yeah.' I hesitate. 'Why?'

'Because it will be very hard for anyone to say no to you when you're wearing that.'

She winks at me and hangs up.

The moment I walk into the yoga studio, I see him. He's sitting on a mat in the back row of the room in a white t-shirt and dark shorts, scrolling on his phone before the class starts. Now, I'm not sure if I believe in fate, but it just so happens that this is a very small studio and the only free mat left is the one at the back next to his.

Okay, fine, I believe. Thank you, Fate. You've done me a solid.

I slink across the room and sit down cross-legged on the free mat as elegantly as possible, smiling at the teacher at the front of the room, who gives a small nod in acknowledgement of my arrival. Leo glances over and does a double take.

'*Iris?*' he says in disbelief, his eyes widening as I pretend to have only just noticed him.

'Oh! Hi Leo. You take this class too? Weird.'

'Shall we begin?' the teacher announces, sitting down on her mat at the front of the class, facing us all. 'We're going to start today on the flat of our backs so when you're ready, lie down on your mat. Take your time, lie down and tuck your chin slightly and ease into things. Let's take a moment to centre ourselves and let go of our day by closing our eyes.'

Following her lead, I do as she instructs, straightening my legs and lying back, before shutting my eyes. I'm soon interrupted.

'What are you doing here?' Leo hisses.

'Yoga,' I whisper, without opening my eyes.

'I mean in this class. *My* class.'

'Do you own the class?'

'What? No, I don't mean—'

'Let your arms and legs relax,' the instructor says soothingly. 'Allow my voice to guide you through our practice today. Take a deep breath in, that's it.'

I inhale deeply through my nose.

'I know what you're doing,' Leo whispers.

I exhale through my mouth.

'I hope you don't expect me to talk to you here,' he grumbles.

Turning my head slowly to look at him, I open my eyes and try not to laugh at how ridiculous this situation is, the two of us lying down next to each other. He's glaring at me.

'Would you mind being quiet? You're disturbing my zen,' I say softly.

'*I'm* disturbing *you*?'

The instructor clears her throat at the front. 'Whatever is going on with you in your external life, now is the time to kindly let go as we go inward, deepening our breath and relaxing our body.'

'I really—' Leo begins in a low voice.

'Why don't we talk after class?' I suggest politely. 'Unless you want to carry on disturbing everyone in this room?'

His jaw clenches. But he gets the hint and turns away to look up at the ceiling. I do the same, fighting the urge to smile triumphantly and instead listening to the soothing tones of the instructor as she guides us through the class.

With my recent work load, it's actually been a while since I did any yoga and, although admittedly, I purely came to seek out Leo, now that I'm here, I'm invested. Throughout the class, I focus on tapping into 'the power of self-love' as the instructor tells me to, and the fact that I can't help but notice Leo glancing over at me suspiciously every now and then is an added bonus. There's no chance that he's leaving here without talking to me, even if it's to tell me off some more. At least we'll be communicating.

Another bonus is that I get the chance to steal glances at *him* during the class too.

I never realised how sexy it is for a man to do yoga, but fuck me, the way his muscles flex and move as he changes positions, watching the curve of his upper arms bulge as they take his weight when he balances, so powerful and strong.

It's a shame he's such a pain in the arse, because he really is pretty to look at.

When the class finishes, I make a point of going up to the instructor to tell her how much I enjoyed it and she encourages me to come back during my stay. Our conversation means that I'm the last student to leave. Grabbing my bag that I left at the side of the studio, I thank her again and push through the doors.

Guess who's waiting for me on the other side?

'Iris,' Leo calls out, as I pass him on my way out without stopping. 'Iris!'

I pretend to not hear him, marching onwards.

'Hey! Hey, *London*!'

I stop in my tracks, turning to give him a strange look as he catches up.

'Did you just call me "London"?'

'I need to talk to you.'

'Okay,' I say, continuing my walk home, 'what's up?'

'*What's up?*' He looks baffled as he falls into step with me. 'You showed up at my yoga class, unannounced.'

I shoot him a strange look. 'Do I have to tell you what I'm doing in advance?'

'You know that's not what I'm saying.'

'Good, because that would be creepy.'

'There are other yoga classes you can take,' he mumbles.

'I like this one. I plan on signing up to lots more during my stay.'

'Those classes are really important to me. I don't want any disturbances.'

'As I recall it, the only disturbances in that class came from you.'

'Hold on.' He hurries ahead so that he can round back and face me, stopping me in my tracks. 'I mean it. Those classes,' he gestures at the studio behind me, 'they help me to get out of my own head. That's something I really need to do the next few weeks.'

'You could always do another yoga class. Or take private ones.'

He shakes his head. 'I can't.'

'Why not?'

'Because... I feel safe in that class. I know the instructor and the other students, and I... trust them. I like to do yoga with other people in the room; it's like you're part of something. A community or whatever. I began yoga in that class with that instructor, and I want to continue under her guidance.' He sighs, putting his hands on his hips. 'I like the routine of it. Without the calm and focus of that class, my head goes... wobbly.'

I break into a warm smile. 'Okay, Leo. I won't come to that class again. You don't need to worry. I'll find another one.'

His eyebrows shoot up in surprise. 'Really?'

'Yeah. Sorry if I made your head go... wobbly.'

He's still confused, but the corners of his lips twitch. 'Oh. Thanks.'

'It's been nice getting a glimpse of your routine,' I admit, omitting the part about how *very* nice it was to observe him doing yoga and how disappointed I am that I won't get to see the show again. I tilt my head at him. 'You know, if you'd turned up yesterday and mentioned the yoga, and said everything you did just then, I wouldn't have had to find that out on my own. I did ask what else you're doing to prepare for the competition other than surfing. Sounds like yoga and the gym are two big components of your process.'

He glances at the floor and then brings his eyes up to meet mine, a knowing smile creeping across his lips. 'You talked to my dad today.'

'I did.'

'He's the one who got me into yoga.'

'I know.'

He nods, looking thoughtful. 'Okay I get what you're saying. We should talk.'

'We should. But you said that to me at Marina's Bar, like you were fully on board, and then stood me up later,' I remind him, sticking out my chin. 'So.'

'So... what?'

'So, I'm good at my job, Leo,' I tell him, allowing a touch of exasperation to filter into my tone. 'If you want me to write things about you that have the potential to impact not only your career in a positive way, but also that of your mother's and your father's business, then you need to start showing up.'

He looks down at his trainers guiltily, but I carry on, unaffected by any remorse he's showing. This isn't personal; it's business. And suddenly, it's as though his reaction gives me full permission to get everything off my chest that I've been wanting to say to him. So I continue brazenly, letting it all out without much thought.

I think the yoga has relaxed all of my body, including my tongue.

'I've already said to you that this feature is going to be written. Right now, you're not coming across as the kind of man people tell me you are – but that's not my problem, it's yours. I write the truth of what I get to see. If you want to keep brushing me off as this tabloid journo here to ruin your life, then that's up to you. Mess me around, be the arrogant, selfish arsehole the press painted you as a lifetime ago. But you have the choice to just be *you*. I've said how I want this to play. I've made my intentions clear. Now, it's on you.'

Whoa.

My rant has surprised even me. In my defence, all of that was true. Normally, I wouldn't tell a star athlete that he was coming across as an arrogant, selfish arsehole, but I get the feeling that Leo Silva needs to be spoken to plainly. All cards on the table, no one trying to bullshit anyone else. I think he may appreciate that.

I hope so, anyway.

'Okay,' he says finally.

'Okay what?'

'Okay, let's talk,' he says, shoving his hands in his pockets. 'Are you free now?'

'I… yeah. I am.' I put a hand on my hip. 'Where shall we go?'

With a hint of a smile, he gestures for me to follow him. 'I know a place.'

Ten

The beach. *Of course* that's where he, a pro surfer, wants to chat.

Jesus, he could have been a bit more original.

But if this is where he wants to talk, then I guess this is where we'll talk. He's already pointed out that sitting on the sand with no one around has the distinct advantage of privacy compared to a bar or restaurant. I mean, so does his flat or my flat, and neither of those require getting sand all over my leggings, but I'm not going to kick up a fuss now. Not when he's finally ready to be interviewed.

'At least you're wearing shoes that are more practical for the sand today,' he notes.

'I don't choose shoes for their practicality,' I grumble, kicking sand off the toe of my trainer.

'Funny enough, London, I've noticed that.'

'Are you really going to keep calling me that?'

He chuckles to himself in response and I roll my eyes.

He finally chooses somewhere, plonking himself down.

'Are you warm enough?' he asks, as he gestures for me to sit down next to him while taking off his shoes and socks, placing them neatly to his other side. 'I can run to the shop and get some hoodies if we need; I have a couple in there.'

'I'm fine,' I say, even though it is getting a bit chillier.

I carefully place myself down on the sand next to him, aware that he's watching as I try to do so as elegantly as possible. I catch a glimpse of him smirking when I brush some sand off my bag once I've popped it next to me.

'What?' I ask, bristling.

He fights a smile. 'Nothing.'

'Oh, I get it. I'm being very *London*, is that it?'

He doesn't say anything.

While I get my phone and Dictaphone ready – I had made sure they were both in my bag on the way out to the yoga class, just in case my invasion into his yoga practice did have a positive impact – he bends his knees up, resting his forearms on them, and digs his toes into the sand.

'Will the sound of the waves be a problem?' he asks, looking out at the ocean getting darker in the evening light.

'No, we're far away enough from the water,' I say gratefully, placing them on the stretch of sand between us. 'Are you happy for me to hit record?'

He nods, keeping his eyes fixed ahead, his jaw tense. He's getting nervous now.

'That was an impressive speech you made back there,' he remarks as the recording begins. 'I wasn't expecting it.'

'Me neither,' I admit.

He gives a wry smile. 'I must have pushed you over the edge.'

I hesitate. 'Leo, I know this isn't something you wanted to do—'

'But we're here now,' he interjects, turning to look at me. 'I can't back out. My dad reminded me of that this afternoon when he came back from your lunch.'

'It was a very nice lunch.'

'Yeah, I noticed he'd had a few.' He raises his eyebrows. 'Your influence?'

'All him.'

'Sounds about right.' He sighs, throwing his head back to look up at the sky. 'Go on then. I'm ready. What's the first question?'

I stretch my legs out in front of me, leaning back on my elbows. Just like when I ordered the wine in the bar with him, I'm making a show of this being as informal as he likes. If this is going to go well, he has to relax into it. That means I do too. Or at least give the impression that I'm doing so.

'Do you remember the first time you surfed?'

He turns to look at me in surprise. 'That's the first question?'

'You don't think it's a good one?'

'No, I... it's fine.' He's folded his arms across the top of his knees and he's tapping one of his fingers on his elbow nervously. 'No,' he says. 'I don't remember it.'

'You were young when you started, your dad was telling me.'

He nods silently.

Fuck's sake. I knew it was going to be like drawing blood from a stone, but I really hope it gets better than this otherwise I'm going to have a huge job on my hands hitting the word count for this feature.

'Did you love it straight away? What drew you to it in the first place?'

He shrugs. 'I don't remember. My dad surfs.'

I wait for him to embellish his answer, but he seems to think that's good enough.

'What's the next question?' he prompts when I continue to stare at him expectantly.

I sigh, sitting up and making a point of turning off my Dictaphone.

'What are you doing?' he asks, brow furrowed.

'It's not working.'

'What's not working?'

'This. Me asking you questions this way,' I attempt to explain vaguely, shoving the Dictaphone back in my bag.

'You haven't asked many.'

'Enough for me to know we have to do this differently,' I say, waving him off. 'Let's just sit here and talk.'

He swivels towards me slightly. 'I don't understand.'

'Don't worry about it,' I insist, before returning to my position of lying back propped up on my elbows. Time to try another tactic. I breathe in the salty sea air. 'Can I tell you something?' I pause for dramatic effect, before blurting out, 'I don't like the beach.'

His jaw falls open. 'What?'

'I don't like the beach,' I repeat.

'How can anyone hate the beach?' he asks me in disbelief.

'I like *looking* at it! Don't get me wrong, I love the view of a beach. But I don't like being on it. The sand gets everywhere, and I hate the feeling of it between your toes.'

I shudder, glancing at his toes as he scrunches them on purpose. 'I hate going into the sea because it's cold and salty and you can't tell if you're going to step on a crab – which, by the way, happened to me as a kid – or if slimy seaweed will wrap around your ankles. And I hate coming out of the sea because it's even colder and the sand sticks to the edges of your feet no matter what you do and you can taste the salt on your lips which makes me want to be sick...'

The whole time I'm talking, he's watching me intently, stunned into silence.

I heave a sigh. 'So yeah, in conclusion, it's not for me.'

There's a beat of silence before he bursts out laughing.

'What's so funny?' I ask, frowning at him.

'Everything you've said is true,' he says, 'and that's why I love the beach.'

'You *like* all those things?'

'Love them. Maybe not stepping on a crab, although I can't say I've experienced that so far in my career.'

'Lucky you. Have you ever been stung by a jellyfish?'

'Yes. I wouldn't recommend it.'

'Where did it sting you?'

He winces. 'Just beneath my butt, actually.'

'Ouch, that must have been sore. Did someone have to pee on you?'

'No, luckily I made it through without that remedy,' he says, breaking into a smile as he leans back on his hands. 'It was nasty, though.'

'Did a shark give you that scar on your wrist?' I ask, nodding to the faint line I'd noticed in yoga earlier.

He glances down on it and then back at me, raising his eyebrows. 'Would it sound impressive if I said it was?'

'Depends on the type of shark,' I shrug. 'If it was a great white, then yeah. But if it was one of those granny sharks, probably not.'

He throws his head back and laughs. It's a nice laugh. Kind of mischievous and boyish, with crinkles appearing around the corners of his mouth. A laugh that makes butterflies dance in my stomach.

'What the fuck is a granny shark?' he demands to know.

'The ones with no teeth! Hammerheads, I think.'

'Hammerheads have teeth.'

'No, they don't.'

'They do. They're kind of hidden because of their—' He tries to gesture what he's talking about.

'Their... hammer-heads?' I offer.

'Right.' He grins at me. 'But yeah, hammerheads have teeth. You're thinking of basking sharks, I reckon. Although, fun fact, they do have teeth. They're really small, though.'

'That is a fun fact, thank you Leo,' I say drily. 'So is that what got you on the wrist? A basking shark?'

'I wrestled it with my bare hands when it tried to attack an orphaned puppy.'

'Uh-huh.'

He sighs wistfully. 'Nah, that scar is from... a wipe-out.'

'A bad one?'

He nods. Clearing his throat, he points to another more recent scar on his other hand. 'This one, however, is from when I tried to bake recently.'

I tilt my head at him, intrigued. 'You bake?'

'I said "tried" to. I was making a cake for Dad's birthday. Fucking disaster.'

'I think it's sweet that you tried. You and your dad seem really close,' I remark gently.

'I'm lucky to have him nearby.'

'You surf together a lot?'

'All the time. You can't keep either of us away from the water.'

'Your dad said that when you grow up near the water, you have a connection with it.'

He nods in agreement. 'Maybe. Although I don't think you can't *find* that connection if you come to surfing late in life. You can. You don't have to be on the water from a young age to understand it. But I was lucky to pretty much grow up on the waves in Australia. I don't remember a time *before* being out on the water. It's always been my life.'

'It didn't frighten you? Even as a kid?'

'Right from the word go, it gave me this rush that I can't describe.' He gazes out at the ocean. 'Being out there is, like, the only place where you're completely living in the moment. Everything else washes away. Your head clears and it's just you and the roll of the wave.'

'It can't be like that at the beginning though, when you're learning. That part must suck. Not that you'll be able to remember that, you know, being a pro.'

He laughs. 'I remember the first time I stood up on a board. You don't forget that. The feeling of getting the balance quite right. My legs were shaking and my dad was cheering.'

He can't help a grin flooding his face, the genuine warmth of it forcing me to reflect it back at him as he turns to look at me. My chest aches at the pure joy in his expression.

God, he's beautiful. Annoying, but beautiful.

'It wasn't for very long and it wasn't graceful, but it didn't matter,' he continues. 'I'd done it. That elation, it was pure joy, you know? I was gliding with the water – shakily – but still. That was it. I knew as soon as I crashed into the water afterwards that there was nothing else I ever wanted to do.'

'You were a natural.'

'I don't know.' His eyes fall modestly to his feet as he scrunches his toes into the sand again. 'Dad's never pressured me into it – you've met him, he's not like that. He loved it as a hobby and a passion, and so did I.' He pauses, his forehead creasing in thought. 'But it somehow also felt as though I never had a choice. I had to be out there on the water, there was nothing else for me. Does that make sense? I'm talking shit.'

'No, I think it does make sense,' I assure him. 'Would it sound too much of a wanker thing to say that… you feel as though the ocean chose you? It's part of your soul.'

He chuckles. 'It does sound like a bit of a wanker thing to say. But yeah. Something like that. Do you feel the same about writing?'

I wasn't expecting the question. The focus is meant to be on him.

'Uh… I… I don't know. Maybe. It's something I've always done.' He's watching me intently waiting for a proper answer, so I take a moment to think about it. 'I guess… I can't *not* write.' I shoot him a look. 'That sounds like a wanker thing to say too.'

'It does. But hey,' he shrugs, 'I get it.'

He smiles in a way that makes my breath hitch. There's something about the way he's looking at me, his eyes softening as his smile broadens, that makes my belly pool with warmth and I realise that my tactic is working. Right here, right now, he's not seeing me as a journalist, sent to interrogate him and ruin his image. He's simply talking to me, Iris, about his passion in life while we sit on a beach. We've had a breakthrough.

I tear my eyes away from his to look out at the water.

'It must be different surfing here to Australia, though,' I reason, steering our conversation back on track.

'It is. Different waves, different people, different vibe.' He nods thoughtfully. 'Both are good in their own ways. I have... missed Australia, though. I've missed it heaps, to be honest.' For a moment, he looks pained. 'I'm looking forward to going back next month.'

'Do you feel like you're going home?'

His eyes lock on mine, his eyebrows knitting together, as though I've asked him something he hadn't considered before.

'No,' he says eventually, refusing to look away. 'It will always mean a lot to me, but this is my home now.'

'I can understand why. It's...' I raise my eyes skyward, searching for the right word '...calm here.'

'Definitely calmer than London,' he comments.

'Most places tend to be. I like that it's busy, though.'

'You always want to live in a city?'

'I don't know. London is all I've ever known.' I hesitate and then decide to divulge more information, if only to continue the connection we're forging. 'My parents wanted me to buy a small flat somewhere – I've been saving up the deposit and they were happy to help too. But... it didn't seem right. I don't know why.'

He digs his heels into the sand, pushing his feet out to

straighten his legs. 'You can't settle for somewhere if you don't have the gut instinct that it's the right place for you.'

'Is that how you feel about Burgau?'

'Yeah. I always felt restless in Australia. My life was different. Here I feel like... I can breathe. Do my own thing. No pressure.'

'As in, no one expects anything of you here? Is that how you felt when you were living in Australia?' I ask cautiously. 'Like you had to live up to something? Maybe because of who your mum was, or because you were successful so young?'

His expression darkens. 'That sounds like an interview question.' Suddenly, his eyes widen. 'You record on your phone.'

'Sorry?'

'You record on your phone,' he repeats. 'It was that other thing that you turned off and put in your bag, but not your phone.'

As he spots it still lying in the sand between us, he moves to reach for it but I snatch it up before he can get it.

'You've been recording this conversation this whole time?' he asks angrily.

'Yes, I have,' I tell him honestly, pressing stop and saving it.

'So you've been lying to me.'

'I never said that I was ending the interview formally. I said it wasn't working me asking you questions like that, and that we had to do things differently.' I give him a stern look. 'Do you want me to delete it? I will if you like, but do you honestly regret anything you've told me this evening?'

He opens his mouth to protest. Then, he closes it.

'You see?' I say smugly, sliding the phone into my bag. 'I really enjoyed our conversation and I think you did too. That was all this needs to be, Leo. I had to get you to relax into it, and you did.'

He doesn't say anything.

'There were some really lovely quotes in there. It was exactly what I was after; all those moving things you were saying about the first time you got up on a board, it's really—'

'I won't talk about what happened in Australia,' he says in a low, serious voice, completely different to the way he was talking to me before.

The walls are back up. He's a different person.

'Leo, that's not what I—'

'You won't trick that out of me,' he growls, his expression hardened. 'You can try to play me about other stuff – my hopes and dreams when I was a kid, my life here now – but don't pretend as though you would go ahead and delete the recording if I'd just spilled my sad little story to you about why my career finished. Don't pretend to be the good guy.'

I stare at him, stunned. 'Leo—'

'This interview is over,' he says abruptly, getting to his feet. 'You got what you came for.'

'Can we—'

'Will you be okay getting home?' he cuts in.

If it wasn't for the hate radiating off him right now, I'd have appreciated how nice it is for him to ask.

I sigh, defeated. 'Yeah. It's about two minutes from here.'

With a sharp nod, he bends down to pick up his shoes and walks away off the beach. I turn to watch him go as he strides forwards furiously.

I glumly get to my feet, attempting to wipe some of the sand off my leggings.

Tonight was, technically, a huge success.

But it doesn't feel that way.

Eleven

As I make my way to the bar for Marina's girlfriend's birthday party on Saturday, I feel nervous. I haven't spoken to Leo since Thursday night at the beach – or rather, he hasn't spoken to me. My messages have gone unanswered and I had to resist the urge to rock up at the surf shop. I appreciate that it maybe didn't look so good, me giving the impression that the interview was over when it wasn't. When I think about it, maybe it was a little underhanded. I realise that I may have played into his belief that all journalists are tricksters out for a good headline, no matter the ethical cost. I wanted to give him some time to calm down and I thought that Marina's party is the perfect place to approach him in a relaxed, non-professional setting. We need this to re-group.

I could also do with a day off.

Mum called when I was getting ready for the party.

'I spoke to an estate agent yesterday,' she informed me. 'About the house.'

I'd paused midway through applying my lip liner. '*Our* house?'

She cleared her throat. 'Yes, the family house. Which isn't really a family house anymore. Your father and I have both agreed that we should sell it.'

I don't know why this news hits me so hard, but it does. I should have been expecting this. Did I really think Mum would go on living there forever? Surrounded by all those memories? It is a big house for one person. It makes sense to sell it. Of course it does.

But I felt winded. I even had to sit down on the edge of the bed.

'Iris, are you still there?' Mum asked nervously.

The concern in her voice catapulted me back into reality. She had enough on her plate without me being unsupportive. I'm a grown-up, not a child. It's just a house.

'Yes, sorry, I was concentrating on my make-up,' I said hurriedly. 'That's great that you spoke to an estate agent! Was it all positive? How did you feel about it?'

She assured me that she was all right and it was for the best, and she said the estate agent was extremely complimentary, confirming that the house was in a desirable location. The perfect home for a young family, apparently. He thinks they would get an offer within the first week of it being on the market.

I mentioned that I had to rush off to the party, so we said goodbye and hung up.

It took me a few minutes to go back to the bathroom mirror to finish my make-up. I had to focus on blinking back the hot tears at the back of my eyes, threatening to spill over and ruin the eyeliner I'd already applied. I was embarrassed for myself. What a stupid reaction to something that should not be such a big deal.

'Pull yourself together,' I scolded myself.

The whole debacle made me change my outfit. I'd been wearing wide-leg linen trousers and a strap top, but fuck it, I wanted to feel sexy. I changed to a green dress with a plunging neckline and block heel shoes, throwing on a faded-black, baggy denim jacket to make the outfit more casual. I boldened my eyeliner and I put on gold statement earrings, letting my hair down from its satin heatless curling headband. It fell in soft waves past my shoulders.

I lifted my chin as I checked my reflection.

'Better,' I said, shaking off any sadness about saying goodbye to my childhood home.

As I approach the bar, the nerves flitting around my stomach intensify. I try to rationalise why I feel this way. My job isn't about personal feelings, so I shouldn't be upset that I may have affected Leo's. I think it's because he proved that, beneath the hardened exterior he puts up for strangers, he's actually very easy to get on with. Naturally chatty, funny, thoughtful, he asked if I was cold, offering a hoodie. That was sweet.

But I need to remember that he's not my friend.

He's a job.

'Iris, you made it!' Marina calls out, beaming at me as I arrive at the bar, which is full of people. She weaves around a huddle of friends to greet me, pulling me into a hug, and I try to pretend I don't notice all of them peering at me, intrigued.

'Thanks again for inviting me.'

'Here,' she turns round to tap someone on the shoulder, 'meet my girlfriend, Anna.'

With cascading, blonde hair and a blunt fringe that frames her delicate oval face, Anna has a striking smattering of freckles across her nose and cheeks, and a smile as big and warm as Marina's. A bit like Flora, she just *looks* friendly.

'You must be Iris,' Anna says in an English accent, before Marina has had the chance to introduce me. 'It's so nice to meet you. Marina mentioned you'd come.'

'Thanks for having me,' I say, before turning to Marina in surprise. 'You didn't tell me she was a Brit.'

'She did tell *me* that you were, though,' Anna says excitedly. 'Nice to have some reinforcements. They're always taking the piss out of me here. I'm from Norfolk but went travelling on my gap year and never came home. As soon as I met Marina, that was it. Made Burgau my home.' She grabs my hand and squeezes it. 'I highly recommend the move. You should be here in the summer when it's hot.'

'I'll have to come back.' I smile. I hold out the paper bag carrying the boxed candle I bought from one of the local shops yesterday. 'Here, a little something for your birthday. Sorry, I wasn't really sure what you like so it's not very exciting.'

'That is so nice of you!' She peers into the bag, before holding out the gift so the others can admire the pink and gold wrapping paper and gold ribbon. 'Oh my God, you wrap presents like a professional. Look at the bow and everything. How come none of my friends are this sophisticated?' She holds out her arms and pulls me into a hug. 'Thanks Iris. Come on, you have to meet everyone.'

'She needs a drink first.' Marina reaches for one of the

bottles of white wine already out on the bar, grabbing one of the glasses alongside it. 'Wine or something different?'

'I think I'll go with what I know for now,' I say, taking it gratefully once it's poured.

'You're going to need the Dutch courage,' Anna says, lowering her voice. 'Some of our friends have made enquiries about you. I think they've seen you around.'

'What does that mean?' I wonder whether Leo has started to turn the locals against me. 'Do people not want me here?'

'What?' Anna balks. 'The opposite!'

'Okay, we have some single friends,' Marina sighs, rolling her eyes. 'But we weren't sure if you were interested. We know you're here to work, so...'

'So tell us to fuck off if we're being inappropriate or if you're in a relationship already, basically,' Anna finishes bluntly for her.

'Oh.' I smile, taking a large gulp of wine. 'I could be interested.'

'*Yesss*,' Anna says excitedly, holding up her glass to clink it against mine. 'Is there anyone who you've got your eye on? What's your type?'

'She only just arrived, Anna; you're embarrassing her,' Marina scolds, grabbing my hand and pulling me away towards a group of people hanging at the front of the bar, leaving Anna giggling into her glass. 'You have to forgive her. She likes to play matchmaker. Here, these are two couples so you can relax. They speak English very well too. Everyone,' she raises her voice, stepping into the huddle of four, 'this is my new friend Iris.'

I'm grateful for the introduction and soon ease into conversation with Marina and her friends, who politely ask why I'm in Burgau and then move into a debate about the best surf spots along the coast. While they talk, I try to stealthily spot Leo amongst the crowd of people here, but I'm busted within a couple of minutes.

'Looking for someone?' Marina asks innocently, leaning towards me.

'No, not really.' I shrug, but then buckle under her pointed look. 'Okay, fine, I was wondering if Leo might be here. You said he was coming.'

She gives me a triumphant smile. 'I thought I saw you two getting cosy on the beach the other night.'

I splutter, dabbing my mouth with the back of my hand. 'That was work! It was the first interview. I finally managed to pin him down and get him to talk to me.'

'On a beach in the moonlight,' she says dreamily, nudging me with her elbow.

'It was not moonlight; it was early evening! And he chose the beach. Anyway, it didn't go well.'

She looks confused. 'Really? It looked like it was going *very* well from here. He was laughing, you were laughing. He looked… relaxed, which is a good step. The only time he's truly himself is when he's on a board in the water. I think in another life, he was a merman.'

I look down at the floor guiltily. 'He was fairly relaxed at the beginning, I think. But I messed it up. I think he's mad at me, actually.'

'Well, I don't know what happened in the end, but I can tell you that from over here, I could see that big smile of his,' she says sternly, forcing me to look at her. 'And he doesn't smile like that for anyone.'

I'm distracted by the crowd parting behind her – and there he is.

He's with a couple of guys, wearing a relaxed white shirt with the sleeves rolled up, highlighting his gorgeously tanned arms, and navy board shorts with flip-flops. Even though he's not just stepped out from the sea, his thick, brown hair is tousled and messy. His hands in his pockets, he's laughing at something the guy next to him is saying, the two of them joking with each other. He looks so at ease with his friends – the real Leo I got a glimpse of at the beach – so different to what he's been like with me.

He glances over and our eyes meet.

My breath catches and my stomach flips. I really shouldn't allow him to have this kind of physical effect on me, but my body doesn't seem to care.

Marina follows my eyeline before turning back to face me with an *I-told-you-so* expression, so I quickly feel the need to explain.

'I kind of tricked him into talking to me,' I say hurriedly, as he turns purposefully away. 'I didn't mean to. Well, I did. But I wanted him to talk as though he wasn't being interviewed, but…' I sigh, dropping my shoulders, defeated. 'I may owe him an apology.'

'Then apologise,' she says simply.

I take a swig of wine. 'Not my forte.'

'Yeah? No shit.' She grins at me. 'Iris, don't worry. He'll come to you anyway.'

'I don't think so.'

She shoots me an all-knowing smile. 'In that dress? He'll come to you.'

As kind and positive as Marina is being, she's wrong. He doesn't come to me.

I'm introduced to several of Marina and Anna's friends, and I try my best to focus on the person I'm talking to, but my eyes are always drifting to where I last saw him, wondering if he's still there and whether he's getting closer. At some point, I know I have to bite the bullet and apologise. I'm not going to be able to enjoy myself at this party if I think that the article has gone sideways. Once Leo has forgiven me, I can focus on relaxing.

Craning my neck to try to spot him a bit later, I get a tap on my shoulder.

'Can you do me a favour?' Anna asks loudly above the music that's been turned up, as I spin round to find her right behind me. 'Can you go to the storeroom at the back of the bar and grab another few bottles of wine? There's no more in the fridge and I can't find Marina anywhere. I would do it myself, but—'

'Of course, you can't get the drinks for your own party!' I put my empty glass down on the bar. 'Leave it with me.'

'You seem like the kind of girl who would know the best wine to choose,' she says, placing a hand on my arm. 'These losers don't have classy taste like you.'

As her friends pretend to act offended, I laugh and leave them to it, walking round the bar and through the door to the room at the back. As the music descends into muffled background noise when the door shuts firmly behind me, I take a moment to appreciate being on my own. It's been nice meeting everyone, but a little overwhelming. One guy seems insistent on telling me all about his deep-sea fishing adventures and, while interesting, I'm a little grossed out by the series of pictures I've been taken through.

Putting my hands on my hips, I survey the room in front of me. The wall at the back is lined with fridges, and across the middle of the space, there are rows of wine cases and branded beer boxes. I might as well take my time with this task. I don't want Anna to think I grabbed the first bottle I came to.

Stepping round the first aisle, I jump about a mile in the air when I see someone.

'Oh my God!' I gasp, putting a hand on my heart as Leo starts at my appearance. 'You gave me a heart attack. I thought I was alone. What are you doing in here?'

'I could ask you the same question. Did you follow me in?' he asks accusingly, holding a bottle of wine in his hand.

'No! We've run out of wine. I was coming to get some more.'

He holds up the bottle. 'Me too. Anna asked me to pick something.'

Ah. I see what's happened here.

'Yeah, me too,' I grumble.

While he carefully places the bottle back in its box, I stand there awkwardly.

'Okay, good. I guess it's covered then,' I say eventually, before smoothing out a non-existent crinkle at the side of my dress and turning on my heel to march back into the party.

'Hey London,' he calls out after me, stopping me in my tracks.

The nickname is weirdly comforting; if he was angry at

me past the point of no return, he'd be more formal. I know it's a mocking title rather than an affectionate one, but I don't care – it still feels like hope. I turn back around as he strolls round the corner of the aisle, leaning on the rack and folding his arms.

'As much as I don't want to admit it, I might need your help here,' he says, gesturing to the wine cases. 'Choosing a good wine isn't one of my key attributes.'

'Well, luckily for you, it is one of mine.'

'I thought it might be.'

I walk back towards him, swanning by to study what's on offer. He turns to watch me, but doesn't say anything, remaining silent while I read the labels. I know this is my opportunity to apologise. Or, at the very least, to address what happened the other night. But irrationally, I find myself irritated at him. I *did* message him after we spoke; I reached out. He's the one who didn't reply.

Selecting a bottle, I hold it out to him. 'Here. This is a good one.'

'We should grab a few then.'

The silence that falls between us is broken only by the clinking of the bottles knocking against each other as I pass him another two. I can feel his eyes boring into me as I turn my back to him so I can survey some of the others that Marina stocks. I brighten on recognising one of the labels, immediately reaching forwards to select the bottle.

'Hey, this is the one I drank with your dad at our lunch,' I say, smiling as I study the label. 'It was really nice. I'll bring some of these through too.'

'Great,' he says.

'Great.'

Clutching the bottles in my arms, I stalk past him towards the door.

'You know, London, I don't get it,' he says suddenly.

'Get what? Wine?' I ask, swivelling round to face him.

He gives me a deadpan look. 'No, not wine. *You.*'

'What do you mean?'

'Didn't you come here to… I don't know…' he shrugs as well as he can while carefully balancing a load of bottles in his arms '…talk?'

'I got the feeling you didn't want to talk to me, Leo, since you haven't replied to me. And I didn't want to bring our… professional tension into Anna's party.'

'Professional tension,' he repeats, as though it's a stupid phrase. Which it kind of is, but I have no idea how else to put it. He brings his eyes up to meet mine. 'I thought you wanted to apologise.'

I blink at him. 'Excuse me?'

'Marina hinted that you felt bad about tricking me into an interview the other night.'

'Did she.'

'Do you?'

'Do I what?'

'Feel bad,' he says impatiently, his eyes locked with mine.

I shift my weight from one foot to the other. 'I… well, I think what happened is that you misunderstood what was going on and if you'd listened to my—'

'You can't do it, can you?' he interrupts, taking a step towards me.

'Do what?'

'Apologise.'

I narrow my eyes at him. 'I apologise when I've done

something wrong, Leo. I won't apologise for doing my job,' I state defensively, despite the fact I've literally been telling myself all day that's what I need to do. 'I obviously don't want you to be upset with me' but—'I wasn't upset with you,' he claims, his forehead creasing slightly.

'You seemed upset when you stormed off from the beach and then didn't reply to any of my messages asking to meet.'

'I didn't storm off,' he corrects. 'The interview was over. I had to go home.'

'Okay, sure.'

He lifts his eyes to the ceiling. 'I was annoyed at myself.'

'*Why?*' I ask, exasperated, moving closer to him. 'Everything you said was so good! Trust me, Leo, you gave some really moving and brilliant quotes. Why would you be annoyed?'

'Because you made me forget myself,' he blurts out, bringing his eyes back to mine.

I stare at him. His eyes flicker down to my lips and back up again. He swallows.

Somewhere in the pit of my stomach, a flurry of butterflies burst into dance.

The door to the storeroom swings open, the creaking making both of us jump. I take a step backwards, only just realising how close we'd been standing.

Standing in the doorway, Marina smirks.

'Oh hey you two,' she says nonchalantly, 'I thought I heard raised voices. I wanted to make sure you were being nice to Iris, Leo, the person who is hopefully going to write nice things about you, Burgau and this bar, *which could use some more tourists spending their money here.*'

She gives Leo a pointed look as she finishes her sentence

through gritted teeth. He doesn't say anything, his brow furrowed.

'It's all good,' I assure her, plastering on a smile. 'I was… apologising.'

Out of the corner of my eye, I see him look to me in surprise.

'Great,' Marina says, her expression relaxing. 'You want to bring the wine through now? You don't normally take this long to choose, Leo.' She addresses me. 'Did he bore you with all his wine knowledge? It's great that he's so into it, but he is such a snob, isn't he?'

Rolling her eyes at him, she spins round and leaves, the door swinging closed behind her. He doesn't hesitate to follow her out, striding past me and leaving me alone, clutching the bottles of wine in my arms, my mouth falling open as he goes.

Twelve

It's more than an hour later that we find ourselves next to each other again. I don't know if he'd been purposefully avoiding me, but for whatever reason we'd been caught up in different huddles of people until now when I turn round to lean back on the bar and find my elbow brushing against his as he slides in next to me. I can tell from his expression that he didn't know it was me standing here and he'd rather it wasn't. He does, at least, stick around long enough to acknowledge me.

'Hey,' he says.

'Hey.'

We stand next to each other in silence, looking out at the other guests. The party has been a lot of fun so far thanks to Marina and Anna both seeming determined to make sure I'm not left out. I guess I am a bit of an oddity; most of their guests seem to know each other, whereas it's obvious I am here on my own. The language barrier hasn't been a problem; it's almost embarrassing how good everyone here is at English whereas I can barely speak two words of Portuguese and yet we're *in* Portugal.

As I do whenever I travel somewhere new and inevitably feel the same way, I make a promise to myself to make the effort to learn another language.

All of their friends have been so warm and welcoming to me, even after I explain what I'm doing here. Any time someone asks, I prepare myself for them to suddenly come to Leo's defence or make snide comments about prying journalists, but apparently Leo's attitude has made me over-worry. If anything, his friends are impressed and excited by the prospect.

Thanks to Anna's overzealous matchmaking skills, I've had a couple of mildly awkward conversations – that deep-sea-fishing guy, Diogo, cornered me again and asked if I would like to go out in his boat some time. I said I wasn't sure I'd have the time while I was here, but thanked him for the offer. It was also very obvious that Anna and Marina were encouraging their musical friend Luís to make his move, but as soon as he threatened to play a song for me if he could find a guitar, it became clear that he and I weren't a good match.

I did consider asking them if they might know José, my handsome landlord, in case I should prepare myself for his imminent arrival. It wasn't so much of a stretch that they might know him; he's obviously local to the area and maybe stops by the bar for a drink some time. But the party is well under way now, the music getting louder, people getting rowdier, and he hasn't made an appearance, so I doubt he's going to arrive now.

I hope he asks me on that date soon. I've only got one week left.

'Are you enjoying the party?' I ask Leo, purely to make conversation.

He nods, watching the guests spilling out onto the decking at the front to dance.

'People seem to like the wine,' I note, my eyes flickering to the glass of sparkling water in his hand. 'Did you not approve of my choice?'

'It was an excellent choice,' he says without looking at me. 'But I'm not drinking.' He nods to my near-empty wine glass. 'Would you like a top-up?'

'No thanks,' I say, as he reaches for the bottle in the cooler nearby.

His hand drops to his side. 'So have you got heaps of quotes?'

'Excuse me?'

'For the article,' he explains. 'You've been speaking to my friends today.'

'I'm not here in a work capacity,' I remind him a little snappily. 'I may have mentioned what I do and why I'm here, but I didn't go behind your back trying to collect quotes for the article. I wouldn't do that to Anna. It's her birthday party.'

It's funny, but with other athletes I've worked with, I've been able to keep them at a distance in my head – even if they annoy me, I don't let them in on that. I try to see them as a colleague, just one I admire. If they are ever difficult or grumpy, which can happen since they're under a lot of pressure mentally and physically as they gear up for a life-changing event or competition, I don't take it personally and I don't let it bug me. I treat them respectfully and calmly at all times, and let any of their gripes go.

But with Leo, I've let myself slip a couple of times.

I'm not sure it's fair of me to be snarky. It's not too unreasonable for him to question whether a journo writing about him might seize on the opportunity to talk to so many of his friends all in the same place at the same time. But here I am, pissed off at the insinuation. I'm annoyed he thinks that's what I've been doing.

Almost as if… his opinion of me matters.

'That maybe was a bit unfair,' he says to my surprise. 'I'm sorry.'

'No, it's fine,' I mumble, placing my glass on the counter. 'I should have realised that me being here might make you uncomfortable. I didn't think. I'll go.'

'That's not… I wasn't saying…' He stops me as I go to walk round him, his fingers lightly resting on my arm. His touch sends a shiver down my spine. I stare up at him as he drops his hand to his side. 'You don't have to leave. I'm not uncomfortable with you being here.'

'If you're sure—'

'I'm sure.'

Nodding, I slide back into my space next to him.

'Maybe this is a good thing,' I blurt out. 'I get to see you in a setting where you're not worried about anything you do or don't say. Unlike our interviews, you can relax here.'

'Likewise,' he responds with a shrug.

'I'm relaxed when we're interviewing.'

He shakes his head. 'I don't think so.'

I raise my eyebrows. 'Excuse me?'

'Come on,' he says, giving me a pointed look and shifting his body ever so slightly towards me, resting his elbow on the counter of the bar. 'You really think that you're completely comfortable when you're interviewing?'

'Yeah, I do it all the time.'

'You're very good at pretending to be relaxed, but you're working too hard to give that appearance,' he says, angling himself even more towards me, blocking whoever's on his other side. 'You're on the job. I've seen you when you've been genuinely relaxed and you're... different.'

'Oh, what, in yoga? That doesn't count. It's a class *training* you to relax.'

He shakes his head, looking entertained by my riled-up reaction. 'Not what I was talking about. I was talking about when we were on the beach.'

I quirk a brow at him. 'You do realise you're proving my point? I was interviewing you on the beach. That's why you're so cross at me, remember?'

'There were moments during that conversation that you let your guard down too. There were times when you weren't being an interviewer; you were being yourself.'

'Maybe I'm really good at my job.'

'No one's that good.'

I stare up at him. His eyes bore into mine.

'Either way, it was nice to see you... stop for a bit,' he adds casually.

'*Stop?*' I repeat, puzzled.

'Yeah, London,' he says, breaking into a warm, annoyingly inviting smile, the crinkles appearing in all their glory. 'You were relaxed. As in, *properly* relaxed. You can say you were feigning it by trying to trick me into talking to you. But it felt real.'

He takes a swig of his water, letting me soak in his words.

When I still haven't responded after a while, he gives me a prompt: 'You all right? I don't mean to insult you or anything.'

'No, I'm not… I'm not insulted. I guess I see what you're getting at,' I admit, not entirely comfortable with the realisation that he may be right. 'I did enjoy the conversation. Even if it was on the beach, which I hate.'

He rolls his eyes at that. 'No one hates the beach.'

'I do.'

'Maybe you haven't experienced it with the right people,' he says, shooting me a look. 'You didn't mind it Thursday evening.'

'I…'

My mind is racing and Leo chuckles at my furrowed expression.

'It's a good thing, London,' he insists. 'Like I say, nice to see you chill out a bit. Your natural state seems to be so busy, alert and vigilant, always looking for the next thing you should be doing, scheduling it into your phone, planning to make plans.'

I snort. 'Oh yeah, "city mode". Busy, alert and vigilant – you're making me sound like a meerkat.'

He brightens, 'Hey, you could do worse than a meerkat. Fun fact—'

'Last time you said that, it turned out to be about a shark's dental capacity.'

'Which *is* a fun fact,' he argues defensively. 'As is the knowledge that a group of meerkats is called a mob. I don't know why, but I love that.'

I break into a wide smile. It's the way he said that: so delighted with himself.

Uh oh. Is the emotionally-distant, guarded Leo Silva secretly... *cute*?

'So what I can surmise from this conversation,' I begin, clearing my throat and looking back out at the party, hoping to distract myself from inappropriate thoughts, 'is that you're full of random animal facts and you think I have a stick up my arse.'

He bursts out laughing, drawing the attention of Marina and her friends before they go back to their dancing. It thrills me that I made him laugh like that.

'You know what, Leo? I might actually take you up on that offer of a top-up.'

His eyes gleam at me, before he grabs the bottle of wine and fills up my glass. As he concentrates on pouring, I find myself studying him, those long eyelashes, the sharp jaw, full lips and rumpled, brown hair that gives him an easy-going, natural handsomeness. Gazing at him, you'd easily forgive him for being superior and arrogant. But now I'm not sure he's either of those things. My eyes run down the slope of his neck to his broad, muscled shoulders and back up to his Adam's apple.

It strikes me that he has a really good neck.

I think about what it would taste like and a warmth throbs between my legs.

'Here,' he says, his throat bobbing as he speaks, jolting me from my daze.

My cheeks burn hot as I pull my glass back towards me, hoping he thinks I've been standing here thinking completely normal thoughts and not been passing the time strangely fixated on his neck.

'Thank you,' I whisper, my cheeks flushing with heat.

'Cheers,' he holds his glass up to mine.

Tapping my glass against his, I take a sip, both of us turning to look as Marina squeals in embarrassment when Anna grabs her hands and forces her to dance in the middle of the circle out on the decking.

Out of the corner of my eye, I see Leo observing them with a smile on his lips.

'How did you and Marina meet?' I ask him, dragging his eyes from them to me. 'Did you find yourselves floating next to each other in the water one day or was it here in the bar?'

'Would it be embarrassing to admit we were introduced through my dad?' he says, wrinkling his nose as he smiles.

'Not at all.' I laugh. 'Your dad seems all-knowing. In fact, I'd be keen to be introduced to others through him. Bet he has some great friends.'

'Yeah, he's a lot of fun when he wants to be,' Leo agrees, nodding. 'He's lived here a long time and knew Marina well – both local small business owners. I wasn't in the best place when I arrived. It took me a while before I was ready to meet new people. After a long time of me moping around and when I was ready to get back in the water, Dad arranged for us to all go surfing.'

'Surfing brought you together.'

'You could say that.'

He catches me smirking into my wine glass and frowns.

'What?' he asks. 'What are you thinking?'

'That you lied to me.'

'When?'

I look him right in the eye. 'When you said you were a lone wolf.'

He opens his mouth to protest, but thinks better of it,

his shoulders slumping slightly as he concedes. I have him there.

'You're lucky to have such a great support network,' I continue, enjoying the light atmosphere between us. 'Your dad is your coach and your fellow surfers are your friends. It's nice. You find your inspiration in and out of the water, you could say.'

He shakes his head at me with a teasing smile. 'I'm not sure you even realise you're doing it.'

'Doing what?'

'Putting quotes in my mouth.' He gives me a pointed look. 'Come on. Referring to my family and friends as "inspiration in and out of the water". Sounds like a well thought-out caption beneath an adorable group photo.'

'How do you know I'm not poetic at all times?'

'Well, I'm not, so don't try to make me say shit like that,' he says, before propping his elbow up on the bar again. 'So, what about *your* inspiration?'

'For what? Writing?' I gave him a quizzical look. 'I guess in this case, that would be you.'

He laughs, properly laughs, the crinkles forming in all their glory, his brown eyes gleaming with surprise. When he laughs like that, his eyes become gentler.

'Not what I meant, but I'm honoured to be your inspiration, London,' he says, still chuckling. 'You said that I was lucky to have this support network.' He gestures to Marina, who is twirling Anna to the background noise of cheers from their adoring crowd. 'I was asking you about *your* support network. What are they like, your family and friends?'

'Oh!' I blush, tucking my hair behind my ear. 'They're great. Really great.'

He watches me expectantly while I knock back my wine.

'That's it? That's all I get? They're "really great".' He sighs with disappointment. 'I thought you were meant to be poetic.'

'It's not like I got much better! Do you know how hard it is to get you to talk about anything properly?'

'Okay, well inspire me then like I inspire you,' he teases playfully. 'Show me how it's done.' He tilts his head at me. 'Tell me about you. Otherwise, I'll just have to imagine the life you lead back in England.'

'Now, that's something I'd be interested to hear,' I say, before grimacing. 'God, come on, what sort of life have you imagined for me? I highly doubt it will be complimentary.'

'I picture you growing up in a big family in an amazing, tall town house in Chelsea or something. Top grades at school, you were probably Head Girl, but not a nerd one, an intimidating one who rules the place. And now you attend heaps of exclusive posh parties with CEOs where everyone is holding those fancy, circular, champagne glass things.'

I burst out laughing.

'What? Am I close to the truth?' he asks eagerly.

'No!' I roll my eyes. 'I mean, I grew up in London and I think that's all you got right. My mum maybe has a set of champagne coupes.'

'Coupe,' he repeats, clicking his fingers. 'That's what they're called.'

'I'm pleased I give off a Head-Girl vibe though,' I reason. 'I wasn't, though. I didn't even make prefect. And I do not party with CEOs. I'm a sports journalist, remember? A very different kind of network to the people your mum would hang out with.'

'So tell me about it, then,' he insists. 'Who *do* you hang out with?'

I heave a sigh, raising my eyes to the ceiling. 'Fine. Okay, well, there's my best friend Flora. In the big scheme of things, we haven't actually known each other that long. We met at the paper I worked at and got to know each other and... it feels like I've known her for much longer than I have.'

'She's the one dating the tennis player.'

'Yes, Kieran O'Sullivan.' I nod, before narrowing my eyes at him. 'Hey, how did you put that together?'

'I told you I read your articles,' he says simply. 'So, Flora is your best mate. Do you have family in the city, too?'

I nod, wrapping an arm self-consciously around my waist. 'Yeah. I do. My mum still lives there, in the house, I mean. My... childhood home.'

He watches as I bring the glass to my lips, taking an abnormally large gulp.

'Are you okay?' he asks, his tone soft and low as his brow furrows.

'Yeah, yes, of course,' I remind myself, fixing a smile. 'It's... complicated.'

'We don't have to talk about it,' he says, waving it off. 'We can talk about something else. Anything else. I didn't mean to—'

'No, it's fine.'

I exhale and then, before I can think properly about what I'm saying, I find myself wanting to talk about it. I don't know why. It's not an appropriate place, this party, and it's not an appropriate companion, my interviewee. But out it comes before I can stop it.

'My parents are divorcing, which shouldn't be a big deal.

They don't get on and, despite all these years together, it's like they just… don't understand each other anymore. They don't want to, anyway. I want them to be happy and it's better that they go their separate ways, but I can't stop myself feeling sad about it.'

He's listening so intently that he's shifted towards me a little more, ever so slightly closing the gap between us.

'I'm sorry,' he says quietly, and I can tell he means it.

I shrug. 'It is what it is. I'm in my thirties, I know they're their own people with their own lives. I need to be a grown-up about this. But my mum called today and she told me she's selling the house.'

Something about saying it out loud hits me harder than I expected and my words become stuck in my throat, tripping my breath up on its way out so it's shallow and shaky. Hot tears build up behind my eyes and I panic. I won't cry about this. Not on my own and certainly not in front of anyone. Luckily, I'm a seasoned pro at this sort of thing. These tears will not be spilling over any time soon. I force them back, my lips twist into a smile and I hold my chin up.

I'm fine.

'Anyway,' I continue brightly, swirling my wine around its glass, 'in answer to your question, I have a great support network too. The shape of it is… evolving currently, but that's okay.'

He nods slowly. 'How do you feel about the house?'

'Mum moving? I think it's great! That house is full of old memories. She deserves a new space that she can make her own. Dad does too. In fact, I'm hoping that Mum might take the opportunity to go travelling like she's always wanted to. She married young and didn't get much of a chance to see the world. She keeps making excuses, though. Maybe selling the house will give her the push she needs. New adventures for both of them.'

I take a drink and when I turn to look at him again, his expression takes me by surprise. It's not awash with sympathy or anything as excruciating as that, but it's thoughtful and considered, as though he knows something I don't. It's both disconcerting and comforting at the same time. Almost as if he cares.

'When my parents broke up, I was young and very upset about it,' he says calmly, his eyes remaining fixed on me. 'They should never have been together – I think they thought that opposites attract and everything, but in the end, it was a disaster. But it's still a big change for a kid and I relied heavily on surfing to help me deal with it. I could forget about everything when I was surfing. But one thing that hit me hard was leaving my childhood house. It was only a house, so it shouldn't have mattered, but it felt like... it was the final thing, you know? Like it was real. The house was gone. So was the family I'd known.'

I watch him as he lifts his drink to his lips, tips his head back and swallows, before lowering his glass.

'Change is never easy, even if it's for the better. Even if you're in your thirties,' he continues matter-of-factly, glancing out at the other revellers as we remain amongst the few not dancing now. 'Sometimes being a "grown-up"' – he forms quotation marks with his fingers – 'about it makes it heavier and harder. You expect more from yourself. You put a face on it.' He sighs heavily. 'I know how that feels. It's... lonely.'

I swallow the lump forming in my throat.

He turns to look back at me. I feel nervous under his intense gaze, a swarm of butterflies fluttering about my stomach, heat rising up my neck.

Leo's eyes are searching mine. I have to break away. I *have* to. This isn't… right. I'm not meant to get close to my interviewees like this. I never get personal.

Luckily, my rescue comes in the form of Diogo, the deep-sea-fishing man.

'Iris!' he bellows, suddenly next to me, swaying unsteadily and stumbling between me and Leo, thankfully splintering whatever it was between us that was not meant to be forming. 'You have to come dance!'

I don't want to dance. I definitely don't want to dance with Diogo, who is pissed.

But I giggle at his silliness, letting him take my hands in his and drag me away, offering Leo an apologetic smile as I'm pulled into the crowd. When I build up the courage to glance back at him, he's not there anymore. I can't see him anywhere. He must have left.

I'm relieved and devastated all at once.

Fuck.

Thirteen

Something has shifted between me and Leo.

I've had to interview people before who intimidate me or make me work hard to get what I need from them, but there's something about this guy that means whenever I'm around him, I feel...

...nervous.

Ever since the party, things have been different. It may just be coming from me – maybe he doesn't feel different at all – but I've noticed that in the two interviews I've conducted with him since then, I've been more fidgety and distracted.

Like a fucking meerkat.

Suddenly it's harder to focus on what I'm supposed to be asking him next and instead, I'm thinking about how best to get those crinkles round his mouth to form again, the ones that appear when he laughs, or how it might feel to run my fingers through his hair, or how my stomach seems to tie itself in knots when he holds my eye contact too long.

I think about how nice it was to talk to him at the party, how he listened and seemed to really care.

Christ. He's making me lose my head a bit. And I never lose my head.

There's no reason why this should be happening. Sure, he's unbelievably hot with those deep-brown eyes, his chiselled jaw and billowy bottom lip... but I've been in the presence of good-looking men before – my job is to pretty much constantly be in the presence of *athletes*, for goodness sake – and, I admit it, I've been attracted to one or two of them before. With that much muscle on display, it's hard not to be. I may be a professional, but I'm also human. But none of them have made me feel so... self-aware.

I think it's his eyes. I blame the long, dark eyelashes. They make his eyes too intense. Too *prying*. It feels like he's trying to work me out. And that's not fair, because this is about me trying to work him out. You know, for the feature.

Not that I'm having that much success there. If I was under any impression that our white-flag-waving conversation at the party might mean he would open up to me more during the interviews, I was very much mistaken. If anything he's tenser. Warier.

Even more closed off than when we first met.

When he agreed to see me for the next interview the day after the party, I was almost *excited*. A barrier had been broken between us; mutual respect had formed. I'd let him have a glimpse of what was going on with me so surely he was going to be completely at ease in my company and tell me all his secrets.

That did not happen.

He was quiet and cautious, lost in thought. His answers

were nice, but shallow. I felt like I was getting nowhere. I cut it short and asked if we could meet again, maybe on the beach. I was trying to recreate the chilled beach vibe he seemed to like, but he was on to me.

What is truly infuriating is that I can't be annoyed at him because technically, he's doing what's required of him. He's cooperating, he's meeting me for interviews, he's answering questions. Ultimately, the problem is me. I'm not getting out of him what I need.

Before the party, I was able to keep calm and level-headed around him, but I find the way he looks at me extremely distracting. Sometimes, I think I'm searching for something that isn't there in his expression; do I *want* him to be interested in me? Maybe that's why I can't sit still around him anymore, why I keep crossing and uncrossing my legs, sweeping my hair round one shoulder then back behind my neck again, pretending to check my phone just to have something to do with my hands. The whole thing is exhausting and I have no idea if it's solely in my head.

Worst of all, it's affecting my work.

If I need confirmation of that, I get it from Toni on Tuesday morning after sending her a draft of what I have so far.

'Iris, hi,' she says down the phone when I pick up, having just made myself a second cup of coffee. She's only said two words, but I can already tell she's desperate to make this quick. 'I've read the draft paragraphs you sent through.'

I pause, my coffee midway to my lips. 'What did you think?'

This is an unnecessary question. We both know it. Toni doesn't bother to make phone calls unless absolutely essential, especially not to journalists on a job. She doesn't need, or want, to hear about any hiccups one of her writers might come across whilst on a project – you go away and get the job done. That's it. She doesn't have time to reassure newbies or massage the fragile egos of writers desperate for praise.

If she has something to say, her assistant will say it.

If it's something you *really* need to hear, she'll call herself, and there will be no mistaking that it's a damn inconvenience for her to do so.

Which is why I lower my mug and sit down on the sofa, bracing for impact.

'Iris, I know I can be straight with you and you won't take it personally,' she begins.

Oh bollocks.

I swallow. 'Mm?'

'It's boring. My God, I didn't even read the last couple of paragraphs. I gave up.'

'Oh.'

'I'm not saying it's unsalvageable. To be honest, I'm confused,' she says, and I hear her tapping her desk in the background. 'Usually, I don't ask you to send me drafts. I don't ask anyone for drafts. But with the Michelle Martin link – well, I thought it best to see how things are shaping up. Maybe all of your drafts are this dry at first, I don't know.'

She pauses and I realise that she's waiting for me to confirm or deny.

'Uh, sometimes, maybe.'

I'm lying. She knows it. I know it. I can't be arsed to keep it up.

'Actually, no, they're not,' I admit, tilting my head back

against the cushion and looking up at the ceiling. 'Usually by this point, I've got more from my interviews.'

'All I've read about this guy is that he liked surfing when he was little, he has a supportive father and he's looking forward to the competition. I mean, come on.' She sighs with exasperation. 'My five-year-old niece would be bored to shit by that fairy tale. I could have guessed all that myself. There are sweet moments, for sure. But where's the *meat* of the story, Iris? Where's the personal struggle and turmoil? Where's the journey and the meteoric rise? You can't have a hero without any challenges, yes? That's what makes them heroic.'

'I know, I know.'

'I know you know. So what's going on? Are you nervous to ask the difficult questions because he's Michelle Martin's son?'

'No! I want to ask those questions.'

'Why aren't you, then?'

I exhale, closing my eyes. 'He doesn't want to talk about that stuff.'

I'm greeted with silence. I knew I would be.

The silence grows. I know she's waiting for me to respond to my own dilemma. I envision the sports editorial director job slipping from my grasp. Swirling in the silence, I hear her thoughts: *she can't even handle an athlete who doesn't want to talk about his past, so how can she manage this huge responsibility?*

I clear my throat. 'Don't worry, Toni. I'll get the story.'

'Better,' she states, satisfied. 'You're the right person for this, Iris. There's no one else I wanted to send. Is that the vote of confidence you need to get your arse in gear?'

I smile into the phone. 'More than enough.'

'Great. Don't send me shit like that again. You're better than this.'

'I know.'

'I know you know. Oh bollocks, I have to go. I'm late for a meeting with advertising.'

'Enjoy.'

'Funny one,' she mutters. 'Bye, Iris.'

I hang up and toss my phone down next to me on the sofa, annoyed at myself. When I cobbled those paragraphs together yesterday morning, I knew they weren't up to scratch. It's all surface stuff. I need to get more from him. We have to go deeper.

Forcing myself up on my feet, I wander out onto the balcony of the apartment and lean on the railing, gazing out at the sea. There are a couple of surfers braving the water this morning, paddling out and turning to face the shore, lying forwards in wait. Leo isn't one of them. I know, even from all the way up here, because I've watched Leo out in the water and he's much more fluid than them. Out there, he seems weightless. It's like he's not even trying. The surfers I'm watching now are putting the work in and you can see it. You can feel their focus and concentration. Whereas when Leo surfs, he's just... being.

Suddenly, I remember what Marina said at the party: *the only time he's truly himself is when he's on a board in the water.*

'No, no, no,' I groan, burying my face in my hands.

I think I know what I have to do.

*

The next morning, Leo is at the counter of the shop when I walk in. He glances up at the sound of the bell ringing on my entrance. Confusion flits across his face as I stroll past the line of surfboards towards him.

'Hi, Leo,' I say, trying to suppress the nerves threatening to make my voice wobble.

'London,' he says with a small nod of acknowledgement.

Whenever he uses this nickname, there's a gleam of bemusement in his eyes, as though he's congratulating himself on his humour. It's both irritating and alluring.

'Iris!' Adriano cries happily, barrelling through from the back room, looking much happier to see me than his son. 'A pleasant surprise.'

'How are you, Adriano?'

'Very well.' He pats Leo on the shoulder. 'How is the feature going? Leo tells me nothing. That will not surprise you.'

'It's coming along,' I say vaguely, pretending to be interested in the little surfboard keyrings hanging on a stand on the counter.

'And you had fun the other night at the party, eh? I heard you were there.'

As Adriano beams at me, I notice Leo shoot him a glare.

'I was,' I say, wondering if it's a good or bad thing that Leo mentioned my presence to his dad. 'It was fun. Great to meet Anna and Marina's friends.'

'A good bunch,' Adriano nods. 'Surf obsessed.'

'There was a lot of surf talk.'

He laughs, waggling his finger at me. 'Perhaps we can win you over and you'll fall just as in love with it as us locals – when do you head home?'

'My flight is booked for Saturday.'

'Too soon,' Adriano says, his shoulders slumping. 'Anyway, I'm glad the party was fun. I hope they were serving good wine at least?'

'Oh yes,' I nod, glancing at Leo. 'Leo made sure of that.'

He suddenly looks very interested in the till, refusing to meet my eye. We never actually addressed the fact that he pretended not to know anything about wine before his lie was rumbled by Marina.

'He learnt everything he knows from his old man,' Adriano tells me, nudging him with his elbow. 'Feel free to put that in the article.'

'I'll think about it.'

'So how can we help you? Are you here to talk to Leo? I would have thought by now you'd be bored of hearing him talk.'

'I can't,' Leo says, finally speaking up. 'I have a lesson booked.'

'Yes. I know,' I say.

'I thought we were quiet this week. Who is it with, Leo?' Adriano asks.

'It's a last-minute booking, made yesterday online,' he explains, typing something into the computer while both of them peer at the screen. 'Someone called—'

'Flora O'Sullivan,' I finish for him.

They both turn to face me.

'You know her?' Adriano asks, intrigued.

'In a manner of speaking.' I swallow the lump in my throat. 'I... I am her. I made the booking.'

Leo stares at me, his forehead creased.

'You are… Flora O'Sullivan?' Adriano checks, puzzled.

I nod slowly. 'Yep. Sorry, not the most original fake name. Flora is my best friend and O'Sullivan is the surname of her partner. Kieran O'Sullivan? You know, the tennis player.'

Leo looks baffled, glancing down at the screen and then back at me. 'But Flora O'Sullivan is signed up for a course of three surf lessons.'

'That's right. Today, tomorrow and Friday. I booked it under a fake name so that you wouldn't be put off by, you know,' I gesture to myself, 'teaching me.'

'I think this is great!' Adriano exclaims. 'You are in safe hands, Iris. I'll leave you to it, I have things to do, but good luck to you both!'

He disappears back through the doors behind the counter, chuckling to himself.

'I don't understand,' Leo says, lines etched into his forehead. 'You don't want to surf.'

'What, because in your head, I'm a duchess wandering around London town with a champagne coupe in my hand?' I ask defensively, crossing my arms.

He gives me a hint of a smile. 'I don't remember giving you a title.'

'I added that detail.'

'The fact that you may be a city girl has nothing to do with it, Your Grace,' he assures me, amused. 'The reason I'm surprised is because you told me that you hate the beach, so why would you suddenly be interested in surfing?'

'It looks fun.'

He doesn't seem convinced.

I sigh, tapping my fingers impatiently on the counter.

'Look, are you going to teach me to surf or not? Because if you refuse then I would like my money back.'

As his eyes search my face, I stare back at him defiantly.

'All right, London,' he says eventually, 'let's go shred.'

Fourteen

He makes it look so easy.

When I've seen him out in the water surfing, Leo paddles gracefully with the swell of the wave, pushes his chest up with his hands and pops up onto his feet, hovering steadily on his board as he glides forwards. The whole process is one fluid motion. It can't take that long to master, right?

Wrong.

I've been practising how to 'pop up' on a surfboard for almost half the lesson and I still don't feel like I've got the hang of it. We haven't even got close to the water yet.

'That was good,' Leo says, as I step off the board after my latest attempt. 'You're getting it. Remember to look forwards, not down at the board.'

'There are too many things to think about,' I groan, throwing my hands up in exasperation. 'I'm trying to remember to only push up with my shoulders and chest and that my thighs remain in contact with the board. Then

I have to think about bringing my front foot forward, letting my body twist, making sure my feet are the right width apart, keeping my knees bent low, and having my arms out to balance. And, of course, making sure my eyes are looking forwards.' I pause for breath. 'I need to write this all down.'

Leo hits me with yet another of his amused smiles. I've had to endure a barrage of them during our lesson.

'I know it seems like an overload of information, but that's always going to be how it goes when you're mastering a new technique,' he says with a shrug. 'When you get it, you won't have to think about it. All of that happens naturally.'

'I have a photographic memory so I really work best with bullet-point instructions.'

'I'm not letting you take notes, London.'

I put my hands on my hips stubbornly, but he remains unfazed.

Despite the challenges of the lesson and the fear of what's to come, I maintain that this is a good idea. Already, I've got a fresh angle of his character for the piece: Leo, the surf teacher. And it's a good one. He's patient, encouraging, funny. He knows what he's doing – he's comfortable and relaxed in this role, so self-assured and dedicated. There's something very sexy about him taking control of this lesson.

I probably won't put that last bit in the feature, though.

His passion for surfing is obvious through the infectious enthusiasm of his teaching style. He wants his student to be good, but only so that they'll be safe in the water and have the right technique and ability to enjoy the sport more. He hasn't made me feel stupid even though I *do* feel stupid. I felt stupid the moment I pulled on the wetsuit over my yellow halterneck bikini, like I was completely out of place. Which I am.

'All the gear and no idea,' I muttered when I stepped out from behind his truck in the wetsuit he loaned me. 'Can you help zip it up all the way at the back?'

After he complied, I turned round, ready for him to take one look at me in this get-up and laugh at me for looking so... unlike me. But he didn't laugh. He was looking at me in such a captivating way, it made me smile shyly.

'Sorry you had to wait so long for me to get into this thing,' I said, forcing a laugh as I tried to break the tension.

He swallowed, his Adam's apple bobbing.

'Don't worry,' he said, a warm glint in his eyes. 'It's easier to take off.'

I blinked at him, stunned. What was I supposed to say to *that*? His words were so fucking *suggestive*, but I wasn't sure if he'd done that on purpose, so I stood there, shocked into silence until he jerked his head in the direction of the beach and went, 'Shall we?' as though he hadn't just caused goosebumps to cover every inch of my skin.

I knew then that this scenario was probably not going to be healthy for the ever-so-tiny crush I seem to be developing for Leo Silva. A private lesson on a near-empty beach with him demonstrating how to go from lying on a surfboard to standing on one was almost certainly a recipe for disaster. Popping up on a surfboard is essentially a glorified press up.

'Watch the positioning of my hands and my arms,' he had instructed at one point as his hands pressed flat on the deck of his board before the muscles in his arms flexed as he extended them, pushing his upper body from the board.

He was telling me to watch him. I had no choice. Not just

once either, I had to observe him perform this art over and over and over...

My mouth was so dry, I had to lick my lips when he wasn't looking.

'You want to try again?' Leo asks now, as I stare at the surfboard in front of me, willing myself to be magically good at it. 'I know it might not feel like it, but you're getting better every time.'

'I'm exhausted.'

'Nah, you're fine,' he says with an easy grin. 'I've seen you practise yoga. You've got what it takes to pop up on a board. Come on, give it a crack. Get back down there.'

I swear it takes all my will power not to say, *Make me* with a seductive smile.

Argh, this is wrong. This is *so* wrong.

I want to flirt with him. And he is very much *off limits*. If anything happened, I'd be really crossing a line – not only is he the subject of my interview, he's also the son of the media corporation's owner, a very powerful woman who has put her trust in me to treat this task with the upmost professionalism.

Desperately trying to shake this attraction out of my head, I reluctantly do as he says and get back to concentrating on his teaching: what I've been struggling to do all lesson.

After a few more tries, he says the words I've been dreading. 'Okay, good news, London: you're officially ready to get in the water,' he says, applauding my recent pop up.

I shake my head. 'I... I think I need to practise some more.'

'Yeah, but this time, you're going to practise in the water. We need to work on your paddling and you're building up muscle memory so that—'

'I've already forgotten everything you've said about the position of my feet,' I stammer, tripping over my words as I blurt them out, the blood pounding in my ears at the thought of the ocean beckoning to me beyond. 'We need to run through it again.'

'Hey, trust me, you're good,' he says, moving in the direction of the water. 'Natural to be nervous, but you'll be fine. Come on, let's get in there.'

As I bend down to pick up my board, I feel my legs turn to jelly.

Willing myself forwards, I start to follow him down the sand. He's glancing back at me over his shoulder with an encouraging smile, waving me towards him. The rail of the board dragging through the sand behind me, I edge nearer and nearer to the water, my heart pounding so hard against my chest, I think it might burst right through.

I've tried to get myself in the water since the Cornwall incident happened. I'm not the sort of person who tends to just give up on things or make a fuss, and there have been times when it's been almost unavoidable to be near the sea. Like when I was in Mallorca with a group of friends and we went to a bar that was perched on the rocks. The idea was that after lunch, we'd all stroll down to the beach next to it and go for a swim. No one knew about what had happened in Cornwall a few years back and I didn't want to bum anyone out by talking about it, so I went along with the plan.

Until I couldn't. As in, I *physically* couldn't.

As my friends all waded out into the water, I froze at the edge of it and then my breathing grew fast and short. I felt sick with dizziness and thought I might collapse until

I felt Naomi's arms propping me up, helping me move away and then duck into a crouching position where I stayed until I had the strength to beg her to get me off the beach before I embarrassed myself completely. Falling apart in public is not my vibe. We went up to the bar to wait for everyone there. I told her what had happened in Cornwall and why I had that physical reaction to the water. When the others came back, she told them that she thought I may have eaten something funny at lunch.

I know my fear is irrational, but against all sense and all logic, it seems to be able to get the better of me. Like right now.

The sand beneath my feet is feeling damper and heavier as I get closer to the water lapping onto the beach. It's a good day for a beginner to surf, Leo said earlier, because the waves are slow and gentle, but the sound of them breaking roars in my ears. My mouth is dry, my breath is rapid and shaky, my throat is closing. The surfboard is slipping from my grip.

'Hey.'

Leo's voice cuts through the panic growing in my head; his fingers brushing against my arm make me jump. The board drops, slamming on the sand.

'You all right?' he asks, bending down to pick it up for me. 'Are you worried about wiping out?'

'S-sorry?' I stammer.

'Falling is part of it,' he says with an easy smile. 'We're not going to do anything crazy, okay? No need to look so worried. It's your first lesson; we're here to have fun.'

I shake my head. 'I can't do this,' I whisper.

'Iris,' he says gently, his eyebrows pinched together. 'It's—'

'No, you don't understand... I actually *can't do this*,' I tell him, shutting my eyes, my heart being squeezed by the panic making my chest tight. 'I'm scared of the ocean, Leo.'

I'm not sure what I expect him to say to that. Maybe laugh at me. Say that it's a stupid fear. I don't know. But I'm not expecting what he does say, which is, 'Me too.'

My eyelids flutter open in surprise. He's watching me, deadly serious.

'Y-you are? How is that possible?'

'Because it's the *ocean*,' he emphasises, his expression softening. 'It's powerful and unpredictable. It's natural to be afraid.'

'How can you possibly surf like you do with that fear?' I croak.

'By controlling the controllables. I practise every day: my balance, the manoeuvres, reading what I can of the water. I'm always learning, often falling. That's how surfing goes. You can't be the best at surfing, only the best that day on that wave in that moment. You never know how it's going to go. That's part of the thrill.'

I tear my eyes from him to look back out at the rippling blue water.

'Without that sense of fear, you wouldn't get the same adrenaline when you catch a wave,' he continues. 'When you surf, you have to give in to the movement of the water. That's a huge part of surfing: letting go. You can't fight against it; you let the water carry you with it as it travels. It's like nothing else, that feeling: a real rush. It's addictive. Once you've experienced it, you won't forget it. You want more.'

'You make it sound... spiritual,' I murmur.

'It is. Bet you're wishing you had your phone recording now.'

'You have no idea.' I swallow. 'Leo, I've never been good at letting go.'

'That doesn't surprise me, London,' he says, and I can hear the smile in his voice. 'I read this cool thing once that I reckon might help. Something like, "There's a freedom found in forgetting to stop and wait at the edge of a ridge, peering down at what's to come – instead, you keep going, fully present in the moment, conquering and falling all at once."' He hesitates. 'I may have got some of the words wrong.'

Closing my eyes, I break into a smile. 'You got most of them right.'

'I've never quoted a line to its author before.'

'I've never been quoted before.'

'Now that *does* surprise me,' he says. 'That ski article really was something. I hope the surf one will measure up. Guess a lot of that is down to me.'

My eyes flash open as a fresh rush of determination runs through my body.

Swivelling to face him, I clench my fists, taking a deep breath. 'Leo, I need to tell you something. Something… personal. But I think you need to know.'

'Okay.'

'When I was fourteen, I was on holiday in Cornwall with my family. We used to go there a lot in the summer and we'd go with family friends, so there was a crew of kids my age. We used to hang out a lot, chill at the beach, swim in the sea. I was a strong swimmer; I loved it.'

I take a moment to steel myself in telling the story, but Leo doesn't flinch. He waits patiently.

'I... I was trying to impress this guy. There was this dare to swim out to the furthest buoy and swim back. No one wanted to go out that far. The sea wasn't calm, we shouldn't have even considered it. But we were idiots, and it turned out I was the biggest one.'

A muscle in his jaw twitches. He knows what's coming, but he waits for me to tell it.

'I thought I could do it. I was the best swimmer in the group. I ignored the warnings and I went out and I kept going. But I got into trouble.' It's hard to get the words out as a lump rises in my throat, the memory seeping into my head. 'I don't remember exactly what happened, but I remember being dragged under and that feeling of powerlessness. I couldn't breathe, I wasn't sure which way was up, it was disorientating and terrifying and so... dark and quiet and...'

I have to stop for a moment to gulp in some air, my mind racing. I press a hand against my heart as it pounds heavily.

'Hey, it's okay,' Leo says in barely more than a whisper. 'Deep breaths.'

When I look in his eyes, I notice something different about them – a tenderness that wasn't there before. I'm determined to finish. It's the only way I have a chance of moving on from this, so I keep going with my story, no matter how much my chest aches.

'I thought I was going to die there alone, swallowed up into nothingness. Obviously, you can see that everything turned out fine.' I attempt a nervous smile, lifting a shaky hand to push my hair back from my face. 'I managed to come up for air and the lifeguard came out to help me back, but since then I... I haven't been able to go in the sea. I look out there and,' I gesture at the water, 'all I feel is panic. The same panic I felt then.'

I drop my head.

He doesn't say anything for a moment, letting the story sink in.

'Thank you for telling me,' he says eventually in a tone that I'm not sure I've heard him use before: low and protective. 'I'm sorry that happened to you. Iris, you don't have to go in the water. Just by being here, you've done brilliantly already.'

'No, that's not... that's not why I told you that,' I say, bringing my eyes up to meet his. 'I want to try. I want to find a way of going in the water again. I just don't know how.'

He nods, putting his hands on his hips and squinting out at the ocean with a pensive expression while I catch my breath.

'You think I'm a hopeless case?' I ask, nudging the board on the sand with my toe.

'No,' he says firmly without a moment's hesitation. 'I think we go about this differently, that's all.'

'How?'

'First, we re-introduce you to the water. Then when you feel a little more confident, we see how you feel about getting on the board. One step at a time. Sound good?'

I nod.

He holds out his hand.

I stare at it. 'What?'

'Take my hand,' he says gently.

'Why?'

'I'm going to lead you into the water.'

'You won't pull me in,' I say, folding my arms across

my chest and tucking my hands away, the panic rising up my throat once again. 'Or throw me in there.'

He shakes his head. 'We'll go in together, we'll focus on our breathing, and we'll just put one foot in front of the other. The water is calm today; it's a good place to start. Hey, London, look at me.'

My breathing has quickened, and he's ducked his head to come down to my level. I force myself to bring my eyes up to his.

'I won't let you go unless you ask me to,' he tells me.

I swallow. 'Promise?'

'Promise.'

I slide my hand into his, instantly finding comfort in his warm grasp. His hand is much bigger and stronger than mine, gripping it tightly, promising security and safety. He's over-emphasising his breathing for my benefit, encouraging me to copy his deep breath in and long breath out. As I fall into the same rhythm, he gives me a small nod and edges forward with one foot. I do the same, slowly and carefully moving towards the water.

When the cold water first laps over the skin of my foot, my breath catches.

Leo can sense my hesitation and his hand squeezes mine, reminding me that he's right here with me. Focusing on him and keeping my breathing as steady as possible, I let him lead me further into the water, feeling the water swirl around my ankles and slowly edge up my legs with every step forward.

As we get deeper, the resistance of the water grows, slowing us down, and it's harder for me to keep calm as the break of the wave hits against my thighs. But I've come this far. That in itself drives me onwards, looking back to see how far I've come.

I don't even realise I'm smiling until I hear his chuckle carry in the light breeze.

'Feels good doesn't it?' he says. 'Realising what you're capable of.'

I nod, unable to express what I'm feeling right now: relief, elation and fear all at once.

'You want to try having a little swim?' he asks lightly.

'That would mean letting go of your hand,' I point out nervously.

'Yes,' he says, 'but I'll stay within reach.'

'Promise?'

'Promise. And I won't let go until you ask me to.'

It takes a good few moments for me to build up the courage to give him the go-ahead and free my hand from his. He keeps his hovering near mine until I've fully pulled away and then waits patiently for me to lower myself into the sea. I wasn't lying when I told him that I used to be a strong swimmer; I was good at it and I loved it too, that feeling of weightlessness as you move through water, the way it stretches out your body and works your muscles. I don't expect to simply plonk myself into the sea and return to the confident swimmer I once was, but my body hasn't forgotten.

The instinct kicks in, I want to swim to keep warm in the chill of the water as it soaks my wetsuit despite the fear running through my veins and how a small, panicked voice in my head is crying out in protest, begging me to put my feet back on solid ground. But Leo is there, right beside me, talking to me the whole time, reminding me I'm not alone.

'Bet this beats the lidos you've got back home, London,' he's saying, floating along nearby. 'How are you feeling? You good?'

'Yeah,' I say, my blood pumping through my body as I swim back towards shore, before I stand up in waist-height water, clutching my heart, unable to believe it.

He's there at my side as I stand.

A grin breaks across my face, my breathing heavy as I try to wrap my head around what I've done. I reach out to take his hands in mine, still not entirely confident. 'Leo... I can't believe it. I can't... Thank you. Thank you for today.'

'The lesson doesn't need to finish yet if you don't want it to,' he says, his eyes twinkling, keeping one hand clasping mine as he slowly leads me ashore. 'You know what feels even better than swimming?' He points at my surfboard, waiting for me on the sand. 'What do you think?' he asks.

'I think... I think I could go for a paddle,' I say breathlessly.

'Yeah,' he grins, his hand still holding mine as though he's forgotten to let go. 'Me too.'

Fifteen

It's difficult to put into words how much today meant to me. It's not like my fear has been magically cured – I know that it doesn't work like that – but I never thought I'd be able to enjoy a beach ever again. And I certainly never imagined I'd swim in the ocean again. I think today I found a resilience I didn't know I had; I've learnt that the fear doesn't have complete control over me. And that means a lot.

I even *enjoyed* paddling out on the surfboard. I didn't attempt to pop up, despite how much practice I'd put into it on dry land, but that's okay. I was amazed to even be in the water, and when, thanks to Leo's guidance, I managed to get past the waves lying flat on the board – which takes a lot more strength and effort than I realised – I turned round and paddled with all my might to keep up with the lift and swell of the water before I let the wave carry me towards the shore. That was when I experienced a smidgen of the feeling Leo has attempted to describe: the thrill of travelling with the water.

The way Leo cheered, anyone would have thought I'd stood up on the board for the first time. But he seemed to understand how big a deal it was to me.

It was exhausting and any time the board wobbled or the salty water splashed in my face, I felt a rush of panic, but the adrenaline pumping through my veins from drifting in safely towards the sand triumphed over it.

I did it. *I did it.*

And I had to do it again and again. I was on a total high, ignoring the ache in my muscles that was beginning to set in from the physical and mental exertion of the lesson.

By the time we drag ourselves out of the water and up the sand to Marina's Bar, my muscles are aching so much, I can barely walk, but that in itself feels great: the rush of endorphins you get from pushing your body. My spirit feels lifted; I can do anything.

'That was incredible,' I gush, squeezing the water out of my hair. 'I can't believe I just did that!'

'You were amazing.' He grins, holding up his hand for me to high-five. Just lifting my arm to reach up feels like a huge effort. 'A total natural.'

'Hardly. But thank you for being so patient with me. I mean it, Leo. I can't imagine I'm your ideal student, but you were… you were great.'

'It was fun; I'm stoked for you.'

'Iris, you had a surf lesson! How did it go?' Marina asks, appearing on the decking as we smile up at her from the beach. She lowers two bottles of water to Leo's outstretched hands and he passes me one.

'I think I'm starting to see why you live here,' I say, before taking a swig of water.

She laughs. 'You looked great out there.'

'You saw me?'

'Oh, I saw everything,' she says, her eyes drifting pointedly to Leo.

He frowns at her before turning to face the ocean, unscrewing the cap of his water bottle. I realise that for an outsider, the lesson might have looked a little... unorthodox.

'Leo is a brilliant teacher. I hadn't warned him about a couple of issues I have, but he made sure I felt safe and comfortable,' I explain hurriedly.

'You're glowing! I can tell you loved it. A great start to your surfing career,' she says, giving me a thumbs up.

'Tomorrow, I hope I'll be able to stand on the board.'

'You will. Practice and confidence are all it takes. Keep up your lessons with Leo and in a week or so, you'll be out surfing alongside us bigging up Leo before he heads to Australia for Bells Beach.'

I hesitate. 'In a week or so, I'll be back home in England.'

'Ah.' She nods, disappointment flooding her expression. 'Of course. I forgot. Well, once you get the surfing bug, you don't stop. A good excuse to come out here again to visit us.' She glances over her shoulder as customers enter the bar. 'I better go. See you later – seriously well done for today.'

Neither of us say anything as she leaves, Leo still looking out at the waves and sipping from his bottle of water as though deep in thought.

'Do you want to grab a drink or something?' I suggest hopefully, the adrenaline from the lesson knocking aside any inhibitions.

I don't think I want to tear myself from his company quite yet.

Leo glances over at me. He frowns, his eyes falling to the sand.

'You should go get warm,' he says.

'I'm fine!'

His lips ease into a smile. 'You're shivering. You should head home.'

My heart sinks a little at the rejection, and I kick myself. At least one of us is acting like a professional. I seem to have forgotten the reason I made today happen in the first place: so I could talk to Leo about his past while we were out surfing together. Instead, all I've done is talk about *my* past. In my next lesson, I need to keep my game face on and pull it together.

'Right. Yes. I should,' I state, hands on my hips, back to being myself and not a swooning teenager with a crush on her surf teacher. *Ugh*. How cliché. 'Thanks for the lesson, Leo. See you tomorrow.'

Turning away from him, I start treading through the sand towards his truck in the car park where I left my bag. Walking back home in my sandals with all this sand stuck to my feet is not going to be particularly comfortable, but I don't seem to care.

Huh. How much can change in a day.

'London, wait up,' I hear Leo call behind me and I spin round to see him following.

'Oh shit, the wetsuit,' I say, realising why he wanted to catch me before I left. 'Sorry, I forgot you need that back. Here,' I turn my back to him and pull my wet hair over one shoulder, 'can you unzip it for me?'

For a moment, nothing happens and I stand still, waiting, wondering what's going on back there. I'm about to turn around to check he hasn't walked off when I feel his fingers at the nape of my neck, gently moving the strands of hair still plastered to the wetsuit out of the way. With one hand holding the top of the suit at my neck, he draws the zipper slowly down to the bottom. Turning my head slightly to one side, I can feel his eyes as well as the cool breeze on the exposed skin of my back. His hands linger a beat too long.

Eventually, he takes a step backwards and I turn round to face him.

'Thanks,' I say, as I note his jaw tick. He looks furious.

He gives me a sharp nod.

My face on fire, I start peeling the wetsuit off me, shimmying it down to my waist, and he quickly looks away out at the ocean. When I'm standing in my bikini, I hold it out to him but he doesn't move. I realise that he probably wants it in the back of his truck anyway, so I toss it in there as I reach for my bag, pulling out the white top I was wearing earlier and pulling it over my head.

'The wetsuit was not why I came over here,' he says suddenly, glancing back at me.

'Oh?'

I balance against the side of his truck to pull my shorts up over my bikini bottoms, doing up the button at my waist.

Frowning, he wets his lips. 'What are you doing tonight?'

'Tonight?' I reach in my bag for my sandals. 'Why?'

'I've got my dad coming over for some food and I thought…' He trails off, staring at me and seeming uncertain of what he's trying to say, before collecting himself. 'You could join us if you're not busy?'

'Oh!' I'm taken aback by the invitation, a thrill rushing through me that he doesn't want the day with me to end here, either.

'You don't have to if you don't want to; maybe you're writing or, I just… we'll be talking tactics and nutrition, you know… important surf stuff, so I figured you might want to be there. For the article,' he concludes, running a hand through his hair.

'Oh.' That makes more sense. *For the article.* I hide my disappointment, embarrassed yet again for thinking that he wants me to be around on any kind of personal level, *which would be hugely inappropriate, Iris.*

'Yeah, that sounds great,' I say with a polite smile. 'Good idea.'

'Great. I'll message you a time.'

'Okay.'

He nods, but doesn't leave. I stand awkwardly, one sandal still in my hand.

'Right, I should go,' he says, almost as though he's reminding himself. 'I'll message. About the time.'

'Yes,' I say, breaking into a grin. 'You said.'

'Yeah.' He laughs at himself. 'I did.'

Leaning on his truck again, I wipe as much sand as possible from my foot and slide it into my shoe, securing the strap round my ankle. I repeat the process for the other foot and find Leo still lingering when I straighten up.

I throw the strap of my bag over my shoulder. 'So, just to be clear, you'll message me a time for tonight?'

He smiles playfully at my teasing. 'Wouldn't want you to be late, London.'

*

I'm still grinning to myself over the exchange by the time I get back to the apartment, allowing my mind to wander freely into idiotic, pointless thoughts about the feel of his hand clutching mine in the water. I'm so caught up in the forbidden excitement of it, I don't notice the man waiting for me by the door to the building until I'm practically walking into him.

'José!' I say, stepping back, the key in my hand.

Dressed in a sharp, grey suit and silk red tie, he takes off his sunglasses and slides a hand over his styled hair to shoot me a winning, pearly-white smile.

'Iris, hello,' he says, looking me up and down, his eyebrows raised. 'You have been at the beach today?'

'Yes, I had a surf lesson,' I admit, before I quickly run a hand through the tangles of my wet hair. 'How come you're here?'

'I was looking for you. I wondered what you were doing tonight.' He folds his sunglasses, sliding them into the inside pocket of his jacket. 'I wanted to take you for dinner.'

'Oh!' I smile, blushing. 'I'm so sorry, I can't tonight.'

'Ah. Tomorrow night?'

'Tomorrow night I'm free.'

'Not anymore.' He grins triumphantly. 'I'll come pick you up at eight.'

'Okay. Great. Thank you.'

He reaches for my hand and lifts it to his lips, pressing a kiss onto my knuckles without breaking eye contact. Then, he turns to leave, strolling away down the road, glancing back to flash a winning smile at me over his shoulder. I have to give it to him: he knows what he's doing. All of it was incredibly charming and sexy.

But I can't help wishing I was going on a date with someone else.

The main living area of Leo's flat is spacious and light, fairly minimalist with a few personal touches here and there – a bookshelf in one corner of the room, well-kept house plants dotted around on glass tables, some framed photographs of him and his dad, and friends – but the main draw is the balcony. It's huge, with a stunning view of the rooftops of Burgau sloping down to the beach.

'Wow,' I whisper, wandering over to the edge to look out.

'You like it?' he asks.

'I'm not sure anyone could *not* like it,' I remark, unable to tear my eyes away. 'I thought my balcony was good, but I think yours might win. It's about four times the size.'

'I remember saying to Dad when I found this place that it suited me because more of the apartment felt like it was outside than inside,' he recalls, leaning his elbows on the side of the balcony next to me. 'I was worried I wouldn't find anywhere I really loved here, because the village is so small. But this came up for sale the week I decided to start looking for my own place. I put an offer in straight away.'

'Fate.'

'Something like that,' he says, checking his phone either for the time or for a message from his dad who he's already told me is running late. 'What would you like to drink?

Wine or beer or soft drink? I have a variety of all of those, so take your pick.'

'Soft drink please. What are you having?'

'A very exciting glass of flavoured water with ice.'

I break into a smile. 'That sounds perfect.'

'Coming right up.'

As he heads back inside, I wander in behind him, taking in his home and picturing him living here. I've almost always been invited into the house of the person I'm interviewing; a lot of people feel more comfortable chatting to me whilst lounging on their sofa, surrounded by home comforts. Others might do it to show off their impressive interior design or to prove to the readers that they're not too flashy, that they're relatable with their kids' toys shoved into the corner of a room out of the way and their dogs jumping up for a cuddle on the sofa. But I actually get the feeling that, although it's helpful as a journalist to see his home, I haven't been invited here as one.

'Make yourself comfortable,' he offers, nodding to the wide, grey sofa as he opens the large, silver fridge in the kitchen to grab a bottle of water from inside the door.

I perch on the edge of his sofa, fiddling with the hem of my burnt-orange playsuit.

Picking an outfit for tonight was a difficult call; I had to find something that wasn't too formal as I knew it wouldn't be that kind of occasion, but it also couldn't be too date night or too casual. In the end, I had to video call Naomi to confirm that it was appropriate. I would have asked Flora's opinion, too, but she has enough on her plate with Kieran's dad rocking up and preparing for the baby's arrival.

Also, I knew she'd ask a lot of questions about why this was so important when I was just popping round for dinner with a client and I didn't want to answer them.

'The wedges are maybe too much?' I suggested, as I held up the phone to show Naomi my reflection in the full-length mirror.

'No, your legs look insane. Is it really hot over there or something? How come you're so tanned?' Naomi asked enviously.

'There's this amazing invention where they bottle tan and you can cover yourself in it.' I'd laughed. 'It's fake, Naomi.'

'You've done a bloody good job.'

'So you don't think the wedges are too much?'

'Wear the wedges,' Naomi insisted. 'They're not too high, so I think you can get away with them being fairly casual. Glam-casual, shall we say.'

'I do have gladiator-strap sandals, which might be easier on the walk to his place.'

'Like a long walk has ever stopped you before. Weren't you born in heels?'

'So the legend goes.'

'I guess you have to ask yourself the following questions,' she began, shooting a sly smile at the camera. 'Do you want this guy to see you in a purely professional manner? Or do you want to leave the dinner knowing that he's going to be fantasising about you and your long legs all night? If it's the former, then you need to pick a different outfit and a different pair of shoes. If it's the latter, you're good to go.'

I pretended to think about it.

Anyway, I'm glad I made the effort because Leo has too. Well, as much as he can, I guess. He's wearing a crisp, white, linen shirt and pale-salmon-pink shorts. He's done something different with his hair – although it still looks dishevelled, if stylishly – and when he invited me in earlier and I walked past him, I got a whiff of the cologne he'd sprayed on.

It smells musky and delicious.

'So what's on the menu?' I ask as he comes to sit down next to me. 'After hearing of your baking success, I'm looking forward to experiencing your culinary skills.'

'Aren't writers meant to be observant?' he asks, placing our drinks down on the coffee table and leaning back into the cushion, his body twisted towards me. 'You haven't noticed the lack of cooking smells or the fact that the kitchen is spotless.'

I glance over at the bare kitchen.

'My dad will be providing the food for tonight,' he informs me in a hushed voice.

I lean forwards, lowering my voice to a hush to match his. 'I'm a little bit relieved.'

He grins at me. 'I would be if I were you.'

Giggling, I sit straight again and reach for my glass before something catches my eye on the wall behind him. A charcoal sketch of a sailboat in the same style as the one in Marina's Bar and in his dad's shop. He notices my expression and turns to follow my eyeline.

'What?' he asks, swivelling back to me in confusion.

'That artwork,' I say, pointing to it in excitement. 'I keep seeing it. Is it a local artist?'

'Oh, yeah, it is. Very local.' He looks almost pained as he adds, 'It's mine.'

I blink at him. 'Excuse me?'

'When you say you keep seeing it, I'm guessing that's because you've seen it in my dad's shop,' he says, laughing modestly. 'I did ask him not to display it there, but he insists.'

'You… you drew these?'

He nods, shifting in his seat, clearly uncomfortable with this topic.

'Leo,' I say in frustration, leaping to my feet to walk around to the picture and study it properly, 'they're really good! Are you kidding me?'

He laughs at my expression. 'How are you annoyed at me? I can tell you are.'

'Because you haven't mentioned that you're a secret artist! Do you know how gorgeous an angle that is for the feature? Tell me about it!'

'Ah, there's not much to tell,' he insists, looking down at his hands as he clasps them together. 'It's not serious. It helps me think. Sketching is a bit like surfing in that it takes me away from everything else.' He hesitates, adding with a wry smile, 'It's a bit more relaxing than surfing, though. I guess it's good to have a hobby that helps me unwind.'

'How long have you done it for? You're so talented!'

He shakes his head. 'I'm not disciplined at all in it; I only do it when I have the time. I used to be quite good at art at school – probably the only thing I was good at when it came to school. But then I sort of… lost it for a bit.' He clears his throat. 'I took it up again when I moved back here. My dad bought me the stuff I needed, actually; he got me all the charcoal and graphite supplies, encouraged me to give it a go again.'

I point at the sailboat in the picture. 'Why is this one special?'

'I'm sorry?'

'This one must be special to you, it's the only one on your wall,' I note. 'The ones in your dad's shop and at Marina's are surfers, but this one is a boat. You don't have any other ones up here in your home but I assume you have done more drawings than this, so what is it about this one that you like?'

He looks at me, puzzled, his lips slightly parted in confusion, as though he's never thought about it. Eventually, he closes his mouth and swallows, before saying, 'It was the first one I ever sketched here on the balcony, so it felt like a moment,' without taking his eyes off mine.

I nod, folding my arms as I turn back to admire it. 'Charcoal creates such a cool effect. Whimsical almost. Kind of haunting.'

'I saw the boat out there and I wondered where they were going,' he explains, standing up to come join me in examining it. 'Then I realised that they probably didn't care where they were going. They were just... sailing.'

Side by side, we fall into silence. I'm so aware of how close he's standing to me, how if I stretched out my fingertips, they might brush against his and maybe that would lead him to wrap his hand around mine like earlier today and drag me towards him and—

The doorbell rings and I jump.

'That will be Dad,' he says in a low voice, stepping behind me to go to the door.

Exhaling, I shut my eyes while my mind races with thoughts that I shouldn't be having. It's a good thing I have this date tomorrow so I can quash this silly crush with the excitement of dating someone like José, who is quite potentially the Perfect Man. I'm heading home soon, too, so anything that happens with José would be temporary and uncomplicated – just how I like it. I *cannot* develop feelings for Leo. That would be extremely complicated.

What matters here is my career.

And that's something I have to remind myself continually throughout the evening whenever I catch Leo's gaze lingering on me a little too long as I burst out laughing at one of Adriano's stories, or when I find myself admiring Leo's artwork too many times to be subtle, or when I say goodnight and he tells his dad he's going to walk me home, happy to stroll slowly next to me while I totter along in my wedges, putting out his hand to help me balance down the steeper slopes.

'Thanks again for this evening, Leo, it was really… helpful,' I say stupidly, as we get to my apartment building. 'I like your dad's attitude towards your training in the lead up to the competition. He's so calm and casual about it. It's refreshing.'

He shoves his hands in his pockets. 'He makes it seem easy, right?'

'I think that's a good thing. He doesn't want to put too much pressure on you.'

'It doesn't matter; the pressure is there. I don't want him to lose his business.' He looks disheartened for a moment. 'If I win, it could do everyone a lot of good.'

'And what about you? What does it mean to you to ring that iconic bell again?'

He brings his eyes up to meet mine. 'It would do me a lot of good, too, knowing I still have what it takes to compete with the young stars out there.'

I fold my arms across my chest. 'You doubt yourself?'

'Doesn't every athlete have their doubts?'

I smile slowly at him. 'That's why they have their support network to help them overcome those doubts. But not you. You're a lone wolf.'

He grimaces. 'I think I may have to adjust that quote.'

I laugh, rummaging in my bag for my keys. 'I'll see you in the morning bright and early. Your dad has invited me to come watch you surf down the coast first thing.'

'Has he?'

'Is that okay? I should have really been shadowing several of your training sessions by now, so please don't say no.'

'Sure, no dramas,' he assures me. 'You do know that my training sessions are just me surfing, right? There's nothing special about it.'

'I'll be the one to judge what's special.'

He gives me a wry smile. 'You can tell me afterwards whether my doubts are justified or if you think I have what it takes.'

'I don't need tomorrow to make up my mind on that.'

It's bold and it's potentially a little inappropriate, but it's also true. And the foolish part of me wants him to know that.

His brow creases and he looks unsure.

Then he leans towards me and my breath catches in my throat as for one crazy moment, I think he might be about to kiss me. But he goes to kiss me on the cheek, the warmth of his skin brushing against mine sending shivers down my spine.

I clear my throat.

'Night, Leo,' I say in a clipped tone as he pulls back, desperately trying to maintain an air of professionalism after letting my thoughts run riot. I hope my expression hasn't given any of them away.

'Night, London,' he murmurs.

I could be looking for something that isn't there, but I think I hear a note of regret in his voice.

He waits until I'm safely inside before he leaves.

Sixteen

Standing on the beach of Sagres early the next morning, I watch as Leo waits patiently in the water to choose his wave. When he eventually makes a decision, he begins to paddle forwards before popping up, gracefully etching lines across the curve of the wave with his board. My mouth hangs open in awe at such skilled, confident surfing.

'How does he *know*?' I find myself asking hoarsely.

'Know what?' Adriano asks next to me, eyes locked on his son's performance.

'That *that* was the wave to choose,' I explain, gesturing out at Leo. 'There were loads of waves before that one that looked good to me, so I didn't understand what he was waiting for. But he was right to wait – that was the best wave so far.'

Adriano chuckles. 'It's like everything, Iris: practice. In a set of waves, you have to find the best one. Leo has learnt to look at the waves and know what they are going to do.'

'So, when he's bobbing on his board out there, he's studying the waves coming in?'

'Studying is maybe the wrong word,' Adriano muses. 'When you're as good as Leo at surfing, when you've spent as much time in the water as he has, it's intuition. He doesn't study the waves, he… understands them.'

'That makes sense,' I say quietly, as Leo dismounts and makes his way out of the ocean. I try to ignore how I instinctively straighten and my heart rate quickens at the sight of him approaching. 'Two things that are always important to an athlete: practice and intuition.'

Adriano nods. 'And for the *best* athletes, you must add one more: courage.' He waits for me to turn to look at him, his eyes glinting in the early morning sunshine. 'The courage to go after what you want.'

I'm going to pop up on a surfboard today.

The sureness doesn't come from me, but from Leo. He keeps telling me that it's going to happen as if he knows, as if there's not a hint of doubt in his mind that I can do this.

And I believe him.

'Falling is part of it,' he warns, as we stand on the beach, preparing to paddle out. 'And timing is absolutely crucial. You're not going to get it the first time, but that's a good thing, because you learn how to read the waves.'

'You're preparing me for failure.'

'Failing is important in surfing. You're learning to feel the movement of the sea whilst also commanding a board, which is awkward and heavy. No wave is the same; you can't memorise bullet points on popping up and expect to do it,' he smiles to himself, 'but with time and commitment, it *will* happen.'

I nod, too nervous to speak. My stomach is twisting itself into knots as I look out at the waves, however gentle, and I'm doing everything I can to focus on the confidence I discovered yesterday in the water. I focus on slowing my breathing, trying my best to control the fear and panic threatening to stop me in my tracks.

'Remember, London,' he says, turning to face me, his voice low and steady. 'I'm not going to let anything happen to you. You're not alone, I'm right here next to you. We're not going too far out and when you fall off that board, I'll be there. *Every* time.'

It turns out, he really is a man of his word.

At first, I really do struggle. Beginner boards are so long and heavy, it takes me a while to feel in control of it. Then when I do feel like I'm getting the positioning better and paddling well, I have to feel confident with my balance and the swell of the wave to take the chance to stand.

The first time I roll under the water, I feel sick with panic but as I come up for air, there's Leo finding his way to me, reaching for my hands and pulling me towards him so I can rest my arms on his as he takes my weight.

'That was brilliant!' he exclaims as I wipe the salt water from my eyes. 'I swear to God, London, you almost had it. You okay?'

I nod, my breathing heavy and laboured.

'Hey,' he says through a gentle smile, forcing me to look at him as my hands remain gripped to his strong arms, 'you're all right. You're all right, London. You're good.'

He's right. I am good. I'd gone underwater, but I'd come back up. He was there alongside me to help pull me up, just like he said. I can trust him. I'm starting to understand I can trust myself too. Something has lit up inside me, a rush that I can't ignore.

I know that I don't have to be here doing this. I can give up if I want to.

'You need a moment?' he asks, his eyes searching mine.

'No,' I say determinedly. 'I want to stand up today.'

He smiles as though something has just been confirmed for him. 'Let's go then,' he says, and we begin the whole process again.

It takes a few more falls to get there, but then, by some miracle, it happens.

I manage to stand up on the board as it moves with the wave. My legs are shaking, my heart frenziedly racing; I feel the chilled wind on my face, and I can hear Leo's cheering just before the board slips out of my control and I fall backwards into the water, the roar of the ocean slamming against my ears. It isn't until I come up and gulp in the cold, salty air that it dawns on me just how exhilarating that moment was.

I did it. I surfed! Me. Iris Gray. A woman who thought I'd never set foot in the sea again. To anyone else, it's a person wobbling up onto their feet on a surfboard, not very elegantly or brilliantly. But to me, it's extraordinary.

Such a small achievement that makes me feel like I'm the most powerful person on the planet, like I can do anything.

I have to do it again. And again.

I fall *many* more times. I stand three more times. Each time better and more confident than the last. And then in the last few minutes of the lesson, I paddle out with Leo and we sit in the water, straddling our surfboards, looking out at the vast ocean stretching out before us. It feels like we're the only people in the world.

'I've never felt like this,' I tell him quietly after a few moments of silence.

'It's not bad, is it,' he replies, bobbing next to me.

I turn to look at him, barely able to feel my feet, they're so cold in the water so long, but I don't care. 'I understand now. How you couldn't stay away from it when you came to live here. It makes more sense to me.'

He doesn't say anything, but he smiles, gazing out ahead of him.

'This is why I love my job,' I continue, the adrenaline pumping through my veins making it hard to stop saying exactly how I feel. 'The thing about athletes is that they often get defined by what they achieve. How many titles or trophies or medals. But when I do big profile pieces, I get the chance to see what it takes to get there: the passion, the hours, the commitment, the sacrifices, the drive.'

I turn to grin at him and find him already watching me.

'What does it matter what you win if you get to feel like this on the way?' I gush, wiping away the droplets of water on my forehead trailing from my hair. 'This is what sport is about. It's a way of life. And I see that now for you with surfing. The sheer love of it.'

He smiles at my enthusiasm, but I don't care if I'm embarrassing myself.

I mean every word.

'It's so peaceful out here,' I say, twirling my pruned fingers in swirls through the water. 'Being out here on the water puts things in perspective. How amazing to get to do this every day. It must be… I don't know… it must become…'

'Part of your soul,' he finishes for me. 'That's how you put it the other day.'

'A wanker thing to say.'

'But an honest one.'

We smile giddily at each other.

He's right. The ocean *is* part of his soul; he couldn't turn his back on it even if he tried, which I think, at one point, he did. Surfing is who he is, but it's not all he is. These are the thoughts running through my mind as I watch him, floating on top of the water with me, our legs dangling in the ocean. These are the things I'll write about him.

His chest rises as he takes a deep breath. 'I want to tell you about what happened.'

'When?'

'In Australia,' he says. 'For the article. I've decided I want to talk about what happened to me and why I left. If you're ready to hear it.'

A swell of excitement ripples through me. *It worked.* The best way to get to know Leo Silva is on a surfboard. There's no one else out here. It's him, me, and the ocean.

'I'm ready.'

He hesitates, frowning. 'Although you don't have your phone on you to record.'

'I'll remember,' I assure him. 'You can always check it to be sure.'

He shrugs. 'I trust you.'

I nod. *I trust you too,* I want to say. But I stay silent, waiting for him to speak.

'When you said just now that it's easy to define athletes on their achievements, you basically put into words something I struggled with every day at the peak of my career,' he says pensively, his brow furrowed. 'You become so focused on the next win, you forget why you started competing in the first place: the love of the sport.'

A shadow of sadness crosses his expression and he takes a moment to collect himself before he continues, his chest rising as he inhales deeply.

He turns to look at me.

'When I was learning to surf in Victoria, I was surrounded by some great people. Everything was easy and fun; we all loved surfing. But when I started getting attention, signing sponsorship deals and earning competition winnings, things changed. It felt good to be so admired; I'd grown up thinking I was going nowhere. My grades were terrible, my academic motivation non-existent. The only place I felt happy was out on the water. I'd grown used to feeling like a disappointment, which was… difficult, considering who I was.'

He looks pained, his eyes falling to his board. I think he might be talking about his mother, but I don't want to ask. This isn't the right moment for interjections.

'I got caught up in the whirlwind of attention I was getting,' he sighs, deflating. 'I liked what fame meant: the money, the admiration, the places it got you. I threw myself into relationships with people who made me feel important. They hadn't known me when I was a goofy grom, fucking up on waves and wiping out. They only knew me as a winner. A rich and famous World Champion. I pushed away anyone who'd ever cared about me: Dad, all my old mates. I shut them out, made them feel like they didn't matter.'

He shakes his head, still annoyed at himself. The old video of him and Ethan Anderson as a couple of grinning, surf-obsessed teenagers flits across my mind, and I wonder if he's included in this group, if their former friendship fuelled the intensity of their rivalry.

'I partied a lot, spending all my time with people who told me I was the best,' he mutters. 'People who didn't ask me real questions about me or my future, because they cared way more about themselves and their own fame. They all thought I was this successful, arrogant bloke with the world at his feet – and for a while, I was. But I look back now and all I see is a scared little kid desperate to prove himself.'

His eyes flicker across nervously to me, and I get a glimpse of the boy he was then, so lost and vulnerable, desperately trying to make his mark. An ache erupts in my chest. I have an urge to reach out to him, to take his hands in mine and tell him that it's okay.

But I can't. All I can do is sit on my board and listen.

'The funny thing was, no matter how many competitions I won or big deals I got, I still wasn't good enough. I remained, at the core of it, a disappointment.' His throat bobs as he swallows. 'I dimmed that sense of inadequacy with more drinking and drugs. And any time I was photographed pissed off my face or high, and it got splashed about the press, I laughed about it. I tried to convince myself I was done attempting to live up to someone else's image of what I should be.' He hesitates, frowning at me. 'I'm not trying to justify the way I acted back then. I think I'm still trying to get to the bottom of it myself. I want to understand why I became that person I don't recognise anymore. Does that make sense?'

'Yes. It does.'

He runs his hand through his hair, his fingers getting caught momentarily in the crisp, salty tangles. 'All of that behaviour numbed the fears and anxiety that haunted me. The thrill of winning, the applause and acclaim – that's addictive. When everyone expects you to win, your self-worth becomes tied to it. Like you say, you define yourself by the wins. I *had* to keep winning. Otherwise, what was I? Nothing. People wanted to spend time with me because I was a winner, that's all I was. Even the thought of losing, I couldn't... cope.'

Hanging his head, he exhales all the breath from his body.

'Leo,' I say, a lump in my throat as I worry he might crumple beneath these memories at any moment, 'you don't have to talk about this now. If you need a break, we can—'

'No, it's okay,' he says, lifting his eyes to meet mine. 'I want to. Your articles aren't just about the athlete's self-promotion, right? They speak to people. This might make someone out there feel less alone.' He offers a sad smile. 'That's important.'

'Yeah,' I breathe, captivated by his gaze, 'it is.'

We fall into silence as he gathers his thoughts, the rhythmic sound of the waves in the background rallying him to speak.

'The thought of losing was one thing, but when it started happening...' He grimaces as he trails off, working out the best way to put it. 'Honestly? I was fucking confused. I was so arrogant, I thought it was a blip. So, I partied harder because I needed to numb the fears that were starting to come true. I was *terrified*. If I'd bothered to take anything seriously, I might have noticed that there was someone else getting better and better. Someone who put the work in.'

I hazard a guess: 'Ethan Anderson?'

A muscle in his jaw twitches. 'I'd never considered Ethan as real competition,' he admits in a low voice. 'I underestimated him. He was better at handling the sport mentally and physically, and he was determined to beat me. We'd known each other since we were groms but... it got hectic between us. When he took the World Champion title the first time, it felt as though everything I was had been ripped from me. I was *nothing* without it. But I couldn't admit that to anyone; that would make it real.' He pauses and turns to look at me. 'Do you ever feel like that?'

The question takes me by surprise. 'Huh?'

'Like, if you say something out loud, if you confide in someone, then you might fall apart. But if you pretend everything is fine, you convince yourself the problem doesn't exist,' he explains, studying my expression. 'You ever feel like that?'

'I... I don't know. Maybe. Sometimes.'

All the time. *All the fucking time.*

He nods slowly. 'Instead of blaming myself for my failure, I blamed Ethan. I hated him, and that hatred drove me off a cliff. I partied more to show the world that I wasn't bothered; I was still the big winner they knew me to be. I hung out with people who told me I was better than him as they poured me a larger drink and cut me a bigger line. My motivation to compete worsened with every loss. When Ethan won World Champion for a second time, I decided that was it for me. It was all or nothing – and I was nothing.'

He hesitates, shooting me a worried look.

'What is it?' I ask, frowning.

'You must be cold,' he says, glancing back at the beach. 'Let's go in; we can talk about this somewhere else.'

'I'm fine,' I tell him firmly, well aware that if someone is interrupted at a crucial moment in the story, sometimes it's impossible to get them back to where they were. 'Carry on if you're happy to.'

'I promise I'm almost done.'

'Leo, I'm *fine*,' I say, breaking into a reassuring smile. 'Go on.'

He's comforted by my expression, if a little unconvinced. But thankfully, he decides to listen to my instruction and after a heavy sigh, he speaks.

'The day Ethan was announced as World Champion, I went to a party, got pissed and announced to whoever was listening that I was quitting surfing for good. I remember people cheered. They were all so fucked, they probably didn't know why they were cheering.' He closes his eyes for a moment. 'And I remember when I got home, I decided not to go to bed. I should go for one last surf.'

I inhale sharply. 'That night?'

'Technically, by now it was early in the morning. But yeah. I grabbed my surfboard and I went to Bells Beach. The weather was bad, the waves weren't right. I was drunk, I was angry and I was helpless. I went against every gut instinct I had as I paddled out – one of the worst mistakes you can make in surfing.' He bites his lip, his eyes set on the rippling water ahead of his board. 'The person who saved my life told doctors it was one of the worst wipeouts they'd ever seen. They thought I was dead but they still pulled me from the water anyway. I don't... I don't remember it. Any of it. Probably a good thing.' He holds up his wrist, pointing to the scar there. 'The small memento l was left with.'

'Oh my God, Leo,' I whisper, before I can stop myself.

He brings his eyes up to meet mine. 'When I woke up in hospital, I was so frightened. And humiliated. And racked with guilt about... everything. Mum and Dad were both there – Mum from London, Dad from Portugal. The incident and my hospital stay were kept out of the press, but still, not one of my so-called friends messaged during that time to check if I was okay. They didn't even notice I wasn't around.'

'What about the person who rescued you? Were they a friend?'

His frown deepens. 'No. Anyway,' he clears his throat and gestures to the beach behind us, keen to avoid the answer, 'that's how I came to be here. I needed a change, an escape, so I flew home with Dad. I could live here in Portugal with my dual-citizenship and Burgau saved me. The longer I stayed here, the more I realised this is where I belong. With some encouragement, Dad got me back on a surfboard. The ocean drew me back in.'

'You're connected.'

'Surfing is a humbling sport,' he tells me with a wry smile. 'It can quickly remind you who's in charge here. You don't get to control the swells or tides, or what the weather is going to be like that day. You try to control what you can: your fitness, your mobility, your focus. That's all you can do. The rest of it is whatever that moment brings.'

He gazes out to the ocean again, the weight of reliving his past lifting in an instant. With a light shrug, he's back in the present and happy to be here.

I break into a smile. 'You put that very nicely.'

'Yeah? Poetic enough for you?' he asks, raising an eyebrow.

'Too poetic,' I say, giving a dramatic sigh. 'How am I meant to remember all these remarkable quotes? I'm going to need you to come over to mine so I can write this.'

'If that's what you need me to do,' he says, his eyes locking with mine.

My breath hitches, flutters rippling through my chest. He's joking. Probably. That was a joke. I should laugh. But not now, because it's too late to laugh now and he'll know I'm faking it. *Shit*. I can't think straight.

'You okay?' he asks, while my cheeks burn. 'You want to go in?'

'I have one last question,' I blurt out.

'Just the one? I'm surprised. I really gave the story-telling my all.'

'Okay, maybe a couple hundred,' I admit.

'That sounds more plausible.'

'I'd have double that if you'd let me take notes.'

He chuckles. '*There* she is.'

'But one more question while we're drifting at sea.'

'As it's only one…'

I take a deep breath. 'Leo, it's been a long time since you walked away from it all. So, why did you accept the invitation to compete at Bells Beach this year?'

Pressing his lips together, he considers the question.

Eventually, he answers. 'Bells Beach was my home; it's where I grew up and it's where I gave up – if I can win there again, I can do anything. It's the only competition I'd come back for. It's a bit like you with the ocean. I don't want to be afraid anymore.' He hesitates, his eyes flashing at me. 'And this time, I want to be worthy of the bell trophy.'

I tilt my head at him. 'So this *is* about proving something.'

'My love and gratitude for the surfing community, yeah. And, if I'm honest with myself, I want to remember how it feels.'

'To take part in a surf competition?'

'To take part,' he repeats, before a knowing smile creeps across his lips, 'and to win.'

Seventeen

As we wade through the water towards the beach after our chat, I feel a sharp sting in the ball of my foot as I step on something jagged, but I ignore the pain, amazed at the success of today and looking forward to getting out of this clingy, damp wetsuit.

Suddenly, Leo's hand grasps my wrist, pulling me to a stop.

'Iris, what's wrong?' he says, his expression full of concern as he stares down at the water around my ankles.

'Hey!' I say, looking at him strangely. 'You called me "Iris". I've been getting used to my nickname.'

'Look,' he insists, bringing my attention to the wisps of blood appearing in the sea.

'Oh shit.' I wince, taking the weight off my aching foot. 'I thought I stepped on something.' I gasp, gripping his forearms. 'Do you think it was a crab? Oh my God, why is this happening to me *again*? I swear, Leo, sea creatures *hate* me. They sense the fear.'

'Lean on me,' he demands, ignoring my ramblings.

Sliding an arm around my waist whilst throwing mine over his shoulders, he pulls my body against his before I can protest.

Not that I would.

'I'm sure it's not that bad,' I reason as he leads me ashore, even though now that I think about it, it does actually hurt quite a lot. 'It's probably just a small... *oh*.'

We've reached the edge of the water, and I've lifted my foot up to discover the underside of it is covered in blood.

'How were you *walking* on that?' Leo asks, aghast before looking at me crossly. 'You should have said something.'

I'm unfazed by his anger towards me because his face is so close to mine that it's impossible for me to really focus on anything he's saying or the tone in which he's saying it. He has the perfect lips. They look so full and soft.

'Put your arms round my neck,' he instructs.

Mesmerised by his features so close to mine, I do what he asks, and in one swift motion, he lifts me up into his arms like I don't weigh a fucking thing, and he carries me up the beach. I feel so safe and secure cradled up in his arms like this. And he looks so adorably worried, the creases across his forehead etched with a mixture of concern and determination.

I don't realise I'm holding my breath until we reach Marina's Bar and her voice cuts through the haze I'd floated into whilst admiring the sharp line of his jaw.

'What happened to you?' she asks.

'She cut her foot,' Leo says, lowering me gently into a chair before he swings another one round to prop my foot up onto.

'I can see that, genius; I meant how.'

'I stepped on a crab,' I murmur dreamily, watching Leo pick up another chair to put it right by my leg, before reaching round to unzip his wetsuit, peeling it down to his waist and sitting down to inspect my foot properly.

Thank fuck I got a pedicure before I came here.

As he peers at the injury, I stare at his torso, glistening with water droplets.

'You *what*?' Marina says, wrinkling her nose.

'We don't know what happened,' Leo says plainly, reaching to grab cushions from other chairs to stack under my foot. 'Can you get the first aid kit, Marina?'

'Coming right up,' she says, hurrying off, muttering, '*She stepped on a crab*,' in disbelief under her breath as she goes.

'You're going to be okay,' he tells me as if I give a flying fuck about my foot right now and I'm not fully distracted by the way he carried me in his strong arms. 'We'll get this cleaned up and then we'll be able to tell what we're dealing with.'

Marina returns with the kit, holding it out to Leo, who gets to work straight away, cleaning the cut. With Marina present, I try not to be too obvious when I observe the way Leo's arms flex as he works, and how shimmering and smooth the skin of his carved bare chest looks, and how defined his abs are, even when he's sitting down, hunched over my foot.

Marina clears her throat. 'Iris? Did you hear me?'

I snap my head up to look at her and find her watching me, smirking.

'S-sorry,' I stammer, forcing my face into serious mode. 'Did you say something?'

'Yes, but it looked like you were in some kind of daze there,' she says with a tone of humour swirling round her words. 'I was asking if you were okay.'

'Yes, thank you,' I say crisply, sitting up a little.

'Good, it doesn't look very deep,' Leo announces, as I wince when he dabs it with something that stings. 'The blood made it look worse than it is. You're lucky.'

'And just when you were getting the hang of popping up on the board,' Marina remarks, putting her hands on her hips. 'Not sure you should surf tomorrow; you need to let that heal.'

'That's a shame,' I sigh.

'And no wearing those high heels of yours,' she adds.

'*What?* It's not that bad,' I protest sharply.

I notice Leo smile to himself.

'Glad you're feeling yourself, London,' he mutters, still focusing on nursing my foot.

'I've got to serve these customers and then I'll go get you guys some water,' Marina says, her eyes flickering between us. 'If you need anything else, shout. Otherwise, I'll be back in a bit.' She comes over to rest a hand on my shoulder, squeezing it. 'Well done for today. You looked great out there.'

'Thanks, Marina.'

Leo and I fall into comfortable silence when she leaves, both of us concentrating on the task at hand: he's busy wiping the blood from my foot and I'm taking the opportunity to admire him openly without any judgement from another party.

'Okay, that will have to do for now,' he says eventually, looking up at me. 'How does it feel? Are you in a lot of pain?' He cranes his neck to see where Marina is. 'Once we have some water, you can take some painkillers, then you should get to a doctor.'

'Leo, I'm fine.'

He stands up. 'I think Marina may have been distracted; I'll go get some.'

'No, don't go yet,' I say a bit too abruptly, my hand reaching out even though he's too far away for me to grab and hold onto.

I drop my hand, my cheeks flushing.

What the fuck am I doing? Why am I acting as though I'm a little kid who has hurt herself and needs someone to look after me? I don't need anyone. I'm mortified.

Leo stares at me, a little stunned by the feeling in my voice. I'm not surprised.

'All right,' he says eventually, sliding his chair up so he's nearer to me rather than my elevated foot.

'I just wanted to... thank you for speaking to me today,' I say hurriedly, lifting my chin and doing my best to act like a grown-up again. 'I know that can't have been easy, revisiting the past, especially when you went through such a traumatic event and I don't want you to think I'm not... grateful. That's the wrong word, I think. Hang on, let me think of a better one.'

He smirks. 'It's okay. You don't have to thank me. I wanted to talk about it. I've been thinking about it and if telling my story helps one person out there to feel less alone, then it's worth it. I've been carrying around the shame of it a long time.'

'There's no shame in losing your way.'

'There's shame in treating your friends and family badly,'

he counters. 'I never apologised to them: the mates I grew up with in Victoria. That's haunted me ever since I left.' He hesitates, his dark eyes softening. 'I know they think the worst of me.'

'I'm sure that's not true. Even if it is, they'll read this article and understand what happened,' I assure him gently. 'And you can always apologise to them in person when you're in Australia.'

He grimaces. 'Saying sorry has never come easily for me.'

'I can relate,' I say, laughing. 'But it does feel better when you do. And anyway, they'll forgive you. Come on, you were young. You were mini grooms.'

He laughs and corrects me, '*Groms*. We were on surfboards, not in stables.'

'Right. Mini groms. We're all idiots when we're young. Look at me and the incident in Cornwall. I have no one to blame for that but myself.' I pause, watching him thoughtfully. 'What about your mum?'

He stiffens. 'What about her?'

'Have you ever spoken to her properly about what happened and how you felt at the time? I get the feeling that you're not... close. And you were obviously upset about how she went about organising this article. But tell me to shut up if I've got that wrong.'

'I'm not sure I'd ever get away with telling you to shut up, London.'

'True. Do so at your peril.'

He gives a small smile, rubbing the back of his neck.

'Is this off the record?' he checks.

'If you want it to be.'

He exhales. 'I was surprised that she was so interested in

me taking part in Bells Beach again. I didn't realise it would be on her radar. But, yeah, maybe her pitching this article is a step in the right direction.'

'Sounds like she's proud of how far you've come.'

His eyes fall to the ground, as though he can't let himself believe it. I watch him retreat into himself again; beneath that strong, muscled chest is a heart that's as brittle and delicate as anyone else's. I think it's been broken and taped back together long before now, the heart of a boy who somewhere along the way accepted that he would never be enough to earn the approval he clearly craved.

How I wish I could reach out and hold him.

Clearing his throat, he lifts his head to smile apologetically at me, blinking away any hint of vulnerability. 'Look, I don't want to talk about… that. How are *you* feeling?'

'Me?'

'Yes, you,' he says, the playful side to him re-emerging. 'You stood up on a board today. You surfed.'

'*And* I survived a crab attack.'

He gives me a look. 'You did not step on a crab.'

'Got the cut to prove it.'

'It was probably the edge of a rock.'

'It stuck out its pincers when it saw me coming and went for the kill.'

'That is very unlikely.'

'Bloody villainous crab.'

Using the arms of the chair, I push myself up so my back is straighter, sliding my foot down from its elevated position. Leo instinctively reaches forward to grab my arm.

'What are you doing? You should keep it up,' he says crossly.

'It's fine; it's a cut.'

'You could make it worse.'

'Leo,' I say, forcing him to look up at me, his face etched with concern, 'I'm *fine*.'

It's at that moment that we both realise how close we are, his face just inches from mine. His hands don't move from my arm, his touch comforting and electrifying at the same time. I hold his gaze until his eyes flicker down to my lips as I wet them, my mouth dry, my heart beating a million miles an hour. When he brings his eyes back up to lock them with mine, they seem different somehow, searing and fierce. *Hungrier.* A bolt of desire erupts between my legs and my breath hitches. He tilts ever so slightly nearer; I shift my shoulders in his direction, the charged gap between us gradually closing.

He's going to kiss me.

Leo Silva is going to kiss me.

A clatter from behind the bar brings us both back to reality with a jolt. We spring apart, turning to see Marina helping a colleague with a tray of glasses that almost went shattering to the floor.

When I twist myself back in my seat, Leo is sitting deep in thought. He fixes a smile when I catch his eye. I smile awkwardly back, wondering if he's thinking what I'm thinking, which is along the lines of: *what the fuck just happened?* And, *Thank goodness we were interrupted*, and also, *I wish we hadn't been interrupted.*

'I should go get you some water so you can take some painkillers,' he says, getting to his feet. He looks restless and uncomfortable, like he wants to escape the situation.

'It's fine,' I say, flustered, trying to collect myself as I start to stand up. 'I have some in the apartment.'

'You can't walk home on that foot; let me help you.'

'I can walk a few metres,' I insist, holding up my hand and stopping him from trying to link my arm around him again. 'It's a cut; nothing is broken.'

'Still. You should rest.'

'Thank you, Dr Silva,' I say, rolling my eyes. 'Seriously, though, thank you for everything today and for all your help with my foot. It already feels better.'

'Okay.' He's agitated, his brow furrowed. 'What are you doing tonight? I could bring you some food or something. You really shouldn't be walking around with an injury.'

'I... I'm out tonight.'

'Oh.' He hesitates, looking torn for a moment before he asks, 'Is it an interview for the article?'

He's prying. It could be that he's eager to be kept in the loop about all my research for the feature, but after that intense moment between us, it feels like something is charged. This is no longer a professional relationship.

I don't know what this is anymore.

'No.'

A muscle in his jaw twitches. I don't say anything further. I don't need to; he can guess. For a moment, he looks irritated. Disappointed. *Jealous.* Tingles run down my spine at the very thought of it. *I want him.* I'm not going to pretend to myself like I don't, because come on. He's so fucking hot, but also fun and cute and thoughtful. The way he carried me up the beach, the way he looked at me when we had our almost-kiss moment...

He's so gorgeous, he makes my brain malfunction.

But even if he felt the same way, nothing can happen. I know that. He surely knows that. So, here we are, standing in silence, tense and begrudging. The energy in the air between us is sparking and crackling.

'I'll let you get home then,' he mutters eventually.

I nod, sliding myself past him to begin my agonisingly slow walk to the door.

'Fuck's sake, this is painful to watch,' Leo huffs behind me, before I suddenly feel his hands around my waist again, propping my arm over his shoulders and hoisting me up so that I can lean my weight on him. 'I'm driving you home.'

'The apartment is down the road!'

'At this rate, that will take you weeks.'

'You don't need to fuss, Leo.'

'Yes, I do,' he states so matter-of-factly, it shuts me right up.

He helps me into the truck and we sit in silence for the two-minute drive. When I steal a glance at him, his mouth is set in a hard line. He pulls up to my building, turns off the engine and jumps out to rush round and get the door, lifting me down and leading me to the door of the building.

'Thank you,' I begin, fishing out my keys, 'but you don't need—'

'I'm taking you up to the flat,' he says gruffly, not even looking at me.

And I don't argue with that either. At first, he lets me lean on him as I attempt the stairs, but then he gets impatient and before I know it, I'm up in his arms again being carried all the way up to my floor. I clutch my hands round his neck a little tighter than is necessary.

When he lowers me down in front of my door, I open my mouth to thank him, but he cuts in before I can say a word.

'Have fun tonight,' he says, refusing to look me in the eye.

He's spun round and rushed down the stairs before I can even *consider* saying out loud what I'd like to say. Which is that I'd like to cancel on José tonight.

And against all better judgement, I'd like to invite Leo inside.

Eighteen

This date should be perfect.

I'm in a really lovely restaurant, one of the most expensive in the Algarve, sitting at a table with the most handsome man in the room. He's in a tailored suit and polished shoes; I'm in a black, halterneck, fitted dress and, against Marina's advice, heels. I've got a very padded plaster on the ball of my foot, so putting my weight on it is really not that bad. José is charming, stylish and intelligent. He's currently telling me about the location of his most recent building project which isn't too far from here, a location that has huge advantages because... uh... well, I'm actually not sure why, because I haven't been entirely listening.

I keep thinking about how strong Leo's arms were when he lifted me earlier.

No hint of struggling or straining with my weight, he scooped me right up.

And I fit so snugly, there against his chest.

Like I was made for him.

'...and that's one of its most appealing prospects,' José is saying proudly, as I automatically nod along, 'that it's easily accessible whilst also being close to shops, bars, restaurants, tourist attractions, family activities. There's a relaxed vibe to the town, too...'

You know what else I like about Leo?

How his whole face lights up when he laughs. He was so guarded around me at first, determined to keep me at arm's length, but over the course of two weeks, I've whittled him down and now I know that when he finds something funny, his expression completely transforms. His eyes gleam, his grin broadens and he gets those gorgeous little crinkles around his mouth. It sounds strange, but I think those moments are the highlights of this trip.

The moments when Leo Silva has forgotten himself with me and properly laughed.

'...of course, identifying potential risk factors has been at the forefront of what I've done here,' José tells me, tapping his finger against the tablecloth to emphasise his point. 'Not just in terms of the surrounding area, but also when it comes to budget...'

It means so much that Leo felt ready to talk to me today.

That took a lot of courage, too, to be open and honest about his past mistakes and what he's learnt from them. It feels like a privilege that he could be that vulnerable with me, when he talked about letting down friends and family. It was moving, how wistful and proud he looked when he explained that surfing helps your soul connect with the ocean. How it can humble you and remind you of what's important.

It was profound. And inspiring.

'...it's been a lot of hard work, but it's worth it because of the passion that goes into these projects. Not just from me either, but from the stakeholders and the locals themselves...'

Leo is so hot too. Have I mentioned that? I don't care. He is.

His eyes are achingly pretty, framed by those full eyelashes, and I love how his thick, dark hair is so unruly, constantly dishevelled like he's always just stepped out of the sea.

His sharp jawline, those broad, strong shoulders...

I mean, he's intimidatingly gorgeous, isn't he.

Just thinking about the way he looks at me intently sometimes – like he's trying to work me out, like he *wants* to work me out – is making my stomach flutter.

'...so in answer to your question, yes, I think it's going to be a great success,' José states with a winning smile, picking up his glass of wine and taking a sip.

I'm jolted from my Leo-themed daydream at the conclusion of José's monologue and realise that, despite that closing statement, I never asked him a question in the first place.

He's somehow convinced himself that I was the one who wanted him to tell me all about his fresh achievement. A humourless laugh bubbles in my throat. I cough it back, reaching for my glass and taking a gulp.

'That's great,' I say, fixing a smile.

'Thank you. It's the tip of the iceberg. There's so much untapped potential in this region – Burgau is a prime example. If I have my way, it will really come to life.'

I'm slightly taken aback by the implication. 'It's already… alive, I think. As in, I don't think much needs to change about it. If anything. It's wonderful there. I've really fallen for it, I think. I'm going to be… sad to leave.'

Devastated, actually. But that sounds too dramatic.

'Ah, but think of what it could be,' he insists, leaning forward on the table enthusiastically. 'It isn't prepared for the influx of tourists that will be coming its way. It needs dreamers like me to ready it. No one there has the right vision.'

I suppress a smirk at his referring to himself as a 'dreamer'. Then I realise that's not fair. Maybe he is. Who am I to declare he's not? And although it's become glaringly obvious to me over the course of tonight that I am currently too infatuated by someone else to have any feelings for José, that's not his fault.

In fact, I really shouldn't be letting my crush on Leo overshadow all of José's qualities. I categorically cannot have sex with the athlete I'm interviewing, no matter how much I want to. That would be a very unprofessional move, especially when I'm vying for an incredible new job at a company owned by his mother. I can, however, have fun with absolutely anyone else.

Literally, anyone else. But him.

And here is someone right in front of me who is just as gorgeous. Maybe not quite so fun, perhaps a little more self-involved… but someone who has made it abundantly clear that he's attracted to me by taking me out to this exquisite restaurant. A lot of thought has been put into this impressive date, and he's an impressive guy. He drove me here in his flashy car and, knowing about my foot, has shown himself to be extremely thoughtful, holding my hand and walking slowly into the restaurant with me so I didn't have to hobble in by myself. There. He's ticking many boxes, especially as a temporary fling in a foreign country.

So.

The smart thing to do is to forget about Leo, and focus on José.

'Let's get the bill and then shall we have a drink at one of the bars in Burgau?' José suggests, signalling to the waiter for the bill.

'*Yes*,' I say, smiling sweetly at him. 'Let's.'

Because I am a smart person and I will do the smart thing.

Okay, I admit defeat. I can't do it. This was not a smart decision at all.

We've been sitting at a table in the outside area of this bar for all of two minutes and I already regret not going straight home after dinner. It's not fair on José – I can't muster up any attraction to him anymore. I'll finish this drink and then I'll make my excuses.

'I'm happy it's such a warm evening and we can sit outside here,' he muses, clasping his hands together. 'I hope to open a bar on this street in the near future.'

'I thought you specialised in residential properties.'

'Currently, yes, but I hope to expand the business in a variety of ways,' he says, puffing out his chest. 'If we can finalise—'

He pauses mid-sentence as a flicker of recognition crosses his expression and I follow his eyeline to see the person passing by who has caused the distraction.

'Leo!' I exclaim, straightening, my heart jumping into my throat.

He's standing frozen to the spot on the street right next to our table. In casual board shorts, flip-flops and a faded-grey t-shirt, he looks unbelievably sexy without any effort – and couldn't look more different to my date.

But just the sight of him is making my stomach twist into knots.

It's the confirmation I really didn't need that I am here with completely the wrong person. *What am I doing with José?* I should have cancelled tonight.

I'm about to do the polite thing and introduce them to each other, but something about the way they're looking at each other makes me think that might be unnecessary. They clearly know each other. And from the glowering expression shrouding Leo's face, I'm not too sure they're on the best of terms.

'Evening, Leo,' José says, adjusting the lapel of his suit jacket and looking him up and down with glaring contempt.

Leo doesn't reply, he just looks to me, his eyes flashing with a mixture of confusion and disbelief. He gestures to José.

'*This* is who you're dating?' he asks me, his tone sharp.

'You know each other?' I say apprehensively, glancing from one stony-faced man to the other.

'In a business capacity,' José remarks, prompting Leo to snort.

'Unbelievable,' Leo mutters, shaking his head at him before narrowing his eyes at me. 'This is the man who owns the company pressurising my dad into selling the surf shop so that he can build a block of flats right there by the waterfront.'

Oh fuck.

I gasp, recoiling from my date. 'José, is that true?'

He shrugs. 'I'm trying to promote tourism in this village. I want to modernise it and secure its future. What's wrong with that?'

'Nothing, except when you're trying to tear down the town, its traditions and charm to do so,' Leo argues.

'Oh, don't be so romantic about it,' José says tiredly, reaching for his drink. 'A surf shop is hardly part of this village's *culture.* You can buy your boards somewhere else.'

As he casually takes a sip of his wine, I stare at him in shock.

Taking a deep breath, Leo must decide he doesn't want to get into it because he doesn't give José another glance. Instead, he hones in on me.

'I hoped you might be better than this,' he mutters, his eyes filled with disappointment. 'Maybe I was wrong.'

Whoa.

It may have been lacking in detail, but his tone and expression tells me that I was on the receiving end of a huge insult.

'Leo, wait,' I begin, as he marches away in the direction of his flat.

He doesn't stop and he doesn't look back. He disappears around the corner and he's walking at such a pace, there's no chance I'll ever catch him up. All I can do is watch him go.

How could I have been this stupid?

Adriano told me about property developers and the

tension rising between them and local businesses like his. When José was rambling on about his projects, why didn't I think to check whether his Burgau ambitions lay anywhere in the vicinity of the surf shop? I would have cut the date short as soon as I found that out, fully aware that I might be jeopardising my relationship with my interviewee and his family.

Why didn't I put two and two together?!

I was daydreaming about Leo. That's why. My stupid little crush has caused me a major professional slip up. But it's not too late to save it.

Pushing my chair back, I stand up.

'I'm sorry, José, I have to go.'

He looks up at me in surprise. 'What?'

'Thank you for such a wonderful evening, but I won't be able to see you again like this,' I say, picking up my bag and looping the delicate strap over my shoulder. 'You know how I mentioned I was out here to interview a surfer? *That* was the surfer.'

'You're writing an article on Leo Silva.' He sits back, unimpressed.

'I hope you understand that I can't do anything to upset him. It's important that we're on good terms otherwise he might not talk to me for the article.'

He slowly exhales the air in his cheeks. 'I… I suppose.'

'Thank you. It was a really lovely evening, thanks so much.'

'I'm sorry it has ended this way.'

I give a polite smile in response, unable to say the same.

'Iris,' he says, making to rise to his feet, 'I should walk you home.'

'No! No, that's fine, thank you, enjoy the rest of your drink. Please,' I say, placing a palm on my chest. 'I'll feel even worse if you don't.'

Paused midway to standing, he settles back in his chair.

'If you insist.'

'I do,' I assure him. 'I really do.'

'Goodnight, then.'

'Goodnight,' I say, walking out onto the street without looking back.

If he notices I'm going the wrong way, he doesn't say anything. I didn't want him to walk me home, because that's not where I'm headed.

By the time I get to Leo's building on my injured foot in heels, having conquered all these stupid cobbled hilly streets, I genuinely wonder whether it might have been quicker to charter a fucking jet and fly there.

'Leo, it's me, let me in,' I instruct grumpily as he answers the buzzer. 'I think my foot might need amputating.'

It's dramatic but it does the job. The door opens and I push through it. That's when I realise God is on my side because the elevator is in full working order today.

'Thank you, thank you,' I breathe, shuffling in and pressing the top floor.

I collapse against the back wall, enjoying a moment of rest. I fully started out on the walk in the mindset that I needed to speak to Leo to apologise to him for making such a misjudged decision and to re-emphasise the commitment I had to the article. But it's taken so long to get here and I'm in such a bad mood because of the pain in my foot that now my mindset has switched and I'm annoyed at him for putting me in this position. The way he spoke to me was out of order.

When the doors ping open, Leo is waiting on the other side of them. His presence takes me by surprise.

'What are you doing?' he growls, folding his arms.

'I needed to speak to you,' I begin, quickly trying to gather my thoughts. 'I wanted to explain why I was with José tonight and—'

'No, I meant what are you doing walking all the way here on your *foot*?' he clarifies crossly, before his eyes fall to my feet and he throws his hands up in exasperation. 'And in *those* shoes, are you serious? Would runners kill you?'

'Yes, actually,' I bristle defensively. 'I wear trainers for exercise, but you know they wouldn't go with this dress and...'

My sentence trails off because a tingling warmth is pooling in my stomach, rising through my chest. He's angrier about me potentially hurting myself than upsetting him.

He really cares about me.

I swallow the lump rising in my throat.

The lift doors start to close, but he holds out his arm to stop them. They rumble open again. The interruption pulls me to my senses.

'Look, I came here to emphasise that I had no idea who José was in relation to you, so, as such, I think you owe me an apology,' I state, flicking my hair back over my shoulder.

His eyes widen in disbelief. 'You think *I* owe *you* an apology.'

'Yes.'

'You were out on a date with the man who's trying to destroy my family's business!'

'I didn't know that! You shouldn't have spoken to me in that way.'

'In what way?'

'That thing you said about how you thought I was better than that. That wasn't fair.'

His jaw clenches. 'Fine. Maybe it wasn't fair, but I was angry. Because of you.'

With a loud ping, the doors start closing again. He stops one of them with his fist, and they both retreat. 'Fucking things,' he mutters.

'Surely it was obvious from my reaction at the bar that I didn't know who he was when you explained how you knew him,' I point out. 'So how come you were so angry at me?'

'I wasn't angry at you.'

'You just said you were angry because of me.'

'Yes, angry *because* of you, not *at* you.'

'That's the same thing.'

'No, it's not! I was angry at the situation.'

'What situation? That I was on a date with José?'

'That you were on a date with anyone!' he cries.

The infuriating ping of the lift doors breaks the silence. He puts his arm out to stop it, this time pressing his palm against the door firmly as it draws back into the side to stop it from even attempting to slide out again.

I stare at him, my heart hammering, blood pounding in my ears. His eyes are fixed on mine, his chest rising up and down with the shallow rasps of his breath.

'You… you were jealous,' I stammer, my brain trying to catch up.

'Yes,' he says in a low, gravelly voice. 'I was jealous.'

My heart swells and, my eyes locked on his, I let out the tiniest sigh of relief. 'Good,' I whisper.

'*Good?*'

Something flashes across his expression: surprise. Confusion, maybe.

Then it gives way to another: hope.

'Yeah, good,' I breathe, butterflies filling my stomach. 'That makes me happy.'

His throat bobs. 'Why would me being jealous make you happy, London?'

'Why do you think, Leo?'

His eyes widen, ablaze with heat and determination.

And the next thing I know, he is abandoning his post at the doors of the lift and striding in towards me. His hand wraps round my neck and he draws my mouth to his.

Nineteen

Leo kisses me so deeply, so urgently, I almost stumble backwards, but his other hand is already there at the small of my back, taking my weight, catching me before I can even think of falling. He presses my hips into his, while his tongue caresses mine, sending electric jolts crackling through my entire body, covering it in goosebumps and dissipating any sensible thoughts that were lingering in my mind.

Oh my fucking God.

I'd forgotten what it was like, to be kissed like this.

Luckily, my body remembers how to respond. As his other hand drops to my hip, knocking my bag out its way, my arms fly to his neck, my fingers threading through his thick, messy hair like they've ached to do for days. I arch my back and melt into him, gasping against his lips as he devours mine. Everything about him is intoxicating: his warm, strong hands holding me in place against him, the woody scent of his cologne, the taste of his soft, full lips and the sensation of his tongue gliding against mine.

I give in. Completely, utterly, absolutely. That's how good this kiss is, sending me weak at the fucking knees, my body consumed by a fierce, feverish ache of wanting more of him. My greediness for him makes me breathless as I kiss him back, moaning into his mouth, causing him to press me into him even harder, one hand roaming down the curve of my hip, the other in its place at the bottom of my spine.

A familiar ping threatens to interrupt us, but neither of us seem to care. I hear the doors slide shut, but I'm not breaking this kiss, not yet. It's too good. I'm consumed by the feeling of his lips, the work of his tongue, the smell of his aftershave. I'm at Leo's mercy and when the lift jolts as it begins to go down, he has me locked in place, secured and safe, enveloped in his strong, muscular arms. I can feel him hard against me and the thought drives me wild. Running my fingers through his hair and down to the nape of his neck, I nip at his lip, that billowing bottom lip I've become mildly obsessed with, and he groans, coming up for air to look at me, his eyes ablaze with need and wonder.

'*Fuck*,' he rasps.

The lift comes to a stop and the doors begin to open up to the ground floor. Before I know what's happening, Leo has stepped round so his back is now against the wall and he spins me to face the lift doors, his hands grabbing my hips and pulling me backwards against him, one hand snaking around my waist and locking me in.

Someone is waiting to get into the lift: a guy in his twenties. He starts when he sees us, his eyes brightening at the sight of Leo. I smile politely.

'Leo,' he says, standing aside to give us room to walk out. '*Tudo bem?*'

'Hi Ernesto, it's okay, we're actually going back up,' Leo replies. 'We… forgot something.'

'Okay.' Ernesto steps in and presses the button for the third floor as well as the fourth, looking at me curiously. '*Olá.*'

'This is Iris,' Leo says, holding me in place in front of him.

'Hi,' I say.

'Hello Iris,' Ernesto grins, standing to one side of the lift and turning his back to us.

He knows what's going on here. We know he knows. My cheeks flush with heat.

We fall into silence.

The doors begin to close and up we go.

The air in here is charged with tension.

It must only take a few seconds for the lift to rise up to Ernesto's floor, but it feels like an agonisingly long time. I'm pressed up against Leo's erection and my need for him grows almost unbearable as I feel him hard against my back, my fingernails digging into the skin of his forearm that's around my waist. He's dropped his other hand to the back of my thigh and his fingers are now trailing lightly up my skin, dragging the hem of my dress with them. He brushes his lips against my hair, pressing a kiss to the back of my head. *God, I can't wait to kiss him again.* Now that I've tasted him, I'm a full-on addict. My breathing shaky, I stare at the lift buttons on the wall lighting up one by one as we make our way up the floors, praying for this thing to go faster.

One.

Two.

Three.

Ping. Ernesto glances over his shoulder to give us a wave before he exits at his floor.

The doors slide back towards each other.

Leo spins me round to face him as soon as they shut.

'Well, that was fucking torture,' he states.

'The worst,' I breathe, before grabbing his head with both hands and pulling his mouth to mine.

I think my enthusiasm takes him by surprise at first, but he's more than happy to throw his back into it, his large, warm hands gripping onto my hips as I crush my lips against his, desire pumping through my veins and making me lose all inhibitions.

When the doors open at his floor, he breaks the kiss and his hand finds mine, threading our fingers and leading me out of the lift as quickly as possible. I clasp his hand tightly, biting my lip as I hazily go wherever he wants to take me, my aching feet miraculously cured by the power of Leo Silva's lips. I have to say, I feel a little bereft to leave that lift; I'm kind of fond of it now. It's where Leo first kissed me, the place where I discovered that my ginormous, inappropriate, burning crush is reciprocated. I feel guilty for being mad at it when it was out of order. It is now my favourite lift in the world.

Do people have favourite elevators? Is that a thing? Fuck it, I don't care. I do.

His door is open and we're inside. He's pulling me into him and his hands are back where they belong: all over my body. My back, my waist, my hips, my arse, roaming everywhere and anywhere – his hands are so large and strong that they make me feel tiny. His mouth descends on mine again and my stomach twists with anticipation as I dissolve into the kiss, dropping my bag from my shoulder and chucking it across the floor, before pressing my hands against his solid, sculpted chest. My fingers fall to the hem of his t-shirt at his hips and I try to yank it up without breaking the kiss, desperate to touch him, to feel his bare skin beneath my fingertips. He chuckles against my lips, getting the hint before pulling away and leading me by the hand towards his bedroom.

'I'm pleased to see you're the kind of guy who makes the bed in the mornings,' I remark, noting the neat, white sheets and general tidiness of his room.

There's no clutter anywhere, just a reading lamp and book on his bedside table and a huge, horizontal, framed photograph of turquoise-blue waves crashing on a golden beach in the warm-orange glow of sunset over his bed.

'Throw cushions?' I say, unable to hide my surprise when I spot them arranged against the pillows. 'I didn't have you down as a throw-cushion man.'

'I'm a lot more sophisticated than you think, London.' He grins, crinkles appearing around the corners of his lips, so gorgeous and sexy they send shivers down my spine.

He reaches for my other hand and tugs me towards him, but he slows things down now, lifting a hand to sweep my hair back over one shoulder, his eyes following his fingertips as they brush down the neckline of my dress, branching away across my collarbone. My breath hitches as he looks at me, a muscle twitching in his jaw.

'You look unbelievable in this dress. Fucking unbelievable. I can't believe you wore this on a date with that dickhead,' he mutters in a low, resentful voice.

'You like it?' I ask coyly.

'It reminds me of the bikini you wore for our surf lesson yesterday. It's similar at the top,' he notes, his fingertips resting on my collarbone.

'The yellow halterneck.' I lift my eyebrows. 'In a good way?'

His eyes darken as he runs his hands down to my hips.

'You have no idea,' he growls, pressing his forehead against mine and sending shivers down my spine. 'It drove me fucking crazy, having to undo the zip of your wetsuit, seeing you in that yellow bikini, unable to untie it and touch you like I wanted to.'

I can barely breathe.

'Show me,' I hear myself say in a quiet, urgent voice. 'Show me how you wanted to touch me.'

Time seems to stop for a moment as I meet his gaze.

'Okay, London,' he murmurs, 'since you ask so nicely.' He bends down and scoops me up in his arms again, just like when he carried me up the beach and up the stairs to my flat earlier. He grins at my gasp of surprise as I'm lifted in the air. 'First, let's get you off that injured foot.'

Walking across the room, he lowers me carefully down onto the bed, shoving the throw cushions aside, before moving to kneel between my knees. Lifting his t-shirt, he pulls it off over his head and drops it down onto the floor beside the bed. He takes a moment to gaze at me, my hair splayed out around his pillows, my teeth digging into my lower lip as I seize the opportunity to drink him in too. My eyes scan his tanned, sculpted chest and abs, a torso I've seen so many times over the last couple of weeks but haven't been allowed to touch. Now, if only fleetingly, he gets to be mine. I ache for him to be close.

'In your own time, Leo,' I mutter impatiently.

'I'm not rushing this,' he says, and something about the seriousness of his tone makes my heart race.

He leans over to kiss me but slowly and deeply, nothing like the urgency of the lift, because I'm in his bed now and we have all night ahead of us. His lips brush against mine so tenderly, he's making me feel shy, which is fairly unusual for me. I'm not used to someone being so careful, so admiring, but that's how it feels like, being kissed by Leo. Like he's been longing for this; like he wants to savour and remember every moment of it. He exhales softly against my mouth, his tongue gliding against mine and sending pulses of heat cascading through my body. I arch my back a little, my breasts pressing into his chest, and his breath catches. There's an intensity to this kiss that covers my skin in goosebumps. It makes me nervous. *He* makes me nervous.

Now I'm shy *and* nervous? I don't know what this man is doing to me.

As his hand moves down my side, his fingers must trip over the small, delicate zip to the dress because he smiles against my mouth triumphantly as he pinches it and carefully pulls it down. He hesitates, lifting his head to look at me with a puzzled expression.

'I'm a big fan of this dress, as you know, but,' he brushes his fingers along the satin halter neckline, 'how does it come off?'

I shake with laughter beneath him. 'There's a couple of clips at the back of the neck.'

'So, I unhook them like a bra?'

'Yes, sort of.'

'Hmm.' His eyes flash at me. 'A new challenge.'

Oh God, he's fucking adorable.

His hand slips under my neck as I lift my head a little to help him and I wait while he works it out. He manages to unclasp it quickly, smirking proudly.

'I'm impressed,' I say, nestling back down into the pillows as the straps come loose and he's able to peel the dress down, exposing my black, lace, strapless bra.

He keeps going, sliding the dress over my hips and down my legs, taking me in as he goes, his process considered and unhurried. With his help, I finally pull my legs free of the dress and his eyes flare with heat as I lie in front of him in just my bra and thong.

My stomach fills with butterflies as I notice him swallow.

Maybe I make him nervous too.

'Fuck, you're beautiful,' he says breathlessly. 'I must be the luckiest guy in the world right now.' As I smile shyly, he turns his attention to my towering heels that I haven't had a moment to take off yet. 'Do you know how long I've wanted to do this? Take these ridiculously sexy shoes off your feet and lie you back in my bed?'

One at a time, he unbuckles the strap around each ankle and slips my shoes off, letting them fall to the floor with a soft thud.

'Since I saw you standing on the beach watching me surf the first evening you arrived,' he says, answering his own question.

'I don't believe you. You couldn't have seen me from all the way out there.'

'I knew exactly who you were. And exactly what I wanted to do to you.'

'But then you met me,' I remind him, my breath shaky, 'and you didn't like me.'

He shoots me a cross look. 'Not true.'

'You didn't trust me.'

'I don't trust anyone at first,' he reasons. 'Especially not journalists.'

'But I'm going to assume, since I'm here, you've warmed to me,' I tease.

'Just because I didn't trust you didn't mean I didn't want you. I did,' he says calmly. 'Ever since you arrived, I haven't been able to stop thinking about you. Imagining you like this, how you would feel, how you would taste. It's been very distracting.'

My chest tightens as he runs his warm hands along my calves and leans down to trail soft kisses along the inside of my thighs, the thin fabric of my thong growing damp.

'You have the sexiest legs I've ever seen in my life,' he murmurs, his lips grazing against my skin, 'and the way they look in those shoes…' He lifts his head to give me a pointed look, expelling the air from his cheeks. 'You've tortured me for a *long* time.'

I giggle. 'It's been two weeks, Leo.'

The warmth of his hands desert my legs as he comes up to hover his lips agonisingly close over mine without touching, his warm breath tickling my skin.

'I don't care. That was fucking long enough,' he says, his eyes darkening.

Inhaling sharply, I grab the back of his neck and claim his mouth with hot urgency, done with his teasing and desperate to feel his weight on top of me again.

'God,' I gasp against his mouth, pushing my hips up and

relishing the friction of the hard bulge in his shorts between my legs, 'I *know*.'

His kisses move lower, his lips working their way down my neck over my throat, across my collarbone and along the swell of my breasts. I lift my back and his hand slides beneath it to unhook my bra and throw it off the bed, a groan emitting from his throat as he cups my breasts before kissing them, while his other hand grips my hip, holding me in place beneath him. As his tongue circles my nipple, I suck in a sharp breath, a wave of arousal flooding me. I've always been self-conscious of my small chest but the way he's admiring my breasts with his mouth, teasing and sucking my nipples like he can't get enough, is making me feel sexy and proud of them for the first time ever.

'You're so fucking beautiful, so amazing,' he murmurs, in case his actions weren't loud enough, his kisses moving down to my stomach. He pauses, lifting his head to look at me. 'You sure you want this?'

Has he lost his fucking mind? I'm practically *panting* at this point.

'You're not very good at reading the room, are you, Leo?'

A smirk plays on his lips. 'I need verbal confirmation, London.'

'You want me to beg,' I huff, shifting beneath him.

'I was going for a simple word of consent, but hey,' he grins, before pressing his mouth against the seam of my thong, my skin tingling beneath his lips, 'if you want to beg—'

'Yes, I want this, Leo,' I say, biting my lip as our eyes meet.

'Guess we'll save the begging for later then.'

'You wish.'

'We'll see.'

As he pulls my thong down over my legs, dropping it on the floor, butterflies flutter around my stomach. He parts my legs and kisses along my thighs, teasing and tormenting me in every way he can, before I finally feel the soft pressure of his mouth on me. My head tips backwards as his tongue swirls over my clit, finding the right spot straight away and sending a wave of pleasure rolling through me. I gasp as heat builds beneath the strokes of his tongue, gripping fistfuls of his sheets in my fingers, my legs beginning to tremble.

'You're so wet for me,' he groans in satisfaction, his tongue circling and swirling over me, his hand pressing firmly against my thigh as it shakes. 'Is this good? Like this?'

'Yes, *yes*,' I utter, trying to remember any of the English language.

He increases the pressure and a moan slips out of me as he winds me higher and higher with this heavenly torment, my hips tilting against his mouth, my body slipping out of my control. With his tongue still sweeping over my clit, he slides his fingers inside me and I think I might lose it completely then and there, my muscles clenching tightly around him, tipping me close to the edge already.

'*Leo*,' I gasp, my nails clawing at his sheets.

'Fuck, I love that,' he mutters as I writhe beneath him, his fingers sliding in and out of me, 'I love you moaning my name like that.'

He increases the pace, his mouth covering me again, licking, teasing, sucking, and the ecstasy is rippling through me, wave after wave of pressure building as he coaxes me closer. I'm barely able to breathe, my brain struggling to comprehend how it can possibly feel this good. With one arm bent over my shoulder, my hand clinging at the pillow for dear life, the other flies to his head, my fingers tangling in his thick, messy hair.

'Oh my God, I want you so badly,' I manage to say between erratic breaths. 'Leo, I need you inside me. Please. *Please*. Oh God.'

'You want me to stop?'

'No, don't stop!'

I hear him chuckle and I know he's smug as hell right now because he got what he wanted – he made me beg. His fingers and mouth keep the same pace, perfectly coordinated, reading my reactions. My muscles squeeze around him, pleasure coiling up the core of my body, turning me into a pleading wreck.

'Oh fuck, Leo,' I whimper, and he groans again at me saying his name like that and I know I'm going to scream it when release closes in because it's the least I can fucking do.

The sensation builds and builds until I can't hold out any longer, intense pleasure rolling through and consuming every inch of me as I tighten around him and spasm, his name echoing off the walls of his bedroom as I cry it out. I come hard, my body shuddering and arching beneath him. *Fuck. Ing. Hell.*

My orgasm gradually subsides, my chest heaving up and down as I try to catch my breath.

'Oh my God,' I breathe as Leo presses his lips against my thigh. I think he may be as obsessed with my legs as I am with his lips. 'That was... oh my *God*. Please come here.'

He chuckles softly, finally giving in to my begging and moving up to lie next to me so I can turn to look at him, mesmerised by his strikingly dark eyes, the slope of his nose, his gorgeous lips, the strong jawline – all of him. He's the most beautiful man I know.

You would have the power to devastate me if I stayed here longer, I think.

'You're unbelievable,' I murmur as he kisses along my cheekbone to my lips. 'And you're a psychic. Didn't you hear me begging?'

'I think I must have been a little distracted,' he says playfully. 'What was it you said? Something along the lines of you wanting something...'

'You're going to make me say it again.'

'As much as I possibly can. What was it you wanted?'

Placing my hand against his chest, I slide it down slowly, my fingers tracing along the ridges and dents of his abs before it hits the waistband of his shorts and strokes over his erection straining against the material.

'You, Leo,' I say softly, as he exhales a ragged breath. 'I want you inside me.'

Twenty

'How are these still on?' I ask impatiently, as he sits up to take off his shorts and boxers at my instruction.

He grins, sliding them over his legs. 'There were more important things going on.'

I inhale sharply at the sight of his huge cock as it springs free. *Christ*. The thought of him inside me, filling me, is making me wet again. I wrap my hand around it and feel it warm and throbbing in my grasp, using my free hand to push him back down on the pillows.

'That was clearly an oversight on my part,' I mutter, heat pooling in my stomach as I give his length a slow, firm stroke and enjoy his reaction, his eyes fluttering shut as his head falls back on the pillow, his lips parting with a tortured groan. 'I'll have to make it up to you.'

His shallow breathing and the low, guttural sounds escaping his throat as his hips thrust into my hand makes the aching throb between my legs intensify.

'*Fuck*,' he grunts, his hand reaching out to grip my wrist, stopping me, 'you can't keep going; I don't want to come yet.'

I move to straddle him and he sits up, grabbing my waist as he kisses me urgently, his whole body tensing when I grind my hips against his thick, pulsing length. I've never wanted anyone so badly. I'm impatient and desperate for this man. I need to feel him inside me.

'Condom?' I prompt, my hands resting at the nape of his neck.

He pulls back from me a little to reach across to the drawer of his bedside table. I remain where I am, keeping him secure between my legs, refusing to budge from my perch where I have front-row seats to his arm and torso muscles flexing as he twists to open the drawer, looking for the box inside. As he finds a foil package and break it free of its strip, I study the shape of his eyebrows, how he's frowning slightly in concentration, the tiny creases around his mouth.

I realise something I should have said much earlier than now.

'You're beautiful, you know,' I say quietly, my hands drifting across his broad shoulders as he turns back to face me, holding the package. 'Like, impossibly beautiful.'

He doesn't say anything, leaning back on his hands and allowing me to trace a finger across his cheekbone, raking my fingers along the side of his head through his hair.

He exhales, his eyes fixed on me.

'How could you have been jealous tonight?' I mutter, amused by the idea as I slide my hands to rest on his shoulders. 'It's mad. You must have known.'

'Known what?'

'What I was thinking.'

'When?'

'When you brought me back to my flat after the surf lesson.'

His eyes light up with playfulness. 'I had no idea. I was too busy trying not to think what *I* was thinking.'

'Why, what were *you* thinking?'

'I asked first.'

'I don't care.'

He grins. 'You're so fucking stubborn. Do you *always* get what you want?'

'Yes. What were you thinking, Leo?'

'Fine. I was thinking along the same lines as what I've been thinking for days, like I've already told you.' Leaning his weight on the hand still grasping the condom, he slides his other hand up the curve of my hip as his voice drops low and serious. 'That I wanted to carry you inside to your bed and fuck you so hard, you wouldn't have the chance to even *think* about whoever you were meant to be going out with tonight.'

I bite my lip, nails digging into his skin. 'If only we'd have been better at communicating, because *I* was thinking…' I pause to smile mischievously at him '…I should cancel on José and invite you inside.'

'Hm.' His shoulders lift as he takes a deep breath. 'I'm glad you didn't.'

'What?' I ask, laughing in surprise.

'If you had, we might have carried on being…' his dark eyes rake lustfully down to my chest and back up again, leaving a burning trail on my skin, a thrill of anticipation fluttering round my stomach '…sensible.'

'You think the date was needed to fire us up.'

'Maybe. We might not have ended up like this.'

'And that would have been a crime.'

His fingers stroke up and down my skin. 'A tragedy.'

'So maybe I should go on another date with someone else tomorrow.'

His jaw tenses, eyes narrowing. 'Don't you dare,' he growls slowly.

My stomach dips at this streak of possessiveness. I never thought I was a fan of jealousy. It's been years since I was with anyone long enough for there to be any talk of exclusivity – but it's so unbelievably hot the way he's talking like this so fiercely and surely, as though he wants me to himself forever more. Which is obviously absurd because I'm getting on a plane in two days. But for tonight, we can pretend this is more than it is. For a few hours, I get to imagine that he's all mine too.

'I'll do whatever I want, Leo,' I tease, my fingers dragging down to his chest. His body is so firm, I'm going to be dreaming about it from now onwards. Fantasising. Longing. Remembering.

He quirks a brow. 'I'd better make sure that it's only me you want, then.'

I press a soft kiss to his mouth. 'I'll tell you a secret,' I murmur as he nips at my lips, hungry for more, 'you've already succeeded in that.'

A groan of frustration reverberates against my mouth as we kiss, his tongue a driving force behind the pulse increasing between my legs. He breaks away for a second to unwrap the condom, rolling it on while my hands balance on his chest to push myself up. Leaning back on one hand, he holds my hip with his other and I slowly slide down onto him.

'Oh fuck,' he breathes, his eyes widening as I push myself up again to sink down further, taking him in. 'You feel so fucking good, so tight.'

I don't know how he's managing to form words, because I can barely think, let alone speak as he fills me, my breath hitching at how incredible it feels. He's so impressive, I need to force myself to concentrate on relaxing to be able to take all of him. My hands pressing against the firm, smooth skin of his chest, I push him back down onto the pillows as he guides me into a rhythm on top of him, before reaching to palm my breasts, his heavy eyelids, grunts and moans sending me into overdrive. Seeing him like this, knowing I'm the one to give him this pleasure turns me on so much, making me wetter than ever. When one of his hands sinks between my legs, his thumb finds my clit, sending a jolt of electricity pulsating through my body.

'*Leo*,' I gasp, tipping my head back as I grind and swirl against him.

'If you say my name like that again, I'm not going to last; you feel too good,' he warns through gritted teeth, his eyes glazed as he looks up at me.

Heat ripples through me as I lose myself in the sensation of his thick length inside me, filling me every time I slide down to the hilt, hitting a spot I didn't know existed. I slow things down a little, savouring the delicious torture of the building ache, thrills fluttering round my stomach at the way groans fall from his lips whenever I push down onto him. When I speed up the pace, spurred on by his swirling thumb and guiding hand on my hip, a loud moan slips out of me, a sound that causes his eyes to flare as he thrusts harder and somehow deeper into me.

'Leo,' I cry, the intense, aching pressure building too fast for me to stop. 'I'm coming.'

'Fuck, you look so fucking amazing. Come for me, Iris,' he rasps and it's all I need.

Everything tightens and shakes, muscles clench and squeeze, heat surging through me as I tip over the edge, frenzied pleasure rippling through every inch of my body. I groan loudly, and as I collapse on top of him, limbs still trembling with the indescribable sensation he's given me, he captures my breath in my mouth, his hand holding the back of my head.

In a swift motion, he rolls me onto my back and I hold onto the rippling muscles of his back, comforted by him still inside me, his weight bearing on top of me, wrapping my legs around his hips so he can never leave.

'Too good,' he says, his voice strained as he buries his face in my neck, pushing into me, his hand gripping my thigh. He's digging into my skin so hard, he'll leave bruises and the thought sends a shiver down my spine. 'Holy shit. You feel too fucking good, baby.'

I don't know if he even realises he's called me that, but it drives me wild. As he draws out and thrusts into me again, I clench around him, my heart pounding, before he cries out, 'Oh *fuck*,' and I feel the pulsating swell of his cock as he releases into me. His body is shaking still and I cling to him, wondering how I'm going to find the will to let him go.

As he falls on top of me, his breath fast and hot against my neck, I kiss his warm cheek, tasting the salty sweat of his skin. My fingers trail up and down his back and he gives a satisfying shudder.

When he rolls over to lie next to me, he keeps an arm around my waist as though he's afraid I might leave. I turn my head to look at him, both of us still catching our breath.

'That was incredible,' he says, his eyes warm and heavy.

That was the best sex I've ever had in my life, I want to say.

'You're amazing,' I say instead, smiling at him.

He reaches up to sweep his thumb along my cheekbone. I watch as he parts his lips as though to say something, but then he seems to think better of it, closing them again and smiling back at me. I feel flushed with happiness and exhaustion, my eyes fluttering shut as I emit a sigh into the pillow, breathing in the intoxicating scent of him lingering on the material.

'This smells like you,' I hear myself say drowsily as I nestle into it further.

The sex has made me delirious, and heat flushes through my cheeks as I realise how weird that sounded, my eyes flashing open to check he's still there and he hasn't run for the hills. Instead, I find him watching me, his eyes full of something I can't put my finger on – contentment I think, or maybe just tiredness – as he laughs lightly.

'Is that a good thing?' he checks.

'Mm.' I close my eyes and relax again, relieved that he seems more concerned about what I'm thinking than the way-too-full-on stupidity of what I'm saying. 'Very good.'

I don't know how much time passes but I'm drifting off when I feel his lips press gently on my forehead before the mattress moves. I manage to lift my heavy eyelids to peer at him as he makes his way to his ensuite bathroom, the bed feeling too big and empty without him next to me. When he returns to slip back under the covers, I reach for him.

'You're back,' I whisper happily, curling into him, hooking my leg over his and resting my head on his chest.

I hear him chuckle softly, before I finally drift off to the sound of his heartbeat.

The next morning, I feel the lightest of kisses brush against the top of my shoulder before I hear Leo quietly getting out of bed. My eyes are closed, my head drowsy, but I'm awake. He just doesn't know that. As I hear him pull on his boxers and creep out the room, I smile into the pillow, a sigh of contentment escaping me before I can think too hard about it. I can't get over how well I slept. Cradled in his arms, I was dead to the world.

I could stay in his warm, comfortable bed forever, but after a while, I hear the whir of his coffee machine and accept that it's time to make a move. He'll be needing to leave soon to surf. I throw the cover off me, swinging my legs out of bed and searching for my underwear somewhere on the floor. When I locate my thong, I pull it back on and slip the t-shirt he was wearing yesterday over my head. It smells like his cologne and I lift up the neck of it to fill my nostrils with his scent, grinning like an idiot and biting my lip, heat pulsing between my legs. God, just the smell of him and I'm wet again.

A clattering sound from the kitchen kicks my arse into gear and I slip into his ensuite bathroom to check my appearance before he gets back.

'Whoa, sex hair much?' I say to my reflection, raising my eyebrows.

After doing what I can with my fingers to tame it, I squeeze some of his toothpaste onto my finger and suck it, looking round for something I can use to take my make-up off from yesterday. I can't believe I fell asleep in it; it is so unlike me. My skin will punish me for it later, no doubt. There's nothing left out on the sides – just shower gel and shampoo in his shower – so I open the cabinet below the sink and discover a tidy range of products including a spare toothbrush still in its packaging and a nice-looking cleanser. That will do.

Nabbing both, I study the label of the cleanser while I brush my teeth properly, impressed at the brand. This is expensive stuff. There's something sexy about a guy being on board with skincare. Or maybe Leo is just sexy full stop and everything about him delights me right now. *Shit*. I have to get a grip. I wash my face and dab it dry with a spare towel, carefully folding it and hanging it on the heated rail.

Then leaning my hands on his sink, I stare at myself in the mirror.

As I take a deep breath, the realities of what happened begin to seep in.

I need to give myself a pep talk.

Last night was amazing. Better than amazing. Incredible. Fuck it, it was life-changing sex. The kind of sex that makes me question what the hell I've been doing up until now. But – it can't happen again. It *can't*. For so many reasons.

Firstly, if anyone at *Studio* found out – if *Toni* finds out about this – I'll never write for the magazine again. An editor can't trust a journalist who screws her interviewees, can she? And worse than that, what if Michelle Martin knew about this? She picked me to talk to her son so I could write a moving and meaningful article for her biggest and most successful magazine. And what did I do? I fucked him. I'm pretty sure that's not going to go down well. This could really affect my career, a career I've worked my arse off to forge, and I'm only just getting to where I want to be.

'What have you done, Iris?' I whisper to myself, grimacing.

Secondly, my flight home is booked for tomorrow. I only have today left to cobble together everything I need to write this big feature; I have to write up everything he said yesterday and I need to start structuring the piece so I have an idea of what else I might need to ask or see before I have to say goodbye to Leo for good.

My stomach lurches at the thought.

No. *No.* I don't have real feelings for him, I can't. This is just sex.

And it's not too late to save the situation. Sort of. All I have to do is focus on what's at stake here and resist temptation. Resist *him.* I've only got one day left here, so that shouldn't be too hard. I can control my urges and cut it off now when it's not as complicated as it could get. Besides, he's probably giving himself the same pep talk in the kitchen. We're likely both on the same page and will be professionals from here on out.

I watch my shoulders relax in the mirror. Yes. I've got this.

Twenty-one

By the time I emerge from the bathroom, he's setting a mug of coffee down on my side of the bed. He straightens and spots me, his brown eyes brightening, a smile spreading across his devastatingly handsome face. *Christ*. Look at him. He's still in his boxers, his remarkable, muscled torso on full display. He's so perfect, it almost makes me want to cry. I can't believe I've had sex with this man. I can't believe I've been so lucky.

'Hey,' he says.

It's warm and familiar the way he speaks, just one word and an ache tugs at my chest to be near to him, to tangle my fingers through that unruly hair of his and hold on tight.

'Hey,' I respond, my heart thrumming.

Professional, Iris, my sensible brain reminds me. *Be professional.*

I clear my throat, tucking my hair behind my ear. I've just remembered I'm not wearing any make-up anymore and I drop my eyes to the floor, blushing at my fresh-faced appearance. He's used to seeing me with all my armour on.

'I used your cleanser and a toothbrush; I hope that's okay.'

'Of course. Use whatever you like. I thought you might want some coffee,' he says, gesturing to the mug.

Thoughtful as well as pretty. This isn't fair.

Nodding, I press my lips together. 'Thanks. Do you have to leave to surf?'

'I've got about ten minutes before I need to go.'

'I should be coming with you, but I'd need to go change and get my stuff,' I say regretfully. *See what happens when you act irresponsibly, Iris? You're left facing a walk of shame and missing out on important research for the feature.* 'Are you surfing Burgau?'

He shakes his head. 'I'm going to head to Zavial; there's better swell there today.'

'By the time I sort myself out and get there, I'd probably have missed a lot. I can use this morning to write instead, I guess.' I hesitate, before asking hopefully, 'Will you be surfing later today?'

He grins, a mischievous glint in his eye. 'I did have a lesson booked with a student of mine, but she's suffered a minor foot injury so I guess she and I will have to fill that time with something else.'

I swallow. Okay, maybe he wasn't giving himself the same pep talk as me in the kitchen. My heart rate quickens at the idea of a repeat of last night.

'I meant, would you be training again later this afternoon or evening,' I explain, my voice coming out a tad higher pitched than usual.

He seems unfazed by my awkwardness. 'Probably not. I need to go to the gym some point this afternoon.'

'Tomorrow morning?'

'Should be.' He nods.

'Right. Good. I can come to that session before my flight. I should have time.'

We fall into silence. I'm not usually shy, but I feel self-conscious about the way he's looking at me, his eyes roaming over me hovering in the doorway. Suddenly, the woman in the bathroom telling me to resist him feels like a stranger, a nag who's out to ruin my life.

I desperately try to find my resolve.

'So,' I begin in as firm a voice I can muster, 'we should talk about what happened.'

'Okay.'

'I don't want you to feel uncomfortable, so how do you want to play this?'

He quirks a brow. 'Play what, London?'

'Well, in case you didn't notice, we kind of crossed a line last night.'

'I remember,' he says with a cocky smile.

I respond with a stern look. 'I shouldn't have let it happen. I… should apologise.'

'But we both know *that's* not going to happen. And besides, I wouldn't want you to.' He folds his arms, his eyes fixed on me. 'I don't think either of us should apologise for what we did last night. Something that good should not be apologised for; it should be repeated.'

Fuck.

As I inhale sharply, he gives me a sultry look.

It's so hard to think straight and take charge of a situation when he's standing topless in front of me, reminding me of what we did and said, how he made me feel, how his lips made my skin tingle, how he felt inside me...

Clasping my hands behind my back, I lean against the doorframe. 'Leo, it obviously shouldn't have happened considering our relationship. Our professional relationship. So, how does it go from here?'

'How do you want it to go?' he asks, tilting his head.

'We should keep it professional. I mean, we should get it *back* to being professional,' I say, my voice wavering as the word *professional* loses all meaning in my head with its repetition. 'We should pretend like nothing happened and focus on the article. I think... in the clear light of day, it's, you know, obvious that we should stop this from going any further than it already has, which is already... far. Too far.'

'Lots of "should"s being thrown about here, London. Okay, you've outlined what we *should* do. But that's not an answer to my question. What do you *want* to do?'

My lips part and I wet them instinctively. He reads my reaction and smirks.

'You know, I'm not sure this is the right time for this conversation,' he continues in a playful tone, as though it's been amusing for him to pretend I'm the one in control of the situation.

'Oh? Why not?' I ask haughtily.

He gestures to me. 'You're wearing my t-shirt.'

I glance down at it. My nipples are hard, pressing against the fabric and giving me away. When I look back up at him, I find his expression has darkened, sending a shudder of hot anticipation through me, tingles engulfing every inch of me.

'Very observant of you, Leo,' I say breezily, still trying to keep a grip on things despite my body's betrayal. 'Why does that matter?'

'Because,' he says, his gaze sharpening, 'you look so fucking sexy, I couldn't give a shit about what we should or shouldn't do. I can only think about what I want to do.'

His candour makes me blush and I lower my eyes to smile, while he closes the space between us, moving across the room to me. He slides one hand around my waist, drawing me into him, while the other tips my chin upwards, his thumb brushing over my bottom lip. Flutters erupt uncontrollably in my stomach, my heart pounding so hard, it's drumming in my ears. How is it possible that he can make me feel this way? Like nothing else matters but us in this moment, his dark eyes so entrancing, they make the rest of the world disappear.

'So now we've clarified what *I* want to do, I'll ask again: what do *you want* to do?' he murmurs, his nose nudging mine, his mouth teasingly close. 'You know, in the clear light of day as you say.'

'I...'

'Mm?'

Any hint of resolve left evaporates.

I reach up to kiss him, wrapping my arms around his neck, and melting into him, my body relieved to be attached to his again. The kiss is gentle at first, both of us taking it slow, before my fingers rake through his hair and give it a gentle tug. He groans into my mouth and I smile against his lips. The kiss deepens, my stomach twisting with anticipation.

When I nip at his soft, billowing bottom lip, he responds by pinning me against the doorframe hungrily. My eyelids flutter open for a moment to meet his gaze, his eyes wild and fierce and greedy. His mouth crashes against mine and I love that it feels like he can't control himself anymore, his tongue rough and demanding. My lips are going to be swollen and bruised, but I don't care; I want more from him, everything he can give me, I want it. I can feel his hard erection pressing against my hips and it sends a rippling wave of arousal pulsing through me. His hands travel over my hips down to my thighs before they slip to the back of them and he hoists me up, my legs wrapping around him and squeezing his hips. He moves across the room to the bed, lowering me gently onto my back, and I ache for him to be inside me again when he lowers himself on top of me.

'Oh God,' I say, my breathing ragged as he buries his face in my neck, his hand slipping under my t-shirt, pulling up the material to find and squeeze my breast. I gasp, tipping my head back. 'This isn't how this conversation was meant to go.'

'Really?' he says, his voice vibrating against my skin, heat building between my legs as he toys with my nipple. 'Tell me how it was meant to go.'

'I meant to tell you that we can't do this again. I meant to…' I pause to swallow, finding it hard to concentrate on words when his hand is now roaming down to the waistband of my dampened thong. 'I *meant* to stop this.'

He pauses instantly, lifting his lips from my neck and rolling to one side of me, propping his head up on his elbow. I feel cold and lost without his body pressed to mine and instinctively want to drag his weight back on top of me.

'If you want to stop this, then we stop this,' he says, his voice steady and calm. 'You say the word.'

Closing my eyes, I inhale deeply. 'I don't want to stop this.'

When my eyes flutter open, I find him watching me intently. I lift my hand to cup his face and he rests his cheek against my palm, his expression relaxing.

'You sure?'

'Yes, I want *you*,' I insist.

I only realise the intensity of my statement once I've said it. It's the tone and how I'm holding his face at the same time rather than the actual words, but the whole thing sounded weighted, more meaningful than I meant it to. I was caught up in the moment, floating in the hallucinatory state caused by gazing into his eyes that second too long, and it sounded as if I'm after more than he can give me. More than either of us can give each other.

This should never have happened in the first place. We live in different countries.

It can only ever be temporary.

I quickly drop my hand to my stomach, tearing my eyes from his.

'You know what I think?' he says suddenly.

'What?' I ask, my voice clipped and distant as I wallow in the shame of forgetting myself for a moment there. I'm usually so good at keeping my shit together.

He exhales. 'I think you need to change your flight.'

I blink at him. '*What?*'

'Your flight home, the one that's booked for tomorrow,' he clarifies, the corners of his mouth lifting into an easy smile, 'I think you need to call up your editor and change it.'

A nervous laugh escapes from my throat. 'And why would I do that?'

'Because you need more time to get whatever it is out of me that you need…' he lowers his head to kiss me gently on the lips, my heart thrumming '…and I think you need more time to do some thorough research.' His hand slides over my stomach, his fingers drifting along the top edge of my thong, toying with the lace. 'And… I don't want you to go.'

I feel dazed as he leaves a trail of soft kisses along my jaw.

'Thoughts?' he prompts, his breath warm in my ear and sending shivers rolling down my spine. 'Don't leave me hanging here.'

I swallow. 'Obviously, I'd like to stay here a bit longer. For many reasons.'

'Course, many reasons,' he murmurs. 'If that's what you want, then change the flight.'

'I… I don't know.'

'You don't know,' he repeats, his fingers sliding beneath my thong.

Oh my God. My breath becomes erratic as his thumb drags over my clit, his lips finding my earlobe and giving it a gentle tug with his teeth.

'I guess… I guess I can ask if I can change it,' I croak as he lifts his head to gaze down at me.

'Ask?' he says lightly, his thumb stroking me, the pressure beginning to build between my legs already. 'That's not like you, London.'

'Tell, I'll tell them,' I say desperately, reaching for him and dragging his mouth to mine so I can kiss him hungrily as his fingers slide into me, causing me to gasp at his lips, my muscles clenching round him.

He's breathing as hard as I am and when he pulls back to

look at me, the heat in his eyes flares, as though watching me like this is enough for him.

'Fuck, you're so wet; say that's for me,' he says hungrily.

'It's for you,' I rasp before I emit a quiet moan as his thumb presses on my clit, tightness and pressure building between my legs.

How is he so good at this? How is anyone so good at this? How the fuck am I supposed to write an article about him and not mention this insane talent? Fuck the surfing; this is surely what people will want to know about: that Leo Silva might just be the sexiest man on the planet and has the ability to give mind-blowing orgasms in a matter of seconds.

You can't be real.

'What's that?' he asks.

As the pleasure intensifies and my brain turns to mush, I realise that my thoughts have accidentally slipped out my mouth.

'I'm *what*?' he persists, gazing down at me intently, his thumb and fingers driving me to oblivion. Oh God, how the fuck does he expect me to think straight?

'You can't be real,' I manage to repeat breathlessly.

A muscle in his jaw twitches before he utters, 'Funny, all this time I've been thinking the same about you,' and dips his head to kiss my neck, his thumb increasing the pressure and ache of my clit, winding me higher and higher until I can't hold back any longer.

The pleasure boils over and floods mercilessly through me, and his mouth is there to capture the loud moan he coaxes from my lips, my body arching and trembling, my hips grinding up against his hand.

Trailing a couple of soft kisses along my cheek, he watches me as I catch my breath.

'Oh my God,' I say, my body limp, my head spinning.

I reach for the hard erection in his boxers that I can feel pressed against my hip, but he stops me, breathing out and shaking his head.

'I have to go,' he says, his voice strained with regret.

'What? You're kidding. Where?'

He laughs, dipping his head to kiss me before he forces himself up from the bed. 'Surfing, remember? You know, that big contest in Australia coming up that I have to train for. Kind of important.'

I press my palm against my forehead. 'Oh, shit. I forgot.'

'I'll take that as a compliment.'

'You fucking should.'

He chuckles again, heading to his wardrobe to grab some fresh clothes. 'You can stay here as long as you like. In fact, feel free to stay here all day. All week. All month, whatever.'

Closing my eyes for a moment, I smile to myself, warm flutters expanding in my stomach. 'Playing it cool, I see.'

'I'm a surfer. I'm nothing if not cool.'

'Uh-huh. We'll let the readers decide on that one.' I prop myself up on my elbows to watch him as he heads to the bathroom. 'You got a hoodie or something I can borrow so it doesn't look quite so obvious what's happened here when I shamefully skuttle back to my place?'

'Take whatever you want,' he says, heading into the ensuite to turn on the shower before he re-appears in the doorway. 'You look good in my clothes.'

'Thank you.'

'Don't walk home in those heels; you really should be looking after your foot.'

I give him a pointed look. 'You weren't complaining about the heels last night.'

He grins mischievously at me. 'No, I wasn't. But I'd rather you gave yourself every chance of getting home in one piece since I can't be there to make sure of it. I have some of Marina's old flip-flops. She left them here once when a few people came back for a party – she won't mind you borrowing them.'

'Okay, thanks,' I nod. 'Once you've left, I'll shower then get going.'

He groans, running a hand down his face.

'What?' I ask, alarmed at his reaction.

'It was already going to be hard enough to focus on surfing well this morning,' he says, dropping his hand to gesture at me. 'And now I'll have the image of you naked in my shower in my head. How am I meant to think about anything else?'

I smirk, deeply satisfied. 'You told me, Mr Silva, that when you are out surfing those waves, you're firmly in the present. The rest of the world disappears, right? Nothing else matters but you and the ocean. That's what you said.'

'Yeah, I know that's what I said,' he says glumly, turning round and disappearing into the bathroom. 'But that was before last night.'

Twenty-two

It takes two minutes after I've pressed send on my email to Toni for her to call me. I smile to myself victoriously when I see her number flash up on my screen – I knew it would be unlikely for me to be put through to her if I phoned the *Studio* office, but that as soon as she read my email, she'd want to speak to me directly.

'Iris,' she says when I answer, her voice full of concern, 'what's this about you needing another week over there? Is Leo Silva still not playing ball? You need me to get involved? Tell me if you're really stuck and I'll speak to Michelle's team.'

Sitting on my balcony, I clasp the warm takeaway cup of coffee I got on the way home from Leo's, trying not to giggle. *If only she knew…*

I know it's bad, but the secrecy of what's going on with Leo is actually wildly exciting. I think back on this morning when he pinned me up against the doorframe to kiss me and a thrilling shiver rolls down my spine.

'No, he's definitely… coming around,' I say vaguely, biting back a smile.

'Fantastic. I knew you'd be able to reel him in.'

Oh, I've reeled him in all right.

'Nicely done, Iris,' she adds, impressed. 'I told Sam if anyone could break through a wall of resistance, it would be you.'

'Thank you – but I do need more time out here. There's a lot we haven't covered,' I say calmly, taking a sip of coffee.

'I suppose it took more time than expected to get him where you want him.'

Her comment causes me to inhale sharply and almost choke on my drink, coughing and spluttering, the coffee splashing and spilling out, pooling in its lid.

'Iris, you all right?' Toni checks.

'Fine,' I utter through wheezes. 'Coffee went down the wrong way.'

'Look, I get that this guy has made you work for the interviews, but you've already had two weeks,' she reminds me. 'We're on a strict deadline with this one. Not much I can do about that with Michelle Martin breathing down my neck. It needs to publish early summer; a surf article any other time of year doesn't make sense.'

'I know, I know.' I press my lips together, thinking about how Leo reminded me that I'm not one to ask for something I want. I take it. 'But Michelle wants this feature to be the best it can be, right? It's important to her. So I'm sure she'd understand that I need a bit more time to make sure of that. It has to be perfect.'

I hear Toni exhale at the other end of the phone.

'And I've saved *Studio* a lot of money by staying in

accommodation arranged by my friend,' I add in an attempt to argue my case. 'So hopefully, a change of flight won't be too extravagant when you take that into consideration.'

'Mm.'

Putting my coffee down on the table, I stand up to wander to the edge of the balcony, leaning on the rail and looking out at the ocean. I wish I could see him surfing out there on the water. The waves somehow look empty without him.

It was nice to take my time leaving his flat this morning. I had a long, hot shower after he left, selected a hoodie from his collection and pulled it on over my dress. When I had found Marina's flip-flops he'd mentioned, I'd strolled leisurely back to the flat carrying my heels in a shopping bag I stole from the cupboard under his sink, just in case I bumped into anyone I knew. Carrying heels from the night before would have been a bit of a giveaway.

As I stopped to buy a coffee from the little café I've been dropping into almost daily now, I lost myself in a daydream about my night with Leo, unable to stop smiling. They had to call out to me twice to tell me the coffee was ready and I blushed when they finally caught my attention, as though they might have been able to read my dirty little mind.

Leo was absolutely right – I need to cancel my flight. No matter how inappropriate the situation, I have to admit to myself that last night (and this morning) was so fun, I'm not ready to leave quite yet. I like it here.

'Honestly Toni, to prove my conviction, I'll say that I'm happy to foot the bill myself about this flight if you really can't make it work. I know that to get this story right, I need more time out here. It's a good story, trust me, but it's a complex one. And I want to get this right for you and Michelle, I really do.'

She takes a moment to consider my argument. 'All right. I suppose we can give you one more week on this. I'll speak to Sam about changing the dates of the flight and she'll email you the confirmation.'

'Thank you, I appreciate it.'

'Sounds like hard work. Have you got anything to show me?'

I hesitate. Since deleting the disastrously dry writing I sent her before, currently all I've got is a blank page. 'You'll have some draft paragraphs by the end of today.'

'Good. I'll make a note to read those tomorrow morning before I take my daughter to her football practice,' she says, and I can hear her typing, adding it to her calendar.

Which reminds me of Leo's teasing about my insistence on scheduling everything. I smile into the phone, thinking of him doing so, how cute he looks when he gets that bemused expression on his face because I'm doing something that is ridiculous to him. That smile of his is so sexy, even when he's making fun of me.

'It will be a nice start to my Saturday morning,' she continues. 'I can sit looking out at the pissing rain while reading about beaches, rolling waves and a surfer who won't quit.'

'You won't be disappointed. Hey, would you rather I sent them Sunday evening so you can have a stress-free weekend and read them on Monday instead?'

'Oh God, Iris, how many things were wrong with that sentence? No, I would rather have your pages as soon as possible. Additionally, I do have the capability of leaving a document unread in my inbox should I decide to read them the next day instead. And a stress-free weekend? *Please*. I'm a working mother. Get a grip.'

I laugh lightly. 'I realised it sounded stupid as soon as I said it.'

'At least you realised.'

'You know, Toni,' I say, peering down at a couple strolling towards the sea and putting their feet in the water, letting the waves lap over them, 'you should come to Burgau.'

'Why would I do that?'

'It's beautiful here and very tranquil, especially in the down season.'

'If I want tranquil, Iris, I'll put on my headphones and listen to a podcast.'

I grin. I hope Toni never changes. 'The views are really something. Everyone is friendly, the beach is great, the food is delicious. And they have good coffee.'

She snorts. 'So does London. In fact, we have all of those things you listed right here.'

'You might scrape by with the people and food, but a great beach?' I point out, raising my eyebrows.

'What the fuck do you call South Bank?'

I burst out laughing. 'I'm serious, Toni; if you ever need to get away, you should consider The Algarve.' I gaze out at the ocean and mutter, 'There's something about this place: the community, the pace – it makes you feel... like you're part of something.'

'That's nice. Put that in the piece,' she instructs bluntly, her brisk tone snapping me out of my daze. 'Right, got to go. Sam will be in touch about the flight change.'

'Thanks, Toni.'

'Get those paragraphs to me ASAP; I can already tell you're a sucker for that beach so you'll write it nice and atmospheric, and make me cheer for this guy, yes?'

'You've got it.'

'Bye, Iris. Good luck.'

She hangs up. I take another moment to soak in the view, musing how it makes me feel so still, despite not being still at all. The waves are rolling in one after another, sailboats drift by in the distance, birds are dancing across the top of the water, and the beach is playing host to a walker and their dog, a stunning collie-type. The dog is barking at his owner to throw his ball before he launches himself after it, sweeping it up from the sand before it rolls into the water.

Filling my lungs with a deep breath of air, I turn back to face the apartment and say out loud, 'Right, let's do this,' before I march inside to fetch my laptop. Bringing it out to the table on the balcony, I sit down and open up all the notes I've made for the piece, reading them through, and starting to plot out a structure. That takes a long time, but once I've got a vague idea of how it's going to go, I open a fresh new Word document. Time to make a start.

An email comes up on my phone that I've left out on the table – it's from Sam, confirming my flight date and time change. Smiling smugly, I put my phone back down and do my best to shut down any thoughts of last night and this morning so I can fully concentrate on my work.

'Okay, starting line,' I say out loud to myself, tapping my fingernails below my keyboard. 'I just need that first sentence and I'm good to go.'

The opening line to a feature has to be perfect. It has to grab the attention of the reader and set out the scope of the article. It always takes me a while to land on, and following that, the first paragraph is the one I find the hardest, but once I've got those down on the page, the rest of the feature tends to flow.

I stare at the blank page on the screen.

Nothing comes to me straight away and the pressure riding on this piece begins to feel heavy on my shoulders. I have a lot of people to please here: Michelle Martin, Toni, Leo, the Burgau locals, the World Surf League and the entire surfing community. And myself. I want to get Leo right. It's not going to be easy capturing him on the page, but I'm going to try.

I take a deep breath and look out at the view.

Come on inspiration. Hit me.

Entranced by the water, I wait for the perfect sentence to pop up in my head.

It doesn't.

After a long time of sitting there with nothing to say, I force myself to write a couple of sentences that I swiftly delete. I try wording it a different way but it sounds stupid, so I delete that. I then type out something so bland, I say, 'Boring' at the screen, heckling my laptop as though it's not acting on my orders.

Hoping that a brief distraction might help, I call Mum to tell her about the change in flight. I brace myself for her disappointment, guilty at being away from her longer, but she doesn't seem all that surprised.

'I got the feeling when we spoke the other day that things were going better for you,' she says, referring to the phone call I'd made to tell her I'd gone surfing for the first time.

'You need to strike while the iron is hot. I'm pleased that Toni understands that.'

'Are you okay? Everything all right at home?'

'All well here,' she says, having never answered that question differently.

I lean back in my chair, wrapping my hand round my waist. 'And... the house?'

'It's never been tidier. The estate agent is sending out a photographer next week, so I've been busy clearing out a load of clutter. You don't realise how much rubbish you acquire over the years until you force yourself to pay attention to it.'

I swallow, before lowering my voice even though there's no one around to overhear. 'Mum, if you're feeling sad about the house—'

'I'm fine, Iris,' she chirps, her stock answer ready and waiting before I can ask.

'I know that,' I say firmly, determined to get this across. 'But if ever you're not, I want you to know that you can talk to me. Because selling the family home, it can feel...' I close my eyes, recalling Leo's words at the party '...it makes everything real. So, yeah, you may want to brush over it and pretend it's not a big deal, which is fine... but I wanted to say that if, at any point, you find that it *is* actually a big deal, then I'm here. You can talk to me.'

I'm greeted with silence.

'Mum?' I prompt after a while.

'Thank you, Iris,' she says gently. 'I know it's only a house but... yes.' She sighs. 'Thank you. I'll keep that in mind.'

I nod, the phone pressed to my ear. 'Good.'

'So,' she says, lifting her tone, signalling it's time to move on, 'how is the article going?'

'Funny you should ask.' I sigh heavily, squinting at my screen. 'I'm working on the opening line. It's taken me maybe an hour to write absolutely nothing at all.'

'Always the way. It will come to you. Especially if you're staying out in Burgau for another few days.'

I frown in confusion. 'What do you mean?'

'I don't know, I've just felt you've sounded different on our phone calls – more sprightly, less agitated.'

'Huh. I think that's the first time anyone has ever called me "sprightly",' I shift in my seat. 'Not sure how I feel about it.'

'You're in the right place to write,' she assures me. 'Stop thinking about it so hard and let it come to you.'

Easy for her to say. But she has a point. Often my best lines crop up into my head when I'm doing something different, when I'm on a walk or out with friends or listening to music. It's that classic thing when if you want something too much, it doesn't happen, and then when you don't need it, it comes along no hassle.

After we've hung up, I decide to get in my gym gear and do some yoga with the help of an instructor on YouTube on the balcony, wondering if a bit of exercise might get my brain going. The stretching definitely helps and I do feel better about myself – but the opening line still hasn't made itself known.

Hands on my hips, I huff in frustration.

'Maybe I should... go surfing?' I suggest to myself, watching a couple of others brave the waves out there this afternoon. And then I tip my head back and laugh at myself.

Leo has truly sent me doolally.

Oh my God, I'm actually considering getting in the sea for no reason but to amuse myself and clear my head. What is *happening* to me? I place my palm against my forehead as I look out at the surfers paddling out. Mum's right. I feel different here.

Although I refuse to accept the 'sprightly' description.

When my phone buzzes with a message, I practically launch myself at the table to pick it up, excited to have any kind of distraction.

I break into a goofy smile when I see who it's from.

Twenty-three

I'll be the one to break and message you first. How is your day going?

An overwhelming rush of affection floods through me and makes me slink down in the chair, clutching my phone with both hands, delighted at the idea of him thinking about me.

Leo's typing again. I wait, my breath catching in my throat.

Did you change your flight?

Cute.

He's seen I've read it, so I don't consider making him wait around for a response. Instead, I bite my lip and start typing back.

Yes, I did. I'm here another week

He's still online and the ticks go blue straight away. He's typing again.

Leo

We should celebrate. What are you doing now?

> Writing about you actually
>
> Or at least trying to

Leo

Study break?

Sighing heavily, I glumly type my response. I know I'm doing the right thing, but it really fucking sucks. Usually, I quite like being efficient and responsible, revelling in getting things ticked off my list.

Not today. Today, I want to be back at Leo's flat, tangled up in his sheets.

> I can't
>
> My editor needs some pages by tonight

Leo

How far have you got?

I lift my eyebrows. 'Honestly?' I say out loud, before taking a photo of the blank page on my laptop screen and sending it to him.

> Wow. My ego just took a bruising. Do I not inspire you
>
> at all, London?

His teasing message makes my stomach pool with a rich, comforting warmth, the kind you get when you've been out in the cold, braving the brisk, crisp air, and then you step inside and clasp the mug of a sweet, hot drink, and you take a sip and have that rush of heat trailing down your throat, making your toes bunch up in your shoes. Cosy, safe, secure. I'm not sure I even realised it, but today I've been missing him. I haven't just been fantasising about the sex – which, obviously, I've been doing a lot of, because hi, I'm human – I've also been missing his company. Now I know he's thinking of me and so everything is as it should be.

This crush is *insane*.

> You inspire me just fine
> I've been working on the structure
> Getting an idea of the order of things

Leo

Not one word on that page
I haven't inspired ONE word

> It always takes a long time to start
> The perfect first line will come to me.
> You'll see

There's a delay before his next message comes through. The ticks of my message are blue and it says he's still online, but it takes a few moments before I see that he's typing again. Then his messages pop up.

Let me come over. We can work on the inspiration together

Oh God. I *wish* I could say yes. But if he comes here, I won't want him to leave and I have too much to do. I let out a groan of disappointment. I can't let Toni down when she's been so understanding about my change of plan. It's only one day; I can see him tomorrow.

I type slowly, hating myself and unreasonably resenting Toni.

Maybe tomorrow?
I have to meet this deadline tonight

Leo

I have a busy day tomorrow

Are you now trying to play it cool?

Leo

I don't need to play it cool
It's natural to me
But I genuinely do have a lot on tomorrow

Tomorrow evening maybe?

Leo

I have a dinner with friends

My shoulders slump forwards. It is understandable that he'd be busy over the weekend; I can't expect him to clear his calendar for me. We'll have to wait until Sunday. I think about his lips on mine, his body pressed against mine, the things he said about how much he'd wanted me, falling asleep in his arms so quickly, so comfortably…

Fuck. Sunday is years away.

No worries

Leo

Sunday?

Sunday it is. How was surfing today?

Leo

It was great actually
Weirdly, I was in a really good mood
Can't think why

Argh, I'm literally aching for him. His flirting is making butterflies dance wildly around my stomach, somersaulting and spinning, having the time of their lives in there.

How strange. I'm pleased for you. Any wipeouts?

Leo

One quite big one

My stomach drops at the idea of him being hurt. I'm glad I wasn't there to see it.

But that's okay. It's a good thing.
If I didn't wipeout every now and then,
I'd know I wasn't pushing myself hard enough

I read his messages twice. Something is whirring in the back of my brain, something important, a niggle that is making its way through the jumbled thoughts and—

Leo, I've got to go

Leo

Everything okay?

Yes. Don't let your ego explode
But I think you've just inspired me

Sliding into my seat, I shove my phone on the table and wake up my dozing laptop. The blank word document flashes up at me. Resting my fingers on the keyboard, I take a deep breath in, push back my shoulders, and I begin to type.

Leo Silva is afraid of the ocean.

If that doesn't strike you as strange, then it should, because Leo Silva is a former world champion surfer. After twelve years of retirement, he's now training to compete in a leg of the World Surf League Championship Tour once more: the iconic Rip Curl Pro Bells Beach contest that takes place in Victoria, Australia in just a few weeks. A young surf prodigy, a lifetime of experience, dozens of trophies – this man practically grew up on the water and has rarely been out of it, even since his early retirement. That he should be afraid of it simply doesn't make any sense. And anyone who has the privilege to witness him surfing couldn't possibly think it.

Out there, gliding on the waves, Leo Silva looks fearless.

But I'm slowly learning that this contradiction is what makes him one of the best surfers in the world. It's not just his breathtaking skill, his dazzling talent, his expert mastery of the water. It's that he also accepts that things can go wrong, that mistakes can be made and learnt from, and that sometimes to end up winning, you have to lose first. A lifetime on the water hasn't only inspired him, it's humbled him.

Like Leo proposes to be, I am scared of the ocean. So afraid, I haven't gone near it for years. And I've never surfed before. But on a warm day in March, standing on Burgau beach in Portugal with him, I believe him when he says that by the end of the day, I'll be riding the waves on a surfboard.

That's the kind of athlete he is. The kind that makes you feel like you can do anything.

Lifting my hands off the keyboard, I read through what I've written.

It needs polishing, but it's not a bad start.

Twenty-four

I'm reading my book in the bath on Saturday evening when I hear a knock on the door. I freeze, wondering if I've misheard or if it's a knock for a different flat, but after a while it comes again.

Quickly marking my page, I call out, 'Just a minute!', climbing out the bath and grabbing my towel. As I tuck it round me and pad over to the door, I wonder who it might be – Leo is at his dinner party tonight and when I saw Marina earlier, she said she was going to the same event as him. I think it's a dinner hosted by Diogo, my sea-fishing friend.

Oh shit. I stop in my tracks on the way to the door as I realise who it is.

José.

There's no one else it could be. I did leave him very abruptly on Thursday night after our date without the most extensive of explanations, so maybe he wants to talk about it. He would also know that I didn't get on that plane today since Naomi extended my stay here.

At first, I consider throwing on some clothes, but then I re-evaluate and realise that if it looks like he has disturbed my evening, it wouldn't necessarily be a bad thing. That way, I can get rid of him quicker – which sounds mean, but I'd rather have the evening of pampering and reading I'd planned than force myself through awkward small talk. And after writing all of yesterday, and into the night, to get those paragraphs to Toni, before another full day of writing today, I deserve a bit of relaxation.

Running myself a hot bath was also a bit of a celebration – Toni replied to my email this morning with the following:

LOVE this. You're back on form. Can't wait to read the rest. Keep drinking that "better-than-London" Burgau coffee you bored me about if that's what gets me these results. Best wishes, T

Her approval meant I was on the right path and I barely looked up from my laptop today. Once I started writing about Leo, I couldn't stop. I forced myself to go on a walk to the beach at lunch time just to make sure I didn't stay cooped up in the flat all day, but it was pointless – my brain was whirring with ideas for the feature and I only ended up making it as far as Marina's Bar to say hi before I scurried back to my hovel. But this evening, I admitted defeat. I needed a break and since everyone I know here is busy tonight, a bath and a book seemed like the perfect evening.

Until I swing open my front door.

It's not José. It's Leo.

He's standing outside my door in a dark shirt and shorts, with what looks like quite a heavy bag of food in one hand

and a bouquet of pink flowers in the other. When the door opens and he sees me, his whole face lights up.

Gripping my towel, beads of water from the bath still dripping down my legs, I stare at him, my breath caught in my throat. He looks achingly handsome, his hair thick and messy, the top buttons of his shirt undone low enough to allow a teasing glimpse of the smooth, tanned skin of his chest.

'Hey,' he says, his eyes warm and soft, his smile creeping wider and wider.

This is not how I would have opened the door if I'd known it was him on the other side. I don't exactly look my best right now. No make-up, my hair tied up in a loose, messy bun, and my cheeks flushed from the heat of the bath, growing hotter under his gaze.

'Leo!' I stare at him, wide-eyed. 'What are you—'

I don't get the chance to finish my sentence because he's already stepped forwards and dropped the bag on the floor by the door with a loud thud before wrapping his arms around my waist and dipping his head to kiss me.

And when he does, everything else around us disappears.

His mouth crushes against mine, his hand carrying the flowers staying at the small of my back while his other moves to my neck, his fingers sinking into my hair. As he walks me back a step until I bump against the open door, I exhale a soft moan of relief, joy, pleasure – all of the above – to have his lips to myself again, a sound that causes him to deepen the kiss, his tongue gliding against mine. God, he smells *so good*, his musky sandalwood cologne filling my nostrils and igniting a fire low in my belly. My hands are pressed flat against his chest and I can feel his strong heartbeat thudding against my palm. It was only yesterday that I left his flat but it somehow feels like a lifetime ago, my body melting into his, craving the feeling of his weight pressed against me. My head spins, my stomach twists, my heart races.

This is one *hell* of a kiss.

He eventually draws back to smile down at me. I bring my eyes up to meet his, my poor brain dizzy from his greeting and still scrambling to make sense of his being here at all.

He dips his head once more to gently brush his lips against mine, soft, careful and inviting, like he's had a shot of what he's been craving and he can relax now: the calm after the storm. Or in the case of that kiss, the calm after a fucking frenzied tornado.

'What are you doing here?' I say breathlessly, only just realising that I'm clinging to handfuls of his shirt. I don't even remember actioning my hands to do that. 'You're meant to be at a dinner.'

'I told them I had somewhere else I needed to be,' he tells me, his fingers sweeping back a lock of hair that's fallen loose of my bun, probably because a moment ago, he was tugging on it, teasing it from the hairband.

'Seriously?'

'I wanted to see you,' he admits, pressing his forehead against mine. 'Is that okay?'

Fuck yes.

'Sure,' I say quietly, hoping he can't hear my heart beating at a hundred miles an hour. I run my hands up and down his torso, making sure he's really here standing in front of me and this isn't a dream. 'Although I feel bad you had to cancel your plans.'

'I feel bad that I interrupted yours,' he says, lifting his head so his eyes can drift down to my towel. 'Not that bad. Kind of seems as though I dropped by at a good time.'

I laugh, self-consciousness suddenly getting the better of me as I glance over his shoulder out at the empty corridor. I'd been so caught up in the kiss, I hadn't thought about neighbours passing by.

'Maybe you should come in so we can close the door,' I suggest.

He agrees, stepping back to pick the bag up and come in, while I shut the door.

Placing his things down on the kitchen counter, he surveys the spacious lounge.

'It's not bad, I'll give José that,' he remarks.

'He does have *excellent* taste.'

When Leo shoots me a look, I'm ready to greet it with an impish grin.

'So I should probably go put some clothes on,' I note, gesturing to the bedroom. 'There's iced tea in the fridge if you want some? Sorry, I don't have much else. If I'd known you were coming over, I would have—'

He holds up one hand to stop me and passes me the bouquet from the other.

'I've got all that covered,' he says. 'Here. These are for you.'

'They're beautiful, thank you.' I admire them, breathing in their sweet scent, their paper wrapping crinkling in my grasp. 'Why did you get me flowers?'

'Because,' he begins, and there's an ever-so-slight waver to his voice, like maybe he's nervous about something, 'I thought tonight could be our very first date.'

I frown at him, half-smiling in confusion. 'What? Like, a *proper* date?'

'Yeah, London,' he says, the corners of his lips tilting upwards. 'If we're doing this, we're not doing it half-arsed.'

I'm too stunned to speak for a moment. One moment, I had a free evening ahead of me, soaking in a bath with my book, and the next, I'm being handed flowers at the introduction to a surprise date with one of the sexiest, sweetest men I've ever met. Maybe *the* sexiest and sweetest man I've ever met.

My brain is finding it hard to compute this turn of events.

'But... Leo, we *can't* go on a date,' I say regretfully, looking at him as though he's forgotten what's going on here and who I am. 'If people saw us... We're meant to be keeping this a secret. Lying low. I don't think it's a good idea for us to go out for dinner somewhere.'

'I know. That's why I've brought dinner here,' he says, nodding to the bag. 'I hope you like Italian food; there's a great little place in the village. I got a selection of the menu; I wasn't sure what you liked.'

I stare at him.

'While you go get dressed, I'll get dinner set out on the balcony,' he continues when I don't say anything. 'Take your time; don't rush or anything. We can always heat up the food in the oven if we need to.'

He gives me a strange look as I continue to stay mute, my lips parted, a tingling feeling spreading out from my heart down through every vein, warming my body.

'You okay?' he asks, concerned. 'You look a bit spaced out.'

'I... I just...' My mouth is so dry. I swallow and start again. 'I wasn't expecting this.'

His forehead creases. 'Sorry, you know, now I'm here, maybe this is too much, I should have checked—'

'No! No, it's not too much,' I say, beaming at him, the muscles in my face finally springing into action to yank my mouth up into a proper smile and reassure him. 'It's wonderful. It's so lovely, I can't...' I trail off, taking a deep breath. 'You really want to go on a proper date with me?'

His eyes fix on mine, the worry etched across his face fading away into a warm smile, the crinkles making a fine appearance. 'Yes, I do.' He hesitates, his eyebrows lifting. 'Do you want to go on a proper date with me?'

What a stupid question. Idiotic, mad, adorably foolish.

'Yes, Leo,' I say, my heart thudding. 'I'd love to.'

'Okay then. Let's do this.' He nods to my bedroom door. 'You should go get ready.'

As I turn round, he stops me by saying, 'Oh, wait, you want me to put those in water?' gesturing to the bouquet of flowers.

'No, it's okay, I'll sort it,' I say, smiling shyly as I hug the flowers to my body, unable to admit out loud that I want to look at them while I get ready. 'They're such a beautiful colour.'

'The same pink as the dress you wore the first night you arrived here, when you walked down to the beach,' he says as though that's obvious.

Where did this man come from?

My stomach flipping, I don't trust myself to speak, so I give him a quick nod and then start making my way to the bedroom. I place the bouquet down on the bed and can hear him rustling around in the bag in the kitchen. After a moment of staring at the flowers, I poke my head round the door again. His forehead is etched in concentration as he pulls various items carefully out of the bag one by one, careful not to spill anything.

'Leo.'

He snaps his head up. 'Yes?'

'I haven't seen a florist around here.'

'No,' he answers.

'Is there a florist in Burgau?'

He gazes across the room at me, the hint of a smile on his lips as though he's been caught out. 'No,' he confirms.

I bite my lip to stop a stupidly-wide grin breaking across my face. *'Leo?'*

'Yeees?'

'Did you drive somewhere just to get me flowers?'

'Go get ready, London,' he says, rolling his eyes and returning his attention to the food. 'We don't want to miss our dinner reservation.'

I slowly shut the door, leaning back against it and exhaling, my heart swelling so big in my chest, I wonder if it might burst right out of there at any moment.

Twenty-five

If all dates were this easy, I would take back my comment to Flora about choosing books over men. I know that's a big thing to say, but that's how good this date is.

The thoughtfulness of this surprise evening encouraged me to make an effort with my appearance; if this was going to be a proper first date, I needed to dress for it, like I would any other, even if it was taking place on my balcony.

It's a warm evening, and it felt like a special one, so I slipped on one of my favourite outfits: a burgundy mini dress with a high neckline, contoured bodice and cap sleeves, gold embellishment on the pockets. I had to sneak out in my robe to grab some pointed-toe stilettos from the shoe stand next to the door, scurrying back into my room before he could see the finished look. With my hair swept up into a loose updo, tendrils framing my face, I added some statement gold earrings, a slick of mascara, bronzer and plum lipstick.

When I emerged out onto the balcony, he was in the middle of putting out the cutlery.

As he looked up, the forks he was holding slipped onto the table with a loud clatter. His eyes widened and his lips parted. I blushed furiously under his gaze. Men have looked at me before, and I've known what they're thinking, but no one's ever looked at me like that.

'Wow,' he breathed, his throat bobbing as he swallowed. 'You look beautiful.'

I smiled at him. The way he was looking at me made me *feel* beautiful.

So far, it's been, hands down, the best first date I've ever had. There have been no awkward silences, no forced small talk – the whole evening, we've been chatting and laughing and learning about each other. We're comfortable in each other's company.

Digging into the delicious pasta he bought, I joke about his lack of cooking skills, and when I get ahead of myself trying to make plans for the extra week I now have here, he teases me about being a control freak. I love that his sense of humour means we can take the piss out of each other already, and more than that, he's good at making me laugh at myself.

'Did you always know you wanted to be a writer?' he asks once we've finished eating and he's cleared away the plates, having refused to let me lift a finger all night.

'Actually, there was a time when I was convinced I was going to be a ballet dancer,' I inform him with a playful smile. 'But I peaked in performance too early.'

'How early are we talking?'

'Around seven years old. I was in a widely-acclaimed

production of *Goldilocks and The Three Bears* at my local dance studio.'

'Impressive. Were you a lead role?'

'In a manner of speaking. I played the part of Porridge Bowl A.'

He bursts out laughing. '*What?* You're making this up. That's not a role.'

'It is! There were the three porridge bowls that she comes upon in the house, so there were three of us wearing porridge-bowl costumes, and I was the tallest so I was Daddy Bear's bowl. We had our own little dance and everything.'

'That has to be the cutest thing I've ever heard.'

'Even cuter when I tell you that I got stuck in the door coming off the stage because my bowl costume was so big and circular. I misjudged the space and forgot to go through at an angle. Porridge Bowl B had to shove me through it from behind.'

He cackles with laughter, head tipped back, his whole face lit up.

I love making you laugh like that, I think, watching him, sparks erupting in my belly.

'Here I was thinking you were so sophisticated and glamorous,' he says, shaking his head, still chuckling. 'Porridge Bowl A. Any photos?'

'Mum might have one or two at home.'

'I'll have to ask her to show me them,' he says, without thinking.

His smile falters. A wave of panic flickers across his expression, before he reaches for his drink, taking a sip. My heart sinks a little as we both silently acknowledge that he won't be meeting any of my family or friends any time soon.

No matter how good this date is, all this can ever be is a fling, and a secret one at that.

'She might have thrown them out by now,' I say in an attempt to breeze over the hiccup. 'She told me she's done a big clear-out of the house before it goes on the market.'

He looks at me intently. 'How are you feeling about it?'

'The clear-out? Pretty good. I don't like clutter.'

'No kidding. I meant, how are you feeling about the house going on the market?' he says, his tone soft and serious.

My eyes drop to my hands in my lap. I have the stock answer at the ready for this: *fine*. Everything is always fine. And when things aren't that fine, I laugh them off or fake it. That's how I work. That's how I've always worked. It's not that I don't have the emotional intelligence to acknowledge when things are bad – I appreciate I'm not a robot. I just prefer to handle it myself.

The truth is, I don't want anyone to think I can't.

But Leo will see right through me. I think I've known that about him from the beginning; the way he looks at me as though he's determined to see past the shield I'm wielding. He's been slowly trying to figure me out on the sly, while I've been publicly hammering away at his own defences. There doesn't seem to be any point in pretending with him. And I don't want to.

'Sad,' I admit hoarsely. 'I'm feeling really sad about it.'

He exhales through his nose, his expression darkening. He almost looks pained. 'I'm so sorry, Iris.'

'Me too. I know it's for the best, but,' I furrow my brow, 'I'll miss it.'

He nods in understanding.

I take a sip of my water before continuing. 'You know,

sometimes I worry that I'm remembering things wrong. Making up happy family memories, all the love and security of this… idyllic family unit I could have sworn I felt, wondering if I was naïve to what was really happening around me. I usually pride myself on being so observant.' I chew on my lip, my voice wavering. 'How could I have missed that my own family wasn't what I thought it was? When I let myself really think about it, I end up feeling so stupid.'

He leans forward, resting his elbows on his knees, waiting until I bring my eyes up to meet his before speaking, and when he does, his voice is so earnest and sincere, it makes my chest ache and my eyes well up with hot tears.

'Iris, what's happening now doesn't take away from what happened before. The childhood you had, the happy family memories – all of that still exists. You didn't make it up. It happened. All of that is part of who you are. Things may be different for you and your parents going forwards, but nothing can take away from that.'

As his dark eyes search mine, I expel a shaky breath. I'm so entranced by his gaze, I forget to respond to what he's saying. Finally, I nod, tearing my eyes from his, collecting myself. He leans back in his chair, still watching me, heaving a heavy sigh.

'I discovered that it really sucks when we get that bit older and find out that our parents are humans who make mistakes, too,' he notes.

'Yeah. It does. How dare they live their own lives?'

'Despicably selfish.'

I give a small laugh. 'Thanks Leo, for being so nice about it.'

'You can talk to me any time, London.'

'I did mean what I said at the party when we spoke about this before, though – I do hope the house sale helps Mum to move on. I really do.'

'And your dad?'

'He seems okay,' I tell him with a sigh. 'He's quite difficult to read.'

'Yeah?' Leo's lips twitch. 'Reminds me of someone I know.'

I give him a pointed look. 'Trust me, my dad is much more stoic than I am.'

'I'm picturing the reserved English type.'

'Doesn't talk much, works all the time, keeps everyone at a comfortable distance.' I shift in my seat, unnerved by my own description. 'I know he loves me, but he wouldn't be someone I'd rush to with a problem. He's the reason I do what I do, though.'

'He got you into writing?'

'He got me into sport,' I correct, shooting him an eager smile. 'And Mum encouraged books and creative writing. Put two and two together…'

'And you get England's leading sports journalist.'

I snort. 'Hardly. But I love it.'

He tilts his head. 'What do you love about it?'

'The people,' I say, without having to think about it. 'I get to meet and spend time with the most amazing, inspirational athletes in the world, and…' I hesitate, looking over at his smug smile. 'Ah. Forgot who I was talking to there.'

'Please, *please* carry on,' he encourages. 'You were saying?'

Oh fucking hell, he looks so outrageously pleased with

himself it's annoying. *Almost* annoying. Okay, it *would* be annoying if he wasn't so gorgeous.

Still, I play along, narrowing my eyes at him.

'I was saying that athletes tend to be arrogant arseholes—'

'That's not what you were saying.'

'—who act as though they're God's gift—'

'You were saying something very different.'

'—and I'm going to shut up now.'

He grins at me as I take a sip of my drink. 'On behalf of all amazingly talented athletes, I would like to say: you're welcome. Happy to be a perk of your job.'

I roll my eyes. '*Please*.'

But I can't fake my disdain for long and soon I'm giggling with him.

'I'm actually up for a new job,' I blurt out. I have no idea why. I would blame wine for my loosened tongue but I haven't had any. He didn't even ask me a question that led to this topic. Apparently, I'm spilling my life to him now.

He raises an eyebrow. 'Yeah?'

'Sports editorial director across the European titles of *Studio*.'

'Whoa. Sounds fancy.'

'It is. It's a big role. It would be… amazing. A dream job. I don't know the full details yet, but if I were to get it, I'd have the opportunity to put some incredible and deserving people in the spotlight, making big decisions on the content, managing a team and…'

I trail off, reading his reaction. The whole time I've been speaking about this job opportunity, he's been looking at me strangely.

'Okay, what is it?' I ask nervously. 'What, you think

there's no way I'll get it? Am I embarrassing myself by even entertaining the idea?'

He balks at my suggestion. 'No! That's not... I think you have every chance of getting that role. You're passionate and knowledgeable and talented. The people at *Studio* would be stupid not to give you that job.'

'You looked... confused when I was talking.'

'No, it's only that I know a little bit about the media world thanks to, well, you know—'

'Your mum owning a sizeable chunk of it?'

He smirks. 'Yeah, that might have something to do with it. Anyway, the position you're describing, it sounds like a management role. Like an editor, right?'

'Sort of.'

I have no idea where he's going with this, but he's looking at me expectantly as though I should have got it from what he's already said.

'Iris, you said you loved your job and when I asked you why, you said...'

'The people.'

'Right.' He nods. 'You get to meet these talented, inspirational and devastatingly handsome athletes,' he winks at me, earning himself a scowl, 'and you write about them beautifully, something I know you love to do and you're obviously brilliant at it.'

'Thanks.' I pause. 'So?'

'So, if you were the sports editorial director, you wouldn't get to do either of those things,' he says simply. 'Sure, it may be this really important role and a dream job, but is it *your* dream job? You should do something that gives you that... spark. Surfing is that for me. And

for you, I think it's...' he gestures between me and him
'...this.'

I'm a little taken aback by his answer – largely because...
he's kind of talking sense. I hadn't really stopped to think
about it that way.

I can feel his eyes boring into me.

'Hey, if that job is what you want, then I have no doubt
that you would be the best sports editorial director anyone
has ever known,' he emphasises, his brow furrowed. 'All I'm
saying is that you're fucking good at what you do. And,
I don't know... maybe it's because I've been that person
before, the one so focused on winning the next big accolade
that I haven't stopped to think about what actually makes
me happy.'

'Interesting.' I turn to look at him. 'And what *does* make
you happy, Leo Silva?'

He breaks into a relieved, wide grin, his eyes twinkling
with humour. 'Always at the ready to get a good quote.'

'You can't blame a girl for trying,' I say with a mischievous
smile. 'I'm still on the hunt for the perfect ending to your
story. I have a feeling it will depend on what happens at
Bells Beach, but a back-up quote is always helpful. So, come
on Leo, what is it that makes you really happy? The laidback surfing lifestyle? The thrill of riding the wave?'

His gaze locks on mine, making my heart pound so hard,
it rings in my ears and sends pulses of warmth shimmering
out from my chest to every corner of my body.

'All of the above,' he says, a knowing smile creeping
across his lips, 'and nights like these.'

Twenty-six

'*...and nights like these.*'

All Sunday morning, his words float through my mind countless times, distracting me from every task and making my heart thrum with happiness. Four simple words that I can't shake. The image of him smiling at me and saying that replays over and over and over in my head. I feel like I'm practically skipping around the village. He's literally putting a spring in my step.

I think I'm in trouble here.

Saturday was an unforgettable night, but it didn't quite end the way I'd hoped – Leo didn't stay the night. When he got up to leave and made it clear that he was heading home, I was stunned, and the fear began to creep in. What had I said or done to prompt him to want to leave? It's not like he could have been confused as to whether I was up for it; we'd already had the most amazing sex a couple of nights earlier, and surely the kiss we had on his arrival could confirm for both of us what we wanted.

He must have read the concern in my expression as he put his hands on my hips and pulled me towards him, before his lips brushed against mine, and explained, 'It's our first proper date. I want to be chivalrous.'

I'm ashamed to admit, I deepened the kiss and pressed my body against his, murmuring, 'Screw chivalry', but despite the smile it drew from his lips, he resisted my efforts and stubbornly insisted on going home. Watching him in disbelief head down the stairs from my doorway, I was tempted to shout out a reminder that we only had a week to enjoy each other's company, but despite him leaving me in a state of frustration, I managed to retain some dignity and stop myself from doing so.

I woke up early Sunday to a message from him letting me know he was surfing Burgau, so I got ready and made my way down to the beach in time to see him heading into the water with Marina and a group of fellow surfers, some of whom I recognised from the party. He'd paddled out with them before he glanced back on the beach to see me, lifting his hand to wave. I waved back and even though I was far away, I swear I could see him break into a grin. Maybe I was seeing what I wanted to see.

It was different, watching him surf with this group, compared to his other training sessions. This one didn't actually seem like a training session at all. I could hear their laughter floating across the waves back to me on the beach as they chatted out there together, and I noticed Leo point and gesture at Marina, encouraging her to catch a good wave that was coming in. None of them in the group were out here for themselves; they were sharing a passion, exchanging advice – from their cheers and whoops, I could hear the amount of enjoyment they got from watching their friends surf well.

It reminded me of that video I found of Leo and Ethan Anderson surfing as teenagers, before competitions got so serious and the success got in the way. It made me hope that this upcoming trip to Australia would be healing for Leo, not just in surfing Bells Beach again, but also seeing those from the surfing community out there again.

Before they were rivals, they were friends.

I left the beach before they came in, dropping in on my local coffee shop again – '*Olá*, Iris! I'll get you coffee for your work. You'll write well today because of me!' – and then going straight back to the flat to work.

After a while, a welcome message distracts me:

Leo

Where did you go?

I had to write. I got some ideas

Leo

There I go inspiring you again

How do you know it wasn't your surf buddies that inspired me?

Leo

You trying to make me jealous?

My heart somersaulting, I smile broadly. Leaving my laptop open on the balcony table, I stand up to wander into the lounge, flopping down on the sofa and clasping my phone in my hands like it's the most precious item in the world.

I start typing a reply.

It did work out well for me last time

Leo

Even better for me. What are you doing tonight?

Are you hoping for a second date?

Leo

Yes
But that will have to wait
Dad and I are going to my uncle's house. You want to come?

I pause. This could be an innocent invitation – speaking to family and friends is par for the course when it comes to these big features. Leo's uncle could be a valuable resource, but since I already have my interview with Adriano and I'm hoping to weave in quotes from Marina, or another of his local surf friends here, word count is already looking tight.

And after what's happened between us, meeting other family members just seems a bit… weird. I'd be nervous and confused, naturally wanting him to think well of me, but *why*? Sex is one thing, but emotional attachment is another, and family dinners is the sort of thing that leads to that. I'm already a little too invested in this guy. We're on the clock here.

If ever there was a time for self-preservation, this is it.

I'd love to, but I have to work

Leo

No worries
At least if you're writing about me, I know you'll be thinking of me

How do you know I'm working on your feature?
I might have another commission
There are a lot of talented, amazing athletes out there,
you know

Leo

You really are trying to make me jealous

Is it working?

Leo

Yes. Tell me when I can see you again

Now, my brain begs. But he was the one who wanted to play it cool last night, refusing to stay over, even when I practically begged him to. Maybe I need to regain some control here.

Tomorrow might work

Leo

Second date tomorrow night then?
What are you doing early tomorrow morning?
I'm surfing Meia Praia
We have a Levant swell, can't miss it
I could pick you up if you want to come?
You might be bored of training now

No, sounds good, thanks
I'm just going to google 'Levant swell'

Leo

My dad can talk you through it tomorrow. See you then xx

Kisses. Kisses at the end of his message. My fingers hover over the keyboard of my phone, no idea what to do or how to reply. But he goes offline swiftly after that, concluding the exchange. Concluding it with kisses. How stupid is it that two little letters can cause such an effect? Flirty messages I can handle, but this feels different. Just a simple 'xx' and our conversation feels intimate. Meaningful. Affectionate. I'm glad that message didn't require a reply, because I don't know if I can echo the sentiment.

Not when I'm saying goodbye in six days.

'Levant waves are generated after southerly strong winds create heavy Mediterranean swells,' Adriano tells me the next morning as we stand side by side on the vast, long stretch of sandy beach, sipping coffee from the flask that he very thoughtfully brought along for me. 'They gain power as they head towards our coast. The water is warm; it's a lot of fun. You have to make the most of it when it happens.'

I lower my cup, smiling as we watch Leo riding a wave, the water spraying out in a fan over his head whenever his board glides up towards the lip of the wave and cuts back down, manoeuvring with ease, generating speed as he goes.

'He certainly looks like he's doing that,' I remark, as Leo twists and turns through the wave, adding in a rotation, whooping as he lands the spin, jumping off his board.

Adriano laughs, gesturing out to him. 'Yes, look, he's playful, like the water.'

'Playful,' I repeat, nodding. 'That's the perfect description.' I turn to grin at him. 'You're missing out; you should go join him. I'm fine here on the beach.'

'The waves are good; we could be out there for a while.'

'That's okay,' I assure him, turning to look at Leo as he readies his board to paddle back out. He catches my eye and grins at me. 'I don't mind.'

'All right,' Adriano says in an amused voice, and when I tear my eyes from Leo to look at him, he's giving me a knowing smile.

Blushing furiously knowing I've been caught in a dreamy daze, I quickly frown, looking down at my feet and kicking some sand off my toes. With a soft chuckle, Adriano takes his board towards the water, leaving me to shake off my embarrassment alone.

If he's caught on to anything between me and Leo, at

least he doesn't look annoyed about it. In fact, if anything, he looked pleased.

One thing he didn't look was surprised.

When we make our way back to the truck, Leo is glowing from the joy of the morning, his eyes gleaming, his cheeks flushed from the exercise, his smile unflappable. I laugh at his and Adriano's excitement as his dad throws an arm around his shoulders to share in Leo's rambled gushing about how good it was out there. I've definitely got at least another couple of paragraphs for the piece from this morning: this wonderful father-and-son scene is going to be a killer.

As Leo gets out of his wetsuit, Adriano does the same, throwing on a t-shirt and coming over to give both of us a hug before declaring he'll see us back in Burgau – he has to get back to the shop. Leo waits for his dad's car to disappear before he grabs me at the waist, that adorably dopey smile still plastered on his face as I place my hands flat against his chest, tipping my head back to look up at him.

'Thank you for coming today,' he says, his arms wrapping tighter around me. 'What did you think?'

'I think,' I say slowly, finding it impossible not to smile myself in the face of such elation, 'that you were born to do this, Leo Silva.'

He exhales a wistful sigh before leaning down to kiss me, my hands moving up over his strong shoulders to clasp together at the back of his neck, his lips softly brushing against mine, capturing my breath. It's a long, drawn-out kiss, the kind that makes the world around you fade into a hazy blur of background noise, the kind where you don't care what is happening or who else is there. It's just me and him. The kiss grows deeper, his hands roam lower and I can feel him hard against me. A shiver rolls down my spine as something unleashes inside of me. When he breaks the kiss, I nip seductively at his bottom lip and watch his eyes flare with a rewardingly fierce need.

'Leo, I'm not sure I'm a big fan of how long we're waiting in between our… dates,' I say, our foreheads pressed together, his breathing fast and shallow. 'And I know the other night, you were on about chivalry, which is really sweet but—'

'Fuck that, let's get you home,' he says abruptly, reaching round me to open the door to the passenger side of his truck, ushering me inside.

I burst out laughing as he makes his way round to the driver's side. But if he thinks I have the patience to wait for him for the car journey home, he's deluded. I've waited long enough. I'm not wasting any more time. I need him now. I move fast, hitching up my dress and lifting my arse to wriggle my thong down, dropping it next to my bag on the seat. When he slides in and shuts the door behind him, I swivel towards him and before he can start the engine, I grab his arm and balance on it as I lift myself up to straddle him.

'Iris,' he breathes in surprise. 'What are you—?'

Taking his face in my hands, I stop his question with my lips, covering his mouth with mine, his hands sliding up my legs over the bunched-up skirt of my dress to my hips. I can feel how turned on he is and as I grind against him in response, he groans into my mouth and his tongue becomes as demanding as mine, gliding and caressing, igniting sparks that crackle through my body. He pulls back from the kiss, his eyes darting to look out the windows at the deserted row of spaces either side of us.

'You sure about this?' he says in a raspy, disbelieving voice.

To answer his question, I reach for his right hand and move it to my thigh before guiding it up beneath my dress. His eyes widen and he gulps.

'You're... not wearing any underwear,' he mutters, tipping his head back as I kiss his throat along his neck, tasting the salt on my tongue.

'No, I'm not,' I say smugly, threading a hand through his wet hair as I nip at the warm skin just below his ear. 'Yes, I'm sure about this.'

The confirmation seems to give him the permission he's seeking to be sent into overdrive, surrendering to the reckless abandon of his urges. He's suddenly kissing me again, hungry, ravenous, his fingers clawing at the fabric of my summer dress. Before I know it, he's hoisting it up, lifting it over my head and tossing it onto the seat next to him, his lips smashing against mine again, jolts of electricity ricocheting through my stomach at his fevered kisses. I can feel how hard he is for me and he's so fucking hot, I'm already panting and he's not inside me yet. But I know it's only a matter of time and my core is clenching in anticipation, the air in this truck growing thick and crackling with desire.

'Fuck, I've missed you,' he whispers, one hand tugging the cup of my bra down to grasp my breast, the other digging into the skin at my hip. 'Why did we wait so long to do this again?'

'It's all your fault,' I say, breath hitching as he leans

forward to skim his lips along my collarbone. 'You were trying to be good, remember?'

He draws his head back to look at me, his damp hair more dishevelled by my hands than by the water, his lips swollen, his dark gaze searing into mine.

'That's the last time I try to be good,' he growls, before he moves his hand from my hip down between my legs. My lips part with a ragged sigh and he breaks into a devilish grin. 'Oh, *fuck*, you're so ready for me.'

I whimper, merciless and reckless at his touch. I rock against him and he lets out a tortured groan, the thin material of his board shorts doing little to contain his erection.

He moves his hand back to my hip, frown lines deepening across his forehead.

'Do you have a condom on you?' he asks through gritted teeth.

I shake my head and he closes his eyes, muttering something under his breath that I can't make out. My hands move to the side of his face, cupping his carved jaw, my brain marvelling at this gorgeous man.

'Leo,' I begin softly, but he cuts me off, his whole body tense beneath me.

'I don't have any in the car,' he says, a muscle in his jaw twitching.

'I didn't expect you to.'

His eyes flash open at me and I smile, entertained by his reaction.

'I'm on the pill,' I tell him, leaning forwards to kiss his lips, unable to resist them any longer.

'I'm clean,' he says, his eyebrows knitted together as

I draw back. 'And it's been a long time since I was with anyone. But I need you to be sure before we—'

'You want me to beg you, Leo?'

His breath catches, as I rock against him, the feel of his huge, hard length rubbing between my legs making my body ache with heat and my heart race. I'm not going to last long, I can already tell. My hands fall to his shoulders, using him to balance as I lift my weight up and sink down on him again.

'Is that what you want?' I ask, a thrill shooting through me as he moans, shutting his eyes again, his hips pressing up into me. 'Because if that's what it takes…'

Leaning forwards, I brush my lips against his ear and whisper, 'Fuck me, Leo. Fuck me right here in your car. Now, *please*.'

His hand shoots to his shorts, pulling them down and releasing his cock, pressing it at my entrance before I spread a bit more to slide down on top of him, both of us groaning together in ecstasy. I don't take him fully inside me at first, waiting until I sink down a second time to fill myself with his thick, hard length, gasping as I feel him pulse inside me. His eyes roll back, his lower lip dropping as I lower onto him.

'You feel incredible,' he grunts out, moaning as I lift up and push down onto him again, addicted to watching him like this, wanting more and more.

His hands grab my hips, lifting me up and down on top of him, picking up rhythm, our breathing heavy and laboured. As I lose myself in the pleasure of how full and good he feels, I let my head fall back and roll my hips, grinding my clit against him and moaning loudly. I can't help it, he feels too good, I don't care who hears.

'Oh my fucking God,' he rasps, bringing one of his hands between my legs, his thumb working at my clit, drawing fast circles and making me clench. 'You're so tight, so perfect. So wet and tight. *Fuck.*'

The rough desperation in his voice spurs me on faster and harder, the thought of him being close to coming making a burst of heat erupt through my body, the throbbing ache between my legs picking up at a dazzling rate. I dip my head to kiss him, my fingers tangling themselves into his hair and gripping it, his grunts and groans melting into my mouth, sending tingles down my spine. I love that it's me getting those sounds out of him, that it's me that's made him this hard and throbbing, that it's me he wants.

'Fuck, yes, Leo,' I cry as he moves me up and down, his thumb massaging my clit, making my muscles tighten and flutter around him. 'I'm close.'

He doesn't need to tell me he's on the edge of release; I can feel it, I can see it in his expression. I grind my hips into him, the pressure building and building inside me until I can't hold out any longer. One more deep thrust and I tip over, waves of pleasure unfurling through my entire body, my legs trembling as they clench against him and I ride out the orgasm. He comes at the same time, spilling into me and groaning expletives through shaky breaths, his head slamming back against the headrest before he lets it roll forwards, pressing the top of his head against my chest that's heaving with every breath.

When he lifts it to look at me, his hands reach up to brush my hair away from my face, his eyes full of warmth and wonder.

'Christ, that was...' He exhales, struggling to find the

right word, but I know it's a good one because he relaxes into a wide grin, which is so cute and sexy, it makes me want to fuck him all over again.

'I know,' I say quietly, my heart thrumming in my chest.

'Iris Gray,' he says, pressing his forehead to mine and closing his eyes. 'You may just be my dream girl.'

Twenty-seven

My first and last real summer romance was when I was eighteen years old. I was travelling with a friend through Europe after we'd finished school and we were having the time of our life making our way from one amazing city to another, with no set plans for anywhere at any time. We'd show up to a city, find a hostel where we could stay and if we liked it there, we'd stay for a few days, or if we didn't think it was quite our vibe, we'd pack up our backpacks and head to the next destination. We were young, we were single, we were free of responsibilities and worries – and we met some brilliant people along the way.

One of those people was Romain, who we met in Hvar, Croatia.

Travelling with a group of friends from Paris, Romain was staying at the same hostel as us, and to say he and I hit it off would be an understatement. He was gorgeous, funny, smart, and the French accent is top-tier sexy. I saw him making eyes at me the first night of our stay when his group invited us to join them heading out for the evening, and as soon as we got talking, that was it. I was hooked.

It lasted just under two weeks – very handily, my friend developed a crush on one of his friends, so she was happy to head to Dubrovnik with them after Hvar. It was the perfect holiday fling: we saw sights during the days, got drunk in the evenings, partied together at night – we fancied each other so much, we couldn't keep our hands off one another. But then it was time for us to go our separate ways – he was going back to Paris, we were travelling on to Split and then Italy. We messaged each other for a while, but eventually, our contact fizzled out. It didn't matter, though; it was better that way, better to cut ties before things got complicated and reality set in. He would always be up on a pedestal for me, though: a dream-like fantasy of a guy, the beautiful, perfect Romain.

I've always known that no romance could ever be as carefree and perfect as those two weeks in Croatia. I was wrong.

I was completely, fucking wrong.

Because my God, this past week with Leo has been mind-blowing. Like something out of a film, I feel like I've been living my very own romantic montage. All it needed was a Hall & Oates soundtrack, and *bam*, we've got it nailed.

We've spent as much time as we can together. I've been there at every surfing session, cheering him on, stealing kisses afterwards when his dad or his friends haven't been looking. We've been on coffee dates that are under the guise of interviews for the article, his foot finding mine under the table, our hands lightly brushing against each other as we stroll home, each 'accidental' touch sending tingling jolts up my arm. I joined him at the gym for one of his workout sessions, which was *extremely* pleasant to observe thanks to all the flexing and I think he found my fitness advice very helpful – 'I think you need to do a few more press-ups, that's it, oh yeah, *veeery* nice' – and he let me accompany him to his yoga classes again.

'Are you sure I won't make your head go wobbly?' I checked.

'You already make my head wobbly,' he replied casually, as though that wasn't the most adorable thing to say. 'Why not do it in those sexy leggings of yours?'

I smiled, blushing. 'I wore that set in the hope you wouldn't say no to an interview that night. And it worked.'

'Course it worked.' He shrugged. 'I would have done anything you asked that night.'

I'd giggled and then later that day came to realise that watching Leo do yoga made my *own* head very wobbly. And that night, like every night this week, we've had dinner together in his flat or mine, and no one has left at the end of it. Which means every morning, I've woken up in Leo's arms.

And the sex. Oh my God, *the sex*.

It's been a rarity that anyone has given me an orgasm before, but even rarer that they've wanted to badly. I've never had so many in such a short amount of time, definitely not with someone else at the helm. His attention and admiration make me feel amazing and I love pleasing him, instantly turned on at the idea of making him feel good. The sex is so fucking intense and incredible that I feel like I've been floating around in a dreamy haze for days. Whenever I'm not with him, I'm thinking about him, and when I am with him, I'm so buoyantly happy and excitable and obsessed that I can't tear my eyes off him.

Yeah, I know. This is so more than a crush now.

I don't know what it is.

But I do know what it can't be.

Because it's late Friday afternoon and I'm getting ready for my leaving party this evening at Marina's Bar. It was her idea: nothing fancy or outrageous, just a few of the people I've got to know a bit better over the past few weeks gathering for a drink to bid me goodbye.

I've been dreading it. When I think about it, I feel sick. When I think about my flight tomorrow, it almost brings me to tears. It's so ridiculous. This thing with Leo always had a sell-by date. It's so wildly inappropriate and unprofessional, it shouldn't have happened in the first place, so I have to count myself lucky to have got away with it. But I don't. Instead, I feel so unlucky that I've found whatever this is with this person. Because with anyone else…

…it might be something.

When I arrive at Marina's, Leo isn't there. It's a good thing, because I'm able to focus all my attention on everyone else rather than on the weighty feeling of sadness that sits low in my stomach whenever I think of saying goodbye to him.

'She's going to miss you, you know,' Anna tells me, nudging Marina with her elbow.

I quirk my brow at Marina. 'That so?'

She rolls her eyes. 'All right, I admit it. You're fun and it's nice serving someone with good taste for once.'

Her comment elicits groans from her friends and I laugh

before pulling her into a hug, telling her that I'll miss her too. Adriano is there and I'm in the middle of a conversation with him when Leo finally shows up, greeted with a warm welcome from the surfers, while I linger next to his father, my breath catching at the sight of him, aching to be close to him.

'It's not right,' Adriano says, hauling back my attention.

'Sorry?' I say, turning back to face him.

'You leaving so soon,' he explains. 'You've settled into life here very quickly.'

'Anyone would.' I gesture out at the sunset casting a warm-orange glow over the beach. 'It would be hard not to.'

'I don't know about that,' he counters, to my surprise. 'It's not for everyone. But I've always said that people make a place, and I think you've enjoyed the people here. Or one person in particular.'

He raises his eyebrows at me and then jerks his head towards Leo, who is being handed some kind of mocktail that Marina has created whilst laughing along with the group at a story Anna is telling. My chest tightening in panic, I swallow the lump in my throat.

'What?' I laugh nervously, swirling my white wine round the glass. 'Adriano, I don't know what you're—'

'Iris,' he interrupts softly, 'I have eyes. I can see what is there between you and Leo.'

'Nothing is there.' I take a sip of my drink before fixing a smile. 'But he is a great person and you must be really proud of him. I hope… I hope Australia is everything he wants it to be.' I glance back over at him, my heart pounding against my chest. 'He deserves it.'

Watching me closely, Adriano nods slowly. 'Yes.'

'Would you excuse me a moment?'

'Of course.'

Giving him a warm smile, I totter along to the bathroom – that's the only way I can get anywhere in these Jimmy Choo platform sandals – and lock myself in a cubicle, burying my face in my hands while I use the loo. What is it with the Silva men being able to see right through me? Part of me wants to hide in the bathroom all night and not face everyone out there – I should have told Marina that I'd rather not do anything tonight. That way, it wouldn't have felt like such a big deal. But marking it like this, all of these wonderful people asking me about my experience here, it's only making it harder to accept that it's real. Tomorrow, I'll be back in London and Leo will be another doomed fling.

How horribly depressing.

But I do what I do best and tell myself that I'm fine, emerging from the bathroom having checked my make-up is flawless, my curled hair is still falling in soft waves, and that my orange mini – a really cute dress with bows on the shoulder straps and a square neckline – is hugging my frame as it should be. Nobody will be able to read behind my smile anymore; I'll make sure of that.

I'd make an exception for Leo, but for him to read anything about the way I'm feeling at all would require him to talk to me or even look in my direction. But he does well to avoid both for such a long period of time that I wonder whether I've upset him. It was a bit awkward this morning when he left the flat for training. Neither of us spoke about tonight – he'd banned me from mentioning my flight home all week, because he argued that by lingering on when I was leaving, I wasn't committing myself to enjoying the *now*.

'Like when you're surfing,' he reminded me, when my legs were entwined around his in my bed, his hand resting on the dip of my naked waist, 'if you focus too much on what might happen in the future, you miss what the water is telling you at the time and, whatever you do, it will never be as good. You should live in the moment.'

I thought he made a good point and so I stuck to his instructions. But he was quieter than usual this morning, and more withdrawn. One of us should have had the guts to talk about tonight. Instead, the goodbye that has to come is just hanging in the air, a gloomy cloud of grey seeping into all the colour in the room and making everything else grey too.

'Speech!' Anna cries suddenly when I'm mid-conversation with the owner of the coffee shop I've been spending the majority of my earnings on. 'Iris, time for a speech!'

I try waving her off, but soon the others all join in with her demands, giving me a round of applause before the bar falls silent. Right at the back, I see Leo hovering, his eyes on the ground. My heart lurches. I can't leave it like this. I'm going to have to force him to talk to me at some point. I clear my throat, beaming around at the rest of my captive audience.

'All right,' I say, with a nervous laugh, 'I suppose I can say a few words. *Obrigada.*'

My terrible pronunciation draws a cheer from the crowd, which I wave off with my hand, chuckling with embarrassment.

'I'm afraid that's the extent of my Portuguese, as you all know, so the rest of this' speech—'Not true, you can order a coffee in Portuguese!' Marina corrects me, raising her glass, laughter rippling through the room.

'That's right, I can. Very important.' I take a moment to think about what I want to say as the noise dies down again. Taking a deep breath, I smile out at everyone. 'Thank you all for coming tonight. It means a lot that you're here to wave me off. I can't quite believe it's only been a few weeks; it's felt a lot longer than that.'

'Probably because you had to put up with Leo's conversation,' someone at the back quips, prompting further laughter.

I watch as his friends clap him on the back and he laughs along with the joke, shrugging and shaking his head. I force a laugh, accidentally looking in the direction of Adriano, who offers me a sympathetic smile. Reaching for my wine, I take a large gulp before gathering my line of thought and holding the room's attention once more.

'I have loved my time here and I can only hope that through my writing, I do all of you and your beautiful home justice. It's strange to think that tomorrow, I'll be back in England and, to be honest...' I swallow, my mouth suddenly bone dry '...I'm not sure anywhere else has captured my heart quite like this village.'

My eyes naturally flicker to where Leo is standing. He meets my gaze and holds it, finally. Everyone else in the room falls away. It's me and him. My strength wavers, hot tears pricking at my eyes. I exhale, my breath shaking.

Someone very softly clears their throat. I don't have to look at them to know it's Adriano. He's saving me from myself. Plastering a grin on my face, I tear my eyes from Leo and hold my glass up in the air.

'A friend of mine *very* recently told me that it's the people who make the place,' I declare. 'Burgau has the scenery, it has the weather, it has the food, it has the wine – but, for me, this place truly is made by its people. So here's to you!'

The guests cheer, raising their glasses.

'Oh,' I add, quickly, holding up my hand, 'and if, when the article comes out, you're pissed at anything in there, blame my editor. If you love it, it's all me.'

I receive a satisfactory wave of laughter before an enthusiastic round of applause. I attempt to make a beeline through the crowd for where Leo was standing. I have to speak to him; I don't want to wait any longer. But I'm delayed in making my way through the bar, getting caught up in conversations with people I pass and by the time I reach the back, he's not there. I crane my neck to try to see him, but he's nowhere. After waiting a good amount of time to make sure he's not just popped to the loo, and having checked with Adriano and his friends, none of whom know where he is, it dawns on me that he may have left.

'Screw that,' I mutter under my breath, furious at him as I march out the door.

He's not getting away with slinking out of here without saying goodbye. Not after the time we've spent together, the way we've talked, how intimate it's been. He might be too cowardly to talk about it, but I'm not – and I won't let him be, either. So, if I have to nip out of my own leaving drinks to walk all the way to his flat and have out this goodbye, then I bloody well will.

Walking down the rickety wooden path from the bar to

the pavement, I have a wobbly moment on my heels and almost go over, groaning at the thought of walking all the way to his in these shoes. Why couldn't he storm off after yoga when I was in trainers? Selfish prick.

A figure alone on the beach catches the corner of my eye.

I stop to squint at them and when they put their hands in their pockets, staring out at the ocean, I know it's him. I can see that mop of unruly hair all the way from over here.

Crouching down to undo my shoes, I loop my finger through the ankle straps and then start making my way across the sand to him. He doesn't notice me approaching until I'm practically right behind him.

'Hey,' he says, turning in surprise.

I glare at him. 'Leo! What the fuck?'

He frowns, confused. 'What?'

'You stormed off without saying goodbye!'

'No, I didn't.'

'Yes, you did. You left there to come over here without saying anything to me!'

The corners of his lips twitch. 'You're saying I should have bid you farewell before walking a few metres across the beach?'

'Don't try to twist this back on me,' I huff, narrowing my eyes at him. 'You haven't said a word to me all night. You've been purposefully avoiding me.'

He drops his eyes to the sand, digging the heel of his foot into it.

'What was I supposed to think? I wasn't going to assume you'd temporarily sauntered off to brood on your own over here.'

He can't fight a smile. 'I wasn't brooding.'

'You're on a beach, staring out at the ocean at night.'

'I was thinking.'

'That's what brooding is, pretty much. Just throw in a frown – and you had one of those on,' I say accusingly.

'Fine,' he sighs. 'I'm sorry. I didn't mean to drag you from your party. And I'm sorry because of me you had to take off your shoes. They're very nice.'

I sniff, folding my arms. 'All right, that comment earns you some points. What are you doing over here?'

He shrugs. 'Thinking. I told you.'

'Thinking about *what*?' I ask, exasperated.

He brings his eyes up to meet mine. 'You,' he says gently. 'And what you said in your speech.'

I hesitate, a wave of guilt lurching through my stomach. 'Okay I… I realise I may not have been as subtle as I should have been. Maybe that bit about the village capturing my heart was a bit over the top. But look, Leo, it's okay, I've always known that this is where it, you know, comes to an end, this thing between me and you, and if by making that comment, I've made you feel uncomfortable, then—'

'That's not what I mean,' he says abruptly.

'Oh.'

He fixes me with his determined gaze. 'What if it didn't end?'

My breath hitches. 'Leo—'

'Hear me out,' he requests, taking a step towards me. He licks his lips, his forehead furrowed as he searches for the right thing to say. 'Do you remember when we were here for Anna's party and we were in the back room searching for wine—?'

'When you pretended not to know anything about it?'

'Just to have the chance to talk to you more, yes,' he says, brushing that off impatiently with a wave of his hand. 'Do you remember what I said to you then? About why I felt unnerved by our chat on the beach.'

'You… you said that I made you forget yourself,' I answer quietly.

He nods, his expression softening. 'Yes. It's true, you make me forget myself. That made me a little scared at first. But now…' he takes a deep breath in, before puffing all the air out his cheeks '…it makes me fucking terrified.'

The silence that falls between us is broken only by the sound of the waves rolling and breaking as they near the shore, the kind of comforting background noise I've become accustomed to over the last three weeks. But I don't feel comforted now. I've never been more on edge, frozen to the spot as I wait for him to explain what the fuck he's talking about.

'I'm starting to understand what that means,' he continues, his shoulders relaxing a little, as though it's a relief for him to say this out loud. 'It means that for the first time in my life, I'm with someone who doesn't make me feel like I need to be anyone more than I am. So I don't care that it's only been a few weeks, I don't give a shit about playing it cool, because the thing is,' he breaks into a wide grin, his eyes twinkling at me, 'you make me fucking happy, London. Deliriously happy. So happy, I genuinely do forget myself.'

I realise that my mouth has dropped open while he's been talking. I'm staring at him in disbelief, my heart thudding at an alarming speed, my stomach knotting.

Oh my God.

'I don't want to say goodbye to you,' he adds, a fierce

determination in his eyes. 'And the reason I've been avoiding you tonight is because I've been torn about how to possibly handle everything I'm feeling whilst looking you in the eye and wishing you luck before you get on a plane away from me tomorrow. Then, your speech...' he swallows, giving a nervous smile '...it gave me a bit of hope. Maybe you feel the same too.'

My blood is pounding so loud in my ears, I'm not sure I'm hearing him right.

And I'm way too stunned to form any kind of words right now. The way he's looking at me, so earnest and sincere, his eyes bright with excitement, it's more than my brain can handle. My mind is racing, desperately trying to make sense of what he's saying.

'I'm flying to Australia in a couple of weeks to spend some time surfing there before the contest,' he continues, closing the gap between us by taking another step towards me. 'After twelve years, I'm going back to where it all began and do my best to finally make everyone proud of me.' He looks so vulnerable suddenly, his expression full of worry, his hunched-over frame radiating his self-doubt. 'I'm scared, Iris – I'm scared of the people from my past that I'll have to face, of the people I let down, of what everyone will say about me. I feel like I need to do this, but I also don't know if I can.'

My trembling hands ache to reach out to him. 'Leo, of course you can.'

'Maybe. Maybe if you were there with me.' He smiles nervously at me. 'Come with me to Australia.'

I inhale sharply.

'I know it's a lot to ask,' he says, his eyes searching mine.

'You don't need to worry about having to ask the magazine for permission or anything; I'll pay for your ticket, whatever you need. But I think... I need you out there with me. I need to know when I paddle out to the waves that you're going to be on the shore when I come back in.'

'Leo,' I croak, my voice hoarse and wavering, 'I *can't*.' I lift my hand to rub my forehead, as if that might help sensible thoughts to form into sensible sentences that will come out of my mouth. 'My work...'

'You need an ending for your feature. Why wouldn't you be there at Bells Beach to get it for yourself?'

'Toni made it clear that wasn't on the cards. Leo, even if I didn't ask the magazine to get me there, she would know what was going on between us. Everyone would know. Your mum...' I bite my lip. 'It wouldn't go down well. I can't get blacklisted by the head of Bind Inc.; it would really affect my career. And I can't take time off work like that; I'm already behind on pitching for new commissions. It would be too reckless and... stupid. It just—'

I groan, burying my head in my hands. I feel his warm fingers wrap around my wrists, gently lowering my hands so I'm forced to look right up into his glistening, brown eyes.

'Is it so bad to be reckless?' he asks, his voice low and soft. 'That's how this is meant to be, isn't it?'

'We haven't known each other that long,' I remind him, desperately trying to convince myself as much as him that this is a bad idea. 'You might get tired of me. You'd regret inviting me all the way out there. Things would go wrong.'

He's shaking his head as I'm talking, his hand reaching up to cup my cheek. 'No.'

'You don't know what might happen. It could go bad.'

'Fine, I don't know what could happen further down the line, but, for me, it's worth the risk,' he states. 'All the important things are.'

'Oh God,' I break into a wobbly smile, 'you're about to give a surfing analogy, aren't you.'

'See? We may not know each other that long, but you've sure got the measure of me. Here it is, one surfing analogy coming right up.' He grins. 'London, if I didn't take any chances, I would never ride any waves. Take this one with me.'

Exhaling a shaky breath, I close my eyes, his fingers brushing my hair back from my face. I wasn't prepared for this. It's too sudden, too soon.

'Hey,' he says, prompting me to open my eyes to gaze into his, 'you don't have to make a decision now. I know that I'm asking a lot of you. But will you think about it?'

I cannot fly to Australia to be with Leo Silva. The risk is too great; the stakes are too high. But I also can't tell him that now, not when he's right here in front of me, looking at me so earnestly, it feels as though he might crumple if I say no. I can't tell him that when I can smell the wafts of his cologne in the salty breeze, a scent so intoxicating and comforting it makes me want to jump into his arms and stay there forever.

I'll tell him when I'm back in England, when my heart isn't aching for him, when my legs aren't trembling, when the butterflies in my stomach have dissolved. I'll tell him when everything is back to how it should be and this is all over.

'Okay, Leo,' I say quietly. 'I'll think about it.'

He smiles, gently brushing his lips against mine, exhaling

softly, one hand tracing through my hair, the other moving around to my lower back and drawing me into him. I melt into him, the rest of the world falling away into the sound of the rippling water of the ocean. People from the bar would be able to see us if they looked hard enough, but it doesn't matter. Neither of us care anymore. Because for him, this is a kiss filled with hope.

But for me, this has to be goodbye.

Twenty-eight

The flight home was miserable. I tried reading my book, hoping a page-turning thriller would distract me from thoughts of him, but it didn't work so I stared out the window listening to Lewis Capaldi instead, allowing myself to feel sad. I walked through Gatwick Airport like a zombie, and the first time I managed a smile all day was when I saw that my mum had surprised me by coming to pick me up so I didn't have to get a taxi.

When she gave me a hug and I buried my face into her shoulder, I almost cried.

I hate feeling like this.

I decided to give myself a week to be down about it. I would pretend to be shut away in my flat working when I was wallowing in secret, then I would shake off Leo Silva and whatever he'd done to me and go back to being the busy, no-nonsense, positive person I am. That felt like a great plan.

But almost two weeks later and I can't stop thinking

about him. I've done well to hide it, brainstorming ideas that I've pitched to various publications and bringing in several commissions, and I've plastered on a smile to attend press events and at the pub with friends. I've even managed to find the strength to all but finish the feature, waiting for the results of the contest to add the finishing touches. That was the hardest thing to do: write about him. I couldn't hide away from my feelings then.

And my feelings... they're muddled, to say the least.

The truth is, there are things I really do miss. I miss the way he looks at me when I walk in a room, like I've just made his day. I miss how he smiles, the crinkles that appear around the corners of his mouth, and I miss his laugh, the proper one where his whole face lights up. I miss our conversations, the ones about something and the ones about nothing.

I miss sitting on my balcony writing, the words flowing freely, knowing I would get to see him later that day. I miss the way he held me, how I felt so secure and warm in his strong arms, so safe there. I miss kissing him. I miss sleeping with him. I miss the early mornings as we scrabbled to get ready so he could go surfing, laughing and teasing, both fighting the urge to jump back into bed and lose ourselves there together. I miss how he made me feel and how he made me laugh. I miss the fact that for a small period of my life, he made me reckless. *I miss him.*

He's been messaging me since I left. At first, they were cute, light-hearted updates, like *Meeting Marina and some friends to go surfing this morning, beautiful day for it!* or, *I just got coffee from your favourite place. Jealous?* Messages that didn't go anywhere near addressing the giant elephant in the room, notes I could reply to without having to imply any kind of answer. But the last couple of days, in the lead up to his trip, they've got more meaning behind them. *I can't stop thinking about you*, his message yesterday said.

I replied the truth, because he deserves it:

I can't stop thinking about you either.

Then I tossed my phone away on the other side of the bed and screamed into my pillow, wishing that things were different.

And now he's on a plane to Australia. If things *were* different, then I'd be with him. Instead, I've come to Mum's for lunch to try to distract myself from the constant ache that's slowly but surely sinking my heart.

Mum, on the other hand, is in a good mood. The house has officially gone on the market and there's been loads of interest. She's had an offer already, but after a load of eager viewings yesterday, she's waiting to see if anyone tops it.

She's ready to move on.

About ten minutes ago, I presented her with the pages I've written on the feature about Leo so far. If something is really important to me, often I'll print it out so I can bring it along and ask her to cast her eye over it to check for any glaring errors. She is thorough and won't hold back on giving her opinion – she's great at telling me which paragraphs I'm waffling my way through and which ones need a good chop. In another life, she would have made a great editor.

'Iris,' she says, coming into the living room where I'd retreated to flick through a magazine while she read the feature in the kitchen.

I lower the magazine, my face falling at her expression.

It's hard and serious, her brow furrowed, her lips pressed together in such a thin, straight line, they've almost disappeared. As she sinks into the armchair opposite me, I sit up straight.

'You hate it,' I croak, reading her expression.

She takes a deep breath. 'No, darling,' she says. 'Quite the opposite.'

'Oh! Phew.' I heave a sigh of relief, breaking into a smile. 'Jesus, Mum, it looked like you were going to say something bad then. I know you have a good poker face, but you might want to work on lightening your expression if you're pleased with something.'

'I'm pleased with the words, but I'm not sure I'm all too happy with you.'

I blink at her. 'Huh?'

'It's brilliant,' she reiterates, placing the pages down carefully on the coffee table in front of her. 'One of the best features you've ever written.'

'Wow. Thanks.' I hesitate. 'So why aren't you happy with me?'

'Because you lied.'

'What?' I look at her in bewilderment. 'What are you talking about?'

'When I picked you up at the airport, I could tell something was wrong,' she recalls, staring me down so intently, I feel like a teenager who's been caught rifling through her alcohol cabinet – which, incidentally, did happen once or twice. 'I asked you on the journey home if something had happened, and if you were okay, and you said to me you were fine.'

'Mum—'

'Over the past two weeks, when you've been moping

about the place, I've asked you several times if there's anything wrong, and you've said that everything is *fine*.'

'Yes, because everything is fine,' I say with a nervous laugh.

She tilts her head at me. 'Iris, I'm your mum. You can pretend with everyone else, and most of the time, I'll pretend along with you if I think that's the way you want to handle it. But not this time. This time, I'm calling you out.'

I give her a strange look. 'Okay, what is happening here? I have no idea—'

'You like this man,' she says, gesturing to the feature print-out. 'Don't you?'

My jaw drops open. I'm stunned into silence.

'I thought there was something different about the way you talked about him on the phone when you were out there,' she continues, swiping non-existent dust off the knee of her cream trousers. 'Something about your voice and your tone, it felt that he was... becoming someone to you. More than an interviewee. You have this wonderful ability to capture the essence of someone in your writing – it's a real talent, you know – but in this piece, you've captured more than that.'

'Mum, I don't know what you're talking about,' I croak, my weak smile wavering.

'There's so much *heart* in this piece,' she says plainly, causing my breath to catch. 'Did you fall for this young man, Iris?'

'No, no, course not.' I run a hand through my hair. 'Gosh, if you're reading all this into it then I have some *major* editing to do. I mean, I admire him, sure. He's an amazing athlete and a really... a really beautiful surfer.' I get to my feet to start pacing back and forth, too fidgety to sit still. 'And you can tell from his quotes that he's smart and kind – guarded at first, who wouldn't be? When you've been through what he has. But then, beneath that he's... he's wonderful. A really wonderful person.'

Mum doesn't say anything. She hasn't moved an inch. She's watched me tread up and down the room, her back straight, her hands clasped neatly in her lap. As ever, my mother is unfazed. I, on the other hand, have become flustered, desperate to get out of this conversation. Putting my hands on my hips, I glance at the clock on the mantlepiece.

'Anyway, time for lunch? I'm starving,' I lie, knowing I couldn't eat a thing.

'Iris, you told me that I could talk to you about the house and the divorce if I needed,' Mum says, giving me a stern look. 'I know that saying things out loud often means accepting them, and that is daunting. But I really appreciated you letting me know that when it came to it, you would be there. I need you to know that that works both ways. So, here I am, sitting in front of you, telling you that it's okay.'

'What is?'

'To open your heart to someone else.'

I swallow, my chest tightening so badly, I place a hand against it to try to ease the growing anguish. I feel jittery and unsteady. Moving back to the sofa, I lower myself down.

'If you really don't want to talk about it, then that's all right, I understand,' Mum continues. 'But if ever you do want to talk to someone, I'm here. And I don't care how much you deny it,' she gives me a sly smile, 'I know you like him.'

I grimace. 'God.' Resting my elbows on my knees, I sink my face into my hands. 'I can't believe it's that obvious in the feature. I'll have to re-write it.'

'It's not obvious to anyone but me,' she assures me. 'Flora might catch on. But to anyone else, this is a fantastic article about a remarkable person, nothing more. The thing is, I know you, Iris. I know how you write and I know how good you are at keeping a distance. But in this case,' she sighs, 'you let yourself go all in.'

'I'm such a fucking idiot,' I say, my voice muffled in my palms.

'*Language,*' she scolds sharply.

'Sorry.' I lower my hands to look up at her with an apologetic smile. 'Mum, I made a big mistake.'

'How so?'

Deciding to give in, I exhale, slumping back on the cushions. I have to admit I already feel a small sense of relief that someone else knows. Carrying this around for the past few weeks has taken its toll. Finally, I get to talk about him. About what he's meant to me.

'I think there was an attraction between us quite early on, a bit of... tension, you know? A spark,' I begin, chewing on my lip. 'We got to know each other a bit better and when he let me know that he was interested, even though I knew I shouldn't even consider the idea, I couldn't... I couldn't help it.' My mind flits back to the moment in the lift and a thrill rolls down my spine at the memory. 'I let him know that I liked him too.'

Mum nods. 'I see.'

'And it was great,' I say quietly, my stomach clenching.

'It was fun and romantic and... perfect. We both knew it couldn't last, though, for so many reasons. It never should have started in the first place. I was such an idiot to let myself...'

I trail off.

'Fall for him?' Mum suggests.

My eyes fall to my lap. I don't need to answer for her to know that she's hit the nail on the head.

She doesn't say anything, waiting patiently for me to go on.

'It had to end. It just had to.' I sigh, bringing my eyes up to look at her. 'He invited me out to Australia.'

Her eyebrows lift just a tad. I honestly have no idea if she's surprised or not.

'He said he'd pay for my ticket and everything.' I sigh, a weak smile breaking through before I can stop it. 'It was very sweet, what he said when he invited me. All these really lovely things about how he knew it was fast, but he didn't care, he'd never felt so... happy. He asked me to think about it.'

'And have you?'

'I didn't have anything to think about.' I shrug glumly. 'It's a no, obviously.'

'Why is that?' she asks breezily.

I stare at her. She stares back. *Is she out of her mind*?

'Mum, you *know* why,' I emphasise, utterly astounded by her calm demeanour. 'I can't casually pack my bag and hop off to Australia with a surfer for a bit.'

'Personally, I think that sounds rather lovely.'

'*Mum.*'

'Iris, you travel all the time for work,' she says, brushing aside my astonishment with a wave of her hand. 'You've never really felt at home here in London, to be honest.'

I snort. 'Leo would disagree with you there. Having met me, he'd be the first person to tell you that I'm a city-mode kind of person. I'm London born and bred; this is where I'm meant to be, it suits me and just because I like somewhere else, doesn't mean—'

'London is a part of you, of course, it always will be, but it's not where you have to make your home if it doesn't feel right,' she cuts in impatiently.

Stunned at her abrupt statement, I shut my mouth.

'You've never found your place here is what I mean,' she continues brazenly. 'You've searched, but it's never been right, has it? But none of this really has anything to do with an invitation to join someone in Australia for a few weeks. You're a freelance writer; you can work from anywhere. Would there be any harm in you joining him?'

'Um, *yes*.' I throw my hands up in exasperation. 'You seem to be forgetting that he is the subject of an article. Think about what Toni would say! She would know that something was going on if Leo himself pays for me to go out there. Also, let's not forget that Leo Silva is Michelle Martin's son. Do you really think she'd allow this?'

'You're two consenting adults,' Mum says in a blasé manner. 'If anything, she might be pleased that her son is dating the brilliant and beautiful journalist she picked out.'

'God, Mum, we're not dating,' I groan.

'Sounds like he wants to.' She gives me a pointed look. 'You just told me he said you made him happy.' She sighs. 'Iris, does *he* make *you* happy?'

I don't know how to answer.

'Being away from him has certainly made you unhappy,' she remarks, quirking a brow. 'I've never seen you so... deflated. It's been alarming to witness you like this.'

Pressing my lips together, I close my eyes, admitting defeat. 'I've missed him, yes,' I say so quietly, I'm not sure she'll be able to hear me across the room. 'Maybe if things were different – if he wasn't him and I wasn't me – then yeah. He might make me... happy.'

'Iris Gray, you're making excuses and you know it.'

My eyes snap open at her. '*What?*'

'You're not Romeo and Juliet,' she says wearily. 'People meet at work all the time. Once the article is published, there's no reason you can't date. Toni might get a kick out of being the person who brought you together – it's quite a nice story: the interviewer and the interviewee.'

'It's unprofessional.'

'It's life,' Mum counters. 'Sometimes, you don't meet someone in the right place at the right time, but that doesn't matter. When it happens, it happens. It's too rare and special to shrug off and forget. As for Michelle Martin, if her son is happy, I'm sure she would be.'

'She owns magazines I write for. If she thinks that I've been unprofessional, she could tell her editors to stop commissioning me.'

Looking me dead in the eye, Mum leans forwards. 'Then who would be being unprofessional?'

A burst of nervous laughter bubbles up my throat before I can stop it.

To be fair, she's not wrong.

'Michelle Martin is the sort of person who would put

her business before any personal feelings,' Mum says with a wry smile. 'If she wants the best person for the job and you are that person, then she's not going to stop you. Besides, if you're worried, would you need to tell her the truth while you were out in Australia? It's perfectly feasible that you'd be flying out to be there for the final contest and finish your article. You don't have to tell her anything else and then if things got more… serious as time went on, you could deal with that then. Keep it under wraps for now, see what happens.'

I can't believe this is happening. Mum is actively encouraging me to go to Australia to be with Leo. I never would have guessed that this would be her reaction, not ever. I wonder if she's got a bit caught up in the fantasy of it; maybe the divorce is playing with her emotions a little and she's not herself. I feel obliged to remind her of the facts.

'I've only known him for three weeks,' I say firmly. 'If I were to fly to Australia, things would be intense and then they could go really bad. This is a whirlwind romance, Mum, and that might not end well.'

'The long, slow, thought-out romances don't always end well, either,' she says with a shrug. 'You don't get to decide how it's going to go before it's even started. You can't run away from the threat of heartbreak forever. Otherwise you miss out on all the good stuff. It's always worth the risk, Iris.'

I swallow the lump forming in my throat. 'Is that how you feel about you and Dad?'

She gives me a small smile, her eyes glistening. 'Yes, that's how I feel. Things didn't end how I hoped, but look where I am. I'm here with *you*. That means all of it was worth it.

I don't regret any of it.' She hesitates. 'But I do know that if I'd turned your father down when he first asked me out, I'd have regretted that. I'd have always wondered *what if?*'

I nod, not quite trusting myself to speak.

'Iris, your head has always been in charge. Don't you think it might be fun to give your heart the reins for a little while?' she asks lightly.

'Mum,' I whisper, 'we're talking about a trip to the other side of the world.'

'Rather an elaborate date, but it's fun! Certainly different,' she says, a playful smile on her lips. 'I admire his ingenuity.'

I snort, appreciating her lightening the tone. This conversation has zapped all the energy out of me.

'There's another roadblock to this anyway. I can't bring myself to accept his offer of paying for everything,' I admit wearily. 'The idea of me jetting off on his credit card without any thought to my work, ignoring how it might affect my career – something about it doesn't sit right with me. But my bank balance isn't screaming it's in the mood for an expensive trip to Australia.'

'Yes, well, my Iris relies on no one but herself; you've always been this way.' Mum sighs and finally pushes herself to her feet, drifting over to where I am and placing her hand on my cheek. 'But you don't always have to be in it alone, you know.'

'I know,' I say gratefully, my eyes brimming with tears as I look up at her. 'Thanks for the talk, Mum. I appreciate it.'

She smiles down at me and then drops her hand, pulling down on the hem of her blouse to straighten it.

'Right,' she says briskly, marching towards the door. 'Lunch time.'

We don't speak about it again for the rest of the day.

The following evening, I'm attempting to find something mindless on Netflix to watch to distract me from making important life decisions when there's a knock on the door.

Heaving myself off from the sofa, I plod over to open it.

'Mum!' I say, stunned to find her there waiting for me.

'Hello, Iris,' she smiles, bustling past me into the hallway.

'You didn't tell me you were coming over.'

'It was a surprise,' she says, her eyes flickering to the flattened cushions on the sofa. She tries to hide her disappointment, but I can see it lurking there.

'Okay, great.' I put my hands on my hips. 'I've already eaten dinner, but if you want some food or anything, I can—'

'I'm not here to eat, Iris; I'm here to tell you something,' she says, a little flustered.

That unnerves me because my mum doesn't really get flustered, not often anyway.

'Has something happened? Is it Dad? Are you okay?'

'I'm fine, everything's fine,' she says, swatting my questions away with her hand. 'But I've been thinking about our conversation yesterday.'

I groan. 'Mum, do you really want to talk about all that again?'

'Not really,' she says abruptly. 'I thought we should probably do something about it, instead. Or rather, *I* might be able to do something.'

'*Okaaay?*' I say slowly, folding my arms. 'What did you do?'

'Something very unlike me. Something I should have done a while ago. Something reckless and spontaneous and something that quite potentially has overstepped the mark.'

My eyes widen with horror as she rummages in her bag to get her phone out.

For a terrifying moment, I wonder whether she might have called Leo or Toni or even Michelle Martin, but the logical part of my brain assures me she wouldn't go that far.

Would she?

After scrolling for something in her emails, she looks up at me, a wide grin on her face, her eyes twinkling with excitement and mischief.

'Iris, I-think it's about time that you and I grab life by the balls,' she states, before showing me the screen of her phone that's displaying a flight booking to Melbourne. 'How would you feel about coming with me on holiday to Australia?'

Twenty-nine

Hey, can you do me a favour?

Flora

Name it

Don't go into labour early
I have to go away for a bit

Flora

Got it
I'll tell the baby to stay in there
You travelling for work again?

Yeah. Sort of

Flora

Where are you going?

Australia

Flora

WHAT?
Oh my God
You're going for him, aren't you
IRIS ARE YOU GOING FOR LEO???

It's complicated

Flora

No, it's not
Oh God you've made me cry

No, don't cry!
I won't be away forever

Flora

These are happy tears
I'm so happy for you!
I knew he was The One
Ever since you told me about him carrying you from the sea
Oh God I'm crying again
My emotions are out of control

I'm primarily going out there for work

Flora

Sure, yeah, for work
When are you leaving?

Now

Flora

NOW?

I'm at the airport

Flora

THIS IS SO EXCITING

You use capital letters too much

Flora

YOU WON'T DAMPEN MY SPIRIT
I'M TOO HAPPY FOR YOU TO CARE
THIS IS GLORIOUS!

Ffs
How do I get you to stop using caps?

Flora

WHEN YOU ADMIT IT

Admit what?

Flora

YOU KNOW WHAT

We're boarding, got to go
I'll message when I land xxx

Flora

FLY MY FRIEND! FLY TO HIM!

Australia has fast become one of my favourite places in the world. I've only been here a day, but I totally get why people come here and never leave. Melbourne is such a stylish and cool city, and the people seem to be the friendliest in the world; everywhere you go, they're giving off such a warm, easy-going, vibrant energy. We haven't made it to the beaches yet, but I already know they're going to be spectacular.

Ever since we got on the first plane, Mum has been living her best life. She sipped the champagne brought to her by the flight attendant, giggled her way through a couple of rom-com movies, and slept well thanks to her silk eye-mask and ear plugs. She had prepped and brought an entire flight skincare routine for both of us to abide by so that we descended from the plane with glowing faces, and when we landed early morning in Melbourne and headed to our hotel, she didn't 'give a hoot' if I was tired and jet-lagged, she had booked a 'fabulous' place for brunch. She was really taking this whole grabbing-life-by-the-balls thing seriously. Apparently, there isn't a moment to lose.

After a stroll through the streets of Melbourne, marvelling at the amount that's going on here and the buzz of the city, we arrive at Top Paddock, the sophisticated restaurant she's booked, and it's there over cheesecake waffles and coconut, chia and almond granola that we discuss how best to play things with Leo from here. I haven't yet told him I'm in Australia.

'I think you message his dad and find out whereabouts he is, and then you can go there and surprise him,' Mum advises after ordering her third mimosa.

'But then what happens?' I ask nervously. 'I don't want to interrupt his training routine or get in his way. Maybe he'd rather I message him and he can work out when it's best for me to fit around his schedule.'

'Iris, you've flown around the world to be here for him. He's not going to casually message you back saying he'll have to consult his schedule.'

'I don't want to distract him.'

'He *wanted* you to be here. If anything, you'll spur him on. The competition is a week and a half away: plenty of time to get his head in the game.'

'Okay, I'll message Adriano,' I say, getting out my phone. My fingers tingling, I look up at Mum, a smile breaking through. 'I'm so nervous, I feel a bit sick.'

'Naturally,' she says, gratefully accepting her drink from the waiter. 'Nerves and nausea are classic symptoms.'

'Of what? Surprising someone out of the blue?'

She shrugs, but doesn't elaborate. I don't push her for an answer either, afraid of what that answer might be. But I do take her advice and message Adriano to let him in on the secret. It was obvious before I left Burgau that he'd got wind of what was going on between me and Leo – since I'm here, it's a matter of time before he gets firm confirmation.

He replies in a matter of minutes. I'm so jittery, I jump out of my skin at the vibration of my phone, and then relax, laughing at the intensity of his message, all capital letters that I hope expressed his excitement, unless he's done it by accident:

WELCOME TO AUSTRALIA IRIS!

His next message buzzes through straight away:

Leo is going to be so happy

I feel warm and fuzzy, like a sparkler has been lit in my stomach, the excitement ever so slightly starting to overwhelm the nerves. Adriano gives me Leo's address, a holiday house rental in Torquay near Bells Beach, and says Leo will be there this evening. He promises to keep his lips sealed about my being here.

'Now, you mustn't worry about me for the next couple of weeks; I want you to focus on whatever is going on with you and Leo,' Mum insists, sitting back and giving me a stern look. 'You have to be brave, Iris. You have to see where this leads.'

'And what will you get up to?'

She exhales, her eyes gleaming. 'For the first time in my life, I'm going to see where each day takes me. I'll see the sights, do some exploring, a bit of travelling around. I have nowhere to be, no one to see, no one to speak for and no one to compromise with – it's just me making decisions for myself.' She hesitates. 'It's frightening, but I think I might enjoy it.'

'You're in the right place for that kind of adventure.'

'Oh yes, where better to remember how to spread my wings than here in majestic Australia,' she muses. 'I think I'm going to like it here.'

After getting a train followed by a taxi, I finally arrive at Leo's Torquay beach house that evening. Having slept badly on the flights thanks to the butterflies that had set up camp in my stomach ever since I accepted Mum's invitation to come here, I was seriously lagging after breakfast, so Mum let me traipse back to her hotel room for a nap while she checked out some of the city's art galleries. When my alarms went off to let me know it was time to get ready before I left for Torquay, I was so groggy, I considered delaying surprising Leo until tomorrow, but then I thought about how big his smile might be when he opened the door to me and I practically launched myself off the bed and into the shower.

Now I'm here outside his holiday let, I've never felt more awake.

'Oh God,' I mutter under my breath as I carefully make my way up the path that leads to the bright-blue front door, 'please let me have made the right decision.'

When I reach the door, I take a moment to gather my courage. Standing outside in one of my favourite pairs of black block heels, an olive-green dress with a deep neckline, and a light denim jacket, I drop my shoulder bag onto the porch. It feels a little embarrassing to rock up at his house with an overnight bag – pretty presumptuous actually – but I don't fancy travelling the two hours back to Melbourne in a slinky dress first thing in the morning if he needs me to leave when he surfs.

I raise my hand and knock on his door.

It takes him a few moments, but eventually, it swings open and there he is. Leo. *My* Leo. He's so gorgeous, so tall and broad, his hair so thick and wild, so sexy standing there barefoot in a white t-shirt and dark-green board shorts. My resident stomach butterflies are going wild. Fucking hell, *how* did I ever walk away from him?

He starts on seeing me, his eyes widening in shock.

'Hey,' I say, offering him an anxious smile.

'*Iris*,' he says like he can't quite believe it.

'I hope you don't mind me showing up unannounced, I was in the area, so...'

I think he's too stunned to acknowledge my weak attempt at a quip. He's still holding the door with one hand, staring at me wide-eyed.

'I thought about it,' I continue, balling my hand into a fist to try to hide my trembling fingers, 'and I would quite like to come with you to Australia. If the offer still stands.'

Another joke that doesn't quite land.

His mouth is open, his expression remaining bewildered. I start to wonder if this surprise was such a good idea. Maybe I should have given him a bit of warning. While he tries to compute my presence, I carry on rambling, filling the silence.

'I flew over with my mum. Turns out she wanted a holiday here. Such a strange coincidence. I wanted to surprise you;

I hope that's okay. I messaged your dad and he let me know where you were staying. I only flew in this morning, but I... I had to see you.'

His mouth closes now to form a small but definite smile, his eyes glinting. He drops his hand from the door to his side.

'I've been thinking about all those things you said to me on the beach in Burgau and I realised I never actually... uh... told you how I felt.'

I pause, my heart hammering against my chest, part of me wondering whether I'm actually going to do this. And then the other part of me goes, *hell yeah*.

Like Mum said, I have to be brave.

'You make me happy, Leo,' I blurt out finally, and God does it feel good to say it out loud. 'I've been a wreck without you. I have no idea where this is going, which frightens the crap out of me, but you're right, it's worth the risk. And I know you love a surf analogy, so here goes. In short,' I grin as his eyes sparkle at me, 'I want to ride this wave with you.'

'Oh, London,' he breathes, his eyes falling to the ground as he breaks into a grin, before he lifts them to fix me with a hot, blazing gaze, 'I'm going to give you the ride of your fucking life.'

He strides forward and scoops me up into his arms, my hands flying round his neck as he presses his lips to mine. Relief, happiness, excitement – it all bursts out from my aching chest and flows through my body as I arch into his, clutching to him for dear life as our kiss deepens, his tongue gliding against mine, his hands roaming all over my back with his fingers spread, like he's checking that I'm a real-life human version of me and not some kind of mirage.

Whatever happens now, I won't forget this kiss. Not ever. It's so full of hope, so giddy it's almost clumsy, our teeth nipping, our tongues clashing. I can't get enough of him, I want him closer, I want to inhale him, to overdose on his smell, his taste, I won't let him go.

To my dismay, he insists on breaking away from me momentarily so he can bend down to pick up my bag, shoving it inside the door before he swiftly returns to where he left me, crashing his mouth against mine where it belongs, and spinning me round to guide me inside, kicking the door shut behind him as he goes.

'Fuck, I've missed you,' he growls against my lips and I give a satisfied moan, before his hands drop to my thighs to lift me up, my legs wrapping around his waist.

As he carries me in what I assume must be the direction of the bedroom, I thread my fingers through his hair and press my lips against the corner of his mouth where those pretty crinkles form, trailing them along his jawline, aching to devour every inch of him that I have access to. When he lowers me onto the bed and eases his weight down on top of me, he kisses me deeply while I claw away at his t-shirt until he gets the message, kneeling up between my legs to pull it up over his head. He runs his hands slowly up my thighs, pausing to take a good look at me. He grins, that warm, easy, dangerous smile of his that makes my body burn.

'I can't believe you're here,' he says, and the affection in his voice takes me by surprise. He leans forward to hover over me. 'Say you'll stay.'

'I'll stay as long as you want me,' I whisper as his lips graze against mine teasingly.

'Then you should have brought a bigger bag.'

He smiles, and the kiss becomes slow and sensual, the heat pulsing between my legs, my lacy thong growing damp with anticipation. His tongue glides against mine and his hand moves down to the hem of my dress, pushing it up so he can slip his fingers beneath my underwear. The groan of pleasure that emits from his throat when he feels how wet I am turns me on even more and I kiss him back greedily, my hands splayed over his broad shoulders, gripping into his taught, flexing muscles. When he moves his hands to my hips and sinks his teeth into my lower lip, I moan, arching my back into him, grinding against his erection.

'*Fuck*, Iris. Do you know how often I've thought about this since you left?' he asks huskily, his mouth pressing against my throat, my skin prickling with heat beneath every kiss as he makes his way down the neckline of my dress. 'You've haunted me. You and your fucking perfect body.'

'I may have thought about you once or twice,' I say, smiling playfully.

He chuckles against my skin, the vibrations of his voice covering it in goosebumps. When he lifts his head to look at me wickedly, I know I'm going to pay for that comment.

Nudging the shoulder straps of my dress down my arms with his fingertips, he frees my arms before peeling the dress down from my body, taking my thong with it until they're both off over my ankles and shoes. Before he takes my shoes off, he takes a moment to look at me, naked but for my bra and heels, the muscle in his jaw twitching as his eyes flare with longing. The heels come off next and last to go is my bra, my skin prickling with excitement as he unclips it and tosses it to the side of the bed.

Done undressing me, he begins to kiss the insides of my thighs, his lips moving agonisingly slowly up to my hip bone, my legs falling open wider for him. My blood is swirling with heat and when he reaches up to palm at my breast, my nipple taught in his grasp, I whimper, lifting my hips up off the bed.

'Was it really just once or twice you thought about this?' he murmurs.

I can hear the smirk in his voice, before he grasps my hips and traces his tongue down from my belly button, his teeth grazing and searing my skin as he moves lower and lower.

'Maybe three or four times,' I choke out, my heart pounding.

'Hmm, interesting,' he says in a low voice. 'Maybe you didn't want it enough.'

When his tongue drifts across my clit for a split second, I almost buck into him, I'm so wound up. His hand comes back to my breast, squeezing it and driving me out of my fucking mind. He's toying with me. Just like I toyed with him.

I've met my match.

'Okay, fine, I thought about you a lot,' I pant desperately, moaning as he rewards my honesty, applying just a little more pressure with his tongue. '*Fuck*. All the time. All the fucking time, Leo. Why do you think I'm here?'

As his tongue swirls on my clit, he lets out a satisfied groan and I tip my head back, gasping at the flutter of sensation, my hands flying over my head, nails digging into the headboard of the bed, pushing it against the wall with a thud.

'Oh my God,' I moan, as he slides two fingers in, and I clench around him, my body writhing, my core tightening as the agonising sensation builds and builds.

It doesn't take long for him to bring me close to the edge and then I'm falling, floating, closing my eyes as I give in to the hot burst of pleasure rippling through every muscle in my body. Gasping for air, I let the tingling feeling subside as he makes his way up to me before I pin him on his back and press my mouth against the warm skin of his chest.

'Your turn,' I tell him.

I slide my hand over every ridge and dip of his rock-hard abs to the top of his shorts, a thrill running through me when I notice him swallow. Pulling his shorts and boxers down his muscled legs and dropping them to the floor, I sweep my hair back so it won't get in the way as I kiss my way down from his neck over his throat to his chest, my hand wrapping around his hard length and stroking him. He groans, his muscles tensing and quivering, his breathing growing more ragged as I move down to replace my hand with my mouth, my tongue circling the tip before I take him in and suck.

He inhales a sharp breath. 'Holy *fuck*.'

Wrapping my fingers around the base of him, stroking and sucking in tandem, his tortured groans become louder and more desperate, heat gathering between my legs as I acknowledge how turned on I am to be the one to give him this pleasure.

'That feels so good, so fucking good,' he grunts through clenched teeth. 'God, shit, I'm going to come.'

'Not yet,' I murmur as I pull back, keeping my hand wrapped round him, my lips grazing up the warm, solid skin of his stomach. 'I want you to come inside me.'

I hesitate, my chest tightening as I realise I need to ask a question.

It's awkward as fuck, but it has to be done.

'You haven't... been with anyone else since I left, have you? It's totally okay if you have, I don't need details or anything, I just want to know if we need a condom.'

I consider how I'd feel if he said we did need to use one to be safe and a sharp jolt lurches in my stomach: irrational anger, desperate hurt, *raging jealousy*.

He props himself up on his elbows to look at me. 'No, I haven't been with anyone else.' His lips curve into a smile. 'I was waiting for you.'

As relief floods me, I can't fight a smile, quirking a brow at him. 'What if I'd never shown up here?'

'Then I guess I would have been waiting a long time.'

I sigh, my heart thrumming. 'I think I was always going to show up eventually.'

'I know.'

Moving up to straddle him, I gently press my mouth to his, my hands pressed flat against his chest. He tangles his fingers in my hair. There's something different about this kiss. It's slow and sensual and caring. It's weighted with meaning, an unspoken agreement of what this is, what it could be. I dig my teeth into his soft, full bottom lip, letting out a sound of approval.

'I'm obsessed with your lips,' I murmur against them.

'I'm obsessed with you.'

He crashes his mouth against mine and I respond to the

surge of passion by grinding my hips, feeling him pulse beneath me, moaning into his mouth. He tugs at my hair and I roll my hips against him once more, sending both of us into a wild frenzy. Our mouths become hungrier and more demanding, nipping, tasting, licking. He rolls me off him onto my back and moves his hand down to sink his fingers into me, a low, guttural sound emitting from his throat as he feels how ready I am for him.

'Fuck,' he growls.

'I need you now,' I whisper in response, arching into him.

He doesn't hang around. As he buries his face in my neck and slowly pushes himself into me, his free hand finds mine, and lifts it back behind my head, his palm flat against my wrist, pinning it there against the headboard. My breath catches at the full feeling of him sinking into me, the pressure and the pleasure that builds with every roll of his hips.

'God, I've missed this feeling,' he's murmuring into my neck, his raspy voice almost drowned out by the pounding of blood in my ears. 'There's only you, Iris.'

He starts with slow and controlled movements, sending shivers down my spine, each deep, considered thrust generating powerful waves of pleasure that roll through my body. Our breathing becomes shallow and ragged, and his rhythm intensifies.

Groaning expletives as his hips rock into me faster and rougher, my muscles clench around him and he frees my hand, lifting his head to look down, his eyes blazing at me. I drag my nails over his shoulders, but then he moves to lift my leg, hooking it over his shoulder and when I bite my lip and smile, my eyes fluttering shut at the incredible sensation of the angle, he thrusts into me deeper and a long moan falls from my lips.

'Oh my God, you look incredible,' he mutters, his skin glistening with a thin sheen of sweat. 'So fucking beautiful.'

It occurs to me that this might have been the sort of thing he was imagining during our yoga classes together, fantasising about angling and stretching me this way. I hope so, because I'll now be thinking about this whenever I have to lie back and lift my leg up, remembering the feel of his shoulder rubbing beneath my calf, the way his eyes are glazing over with pleasure. His hand returns to the heat building between my legs and when he rubs my clit with the perfect pressure, I almost lose it, my body clenching with need. He groans helplessly as I tighten around him.

'I'm close,' I just about manage to say, feeling breathless as I hurtle closer and closer to the edge with every thrust.

When I tip over, he falls apart with me, the pulsing of his length inside me only intensifying the pleasure further. Crying out in pure ecstasy, I clench and flutter around him, the sensation spilling and flowing into every inch of my body, leaving me trembling and shivering beneath him. He collapses on to me, burying his face in my hair and kissing my neck before rolling onto his back to lie beside me.

We take a moment to catch our breath, lying side by side.

'That was incredible,' he says in a daze, lifting his hand to push his hair off his forehead. 'Fucking hell.'

I lean over to kiss him on the cheek, before forcing myself up off the bed to go to the bathroom. I flash him a grin. 'Coming here tonight was a good surprise, right?'

'Good? That doesn't even come *close*.' He exhales,

shaking his head, his eyes fixed on me as I go. 'Best surprise ever.'

Thirty

'Have you seen this?' Leo asks, reading something on his phone at the kitchen table. 'The headline reads: *Battle of the Surf Has-Beens*. It's about me and Ethan, and it's got this really shitty tone to it. The bloke who's written it is laughing at us. Mostly at me.'

I move to stand behind where he's sitting, wrapping my arms around his collarbones and resting my chin on his shoulder to read the article. It's the first day of heats for the Rip Curl Pro Bells Beach competition and he was up insanely early – it's still dark out. This is the first time I've seen him sit down and he's already fidgeting.

'Stop reading those stupid articles. There's loads of good ones about you, saying how excited the surf world is to welcome you home. Everyone is talking about you.'

'Talking about how washed-up I am,' he grumbles.

'No, talking about how you're a *hero* to a lot of the surfers competing today,' I correct, grazing my lips against his cheek. 'They just want to see you surf again.'

'A *has-been*,' he repeats in a low, resentful mutter. 'Fucking hell, I know it's been a long time since I was in the game but it's brutal to read that about yourself.'

'Which is why you shouldn't be reading anything about you at all. It's toxic. Who cares what people like that think? Come on, Leo, you know those articles are written and published by morons who just want clicks,' I remind him, kissing down his neck.

'Morons like my mum?'

My lips pause on his skin, and I lift my head back to peer at his phone again. 'This is one of your mum's magazines?'

'Their online site, yeah,' he sighs, turning off his screen and setting his phone down.

I straighten, resting my hands on his shoulders and rubbing them. 'Hey, she has a few trashy magazines on her books and she can't check over everything they publish, especially online. Trust me, stuff like this is probably written by a junior writer in like five seconds before it's shoved up online and they start writing about the next thing. Seriously Leo, she'll have nothing to do with this.'

'I know,' he says, closing his eyes and tipping his head back. 'Fuck, I'm nervous.'

'Nerves are good. You want the adrenaline to be ready and alert. I've never been in a surf contest but I'm guessing nerves are normal.'

'It's not just the contest,' he admits, opening his eyes to gaze up at me. 'My mum's going to be there.'

I move to pull out the chair next to him. He grasps one of my hands as it slides from his shoulder, lifting it to his hips and kissing along my knuckles. For the past couple of weeks here, it's been like this – any time we spend together, we seem to be always touching, as though terrified the other one might slip from our grasp.

Not for one moment have I regretted getting on that plane to Australia, I only wish I hadn't wasted time moping about in London while I came to a decision.

Victoria is a breathtakingly beautiful setting – spectacular cliffs along the coastline, long, sandy beaches, sparkling, blue seas – and when I've not been taking in the sights, I've had plenty of time to work out here on various commissions while Leo's spent long hours of the day surfing, working out, practising yoga and meditation, and sketching when he needs a break from all the surf stuff. Some of my favourite moments have been the quiet ones in the evenings when he's needed some downtime. I've been working at the table while he's sketched on the sofa. I can't wait for him to meet Flora; they can chat about art together. The thought of him getting on with my friends makes my heart do an excitable little flip.

Sports reporting has been a little harder for me to do because of the time difference, but I've made it work, staying up if I need to watch a specific event to report on, and interviewing people over zoom to get one or two quotes. As far as Toni is concerned, my coincidental trip to Australia is a wonderful surprise that we can turn to our advantage: I'm there to witness and capture the climactic point of the feature *and* she doesn't have to pay a penny for me to do so. Toni's not an idiot. She is suspicious, especially considering I've not just gone anywhere in Australia, I happen to be in the Bells Beach area – but when the good outweighs the bad where the magazine is concerned, she'd rather not know the gritty details.

Mum's been having the best time travelling the country and sending me daily updates and photos, and around Leo's training, he and I have been making the most of being together in this happy, enchanting, exhilarating bubble. We've sat on the porch of his beach house in the evenings, talking and kissing, letting him unwind after an exhausting day; I've had dinners with his dad, who seems over the moon that I'm here to stay, and has embarrassed Leo countless times by harping on about the improvement in his surfing because I'm here now so 'his heart is full'; and at the end of each day, Leo and I have spent the nights, bodies entwined, falling asleep in each other's arms. We've had so much fun and laughed so much together, my jaw is constantly aching.

The truth is, every moment I'm with him, I fall harder and harder.

And seeing him like this today, nervous and fragile, I realise that I want to always be the one to comfort him when he needs, to protect him from the bad out there. I've fallen way too far to ever come back unscathed. I should be freaking out about that. I should be worried about what that means, what I'm exposing myself to. I should be being more sensible and careful, more practical and guarded. I should be terrified.

But I'm not. When I find myself thinking like that, I hear his voice in my head:

A lot of 'should's being thrown around here, London.

I'm not listening to the 'should's. Instead, I'm going with my heart. For the first time, I'm embracing uncertainty, letting Leo take my hand and drag me head first into a freefall. And I know it's early days, but so far, I can safely say it's the best thing I've ever done. I feel lighter but stronger, more powerful and confident; my head is clearer, my writing is flowing better, my creativity coming faster. The world is that bit brighter.

He might just turn out to be the best thing that's ever happened to me.

As I sink down into the chair next to him, I clasp one of his warm, strong hands in mine, meeting his gaze.

'Has your mum messaged to say she's going to be there today?'

'When her publicist got in touch to talk to me about your article, she mentioned that my mum would be out here around the time of the contest filming scenes for her documentary. She's hosting some big gala event or something.'

'Toni, the editor at *Studio*, mentioned the documentary.'

'Yeah, well her publicist phoned me later to say that she'd come support me in as many heats as possible,' he reveals. 'That feels big for me. She hasn't watched me compete since I was about fifteen.'

'*What?*' I don't mean to sound so surprised, but I can't hide it. 'What about the years when you won World Champion? Those tours were in your early twenties, weren't they?'

'Yeah.' He exhales a deep breath, his knee shaking impatiently beneath the table, his body raring to face today. 'I get it, though. Those contests take place all over the world. She was working all the time; she couldn't just fly over to Hawaii or Brazil or Fiji or whatever, you know?' Drawing his hand free from mine, he folds his arms across his body, a defensive, self-preserving position. 'Obviously, I would have liked her to have wanted to be there. At the time, most of our contact was when her office would send me warnings about my "embarrassing behaviour" once the contests were wrapped up.'

He heaves a sigh and then his expression brightens with hope.

'But she's making the effort to be there this time. She wants to support me. I've got my shit together now, so I'm going to make sure it's worth her while. Kind of cool that it's back on our home turf.'

'Leo,' I say gently, 'you're surfing Bells Beach again for yourself, no one else.'

'I know that. But, when I walk down those steps to the beach, it's nice to know that she'll be on the hill or on the beach with the rest of the crowd.'

I offer a weak smile, keeping my mouth shut on this one. I can't work out if it's a good thing that, after all this time, it's so obvious that all he wants to do is make his mum proud of him.

He claps his hands against his knees before jumping to his feet. 'I've got to get moving.'

'You need anything?' I ask, pushing myself up.

'Yeah, I do actually,' he grins, taking a step towards me and clasping my face in his hands, his mouth descending onto mine.

My heart somersaults as his tongue strokes against mine, my hands digging into his back, our bodies pressed against one another's. A tortured groan rumbles up his throat before he draws back, breaking the kiss and running his hands up and down my arms.

'Better?' I check, grinning stupidly up at him.

'Much.'

He reaches down to grasp at my arse, slapping it playfully

before he saunters off to another room. I roll my eyes, putting my hands on my hips.

'Well,' I sigh, 'I'm glad I can help in *some* way.'

'You do more than help, London,' he calls back over his shoulder. 'You inspire.'

I can see for myself now why this contest is a big draw for surf fans: with the dramatic sand-stone cliffs curving around the beach, along the top of which spectators can find a good spot to watch the action on the waves below, Bells Beach is a natural amphitheatre.

After his warm-up this morning, Leo is desperate to get back out onto the waves. I can see it in his bright expression and fidgeting body language as he stands with his father in his wetsuit, looking out from where we're standing at the top of the cliffs, discussing the water. I'm waiting to the side, soaking in the buzzing atmosphere as the surfers chat and mingle with their supporters. Despite it being the break of dawn, the energy here is electric.

Adriano smiles warmly at me as he leaves Leo to have a moment to himself, stepping back to ask how I'm feeling.

'Good,' I say, wrapping my jacket around me a little tighter, before I lower my voice a notch to add, 'Nervous, but don't tell Leo that. Are the conditions good for his heat today? I don't really know what you're looking for.'

Adriano nods, rubbing his hands together. 'Yes, it's a great start to the competition. Perfect Bells off-shore winds, we're looking at six- to eight- footers this morning, hopefully the odd bigger set. The swell was very big yesterday – eight- to ten-foot faces – so it peaked then, but the conditions will be very pleasing for the rest of the week.'

'Okay, so... good waves?' I translate.

'Good waves,' he confirms, shooting me a smile.

'Remind me how this all works again. Will Leo be surfing first?'

'One of the first heats, yes. They're starting with the men's opening rounds. So he'll compete in a heat with another two surfers, three in total out there in the water together. Each heat is thirty minutes and you can surf as many waves as you like; there's no maximum. You have to choose carefully, though, because of the time limit. The surfers are scored by the judges on each wave they surf out of ten. They then add together each surfer's two best scoring waves to give them their heat total – this is out of twenty. The top two surfers go through to next heat.'

I grimace. 'But one of the three is eliminated from the competition.'

'No, they go into the Elimination Round. The surfers who place last in *that* one are then out.'

'Okay, so even if he doesn't score top of his three this morning, he still has a chance of going through to the next round.' I chew on my lip, my forehead furrowed in concentration. 'How many rounds are there?'

'This is the Seeding Round and then, as mentioned, you also have the Elimination Round – then they go into one-on-one heats for the Round of thirty-two, then it's the Round of sixteen, then we have the Quarterfinals, Semifinals and eventually the Finals.'

I blow the air out of my cheeks. 'It's going to be a busy few days.'

He nods. 'Yes. Of course, you also have to take into account that the competition relies on the natural elements so we're working around the best swells, waves, the wind and the tides – we need to have the right conditions to compete.'

'So we don't know if this is going to be wrapped up in five days or twelve?'

He quirks a brow. 'The weather keeps us on our toes. But, it's looking good to start.'

'Can I ask a stupid surf question?'

'You could never ask me a stupid question when it comes to surfing, Iris!' he insists, clapping me on the back. 'I love that you are interested. Go.'

'When I watch people surfing, they all look good to me unless they, you know, properly fall,' I point out. 'So, how does a judge tell that one surfer is better than another?'

'They are scoring on a few different things,' he tells me, gesturing to the surfers in the water warming up. 'They're looking for speed, power and balance. Then the manoeuvres: the variety and combination of those manoeuvres, how well they are executed, how interesting they are, things like that. But also, the judges take into account the conditions – how difficult they are for the surfers to face. And how committed are the surfers to a wave? The worst is when a surfer gets a good wave but they do not make the most of it.' He flashes me a knowing smile. 'I never have to worry about that with Leo. Remember what I said in Meia Praia? He plays across the wave. Beautiful to watch, beautiful.'

Grinning back at me over his shoulder, Leo comes to join us, his eyes brimming with excitement. I'm trying to work out what he's reminding me of and then I realise it's that video I watched of him when he was a grom: laughing with Ethan, dreaming of a lifetime of doing nothing but travelling the world to surf the best and biggest waves together.

'I think it's going to be a great day,' Leo says, biting his lip.

'You will make it so,' Adriano says, grabbing his son's arm and squeezing it. 'No matter what the result, have fun out there this morning.'

He glances at the ocean. 'If I remember to.'

'You grew up on these waves, Leo; you know what to look for. No one reads them like you,' Adriano tells him sternly. 'Remember how far you've come.'

Leo cranes his neck to look over our shoulders at the rest of the crowd mingling around the area and making their way down to the sand. 'Have you seen Mum yet?'

Adriano's smile falters, but he does well to haul it back into place before Leo notices anything amiss. 'Not yet, but I will look out for her.'

'I don't want her to miss my heat, that's all. I did message her publicist yesterday with a rough schedule of the day.' He winks at me. 'You'd have been proud of my organisation skills, London.'

'She'll make it in time,' Adriano assures him, his eyes flickering to me.

'Yeah, course,' I chip in. 'If she said she'll be here, I'm sure she will.'

He nods, still intent on looking out for her, his eyes scanning the sea of faces. 'Yeah, you're right, I'm being—'

He stops, his whole body tensing. His eyes widen and his jaw ticks. Thinking it must be his mother to prompt such a reaction, I spin round. But it's not Michelle Martin standing just metres away, it's Ethan Anderson. He is shorter than I expected. I think, knowing nothing about them, I assumed all pro surfers to be as tall as Leo, but he looks like he's just under six foot. He also looks younger than he is, a fair-haired, baby-faced man with piercing blue eyes that are fixed on his famed rival.

The sudden tension is palpable. Others have noticed the face-off and are slowing down as they pass by, gaping at the two of them. Leo's hand twitches before balling into a fist. His forehead furrowed, he parts his lips as though he might speak. But then he closes his mouth into a hard, straight line. His eyes dropping to the ground, Ethan turns away and moves along, striding towards the famous stairs that lead to the beach.

Adriano sighs.

'Don't say it, Dad,' Leo snaps, a dark cloud shadowing his expression.

Holding up his hands, Adriano shrugs. 'I wasn't going to say a thing.'

'I'll talk to him when I'm ready.'

'Okay, okay. I know, son.'

Leo looks so troubled that I reach out to take his hand in mine. He turns his attention to me, his frown softening as I gaze up at him.

'When you're out on that water, nothing else matters,' I remind him, smiling encouragingly. 'Forget him, forget your mum, forget us, forget everything else. Like your dad says, read the water and go where it tells you.'

He takes a deep breath, leaning forwards to kiss me gently on the lips.

'I'll see you afterwards,' he says softly, before turning

away to grab his surfboard where he left it propped up and make his way down the steps to the Red Bull Athletes Zone.

Adriano follows him, raising his eyebrows at me, and I realise that we both got a bit caught up in the moment there. We've never kissed in front of anyone before. I blush furiously, quickly checking around to make sure Michelle Martin and her camera crew definitely aren't there. I'm glad they're not for my sake.

But for Leo's, I hope they show up soon.

A wave comes and Leo goes for it.

My breath catches. I've already had to watch the other two in his heat surf a couple of waves and, as far as I could tell, they did very well. I thought he might be facing Ethan this round, but Adriano explained they were in different heats. All being well for both of them, they would face each other much further down the line.

The action is being projected on a big screen, or spectators can watch from one of the many vantage points high up on the cliffs, but I've opted to sit amongst the crowd on the beach, peering out at the three tiny dots bobbing on the water. Adriano is watching from a viewing platform where he can spot the rhythm of the sets coming in easier, but I wanted to be as close as possible, on the sand ready for when he comes out of the water.

Plus, the atmosphere down here is amazing. When AC/DC's 'Hells Bells' started playing through the speakers at the beginning of the first heat, I thought someone had sabotaged the sound system, but it turns out that it's tradition at Bells

Beach for the song to play at the beginning of the first heat of each day to pump up the competitors and the crowd.

All I can say is, it works a bloody treat.

I felt so excited and empowered by the end of the song, I could have grabbed a surfboard and raced out there to shred some waves myself.

Thankfully for everyone, I found the willpower to resist.

And now that it's Leo's turn, I'm a bit more subdued. I'm too nervous to speak or cheer, my heart thudding hard against my chest. The other two surfers hold back as Leo has priority, watching him paddle forwards before he pops up and takes off. I'm unable to take my eyes off him, my chest squeezing so tight, I can't breathe.

He glides so fast, so effortlessly, so *powerfully*.

He's magic out there.

My shoulders relax as I watch him carve across the face of the wave, whipping his board around when it skirts across the lip as the water curls, the white foam cheering him on at the heel of his board. His technique and commitment to each turn is breathtaking to watch as he glides along the water. It's a much bigger and better wave than his competitors took, and he's playing with it, dancing along its surface as it swells.

Speeding up to the lip of the wave, he takes flight.

I gasp as he spins in the air, a full rotation, before his board glides down the white water of the wave. The crowd on the beach erupts into cheers and applause. My hands are clasped over my mouth as the wave comes to a foamy finish and he dismounts from his board, before the jet ski arrives to take him back out there.

Fuck me.

I don't need to hear the points he just earned to know that's going to be one hell of a good score. What a start to the contest! I've never seen him surf like that. I don't know what propelled him to pull out all the stops – seeing his rival Ethan again, the thought of his mum in the crowd somewhere, what his dad said about having fun, being here in Bells Beach after all this time – but something has put fire in his belly and my God, that was breathtaking to witness. *Has-been my arse.* He just performed better in his first wave than anyone else has in these heats all morning.

'Leo Silva is back, baby!' a fan yells out nearby, prompting another round of applause from the crowd.

'You better believe it,' I mutter to myself, grinning from ear-to-ear as I spot him back on his board in the distance, watching the swell and reading the water.

Thirty-one

On the evening before the third round of heats – Round of sixteen – Leo checks his phone to find an email from his mother formally inviting him to her black-tie ball, celebrating the launch of Bind Together For Our Oceans, her new fund that will support projects dedicated to restoring and conserving marine ecosystems.

Dear Leo,

Congratulations on your continued success in the Rip Curl Pro Bells Beach stop of the World Surf League Championship Tour. Although my various work commitments here in Australia have prevented me from attending the early heats, I hope you can attend tomorrow night's event at The Langham Melbourne. Invitation attached.

*Please RSVP to the email address stated on the invitation
by tomorrow morning at the very latest.*

*Your presence would be much appreciated – Leo, I
would love to see you.*

Mx

Sitting on the sofa next to me, my legs lounging across
his lap, Leo is watching me as I read it through, studying my
expression. I do everything possible to give nothing away,
reading the email out loud with a neutral expression and
in as emotionless a tone as I can manage. The room falls
silent as I open the attachment, checking out the elegantly
designed invitation. It looks like it's been sent from a
member of royalty.

'What do you think?' he asks when I lower the phone.

'What do *you* think?'

He drops his eyes, his hands tapping lightly on my
knees. 'It looks like a nice event. Very grand. I'd have to
find a tux.'

'You would.'

'I did miss a call from her publicist this afternoon. She
left a voicemail.'

'What did she say?'

'A lot of it was her gushing about how well I'd done in
the first two heats, how my mum was really happy for me
and disappointed that she'd been forced to miss them. Then
she went on to say that I would be receiving an invitation to
this event and it was completely her fault that I hadn't been

sent one before – sounds like she thought Mum had asked me and Mum thought her publicist had asked me.'

I nod, my eyes fixed on him. 'Classic mix-up.'

'She said Mum was excited that I would be coming.' He lifts a hand to rake it through his hair, leaving it sticking up all over the place in an adorable way. 'At least I know now why she didn't show at the last few heats.'

'True.' I glance back down at the email. 'It's quite formal language.'

'That's just how my mum communicates,' he explains. 'But she did add at the end that she'd love to see me. That's, like, *big*.'

My lips twitch into a weak smile. 'Yeah? I can understand that. My dad always messages quite formally.' I watch him as he heaves a sigh. 'What are you thinking? What do you want to do?'

'I don't know. I should turn it down. I've got Round of sixteen tomorrow, so I'll be tired from that, and I should stick to my early nights. I should be unwinding, getting my head in gear for the next round if I'm lucky enough to get through.'

I tilt my head. 'A lot of "should"s being thrown around here, Leo. What do you *want* to do?'

He chuckles, turning to look at me, his head resting back on the cushion. 'You're so happy to throw that back at me, aren't you?'

'Ecstatic.'

'I think I want to go,' he says, his forehead creasing as though he's confused by his own decision. 'It's been a long time since Mum and I were in the same room. Things have changed and this event is clearly a big deal for her. I want to be there.'

'We'd better find you a tux, then,' I say, passing his phone back to him.

'We'll get you a dress at the same time,' he says, grinning when I blink at him, puzzled. 'If I'm going to this thing, you're coming with me.'

I pause, my stomach rolling with nerves. 'Are you sure that's a good idea?'

'I'm sure,' he says firmly, before shooting me a mischievous smile. 'It's about time you met your boss.'

I'm a sucker for Leo's laidback beach style, but my God, he looks hot in a tux.

I was so nervous, I was kind of dreading the ball – we were wandering into unchartered territory here, considering we were still meant to be under the pretence of my following him to Bells Beach in the name of the *Studio* article – but then I see him in his tux and I almost melt right there on the spot. Maybe this will be a fun night after all.

I meet him at the hotel just in time for the event. Preparing for the ball this afternoon has been wildly chaotic and very expensive – as soon as Leo finished his heat this morning, blowing the competition out the water, I waited to congratulate him on winning but then didn't hang around. I left him with Adriano and got a taxi to the train station, making my way to Melbourne to shop for a gown and get my hair and make-up done.

I threw my credit card at the time-limit crisis and Melbourne came up tops. It didn't take me long to find the perfect dress for the occasion: a dark-green, plunge, halterneck evening gown. With my hair expertly styled into a loose updo, wavy tendrils framing my face, and heavily mascaraed eyelashes paired with bold red lipstick, I finished the look with thin, gold dangling earrings and a pair of towering stilettos.

When I clock his jaw drop as I step out of the taxi, I relax into a smile, pleased to see he approves of my choices. The credit-card bill is worth it.

'You look beautiful,' he says in wonder as I approach him. His gaze running down my dress and back up again, he meets my eye and swallows, his throat bobbing. 'God, you look *unbelievable*. I can't believe I get to walk in there with you.'

Hoping the bronzer is working well to hide my fierce blush at his reaction, I reach out to take his hand, leaning in to kiss him on the cheek, careful not to smudge my lipstick.

'You were amazing this morning. I swear, Leo, you have such a strong chance of winning this contest; everyone was saying it. I'm so proud of you.'

'Iris,' he breathes, still taking me in, 'I couldn't give a shit about the contest right now. I'm about to spend the evening with the most beautiful woman in the world.'

Letting go of my hand, he holds out his arm and I gladly take it, smiling at the doorman, who greets us with a tip of his hat as we head through the glass doors of the hotel, through the grand lobby to The Clarendon Ballroom.

'Remember, we agreed not to tell your mum about us,' I remind him in a hurried whisper as we join the other guests filtering into the event. 'We're colleagues.'

'Not with you in that dress, we're not.'

'I'm serious, Leo,' I say, giving him a look. 'You did explain that to the publicist when you RSVP'd and asked for a plus one, right?'

'Yes, stop worrying,' he assures me. 'Even if nothing was going on between us, I still wouldn't be able to take my eyes off you. No one else will be able to, either.'

I exhale, my breath shaky, betraying my nerves. It would be a big enough deal meeting Michelle Martin in any scenario, but showing up on the arm of her son feels particularly bold. My hope is that she's going to be too busy hosting and focusing on catching up with Leo to pay much attention to me.

Once we're in, I don't hesitate to take the glass of champagne I'm offered, while Leo accepts the mocktail option. One of the girls on the door said she'd let Michelle know Leo had arrived, so we linger amongst the guests at the back, admiring the lavish setting with its sparkling chandeliers and extravagant flower displays. Music is being provided by an orchestra at the other end of the space. No expense has been spared.

There's a camera crew working the room, all dressed in black, doing their best to move around and get involved without disturbing the conversations between guests. I assume they're collecting stock images of the night for Michelle's documentary.

'Do you know anyone else here?' I ask, glancing around the room.

'No one. Not exactly my usual crowd,' he says with a wry smile.

'At least you'll have something in common to talk about should we mingle.'

He tugs at his collar. 'What's that? How restraining a bow tie is?'

'I meant the ocean,' I laugh, swatting his hand away. 'It's a fund to protect and conserve the oceans, right? Stop fidgeting; you look sexy.'

'When can I undo this thing?'

'Not yet. You've been in it all of five minutes. Although…' I hesitate, looking up at him beneath my heavy eyelashes '… you would look even sexier with it untied and your top button undone. I think I'd like to see that.'

A mischievous glint appears in his eye, his hand finding my waist. 'That can be arranged. What are you doing after this?'

Giggling, I nudge his hand from my hip, glancing around to make sure that no one's watching.

It's lucky that Leo and I get on so well, since we're left to our own devices for a while. We bide our time, reading through all the boards they've set up by the door that provide information about the project and statistics about the ocean.

'This initiative is seriously impressive,' I comment, sipping my champagne. 'Your mum must be very passionate about the ocean. Also, as if there's 1,625 different species of fish in The Great Barrier Reef! I can maybe name, like, four types of fish.'

'Go on.'

'What?'

'What are the four types of fish you can name?'

'Fine. Tuna, salmon, sea bass… and cod.'

His lips curve into a smile. 'You're naming the ones you eat, aren't you.'

'Goldfish!' I add on excitedly. 'And that Nemo one.'

'Clownfish,' he tells me. 'Well done, London, you got five and a half.' He gives me a stern look. 'Only half a point for "that Nemo one", since that's not the actual name of the species.'

'Bet you're full of random fish facts.' I roll my eyes. 'Why is it that you have these random animal facts squirreled away in your brain?'

'I like animals,' he answers simply. 'If I learn something interesting about them, I try to remember it.'

'I still can't believe you said I was like a meerkat,' I sigh.

'If I remember correctly, it was you who said I was making you out to be like a meerkat,' he corrects all smugly. 'I only agreed that it was a good animal to be compared to.'

'I should compare you to an animal and see how you like it,' I mutter.

He strokes his chin thoughtfully. 'I think I'd be a manta ray.'

'What? You don't get to choose!'

'Calm, curious, graceful – a creature that inspires a sense of awe and peace.'

I snort into my glass.

He continues, undeterred, shrugging in the face of my mocking: 'It makes sense that I would be a fish.'

'You just said you'd be a manta ray.'

'Exactly.'

'That's not a fish.'

'Actually, the manta ray is classified as a cartilaginous fish.' He shoots me a grin as I stare at him, bewildered. 'There you go. Now you know six and a half.'

*

We've been here half an hour and we still haven't seen Leo's mum yet, so we make the decision to work our way around the room to try to find her.

'She's probably got caught up talking to everyone she tries to pass,' I say to Leo above the music, weaving around the glamorous guests. 'When you're the host, everyone is here to see you. She'll be in a hurry to get to you, but she won't want to be rude to others who catch her attention on the way.'

Finally, I spot her.

In an elegant, long-sleeved, black gown and a statement diamond necklace, Michelle Martin is holding court in a conversation with two middle-aged men, holding a glass of champagne and clearly in the middle of a story, in which her audience is enraptured. Her golden-blonde hair is expertly curled, her brown eyes accentuated with liquid eyeliner, and she oozes confidence and self-importance. You could never have heard of her but one glance and you'd know that *this* is somebody.

Leo follows my eyeline and tenses. His spine straightens, his shoulders rolling back as though he's standing to attention. A fierce protectiveness rages through me as I witness his reaction. Suddenly, it's not important if his mum pays attention to me or not – but she better pay some fucking attention to her son.

It takes her a few moments but eventually, she glances in our direction and double takes. She acknowledges Leo with a thin-lipped smile, holding up one of her fingers to signal she'll be over in a minute. She takes her time to finish her current conversation and then turns away from us to signal for someone to come over. A man all in black with a headset appears at her side and she says something to him, whilst gesturing in our direction. Glancing our way, his eyes light up and he nods eagerly. He says something into his headset. Michelle doesn't move, taking a sip of her champagne, surveying her guests.

I'm confused. She definitely saw Leo and she's no longer distracted by a different conversation, so I wonder what she's waiting for. I thought Leo said they hadn't seen each other in a long time; I'd have thought she'd be a little bit more… eager.

Then it all makes sense. The documentary camera crew appear at her side, having had to jostle their way through the guests. The man in the headset gives them instructions and then turns to Michelle with a short, sharp nod. A go-ahead nod.

Finally, she swans over to us.

Christ.

'Leo, you made it, how lovely,' she says, giving him a kiss on the cheek and standing back to look at him properly. 'On time *and* dressed for the occasion.' Her eyebrows lift in surprise. 'Goodness. I applaud you.'

It's an odd greeting, and I can't work out if it's the sort of affectionately teasing thing a mother would say to her useless-but-loveable son, or if it's a sting. It's hard to tell due to the complete lack of emotion in her tone. With one cameraman in position at an angle behind her to capture us, another roams around behind us, pulling focus on the leading lady.

'Ignore the prying lenses,' she adds, her weak smile fixed. 'They're only here for visuals at the moment. The only audio they'll use from tonight will be my speech later on, so you can speak freely.'

'Great. Well, thanks for the invitation, Mum,' Leo says, sounding different to normal, his voice more clipped and formal. He's on edge. I can't tell if it's because of the camera pointed directly at him or if it's because of her.

'It's good to see you,' she says, her eyes shifting to me, a hint of a frown. 'Please accept my apologies; I don't think we're acquainted.'

'Iris Gray.' I hold out my hand for her to shake. 'It's a pleasure to meet you, Ms Martin.'

She looks at me strangely before her eyes widen with recognition. 'Iris Gray, the journalist?'

'She's the writer doing the feature on me for *Studio* magazine,' Leo jumps in, his hand twitching as he gestures to me, and I think he's fighting the urge to put it round my waist. 'I told your team that she'd be coming tonight. They didn't tell you?'

'We've had a lot going on today,' she says, gesturing around her. She returns her attention to me. 'I didn't realise you were coming out to Australia too.'

'Neither did I at first, but it seemed like a good idea to see the competition first-hand,' I explain, before beaming up at Leo. 'It was definitely worth the trip. He's done brilliantly.'

'Yes,' she says, her eyes flickering between the two of us as Leo stares down at his shoes. She inhales deeply, giving him a tight smile. 'I've heard you're doing well. I know you have a… complicated relationship with Bells Beach. I'm glad to hear none of that is holding you back this time. I did wonder whether it might.'

Leo's jaw ticks.

I clear my throat. 'Tonight is a fantastic event,' I say brightly, hoping to draw her focus back to me while Leo can have a moment to collect himself if he needs. 'Congratulations on Bind Together For Our Oceans; it sounds like a wonderful project.'

'Yes, I've always been passionate about generating a positive impact on vulnerable marine ecosystems, and I hope that my fund and support will help to encourage the use of sustainable solutions that work in harmony with those ecosystems,' she reels off.

I know a well-practised soundbite when I hear one. It never ceases to amaze me how people in the public eye can say how 'passionate' they are about something whilst sounding not the least bit interested.

'I wanted to launch it here in Australia because I wanted to give back to the community in which I was raised,' she goes on, saying all the right things, her tone flat and meaningless, 'and tonight is an opportunity to gather together the country's leading business owners and philanthropists, all of whom are as dedicated to this project's potential as I am.'

I respond through the most convincing smile I can muster. 'It's clearly a great success. Thank you for inviting us; it really is an honour to be here.'

'Of course,' she says, pausing for a moment before she adds, 'Actually, I'm *delighted* you're here tonight.'

Leo lifts his head, a glimmer of hope flitting across his face. At last, a hint of some emotion in her voice, a faint but sure giveaway that it means something to her that he's here.

'You'll be able to work this into your feature, won't you,' she continues to me, not a glance at him. 'I'd like the project to be mentioned; my publicist can send you the press release to make sure you have the facts correct, and any images you might need of course.'

It's horrible to watch someone fighting the urge to deflate right in front of you. The way the creases on Leo's forehead appear before they're ousted in a flash, how his lips part momentarily only to be forced into an upwards tilt a moment later, the hurt that flickers in his eyes before it's blinked away. God, I hate seeing him like this. It's not fair. It's not natural.

How can he be so dismissed?

'Speaking of images, we must get a photo together, Leo,' Michelle says, reaching out to straighten his bow tie, a moment that the camera team bristle with excitement over, darting around to get the best angle to zoom in on it. 'My team are very keen for one.'

'Sure,' he mutters. 'If the team want one.'

'Ah, Peter,' Michelle says, looking over my shoulder at someone who has appeared between Leo and me. 'Thank you so much for coming.'

'Wouldn't bloody miss it, Michelle,' replies our new companion, an Aussie in his sixties with a mop of grey-speckled brown hair, bold eyebrows and a neatly trimmed beard.

His loud voice and zealous mannerisms instantly bring a fresh energy to our circle that clashes with Michelle's – he's lively, jolly and his eyes glint with excitement as he looks up at Leo towering over him.

'Leo Silva, what a privilege,' he says, holding out his hand to shake Leo's vigorously. 'I'm a big fan of yours, mate. Watched you from when you were a grom.'

'Leo, may I introduce Peter Davis, a titan of innovation

and technology projects for a long list of forward-thinking companies,' Michelle says plainly.

'You're a master of flattering introductions, Michelle,' he chuckles, shoving his hands back in his pockets, before beaming back at Leo. 'You, sir, need no introduction. I'm a bit of a surfer myself – not to your level, that doesn't need to be said,' he barks with laughter, and I smile warmly at him, grateful for his interruption to our stilted conversation, 'but I do love it when I have the time. You're retired I know, but do you still get out there?'

Leo opens his mouth to answer, but Michelle gets there first.

'Oh, Leo does nothing but surf,' she says, a hint of disapproval in her voice, adding with a sigh, 'That's all he's done for years.'

Aware that there's cameras still fixed on us, it takes all my control not to let the muscles in my face form the frown they're crying out to do. She's good at this – saying what she means without saying what she means. But it's all there, her blatant criticism seeping through her meticulously constructed words.

I can feel it, and worse than that, I know Leo can.

'Leo is currently competing at Bells Beach,' I say proudly to Peter. 'He won this morning – he's through to the Quarterfinals.'

'Crikey! Brilliant, mate.' Peter reaches for Leo's hand again to give it a vigorous shake, causing Leo to laugh despite himself. 'I didn't know you were back on the Championship Tour again. I haven't had time to keep up with it this year, but if you're there, I'll be sure to look out for you. What's Bells? The fourth stop on the Tour?'

'He's not competing in the World Championship,'

Michelle states. 'He's only back for this one contest by special invitation.'

'Ah, well, that must be a bit of an upset for the younger surfers on the Tour,' Peter says excitedly. 'Showing them how it's done, eh? You were unbeatable then; I'd say you're even better now.'

'I *was* beatable then,' Leo concedes modestly. 'Ethan Anderson proved that, and I'm not the only one providing an upset for the pros – he's not been doing badly himself at Bells.'

'Where have I *been*? Under a bloody rock, it would seem!' Peter exclaims, slapping the palm of his hand against his forehead. 'He's back as well, is he?'

'Came out of retirement to face Leo again.' I say.

Peter nudges Leo with his elbow. 'He was never really a match for you. He had power, but he didn't have your technique. I'll be putting money on you, mate.'

'Thank you.' Leo smiles, his cheeks flushing.

'What a comeback!'

Michelle gestures to me. 'Yes, Iris Gray is the journalist who is chronicling his journey for *Studio*.' Her eyes fix on mine as she offers a thin-lipped smile. 'She's clearly very... committed to the project.'

Fucking hell.

There are a few ways to react to someone when they treat you like this. When their looks and comments drip with poison to make you feel small, to embarrass or shame you. It's easy to shrink away from it, maybe even start to believe that they're right about you.

But I've never been one to run from a fight. Michelle might think she's got me down, but she can bet her arse that I can read her like a fucking book. I'm not daunted by the formidable. I was raised by them.

I hold her gaze and smile right back at her.

'Oh, there's nothing that motivates me more than a good story,' I say directly to Michelle, Peter and Leo no longer a part of this. 'When it comes to one of my articles, you can always count on me to be as thorough as possible.'

There it is: so quick anyone else would miss it, but I see the flicker of fear in her eyes. I know exactly who I'm talking to. It's time she realised who she's dealing with too.

'A journalist, eh?' Peter chuckles, oblivious to our stand-off, his chipper tone drawing both of us back into the room. 'And a Brit! You lot have always been the most ruthless when it comes to the media, isn't that right, Michelle?'

'I can't disagree,' she says gravely, still watching me as I casually take a sip of champagne.

'Iris isn't a tabloid reporter; she's a sports journalist,' Leo tells Peter. 'You've probably read some of her features.'

'I'm afraid I focus on the business pages – boring of me, I know,' he sighs, before nudging Leo. 'You ever been tempted to get into the media industry since retiring?' He winks at Michelle. 'In your blood isn't it?'

'Nah, I've stuck to surfing,' Leo says.

'Yes, that ship sailed a long time ago,' Michelle informs Peter with a forced laugh. 'I did try to get him interested in real work, but it was met with resistance. I'm sure you read all about how entertaining his choices were back then.'

For the first time in this exchange, Peter looks a little startled and then uncomfortable. He attempts to breeze over it by saying, 'When the ocean calls, you have to answer, right Leo? Speaking of which, I must talk to you Michelle about your vision for this fund; I've got heaps of collaborators excited about this one.'

She responds with a polite smile. A woman taps her on the shoulder and whispers something in her ear. I look over to Leo, who has retreated into pensive silence.

'Do excuse me, I'm needed,' Michelle says calmly to us, before exiting the conversation, followed by her camera crew.

As Peter follows suit thanks to being cheerfully greeted by an acquaintance, the woman who had just initiated Michelle's next move steps into her empty space.

'Mr Silva, I'm Jenna, one of Ms Martin's assistants,' she says hurriedly, a bright smile attempting to mask her stress. 'Did your mother mention the photo we'd like to arrange with you? I'll come find you in a bit if that's all right; we have a screen all set up to the side of the room, so it won't take up too much of your time. Thank you so much.'

Leo doesn't say anything, but she doesn't appear to need a response. She turns on her heel and scurries off into the crowd.

'Leo,' I say quietly, 'are you—?'

'Let's go,' he states, placing his glass down on the nearest table. I think I see his hand trembling. 'We never should have come.'

I knock back the last of my drink and reach for his hand. I don't care who sees, not anymore. Threading my fingers through his, I give his hand a comforting squeeze and he leads me around the edge of the room towards the door.

As we leave the ballroom, I feel a wave of relief, as though I hadn't realised how long I'd been holding my breath in there. He grips my hand tightly, striding across the lobby.

'Mr Silva!' A cry behind us comes up. 'Please! Mr Silva!'

He halts abruptly, causing me to bump into his arm, before he turns to see Jenna pelting towards us, her eyes wide with panic.

'You're not leaving?' she asks breathlessly.

'I'm afraid so,' he mutters. 'I have an early start in the morning.'

'Wait!' she pleads. 'I'm sorry, I should have organised the photo earlier. If you have just a moment, we could quickly get that done now. I'll make sure a car is waiting out the front for you so you can get off straight after. But it's very important – you see, Ms Martin noticed you leave and she's keen to—'

'She noticed, did she?' He drops my hand to shove his in his pockets.

'She'll be right here, any moment,' Jenna wills, glancing back at the door to the ballroom. When it swings open, the relief that radiates through her is unmissable. 'Ah, here she is.'

Michelle marches towards us and, naturally, the camera crew come bustling through the door right behind her, lugging their equipment, scuttling after her to keep up.

'Leo, what do you think you're doing?' she asks calmly, clasping her hands in front of her. 'You've only just arrived.'

'Actually, we've been here a while,' he corrects, barely able to look her in the eye. 'You were busy with everyone else.'

She gives him a look that says: *really?*

'I have to get home,' Leo continues, nodding to the exit that is screaming at us to run through it. 'I'm up early.'

'I understand; we'll make this quick,' she says, her eyes

shifting to Jenna. 'Go get everything set up and we'll be there in a minute.'

Jenna nods vigorously at her boss. 'I'll have that car waiting for you,' she promises Leo, before she scurries back into the ballroom.

Michelle turns back to Leo. 'One photo and then you can go.'

'Mum, I really have to—'

'One photo, Leo,' she cuts in. It's a direct order, not a request. 'I think that's the least you can do for me. Surely you can fit that into your hectic work schedule.'

Oh hell no.

That's it. That dollop of sarcasm is the last fucking straw. He doesn't need this, not now, not ever. I'm done letting her treat him like this.

I see red.

Thirty-two

'You have no idea, do you,' I snap, glaring at Michelle as I shift my body to face her full-on. 'You have absolutely no idea how amazing your son is. Well, I do, and I'm not going to stand any longer for the lack of respect you've shown him all evening.'

She stares at me. She doesn't flinch, she doesn't recoil, she responds to my sharp accusation with that iconic hardened stare. My back now turned to him, I can hear Leo breathe in sharply behind me. But I don't care. My blood is boiling, my heart pounding, my face flushed with fury and protective rage.

I'm no longer a busy meerkat. I'm a fuck-off massive, claws-out, roaring bear.

Her glacial eyes bore into me.

I glower back at her.

Bring it on, bitch.

'Would you please give us a moment?' she says, turning her head ever so slightly to address her camera crew quivering with excitement behind her, her eyes still locked with mine. '*Now.*'

Lowering their equipment, they traipse back to the ballroom, hunched with disappointment at missing out on the impromptu, legitimate, juicy bust up with their protagonist at its centre. Real-life documentary? What a load of bullshit.

As soon as the door closes behind them and the lobby returns to silence, she speaks.

'Excuse me?'

'All evening, I've listened to your snide remarks and petty put-downs, and I understand why Leo feels like he has to stand there and brace himself for impact while you go at him with all the tactfulness of a sledgehammer, but I'm not going to leave him defenceless.' I pause to take a breath. 'Michelle, do you have any idea how brilliant he is?'

She narrows her eyes at me. 'I know my son.'

'I don't think you do,' I counter. 'You seem to be happy to dismiss him, but I have spent a lot of time with this man recently and I can tell you now that anyone who has the privilege to know him would never have the audacity to brush him away. Look,' I hold up my hands to initiate a treaty talk, 'I don't want to cause a fuss, I know you're busy and you have an event to host, but I just wanted to make sure you know what you're doing. I won't speak for Leo, but I was under the impression that your extension of the invitation tonight was for you two to begin rebuilding your fractured relationship – but if you treat him like this, I'm not sure you're on the right lines.'

Her lips curl into a venomous smile. 'Am I to believe that I'm supposed to take advice from the journalist who's clearly screwing my son when she was meant to be working with him?'

The arrow flies at my chest.

It splinters before it hits.

'Hey,' Leo snaps, stepping forwards to stand alongside me, but I press a hand gently against his arm.

'It's okay, Leo,' I assure him, smiling back at her. 'It doesn't bother me for her to know that we're together. In fact, I'm relieved. I'd like to shout it from the rooftops that I am the lucky person who gets to be with her son. The bravest, kindest, most incredible man I've ever met.' I look up at him to find his eyes gleaming. 'I don't know what's really happened between you two, but whatever it is, it's led to the man you are today, Leo. And that man is exceptional.'

He exhales, his fingers brushing against mine.

'And boy can he surf,' I add, almost laughing in wonderment. I turn to grin at Michelle, her animosity no match for my radiating enthusiasm. 'I've never seen anything like it. You should see him out there. He is dominating this competition, he's surfing like he never left, and his opponents are bricking it, because they can see what's changed. Everyone's always known that he's got more talent than anyone else – that Peter guy just proved that – and it doesn't take a genius to work out that he has drive, but more than either of those things is that Leo gets more joy from this sport than any of his competitors. And that's dangerous.'

Michelle's lips are pressed together so hard, they're disappearing.

'You know I know sport,' I say, giving her a conspiratorial smile, as though I'm on TV being interviewed by a fellow commentator, 'and I know what it takes to win. You can literally see it when he's out there. The other surfers are concentrating so hard, and they're good, really good. But Leo surfs with the spirit of the water.' I glance up at him. 'I don't care if that's a wanker thing to say; it's true.'

He chuckles, beaming down at me.

'That's all very touching,' Michelle remarks drily, unimpressed. 'But you seem to be forgetting, Miss Gray, that I'm fully aware of his talents and potential. I wouldn't have sent you to profile him if I didn't think he had the ability to come across to audiences as an appealing option to cheer for. But I also know his weaknesses. I know what happens when he gives into indulgences and the consequences that follow. At the heart of it, people don't change. We are who we are, and I know him.'

The arrow hits its mark that time. Leo flinches, stung.

That's the power she wields, swiftly reducing him to the lost boy he took drastic measures to suppress and ignore, the kid who couldn't help but let his mother down. It didn't matter if he was champion of the world. Once, twice, three times, whatever. Surfing was never going to be enough for her. That title was never going to be enough for her.

He was never going to be enough for her.

My heart sinks as I watch him crumple.

'You have no idea what we've been through as a family,' Michelle hisses, her emotion coming through now. 'You have no idea what *he* put me through, what I've had to do to protect him.'

'*Protect* him?' I repeat, baffled by her delusion.

'She's right,' Leo croaks, his eyes dropping to the floor.

'Leo—'

'No, Iris, she's right,' he repeats, his forehead creased in agony. 'I didn't... I didn't tell you everything because I didn't want it in the article.' He glances up at her, before closing his eyes and lowering his voice. 'The night at Bells... when I went surfing drunk—'

'And on drugs,' Michelle mutters, lifting her eyes to the ceiling.

Leo takes the hit. 'Yep, and on drugs. The person who saved me from drowning was there at my house because of Mum. She's the reason I'm here today.'

'Sorry,' I say, frowning, 'I don't understand.'

'When Ethan Anderson won the World Championship title again, I knew that Leo would do something stupid,' she says briskly. 'I was in London at the time, but I sent someone who worked in my Melbourne office to go check on him. It was God-knows-what-time in the morning over here, but I forced that person to get up, leave his family sleeping peacefully, and check in on my son. When he got there, he saw him heading out to Bells Beach with his surfboard, swaying and clearly not of sound mind.'

The tremor in Leo's hand causes it to vibrate against my fingers. He clenches his hands in an attempt to stop it.

'He rescued him,' Michelle continues, folding her arms. 'I did everything in my power to keep the unfortunate incident out of the press, which wasn't easy, let me tell you. A lot of people involved needed... financial encouragement to keep their mouths shut. And his rescuer got a healthy promotion, too, despite being a pompous, brain-dead idiot. I paid dearly for his bump up – but that's best forgotten.' She rubs her forehead and then gives a wave of her hand. 'Anyway, that was when we all decided it was best for Leo to get away from the temptations here and move to Burgau where he could lay low.' Her eyes sharpen at me. 'There. You think I don't know my son? You are very much mistaken. I know exactly who he is. I knew his next actions before he did.'

Leo is silent, his head bowed, his hands still balled into fists.

I process this fresh information.

'You already told her about the Bells Beach incident for the article then, I take it,' Michelle surmises, sucking air through her teeth. 'I hoped that you had better sense than that, Leo – I assumed that you'd skate over the hairy details and make something up about why you quit the country, but I must have underestimated Miss Gray's capability of extracting even the most gruesome of details from her subjects.'

'Gruesome,' I whisper in disbelief, but she doesn't hear me or doesn't care.

'If you must include it then I trust that these extra additions won't make an appearance,' she says in a severe tone. 'I'd rather not be in any way involved.'

I glance up at Leo. He looks smaller somehow. Shrunken, thwarted, beaten.

Michelle heaves a sigh: the martyr who tried to stop this before it started.

'Let's move on, shall we?' she proposes, before gesturing to the ballroom behind her. 'One photo, Leo, and then you can leave.'

'No.'

I hear myself say it before I've thought it through.

Michelle starts, before her lips curve into a mocking smile. 'I was talking to my *son*.'

'He doesn't need to be a part of this,' I say quietly but surely.

Leo has lifted his head now and he's watching me, puzzled, his eyes desperately searching my expression, trying to work out what's going on. Michelle remains bemused by my insistence on getting involved, a pebble jutting out in the middle of the path she's bulldozing through. A minor inconvenience, easily flattened.

'A part of what, Miss Gray?' Michelle asks curiously, the challenge gleaming in her eyes, her smile stretching.

'Your attempts to smooth over your PR crisis.'

She freezes. Her smile evaporates.

'That's what this has been about all along, right?' I say, no longer cocky to have one over on her, not angry and raring to fight. I'm disappointed to have played a part in it and I'm sad I didn't see it before. 'The call for boycotts against your publications on social media, the shift in how the public feel about you. The Bind Inc. board is getting twitchy.'

She gulps audibly.

Bullseye.

'It was your publicity team who set up the feature,' I recall, thinking back on mine and Toni's conversation. 'They were in contact with the *Studio* editor, not you. I assumed it was your idea, but I think it was theirs. I think they've been behind all of this. You know, when I accepted this feature, I openly acknowledged that it was great for your dismal public image – but I somehow convinced myself that was an advantage, not the full motivation.'

'I don't—'

'Were you ever planning on coming to watch Leo's

heats?' I ask, cutting her off, somehow emboldened by the truth. 'You didn't phone him or message him directly. It was your publicist who led Leo to believe you'd try to be there, right? Not you.'

Leo turns to look at her, his jaw ticking. When she doesn't say anything, he prompts her, needing the answer: 'Mum?'

She purses her lips, clasping her hands in front of her again. I picture her in board meetings doing this when she's challenged, biding her time to think of a rebuttal.

'My schedule was always going to be busy, and to be honest, Leo, I... I was worried you would fail in the first heat and I didn't want to watch that – it has been a long time and there's a lot of fresh talent,' she admits. It's the first time I think she might be speaking from the heart, actually. She adds, with a satisfactory pinch of shame, 'I am pleased to have been proven wrong.'

Scrunching his eyes, he runs his hand down his face, muffling an angry groan.

'I hope to attend one of the rounds, Leo,' she asserts. 'Maybe not the Quarterfinals, but perhaps if you reach the Semifinals, I'll be able to shift some things in my schedule.'

He snorts. 'Okay. And what about tonight? Was I ever actually invited? That bullshit your publicist spun about both of you thinking the other one had asked me. Am I only here because I'm doing well? Something you didn't foresee but can happily use to your advantage?'

Her jaw clenches.

'Wow.' He puts his hands on his hips, grinning manically at the ground. 'I'm a fool. What is *wrong* with me?'

'You're not the fool, Leo,' I say quietly, looking at Michelle.

She's masking it well, her regret, but it's there in her hardened features.

'The big deal about this photo. It's a photo *op*, right?' Leo says, his eyes flashing furiously up at her. 'That's the only reason I'm here, isn't it. Your team is scrambling to save your public image, the one you've been fucking up so well recently. The big new documentary, the flashy *Studio* feature, and a photo at your big new charity launch with your beloved son. Holy shit, Mum, congrats,' he claps his hands, 'you played me so well.'

'Leo—' she begins.

'No, I don't want you to try to talk your way out of this,' he says, shaking his hand at her. 'I've always felt like a disappointment, but here we are and suddenly the only disappointment is you.'

She sighs.

His eyes harden; he's focused now, clear-minded. I could burst with pride.

'You made it clear that I owed you the *Studio* feature because of all your effort to protect my image before,' he states coldly. 'I've done that now. I've shown up to your event, your cameras have captured our heartwarming reunion. That's enough. I'm done. We're even.'

She closes her eyes briefly. 'I *was* trying to help you.'

'You were trying to help *you*,' he claps back. He sighs, softening his voice. 'You've never been happy with my choices, and that always felt like my failing, but it's not, it's yours. I wouldn't change anything. Honestly, I'm grateful to you, Mum.'

Her eyes lift to his in surprise.

'I'm grateful for what you did for me back then,' he tells

her. 'But more than anything, I'm grateful that because of you, I said yes to the feature that would change my life.' He gazes at me, reaching for my hand and taking it, holding it tight. 'It led me to Iris.'

Smiling, I reach up to untie his bow tie, leaving it hanging loose around his collar. He finishes the job, lifting his chin to undo the stiff top couple of buttons.

'Better,' I observe. 'We should get out of here.'

He looks back to his mum, growing taller as he straightens, his shoulders rolling back, his free hand sliding into his pocket as though he hasn't got a care in the world.

'Congratulations on the launch of your new initiative, Mum. I'm sure your guests are in for a great evening,' he says, giving her a brief nod.

Then he turns and, hand in hand, we walk away.

Michelle doesn't call after us and we don't look back.

Thirty-three

'We need to make a stop,' Leo tells the driver.

I turn to him in surprise. It's been a long drive from the ball back to Torquay, and although we didn't stay long enough at the event for it to be that late, it's still a long night when you're meant to be up at dawn to surf.

'Of course,' the driver says, glancing in the rear-view mirror. 'Where to, Mr Silva?'

'Bells Beach.'

'Leo,' I say frowning at him, 'please don't tell me you're planning on surfing right now. We should get home.'

'I need a moment there.'

That's it: that's all the explanation he gives me.

The driver nods and makes a turning. Leo looks studiously out of the window and we fall back into silence. We haven't spoken much on the journey, both of us absorbing what just happened, letting it all sink in as the adrenaline from the confrontation ebbs away. The only time he let go of my hand was so that he could take off his jacket, folding it onto the middle seat before he reached to thread his fingers through mine again, his jacket propping up his elbow.

I've been shooting him concerned glances that he's ignored. That's okay, I know he'll talk to me about what went down when he's ready. I stood up to Michelle Martin, a feat that I'm proud of, but will no doubt have its own repercussions. I'm not afraid, though. I know that, come what may, I've done the right thing. That's what matters. I'd rather suffer the consequences of that then look back and wish I'd done more.

But for Leo, there's so much to unpack. He's spent his life trying to please her; even when he resented her, he was still trying to make her proud. Now, he's got to come to terms with the fact that it was all in vain, that even now, she refuses to believe in him, and that ultimately, she would risk their relationship to better her public image. I can't imagine what that's like. I can't imagine how that feels.

So, I don't ask any questions or plead with him to talk. We sit in the back of the car in silence as it trundles towards the Bells Beach car park. When we arrive, Leo asks the driver to wait.

'We won't be long,' he says, as he opens the door to slide out.

The 'we' is welcome because I wasn't actually sure if he wanted me to come with him, but if I had any doubt, he squashes it quickly by appearing at my side of the car to open the door for me, holding out his hand to help me clamber out.

As we stroll in the dark, I link my hand through his arm.

'Do I need to take off my shoes?' I ask.

He smiles. 'Why would you need to take off your shoes?'

'Have you seen these heels? They're like daggers. Not very practical on a beach.'

'When have you ever been one for practicality?'

'When I'm wearing shoes that cost more than my rent. If you think I'm getting a speck of sand on these, you have another thing coming.'

He laughs, shaking his head. 'We're not going down to the beach.'

'Are you sure?' I ask, reaching for the bannister as we start going down one of the sets of wooden steps.

'I'm sure.'

With no idea what's going on here, I grip his arm for balance as we slowly descend until I realise that we're stopping at one of the viewing platforms.

I drop my hand from his arm and watch him as he goes to the edge of the fenced barrier, leaning his elbows on it and clasping his hands in front of him. His hair whipping about in the breeze, he takes a deep breath in through his nose. In the darkness, you can just make out the waves hitting the beach, the sound of them rolling and crashing in a rhythm of their own. For the first time tonight, he looks at ease again.

Hanging back at the steps, I smile, giving him a moment on his own over there.

After a while, he glances back to me over his shoulder. I take it as my cue.

My heels clacking along the wooden boards of the decking, I come to stand next to him, resting my forearms on the fencing. I sneak glances at him, admiring his profile in the dim light of the evening: his full eyelashes, the slope of his nose, the groove above his top lip, the swell of his bottom one, the strong line of his jaw. He looks so handsome, so strong and masculine with the crisp, white shirt stretching against the curve of his biceps, his bow tie undone, hanging around his collar. I wonder at how lucky I am to have found him. And how close I came to letting him go. I exhale a shaky breath.

'This place,' he says softly, gazing ahead of him, 'it has such a hold on me.'

'A good or bad one?'

'Bit of both.' He shoots me a weak smile. 'I can't work out if I love or hate it. It's where I found my love of surfing, and it's where I almost lost everything.'

I press my lips together. We fall back into silence, listening to the water. It's so quiet out here, it feels like there's no one for miles. Just me and him.

'I think it will always be a part of you,' I say quietly. 'I don't think that's a bad thing.'

He nods slowly. 'Every morning I've surfed it this contest, I've been afraid.'

'You haven't looked it.'

'I've felt it.'

'That's good.' I nudge his elbow. 'You're supposed to be afraid of the ocean, remember? You taught me that. It's, like, surfing 101.'

He laughs lightly. 'I keep thinking that if I can win this contest, I can wipe away the memories of what happened. But... I can't. My mum reminded me tonight how weak I can be, especially in comparison to that,' he nods his head in the direction of the water, 'and how quickly it can all go wrong.' He swallows, frowning as he looks out. 'Maybe I'm kidding myself that I can overcome my fear here.'

'Leo,' I begin, twisting my body to face him, 'you can't block out memories. It doesn't work like that. But you can make new ones. Your mum is wrong about you. Anyone can climb to the top, but to fall and start climbing again, that's where the real courage is.'

'My courage seems to be wavering,' he admits, his voice hoarse.

'Yeah, well, you are human,' I say with a wry smile. 'You know, in my interview with your dad, he was talking about how after one wave, there's always another one coming.'

'That's kind of... obvious.' He snorts. 'Good one, Dad.'

'Hey, you're missing the point,' I say sternly, raising my eyebrows at him. 'He was saying that there's always another *chance*. It's not over because you make a mistake. You have the choice to go again.' I reach out to grip his arm. 'You've chosen to surf Bells Beach again, Leo; do you know how brave that is? It's fucking brave.'

He breaks into a smile, his eyes dropping. 'I don't feel brave.'

'You are,' I tell him. I reach out to take his hand, turning it so his wrist is facing up and bringing it to my lips, pressing a kiss to his scar. He sighs as I let his hand fall again. 'And you were brave tonight too. What you said to Michelle, telling her how you felt – that took a lot of guts.'

'Oh, I wasn't the brave one,' he says, turning to face me, one arm leaning on the rail. 'I think you might snag that award. I've never seen *anyone* stand up to my mum.'

'She doesn't scare me.'

'No one scares you.'

'You do.'

His eyes twinkle at me as he smiles. I swallow, gazing up at him.

He reaches out to brush my hair from my face as the breeze does its best to destroy my updo, and dips his head to give me a soft, affectionate kiss. I wrap my arms around his neck, wanting him close, pressing my body into his. That musky sandalwood cologne of his smells so good, it sends heat pulsating between my legs and when I part his lips with my tongue, a groan slips from his mouth.

His kiss becomes more demanding, rougher and urgent, his strong hands roaming down the sides of my dress, following the curve of my waist, hips, back up to my ribs and round to the base of my spine. God, I love the way he touches me, how he makes me feel as though he wants to cover and devour every inch of me. It's cold out here this late, the thin satin of my dress not doing much against this breeze, but his hands are warming my goose-pimpled skin, the strokes of his tongue igniting flares of heat between my legs.

I moan into his mouth.

The sound fires up something inside of him and when he breaks the kiss, his eyes flare at me, dark, wild and searing. As our breaths come shallow and fast, I watch his gaze drop to my cleavage, the plunge design of the dress working its magic.

'Do you like this dress, Leo?' I ask quietly.

He traces a finger down the faint swell of my breasts on show, his jaw clenched tight.

'You know I do,' he says, his fingertip toying with the edge of the fabric.

I trail soft kisses up his cheekbone, my lips lingering at his ear.

'Then fuck me in it,' I whisper.

He tenses. To make sure he knows I'm serious, I take a step backwards to lean against the wooden fencing of the viewing point. His hands resting loosely on my hips, he watches as I drop my hand to the side of my thigh and I slowly begin to lift the skirt of my dress. The cool breeze hits my leg as it gradually becomes more and more exposed, the material drifting up higher and higher as I gather it in my hand. My heart is racing, my nipples hardening as I witness his eyes darken with desire and the muscle in his jaw tick as he clenches. I love watching him like this. Watching him want me.

When I've lifted it high enough, his hand falls to the opening I've created and slips beneath the hem. Relinquishing control, I let go of the dress, leaving it draped across his wrist, my hands gripping into the shoulders of his shirt. I feel like my whole body is throbbing as his fingers follow the thin string waistband of my black thong, brushing over the flimsy strip of lace between my legs to feel how damp it is.

'God, Iris,' he breathes, as I dig my teeth into my bottom lip.

His fingers slide beneath the fabric, circling over my clit. I gasp at the jolts of pleasure, begging him hoarsely for more. A surge of heat gathers beneath his fingers as his other hand holds me still at the hip, his head dipping to my neck to kiss and nip at my skin. When he sinks his fingers into me, I close my eyes and bite back a moan, knowing that we can't be too loud. Oh *God*. If he keeps going like this, I don't know if I can be quiet.

As the pressure builds, I arch my body into his touch, letting my arms drop from his shoulders to lie along the top rail of the fence barrier behind me, my fingernails clawing and digging into the wood. I don't care if I get splinters, I don't care about anything, he's too good at this.

'You look so fucking hot,' he growls, his mouth devouring mine, my hands coming back to the sides of his head, raking through his hair down his neck and making him groan.

'Fuck, Leo, you're making me close,' I whisper breathlessly.

Spiralling as he increases the pressure on my clit, I frantically reach for his belt, fumbling at the buckle. His mouth captures my short, raspy breaths, while I grapple with the button and zip of his trousers, his erection straining against the material. Gripping the waistband of his boxers, I yank them down with his trousers, nudging his hand out the way so I can wrap mine around his cock, feeling it thick and hard in my grasp, my muscles clenching and fluttering at the thought of him inside me.

His hands gripping the back of my thighs, he hoists me up, propping me against the fencing, while my legs spread to accommodate him, winding around his waist, my dress fully hitched up over my hips. He's so fucking strong, I feel so light and secure up here, knowing there's no chance in hell he would ever let me fall. Moving one hand to press against the bottom of my spine, he uses the other to guide himself to my entrance, pushing my thong aside and thrusting deeply into me. I gasp, my blazing core winding tighter as he pulls back and rocks into me again, finding a faster pace, his fingers sinking into my arse as he holds me in place, his muffled groans and pants at my neck driving me wild.

'God, you feel amazing,' he mutters, driving into me harder and faster.

My muscles tighten and tremor, the pressure builds, the angle, the pace, the fullness sending rippling waves of pleasure through my body.

'Oh *fuck*,' he says through gritted teeth as I near the edge, clenching around him.

The pressure inside me erupts and I cling to him as I come, consumed by the sensation, biting into his shoulder as my body squeezes and convulses around him. My orgasm breaks whatever resolve is left in him and I capture his groan with my mouth as he releases. He drops his head to my neck, his thrusts slowing, his breathing warm on my shoulder. As my daze clears, the setting starts to come back into focus. Lifting his head, he kisses me softly, once, twice, before he pulls out, carefully lowering my heels back onto the decking. We sort ourselves out, making sure we look respectable.

Wrapping his arm around my waist, we start to make our way back up the steps, both of us grinning like idiots, cheeks flushed, hair dishevelled, hearts glowing.

'I kind of forgot our driver was waiting,' I remark as we near the car park. 'This is going to be an expensive taxi fare.'

'It is. Good thing Jenna organised it. Actually, that's a great point: since it will be my mum picking up the bill—' He stops, turning to jab his head back in the direction of the viewing platform. 'Want to wait a few minutes and go again?'

Bursting into laughter, I tug his hand and we reluctantly head back to the car, grinning like idiots the entire way home.

Thirty-four

QUARTERFINALS *Heat 3*, Rip Curl Pro Bells Beach
Leo Silva vs Antoine Lambert
AUS FRA

The conditions aren't so favourable today as they have been. The surf size has dropped to three-to-four foot waves and there's a bitter wind whipping across the beach. Wrapped in a puffa jacket I bought this week over one of Leo's hoodies, I'm regretting wearing denim shorts today, my legs covered in goosebumps – it turns out it can get really quite cold around Bells Beach this time of year. Aside from the misjudged shorts choice, I feel like a seasoned spectator, and am sitting on the sand on my picnic blanket, armed with a flask of coffee and snacks, as well as a cap and suncream should the sun decide to make an appearance later on, as the app on my phone predicts. It feels like one of those days where you get all the seasons in one.

I'm waiting anxiously for Leo's heat to start.

Adriano invited me once again to come with him to watch from a higher vantage spot, but I like it here on the beach. If you grew up in the area like Leo, I can understand why you would love it here, but even as a visitor, it's impossible not to acknowledge that there's something special about this spectacular setting, its natural beauty maintained by the Wadawurrung people, the traditional owners of Bells Beach. Once this contest is finished, I want to drive the Great Ocean Road with Leo, I want to explore this coastline, learn everything there is to know about his childhood, where he surfed, where he swam, where he went to school. This magical place is part of him, so I want to be a part of it too.

I take a deep breath in as Leo's heat begins.

The two of them are bobbing in the water together, their hands swirling through the water back and forth as they drift up and down with the swells.

'Antoine is a great surfer,' Leo told me this morning, sipping at his energy drink, his free hand in the front pocket of his hoodie, a backwards cap on – since being back in Victoria, Leo seems to have really leant into that effortlessly sexy, laidback surfer style.

And I can't lie – I'm *loving* it.

'You're a great surfer,' I countered, before adding, 'The best, in my opinion.'

His forehead furrowed, he was too lost in his own thoughts to acknowledge my cuteness. 'He's shown big powerhouse turns this contest that judges love. He's full of confidence.'

'So are you.'

But he looked down at the floor.

I worry that the showdown with his mum affected him more than he's let on. It makes me even angrier at her that she might have dented his confidence midway through the biggest performance of his life. When it comes to Michelle, it's hard for me to say the right thing when Leo has made it clear that he doesn't want to talk about her anymore – he said he's drawn a line under it, that he only wants to focus on the competition.

'I know now who I don't need, and who I do,' he said to me in bed last night, nudging my nose with his. 'I don't need her support to know I can do this.'

Which is great, but in reality, it's always harder to let go.

And when Antoine takes the lead early on in the heat, coming in with good momentum while Leo has a slower start, I worry that he's lost the playful spirit he's found here over the past week. The first wave he takes, he can't quite get ahead of it, the wave sectioning up – when it breaks unevenly ahead of itself – and his ride is cut short. As he disappears under the white foam, I remain hopeful. It was only the first one. But his next attempt isn't much better – he does nicely, but there's little flair to his turns and carves. He seems stiffer, pushing hard through the bumps on the face of the waves. The air feels heavier today, echoing Leo's state of mind.

'Come on,' I mumble, urging him to find the fight within.

The clock is ticking down to that siren that signals the end of the heat.

He needs one good wave, I convince myself, to get back on track. He needs the water to work with him today, give him a little boost. He needs to remember that it doesn't matter what came before here at Bells Beach; what matters is that he's here now. And I hope he knows that he's not a lone wolf; he never has been. Even if his mum didn't have his back, his dad has been his number-one fan since the first time he got on a board. Marina looks up to him as a surfer and as a friend, as do all of his surfer buddies back in Burgau. Even Ethan Anderson was happy to concede that he was better than him back in that video when they were groms – he points out how amazing Leo is to watch on the water.

He needs a reminder of that.

He needs a reminder of that.

Without a moment to lose, I jump up to my feet and cup my hands round my mouth in an effort to carry my voice further, shouting his name and cheering: 'Go on Leo!'

It's a quiet moment in the heat, both of the surfers waiting in the water for the next set. Until my interruption, the beach was in a chilled state of spectators chatting.

'Go on Leo!' I repeat at the top of my lungs, clapping loudly. 'You've got this!'

He's looking out to the ocean, his back turned to the beach, but I see his head turn just a tiny bit. The crowd at Bells Beach is so great that instead of my spontaneous lone cheer being met by silent, sneering judgement, everyone else starts joining in. The beach erupts with support. They're cheering both surfers, Antoine getting as much love as Leo, a wave of whoops and whistles carrying across the water to the two of them.

As the cheer slowly dies down, I settle back on my blanket, my heart hammering with the rush of being centre stage. Leo might not have known what just happened, he might not realise that it was his name that was cheered first – but that noise from the crowd on the shore will have carried out to him and he'll know that my voice was somewhere there amongst the others, willing him to believe in himself.

That has to mean something.

Leo uses his priority to take the next wave that comes in and this time, he comes at it with aggression, power and confidence. He has a whole new energy. His first swoop across the face of the wall draws a gasp from the audience, it's so good, before he strings together a clean sequence of beautiful turns, drawing everything he can from the wave right along to the inside where he springs from the board into the foam. He comes up from the water grinning.

I sigh with relief, breaking into a smile.

'Leo Silva is back, baby,' I whisper into the wind.

SEMIFINALS *Heat 1*, Rip Curl Pro Bells Beach
Ethan Anderson vs Jude Garcia
AUS USA

SEMIFINALS *Heat 2*, Rip Curl Pro Bells Beach
Yazid Bayu vs Leo Silva
INA AUS

After a two-day delay due to on-shore winds and a diminishing swell, the day of the Semifinals has arrived. I'm as pleased as Leo that the contest is back up and running, having had to put up with his pumped-up energy for the last couple of days, fresh off his Quarterfinal win, feeling excited to keep up the momentum. The surf world has been buzzing about the way he stole the show right at the end from Antoine Lambert, whose exit interview was so gushing about Leo, it almost made me cry.

'If you're going to lose, lose to one of the greatest surfers in the world.' Antoine shrugged with a smile when the interviewer asked him how it felt to exit the competition.

Today, Leo faces Indonesian Yazid Bayu, who Adriano tells me is a high-ranking, well-rounded surfer with a smooth, stylish technique; he's also a popular showman, an entertainer who feeds off a good crowd. Surf talent aside, that can be intimidating.

The conditions are good, the waves looking big during Leo's warm up.

'How do you think Leo looks?' I ask Adriano from the steps.

Adriano watches on with a pensive expression, his eyebrows knitted together. He takes so long to answer, I wonder whether he was too focused on the warm-up to hear the question, but I don't bother repeating it, not wanting to interrupt his analysis.

But suddenly, he mumbles something.

'Sorry?' I ask, having been distracted by the cuteness of two little kids in wetsuits, following their mum, a Semifinals competitor walking down the steps with her board.

'Fierce,' he repeats, folding his arms and nodding. 'Leo looks fierce today.'

I raise my eyebrows, impressed. 'Fierce is good.'

'Yes,' Adriano says, a smile playing across his lips. 'Very good.'

Ethan Anderson wins his heat.

It's a major upset, knocking out one of the highest-ranking surfers in the world who was hoping for his first win at Bells Beach this year. My stomach is twisting itself into knots at the beginning of Leo's heat as he heads out, having been quiet and focused all day. Suddenly, it all feels very real – if Leo wins this round, he wouldn't just be facing the Bells Beach final again; he'd be facing Ethan Anderson. The organisers of the event must be beside themselves with anticipation going into this heat. Either way, this is big news: if Leo loses, they still have a former World Champion back to make his mark on the tour for one contest only. But if Leo wins? The interest in the final would surely soar to new heights. Two former champions and rivals, both here on special invitation, one last shot to win.

Fuck. This is big.

My hands are trembling, but not from the cold this time. I shove them into the front pocket of my hoodie and clasp them together, chewing on the inside of my cheek. It seems unfair that Leo's heat is second. More time for the nerves to build. To be fair, Leo looks a lot more relaxed than I feel.

So I guess it's a good thing he's the one surfing and not me.

Yazid Bayu gets things started, tackling an early wave and taking his time to carve his way along it, putting in turns and grinning from ear to ear as he rides into the shallows on the end of it, blowing kisses to the adoring crowd.

I instinctively worry that his charm and style will overshadow Leo and knock his confidence, but I couldn't be more wrong.

As soon as Leo goes for his first wave, the spectators know we're in for a good heat. Picking up speed, he attacks the lip of the wave, the spray curving in a rainbow raining over him as he turns, his surfboard like an extension of his body. I'm in awe, baffled by how it seems glued to his feet, how he can possibly stay on when he's moving that fast, manoeuvring so quickly, defying gravity every time he glides up the face of a wave before speeding down it. To a roar of approval from the crowd at his finish, Leo jumps off his board and comes up grinning, turning to blow a kiss back to Yazid, who bursts out laughing.

They're playing.

They're meant to be rivals right now, but it just doesn't feel that way. As the heat goes on, the two of them up their game, and it feels like they're showing off to each other. You can imagine what they're saying out there to each other:

'*This looks like a beauty of a wave, check this out.*'

'*Oh yeah? Not bad, but look what I can do!*'

They look as though they're having the time of their lives out there, as though they've forgotten there's anyone watching them at all and they're being scored on each wave. Even when they mess up, they don't seem to mind too much. *There's always the next wave.* My heart could burst at how touching it all is and once again, I find myself inspired by this sport and its community.

Scores are looking tight as we near the end of the heat, but I'm not sure anyone watching actually cares that much. We're all having too much fun.

Then, Yazid makes a crucial mistake.

He lets a wave go and Leo takes it.

No one can stop him now.

That's what I'm thinking when the points come in.

The fans waiting on the sand are going wild, their cheers drowning out the commentary coming through the speakers. Leo is wading in from his final wave, his hand scooping up sea water and throwing it up in the air to rain down on his head as he cries out, 'Come on!' in celebration.

My hands feel numb from clapping, tears in my eyes. He's shallow enough to start jogging in now, his surfboard tucked under one arm, his free hand raking through his wet hair that's plastered to his forehead, and he's looking for me. I know he is. He spots where I'm standing, waiting for him. His eyes light up, his smile widens, and my heart soars.

Dropping his board, he strides across the sand to lift me up, saying hoarsely, 'I'm through to the Final! The *Final*!'

Then he kisses me. It's a kiss that I will soon learn makes a great photo – water dripping off him, my hands cupping his jaw, my feet kicking in the air.

In a few minutes, it will fly around social media. It will go viral and cause Flora to phone me later when she wakes up and scream, 'That kiss is so sexy, you almost made my water break!' Naomi will message, *You found the dream surfer! (Does he make piña coladas?)* and Toni will email, *I look forward to the final draft of your article, Iris*, but then WhatsApp from her personal phone on the side, *I fucking knew it. Let me know when you're back and we'll go for wine. I will glug down a large glass of Chablis while you tell me every delicious fucking detail.*

But I don't know any of that yet.

All I know now is this kiss and how happy it makes me.

When he lowers my feet back to the sand, I hold his face in my hands and, eyes locked on him, say through a watery smile, 'Leo Silva, I never had any doubt.'

Thirty-five

'Good morning and welcome to your live coverage of Finals Day here at Bells Beach – the sun is shining, the swell is filling in, the tide is dropping out, the waves are firing and we're about to see what could be one of the greatest contests in the history of this competition. It's going to be a beautiful day here in Victoria, wouldn't you say Kristen?'

'Oh, absolutely, Matty – it's going to be a memorable one. What an honour to be here, the longest-running competition in the surf calendar, the Rip Curl Pro Bells Beach Final.'

'And the surf gods are smiling at us – we had a series of lay days earlier in the week, but then not too bad a day for the Semifinals yesterday, the conditions weren't quite right in the afternoon, but this is the morning we've been waiting for: really clean conditions on the bowl, about six-foot waves at the moment and building.'

'That's right, Matty, the swell keeps pushing in and we're going to see some great surfing, no doubt about that. It's on.'

'We should probably begin with the story that everyone's talking about [*laughter*]. Let's talk about the two finalists in the men's: Ethan Anderson and Leo Silva, both veterans of the tour, both technically retired, and they have wiped the competition, each of them taking down giant names – how did this happen, Kristen?'

'It is quite the story. These two former champions have dominated the contest and given us some monster rides. Ethan Anderson – wow, that power, that focus, he's an icon to so many of the younger surfers here. He's always been a great advocate and face of the sport, so committed, and clearly time has done nothing to dampen that drive to win. And Leo Silva [*exhale*] is it possible to sum him up, the man and his style in a few words?'

'[*laughter*] Oh, I don't think so.'

'You know, Leo has had his fair share of ups and downs out of the water – and ultimately, let's be real here, that did once impact his performance – but that's all in the past and what he's proven over the last few days of this competition is that he is in a good headspace now, and there's no denying it: like Ethan, he really is one of the all-time greats of this sport.'

'I couldn't agree more. No matter the conditions, no matter the wave, Leo Silva can master it.'

'That's it, Matty. He has a unique relationship with the ocean, he understands the way his body has to work with the board and wave; it's beautiful to watch. And from seeing him out there this week, I think one of his greatest strengths is his decision-making ability. He reads the water better than anyone.'

'You were just in the Red Bull Athletes Zone – a lot of

focus in there this morning, knowing that the champions will be crowned today?'

'Absolutely. They're focusing on winning the most iconic trophy in the sport.'

'And now for the question on everyone's lips: any tension between Ethan and Leo? We all know they're not the best of friends...'

'[*Laughter*] I think there's always going to be tension in these situations, you know, they both want it but there can only be one winner. It's natural to keep yourself to yourself. But I have to say, Matty, as I was leaving the tent, I did see Leo approaching Ethan, so who knows what was about to be said?'

'Let's hope they keep the fighting for out there on the waves.'

I watch Leo walking over to Ethan, my heart pounding against my chest. The Red Bull Athletes Zone is mostly empty – just me and Adriano here for Leo, while Ethan's coach is at the other end of the room talking on the phone. One of the presenters was milling around but she's on her way out, so I suppose if he's going to talk to Ethan in the lead up to the Final away from prying eyes, now is a good time.

Leo has been pensive all morning. I figured that was natural, it being such a big day for him, but when we were standing near the top of the steps earlier, looking out at the ocean so he could have a look at the conditions, he heaved a big sigh.

'You're going to be amazing,' I told him.

'Plenty of fun to be had today,' Adriano said.

'No matter what happens, we're so proud of you,' I added.

His forehead creasing, Leo muttered, 'I have to talk to Ethan.'

Adriano and I were both taken aback by the response, neither of us expecting that to be his line of thought. We'd shared a look but before we could comment, Leo emphasised his point: 'Before we go out there today, I *need* to speak to him.'

And then he'd gone back up the steps full of determination, his hands in his pockets.

So, I knew this moment was coming, but I didn't know when. Ever since we entered the Athletes Zone to find Ethan warming up on the exercise bike, Adriano and I have been on edge, glancing at each other, wondering if he was going to take this chance.

As he sees Leo approaching, Ethan looks confused. Then wary.

His pedalling slows, his shoulders tense.

Leo takes a deep breath. 'There's been something I've been meaning to say.'

Ethan stops pedalling altogether, straightening his back, his arms dropping to his side. He doesn't say anything, waiting for Leo to continue. Adriano and I pretend to be busy, but I'm in full meerkat mode: alert and ready to step in if needed.

'I'm sorry, mate,' Leo says eventually, his words coming out fast, as though he's pushing them out along with all the air in his lungs.

His brow furrowed, Ethan stares at him, his mouth in a hard, straight line.

'I'm sorry about the way I treated you. No excuses, I was a shitty friend. You reached out so many times, even when things were really bad between us, but I ignored your offers of help. One of the biggest mistakes of my life.'

Ethan's frown deepens. He looks down at the ground.

'I didn't like seeing you like that,' he mutters.

'I know,' Leo says.

Inhaling deeply, Ethan brings his eyes back up. 'It was a long time ago.'

'Still. I wanted to apologise,' Leo says firmly. 'I wasn't there for you like I should have been.'

Ethan nods. 'I appreciate that. Thank you.'

Leo holds out his hand. Climbing off the exercise bike, Ethan faces him properly, takes his hand and they shake. The tension in the room eases. With this simple gesture, a heavy weight begins to lift. I look over to Adriano to see he has tears in his eyes.

'You've been looking pretty good out there,' Leo comments, a smile playing across his lips. 'Any chance you've been practising since you retired?'

Ethan cracks a laugh. 'I heard the rumour you'd be here, so I thought I'd try to up my game a little. You know I always liked to kick your butt in the water.'

'I don't remember that happening too often.'

'Yeah? I'll have a go at refreshing your memory today.' Ethan grins as Leo chuckles. 'You know, mate, all that bullshit in the press about us being rivals. I never liked it.'

Leo's laughter fades, confusion flitting across his expression.

'I never liked being pitted against you,' Ethan presses, looking at Leo earnestly. 'I know that we... grew apart, but even when we were fighting, I still missed surfing together. When we were groms, you made me want to be better. You and your dad… I learnt a lot from you guys.' He nods over at Adriano, who responds with a watery smile. 'My family never got it like you did.'

Leo smiles, folding his arms across his chest. 'Some good times.'

'Fuck yeah,' Ethan says. 'Some of the *best* times of my life, catching waves here at Bells with you.'

Leo nods, his eyes twinkling at the memories. 'Same.'

'Guess we're lucky to have today, then,' Ethan says, lifting his chin. 'A chance to relive it all. It's going to be fun.' He gives Leo a knowing smile. 'The swell's looking good.'

'Yeah, we'll get some great waves today.'

'Let's hope I'll have priority on the best ones.'

'I thought we were here to have fun again.'

'It's still a competition, mate; don't get too comfortable.' Ethan grins. 'You've always been the best surfer I know, the only one to beat. There's no one I'd rather win against.'

'There's no one I'd rather lose to.'

A beat of silence passes as Ethan looks physically moved by Leo's statement, his eyes glistening. 'Yeah, me neither.'

'Whatever happens, I've got your back out there.'

Leo holds up his hand again. Ethan grabs it and pulls him in for a hug.

'Yeah, always mate,' Ethan says, clapping his back like men do before drawing away.

Having been lingering to the side of them since his phone call ended, waiting for a good moment to interrupt, Ethan's coach smiles apologetically.

'We've got an interview, Ethan,' he says, gesturing to the door.

Ethan nods and with a sharp nod goodbye to Leo, he follows him out. As they leave, Leo exhales with relief. His eyes drift to me and he smiles. He looks lighter. As Adriano dabs at the corner of his eyes, I wander over to Leo and he wraps his arms around me, the palms of my hands resting against his chest. I tip my head back to smile up at him.

'That was a nice line. The "no one I'd rather lose to" one. I'm impressed.'

'I have been hanging out with a writer recently.'

I give a soft laugh as he presses his forehead against mine, closing his eyes. We stay like that for a moment and then he takes a deep breath, lifting his head.

Turning to look at his dad, he receives a nod. It's time.

'Let's go find out how the article ends,' he says, releasing me and moving to take his board from Adriano.

'I'll be on the beach waiting for you when you come in,' I tell him.

He tucks his board under his arm. 'Promise?'

'Promise.'

As Leo and Ethan paddle out together, it strikes me that I'm oddly calm.

Usually, it's around now that I'm feeling sick with nerves, but maybe it's been the build-up to the Final that has actually been the most stressful bit. But he's here now; he made it. He doesn't have anything else to prove. Aside from the crowded stretches of sand either side of me, it feels like one of those calm mornings in Burgau when I'd watch him head out with his friends to surf. He looks relaxed, flicking the water out of his hair after duck diving through a wave, paddling just ahead of Ethan.

Despite the time difference, I've had a flood of messages from people asking me to wish Leo luck. Flora and Kieran, Naomi, Toni, and Marina, who has set up a projector and is screening it live at the bar. She sent me a picture of everyone earlier; it may be the middle of the night over there, but the place is rammed, all the locals out to support Leo. My mum is currently making her way here from Tasmania where she's been for several days.

'Tell Leo I've had a surf lesson!' she told me on the phone yesterday.

'You *what*?' I said, unable to even picture my mum on a surfboard.

'My teacher said I'm a natural,' she informed me proudly.

'That's… that's brilliant! Mum, I didn't know you were going to have a go at surfing.'

'I thought it would be a fun thing to get into. Then the three of us will be able to go surfing together some time.'

It was one of the nicest, most moving things Mum's ever said to me.

Glancing around the excited surf fans crowding the beach, I turn to look back at where Adriano is positioned halfway down the steps to the beach. His eyes meet mine and he smiles, before peering out at his boy, rubbing his hands together apprehensively.

That's when I see her.

My lips part with surprise. Michelle Martin standing near the top of the steps, Jenna tucked just behind her.

I don't think Adriano knows she's here. There's no camera crew surrounding her; there's been no fuss made about her arrival. She's easy to spot in her cream, tailored trouser suit and oversized, designer sunglasses, but it would seem that she's making every attempt to blend in and not cause a scene. As she surveys the beach, she spots me gaping at her. I think about waving, but can't quite bring myself to do it. It might be a trick of the light, but for a moment, I think I catch a glimpse of her giving me a nod.

But I blink and she's turned away, her eyes fixed on the contest.

Following her lead, I return my attention to the waves, a warmth filling my stomach. I may strongly dislike that woman, but I'm glad she's here.

The forty minutes on the clock has begun – they have that bit longer for the Final. The waves look big out there and forty minutes gives Leo and Ethan plenty of opportunity to show off what they've got. When Leo pops up for his first ride of the heat, taking a smaller wave than Ethan, he seems perfectly balanced and connected, looking as though he's barely trying as he puts in four brilliant turns with perfect rhythm, before throwing in a rotation at the end, hopping down into the white foam to an eruption of gasps and applause from the crowd. The scores come in: a seven-point ride, compared to Ethan's starting four point six.

It's a strong start, but if Bells Beach has taught me anything, it's that the tide can change. On these waves, anything can happen.

The competition carries on and no one around me is able to stay composed. There's an incredible buzz on the beach, the crowd making a lot of noise at each turn they put in, and it feels like both Ethan and Leo can feel that energy.

It might be the encouragement from the spectators or maybe he's a little inspired by Leo, but Ethan starts to push that bit harder. He's fighting back. His scores creep up and Leo is no longer dominating the Final; he's winning but not by much. It's two unbelievable performances with one difference – it's clear that while Ethan is so focused, he's stiffer, perhaps that bit more nervous, the dream of winning again after all this time within his grasp and dampening his fun. Where he's climbing the face of the wave, Leo is floating. Ethan returns to playing it safe; Leo is playing with flips.

You can see it in their movement, in their expressions, even in the way they paddle back to position after a wave: Ethan wants to win Bells, Leo's just happy to surf it.

There's not much time left and Ethan makes a decision to take a wave that Leo either hasn't noticed or isn't interested in, because he doesn't even attempt to move with it. He turns his head in surprise when he sees Ethan go for it. It's a mistake on Ethan's part: he's trying too hard, forcing turns, he tries to add in a rotation, but his foot slips and his board leaps out of his control, jutting upwards into the air. The crowd groans as Ethan is forced to dive into the wave, resurfacing and wiping the water off his face, crestfallen.

It won't affect his points – he has two much better scores up there – but time is running out and Leo is now in a brilliant position, while Ethan has to paddle his arse off to get back in time for a chance at another go.

'Leo's going to win,' I whisper, my breath shaky. 'Oh my God. He's going to do it.'

He floats out there in the water, waiting for his chance. Serene and hopeful.

When I accepted this commission, I never thought I'd end up here. There are so many things that have led to this moment that I never could have envisioned.

I never thought that I'd find myself right at home in a small former fishing village on the Algarve coast. I had no idea that I would find the courage to face my fears and swim in the ocean once more, that I would stand up on a surfboard and glide in, however bumpily, with a wave. I didn't consider I might return to London and feel like I was in the wrong place, that I might belong somewhere else.

I didn't predict that the retired athlete I was interviewing would be just as good as any current ranked surfers, that he would still be the best here at Bells Beach and prove as much. I never could have foreseen that I would stand up to Michelle Martin and risk future work to fight someone else's corner. I would have laughed if you'd said that I would end up making my way to Australia and not on my own, but with my mum, who had finally taken the jump and was travelling. Just when she thought things were over for her, it turns out they were only just beginning.

And I would never have believed you if you'd told me in Toni's office, as I gazed at the photograph of Leo Silva on her desktop screen, that I was going to fall in love with him.

Because I am. It hits me like a fucking tonne of bricks as I gaze out at him alone in the water, on the cusp of winning Bells Beach. *I love him*. All of him. And I couldn't give a shit what happens in this competition, I just want him to get his cute, absurdly firm arse back on this beach so I can tell him that. I break into a wide grin, my hands round my mouth.

I can't believe this. I really am in love with this guy. Head-over-heels, delirious-with-giddiness, too-happy-to-breathe love. Fuck me. I didn't see that coming.

Before I flew to Burgau, Mum reminded me that people can surprise you.

I just didn't think I could surprise myself.

'This is going to be a good finish, I can tell,' someone says on the blanket next to me on the beach, getting to their feet.

Everyone is standing up. I join them, my heart racing. There's forty seconds left on the clock. Ethan is only just making it back to Leo now. His arms must be tired, his chest must be aching, his legs must be burning. But the swell is the best it's been, and he's doing everything he can to get there.

'Fuck, that's going to be a good wave,' another person says.

'Watch Leo Silva show them how it's done,' their companion replies.

Standing on my tiptoes, I can see Leo is shouting something at Ethan. He's... he's waving frantically for Ethan to move with him. My smile falters as I peer into the distance trying to work out what's going on. Everyone else seems to be doing the same, a ripple of confusion washing over the crowd. Somehow finding the energy, Ethan is doing everything he can to paddle up next to Leo, who is nearest to the peak of the breaking wave.

'What's Silva doing?' someone cries, as Leo looks back to check Ethan is there. 'He has priority!'

But Leo doesn't take it. He's still yelling something at Ethan as he hangs back and Ethan flies forward, moving to pop up. It's the best wave so far, no doubt about it. It's a huge face to play on and Ethan makes the most of it. He glides and carves, cutting through the water and putting in turns with such drama and power, it draws a chorus of awestruck gasps from all of us lucky enough to see it playing out live in front of us. The wave seems to go on forever, giving him time and room to dance across it, and when it finally comes to a close, he throws in a rotation with such flair that the roar of noise from the spectators almost bursts my eardrums. It's going to be a big score. Big enough to put him in the lead.

The buzzer sounds. The Final is finished.

Ethan Anderson has won Bells Beach.

I look to Leo, still far out in the water. He must have heard the siren, but he looks unfazed, paddling calmly with the water and surfing in on a small wave.

'Silva made *such* a big mistake,' a man sighs to his friend next to me, before joining the crowd surging towards the water to greet the surfers when they come out.

Ethan waits for Leo, the two of them sharing a hug, before Ethan is engulfed by his coach and the rest of his team. The water swirling at his knees, Leo claps for his former rival and friend, while Ethan is lifted onto someone's shoulders and carried all the way to the podium, as is Bells Beach tradition.

I smile to myself. Leo didn't make a mistake. He made a choice.

As the mass of fans cheering Ethan's win drift across the beach to the podium, I stroll in the opposite direction to everyone else, making my way to Leo, who remains in the water, being hugged by his father. Neither of them look disappointed. I wait on the sand until Leo spots me over his dad's shoulder and his face lights up. Adriano glances back at me and grins, wading with Leo out of the water.

'Bet he's made you proud,' I say to Adriano as they approach.

'He always does,' he replies with a chuckle. 'I'll see you both over at the podium for the trophy presentation.'

Patting Leo on the cheek, he leaves us to join the back of the crowd.

Leo sighs, placing his board down on the sand before straightening.

'Sorry you didn't get the Hollywood ending for your feature,' he remarks.

'It's okay.' I shrug. 'I can make this work. I'm fucking good at what I do.'

He tips his head back and laughs, the proper laugh I want to spend my life chasing.

Leo Silva, you make me weak at the knees.

'You were amazing out there,' I gush, looking at him in wonder.

'I had the best time,' he says, beaming at me. 'It was a lot of fun. Brilliant to surf with Ethan again. I wish it wasn't over. I'd like to get back out there, but,' he nods to the crowd with a grin, 'Ethan is having his moment, so I probably need to stick around.'

I tilt my head at him. 'You knew that last wave was the one to catch. You had priority but you gave it to him.'

'Nah, I couldn't have surfed it like he did then. That was fucking incredible. The best man won today.'

You make me want to be better.

'Well, you may not have won but Bells Beach finalist is pretty damn good,' I reason.

'Yeah, not bad for a has-been.' He rakes his fingers through his hair, glancing over at Ethan as he nears the climb to the podium. 'Dad tells me I've got a lot of sponsorship interest and commercial opportunities flying in. And surf-lesson bookings are through the roof. Looks like the surf shop and school in Burgau is going to be safe.'

'That's great news, Leo.' I hesitate. 'Speaking of which, while you were messing around in the water out there today, I've been doing some serious thinking.'

He raises his eyebrows. 'What about?'

'Burgau. It's weird, but I ended up writing really well out there. Despite certain distractions, I was extraordinarily productive.'

The corners of his mouth twitch into a grin. 'Certain distractions can be inspiring.'

You make me laugh.

'Against all logic, yeah, they can.' I kick at the sand absent-mindedly. 'I've been thinking that maybe I could find a place in Burgau to stay for a few months over the summer. Being a freelance writer, I can work from anywhere, and since I write so well there…'

He stares at me as I trail off. 'What about that big role you're being considered for? The sports editorial director.'

'I do think it's a dream job,' I muse. 'But for someone else. I've come to realise I'd rather be out in the field, meeting my sports idols and writing their stories than making big decisions in a swanky office somewhere.'

A smile stretches across his lips. 'And you think Burgau might be a good spot to write those stories.'

'Yeah, I do. Obviously, it's just a thought, I'd need to—'

Leo reaches out and grabs my waist, pulling me towards him and dipping his head to kiss me. Winding my arms around his neck, I melt into him, sparks igniting in my chest as his arms wrap round me tighter, my clothes growing cold and damp pressed up against his wetsuit. But I don't care about that. I don't care about anything.

In this perfect moment, the rest of the world has faded away.

You make me happy.

He breaks the kiss to gaze down at me, his eyes glistening as he murmurs softly, 'I love you, Iris.'

Closing my eyes for a moment, I sigh. Then, I open them to meet his.

'I love you too, Leo.'

In the background, a cheer erupts on the beach as the famous bell trophy rings out over on the podium, the victorious clanging echoing around the cliffs and across the waves. As Leo kisses me again, he goes to lift me up in his arms, but he finds I'm already jumping.

You make me fearless.

Acknowledgements

FIRST AND FOREMOST, a huge thank you to my brilliant editor Aubrie, without whom this book would be a total mess. It has been so much fun to work with you on this project – in fact, thanks to you, it hasn't felt like work at all – and thank you for all your wonderful ideas and excellent guidance. Special thanks to the fabulous Kim, who helped me shape the plot, and continues to champion everything I do, and to Sofia for the beautiful cover illustrations. Thank you to Holly, Sophie, Hannah and the entire Head of Zeus team – I am so very grateful for your dedication, hard work and talent, and feel honoured to work alongside you all.

Without my agents working unbelievably hard behind the scenes, I would be completely lost and have no idea what's going on in my life or what I'm supposed to be doing, so huge thanks to the fantastic Lauren, Callen, Paul, and the wonderful team at Bell Lomax Moreton.

To my family and friends, as always, thank you for your endless support and encouragement, in particular during the past year, my busiest year of deadlines yet – I can't believe how lucky I am to have such brilliant, kind, hilarious people in my life. Huge thanks to Annie and James, my

Aussie experts, and to Ben, Hattie and Bono for always cheering me on.

This book is dedicated to a special group of old school friends, the Wolders girls. Life, it would seem, continues to throw things our way, often unexpectedly, never predictably, and sometimes messily – but we have seen each other through it all, laughing and joking along the way in spite of everything. The strength and resilience of the women in my life continues to astound me and inspires the boldness in my favourite female characters – my Wolders girls have a lot to do with that. Thank you for reminding me of what we are capable of and that the most important things in life rarely come easily – but the juice is worth the squeeze.

Finally, to my wonderful readers and fellow romance nerds, thank you for choosing *Ride the Wave*. I can't tell you how much I loved writing this book. I loved every moment of it, and I mean that. These characters have captured my heart in a way I didn't see coming, and I only hope that you will fall head over heels for them, too. Thanks to you, I have my dream job and I'll always be so thankful for the support of the romance book community. What a journey this has been so far – whatever comes next, thank you for catching this wave with me.

About the Author

KATHERINE REILLY is the pseudonym for an author of several young adult and adult novels, published globally. Under Katy Birchall, she is the author of *The Secret Bridesmaid* and also writes YA novels as Ivy Bailey. Katherine lives in London with her family and rescue dog.

In tennis, love means nothing.

Match Point

KATHERINE REILLY

Discover more sizzling sports romance from Katherine Reilly

In tennis, love means nothing.

For two weeks Wimbledon hosts the most prestigious tennis tournament in the world and this year everyone is talking about player Kieran O'Sullivan, the infamous bad boy of the sport with one last chance to win a Grand Slam.

Everyone, that is, except Flora Hendrix. Flora might live in Wimbledon, but she's renting out her flat for the summer while she explores the fresh start that she's longing for. Except when Flora's plans unexpectedly fall through, the last thing she expects is her house guest to refuse to leave. Especially when it's none other than Kieran O'Sullivan.

Thrown together for the summer, sparks fly between Flora and Kieran. But they're not going to let a few sparks distract them from finally following their dreams. Are they?

Available to buy now.

Stories to fall in love with.

Aria

Thanks for reading!

Want to receive exclusive author content, news on the latest Aria books and updates on offers and giveaways?

Follow us on X @AriaFiction and on Facebook and Instagram @HeadofZeus, and join our mailing list.